Packed Together
The Buckeye Lake "Together" Series
Book Two

Kim Garee

www.MtZionRidgePress.com

Mt Zion Ridge Press LLC
295 Gum Springs Rd, NW
Georgetown, TN 37366

https://www.mtzionridgepress.com

ISBN 13: 978-1-962862-48-6

Published in the United States of America
Publication Date: December 1, 2024

Copyright: © 2024 Kim Garee

Editor-In-Chief: Michelle Levigne
Executive Editor: Tamera Lynn Kraft

Cover art design by Tamera Lynn Kraft
Cover artist: Addison Stewart
Cover Art Copyright by Mt Zion Ridge Press LLC © 2024

All rights reserved. No portion of this book may be reproduced or transmitted in any form or by any electronic or mechanical means, including photocopying, recording or by any information retrieval and storage system without permission of the publisher.

Ebooks, audiobooks, and print books are *not* transferrable, either in whole or in part. As the purchaser or otherwise *lawful* recipient of this book, you have the right to enjoy the novel on your own computer or other device. Further distribution, copying, sharing, gifting or uploading is illegal and violates United States Copyright laws.

Pirating of books is illegal. Criminal Copyright Infringement, *including* infringement without monetary gain, may be investigated by the Federal Bureau of Investigation and is punishable by up to five years in federal prison and a fine of up to $250,000.

Names, characters and incidents depicted in this book are products of the author's imagination, or are used in a fictitious situation. Any resemblances to actual events, locations, organizations, incidents or persons – living or dead – are coincidental and beyond the intent of the author.

The Buckeye Lake "Together" Series:

Pressed Together
Packed Together
Patched Together

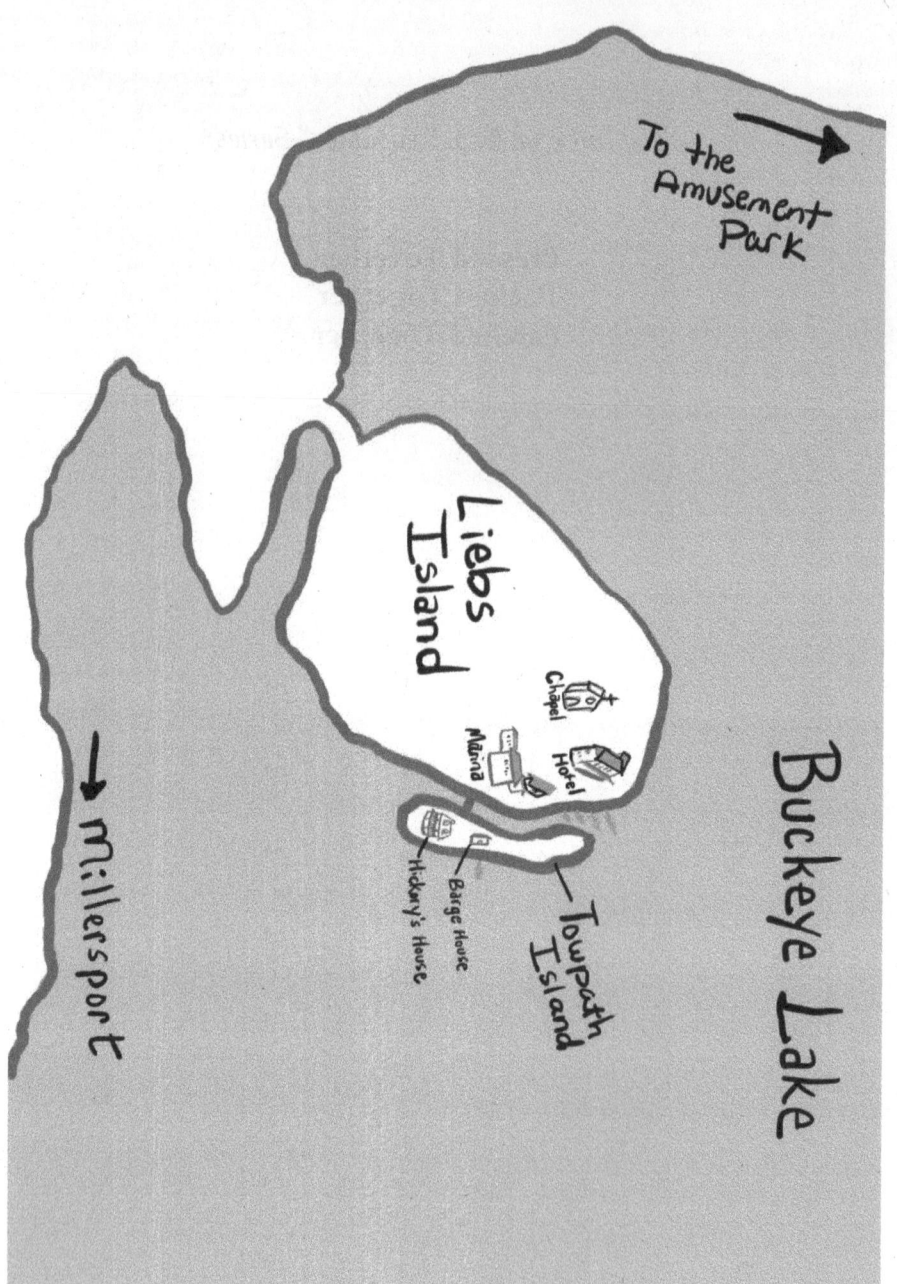

DEDICATION

This book is dedicated to my own mom, Joy. She's always been there for me, living up to her name.

Chapter One

**Delia Stimpson Grade Four
Christmas Journal Project**
Buckeye Lake Public School
December 1946

    Ms. Bailey says our first marks for the new year are this little book we have to write by the time we go back after holiday break. We all know it's her way of making us practice penmanship when school is out when we would much prefer doing pleasanter things, but she says our penmanship is not good at all.
    It is snowing SO HARD today. All us students will probably write that. First thing this morning, Pastor Skip, who I live with now, took me to the Ben Franklin store with my money to buy Christmas presents for the people I love. So, for him, I got a book sort of like this one. I figure he can use it to write down the things he wants to tell me. Rules, mostly. He tells me good things to do and bad things not to do. He tells me those things all day, every day. I figure he should just write them down. Then maybe I can read them when I feel like hearing those things. I don't always feel like it, I can tell you.
    Charlie Graham is my best friend. I got him a comic book. They don't have the best ones here at the lake, but Pastor Skip says the roads are bad and we can't go to Newark. I got Hickory, Charlie's grandpa, lures because he fishes even when the lake is ice. And for Rosie who is Charlie's mom, I got her a pretty necklace with beads of all the colors that remind me of the things she makes. She is an artist. She does not have a husband. She just has Charlie. And she has me. I try to be with her as much as Pastor Skip lets me be.
    I will see them all soon. Tonight is Emily's wedding. Emily is Charlie's aunt, and she is Rosie's sister. She is marrying the park cop, Drew. Pastor Skip says I have to wear the dress with the plaid Mrs. R handed down to me that was her daughter's. Emily said I might have her flowers from her wedding because I like flowers, and now I remember I forgot to buy Emily a Christmas present! Charlie says she gets to go on a honeymoon so maybe she will forget that I forgot. We got to go now. Pastor Skip says the roads are getting real snowy.

~~~~~

    A bride and groom were supposed to understand the whole thing about it being bad luck to see one another before the wedding. Didn't everyone know about that? Rosie Graham figured it was never supposed to fall entirely on the Maid of Honor to run herself ragged all day blocking a couple from cursing their own marriage.

Not that Rosie really believed in luck, per se, but she did believe in traditions rooted in romance. At least, for other people.

"I think it's just that the groom isn't allowed to see the bride unless she also sees him *too* ... at the same time," Drew Mathison reasoned through the crack she'd permitted in the porch door.

"That makes no sense," Rosie told him, standing guard in her fluffiest robe, her red-gold hair in curlers. A wicked swirl of winter teased goosebumps on her legs, and she tried to close the door. Drew's foot blocked it. Classic police detective move, Rosie thought as she shivered.

"C'mon, Rosie. Em and I have things to talk about."

They probably did. A blizzard threatened. Or had already arrived. Rosie wasn't sure when a thing like that was officially underway, but the fact she couldn't make out the lake from right here on Towpath Island for the curtain of blowing snow meant the blizzard had most likely, in fact, hit.

"You'll have the rest of your lives to talk." Traditions were traditions, blizzard or no blizzard. She pushed harder on the door.

Anyway, she'd been hearing her little sister talk non-stop for two dozen years and could attest that most of what she said could certainly wait a few hours.

"Just five minutes."

"No."

"Ask her. She wants to see me, I know."

"It's bad luck, and you know that it's bad luck. Why am I the only one committed to doing this right? I'll pass her a message, Drew, and that's that."

Only, the message he'd given her to pass on was so nonsensical and sappy—not about snow at all, it turned out—that Rosie had refused to repeat it to her sister.

It seemed the couple's long separation in the fall trumped both luck and tradition. They'd barely left one another's sights during waking hours since their engagement.

So, Rosie was reduced to enlisting her ten-year-old son to help keep Emily from sneaking Drew in at the back of the house on their wedding day.

Charlie, whose legs had grown as fast as his cowlick-swirled sandy hair, had taken to the task with his usual zeal. Freckles standing out against the winter pallor of his sweet baby face, he had made himself a soldier, thwarting plots by the lovebirds and reporting back to his mother, the General, on the battlefield of matrimony.

After another hour had passed, he saluted. "Sir," he addressed her. "The groom says he is suffering from frostbite. What would you have me do?" Charlie loved war movies. He knew the drill.

Rosie sighed and scrubbed shortening off her fingers with a dishrag. The frosting would have to wait. She moved reluctantly to the front door once more, this time flanked by her faithful soldier. Outside, Drew was, indeed, coated in frost and snow.

"If you'd go find something useful to do, you wouldn't be cold," she teased, opening the door only two spare inches this time, too narrow a space for a boot. She braced her shoulder against it.

Drew Mathison informed her he'd had to help push her Aunt Cookie's and Uncle Burt's car out of the ditch on Liebs Island, but they were now safely arrived at the little chapel. Rosie peered out again at the storm and considered. The snow seemed to riot not just the sky but also from the ground and everywhere in between. What would they do?

"I need medical care before my digits fall off."

"Your bride is in no way qualified to provide first aid. Go to the barge house with the other men, Mathison. They'll fix you up." Rosie couldn't help but smile at the twinkle in her almost-brother-in-law's eyes beneath brows dusted by snow.

"Hey! Remind Emily what we said. *No postponing*," he called as she stepped back.

"I want to be with the men in the barge house, too," Charlie complained behind her when she'd locked the door against the storm and the persistent, frozen groom. Charlie followed her up the staircase, carrying a small pot of black tea, a domestic task that had effectively dissolved his soldier fantasies and reduced him to whining.

"The fellows are running here and there, dealing with the storm, Sweetheart. You're better off warm here, with us, than next door."

"But I wanna run here and there, *too*. With *them*."

"Release him," Emily put in with an indulgent laugh from Rosie's large, drafty bedroom. She made a move to help with the sloshing tea pot. "I promise to be good if it means Charlie gets to be a guy."

Rosie snorted doubt over the bride's promise to behave, but she tousled Charlie's hair. Both sisters understood Charlie had had precious few opportunities to be a "guy" before Drew had pressed into their lives. "Go put on your wedding suit, and we'll see about you joining the others." The wind howled, which made Rosie add, "You'll need your boots."

He was gone before she'd finished, and Rosie leaned her backside into the bedroom door to shut it. As Emily poured cups of tea, one of Grandma Louise's old Benny Goodman albums played "Jingle Bells." The bride was dressed in her warm, fancy underthings and a thick, not-at-all fancy blanket she'd draped around her shoulders. She carried her own cup to the window, where the pane rattled and the lake was hidden in the white cloud of the storm.

"One of your wedding presents is a bona fide natural disaster." Rosie made her voice as pleasant as possible as she came alongside her sister, sipping the tea.

"Heaven knows we've had experience with the *un*natural ones," Emily said, then flashed her contagious smile. "Might as well try something new."

Anyone would know the pair of them for sisters, seeing them framed in that window, watching it snow out of similar blue-green eyes. Both were on the tall side, leggy like their dancer mother had been rumored to be. The differences between them were in their mouths and hair — mostly the fact Emily's hair and smile were pure, sudden yellow sunshine, while Rosie's hair and grin were the slow, blossoming orange of a sunset.

As they regarded the storm raging on the other side of the glass, it was probably a good thing that neither were prone to melodrama or despair. Those had belonged to their mother; Grandma Louise had not permitted them in the girls when that mother had disappeared.

"The fact is, I've never seen a storm like this," Emily said. "Drew's parents turned back around before they'd made it to the Ohio border."

"I heard. Sorry they can't be here."

Emily sighed. "At least we got to spend Thanksgiving with them, so they know what they're getting for a daughter-in-law." She sipped tea. "For better or worse." Now she shot Rosie a vulnerable glance. "Do you think we should reschedule?"

As if to punctuate her question, the window rattled harder. Rosie wondered how they would make the short distance to the chapel in this weather.

"Do you want to reschedule?"

"I want to get married today, Rosie," Emily said on another sigh. "I overheard Cookie and Burt were already in a ditch driving the few miles out here. What if someone gets stranded and freezes to death just because I'm being stubborn?"

They were often forced to play "mother" for one another in turn. It wasn't a role Rosie took lightly. Being a mom was what she did, even when it meant switching off her "sister" hat. Drew clearly did not want to cancel, either. He practically vibrated with enthusiasm to take these vows. Unsure of what the right advice was, as she was often unsure, Rosie draped her left arm over Emily's shoulders.

"Drew said the two of you decided to stick to the plan. I was supposed to remind you."

"Yes, but ..."

"There are enough people safely arrived to do this thing, Em. The others aren't making the attempt, so they're safe at home. Those who were coming are here, and you wouldn't want that to be for nothing. I promise we will make sure those few get home safely afterward. For now, Pastor Skip and Delia are already at the chapel with Burt and Cookie. Grandpa will head over with us and Charlie, of course, and Drew's set. I think everybody's all set. You can always have a celebration later with those who couldn't make it, after all."

"Hmm. What about Dottie?" Their good friend was supposed to stand up with her during the ceremony.

"Dottie rode over with our aunt and uncle. She's there. So, you know what that means?" Rosie planted a soft kiss on her sister's cheek. "It means it's time to get you dressed, you beautiful bride, you."

Rosie turned to blink away the tears that threatened and pulled Emily's dress off the hanger. It was made of creamy parachute silk, easy to come by after the war, with beadwork of the same hue in a flower pattern over the bodice.

Rosie kept her own movements calm as she helped make sure Emily was satisfied with her appearance. No hurry. No worry. There'd been enough of that, and, if they were going to keep this designated wedding day, then Rosie was determined it not be frantic, no matter how much the house on the towpath groaned in the wicked wind.

~~~~~

Buckeye Lake, dug in another century as a feeder for the Ohio-Erie Canal, now featured a pier amusement park owned by their friend Dottie's family.

Because of that, the lake had become a summer destination for people across the Midwest, an oasis of fun surrounded by miles of cornfields. It had quieted a bit during the war, but 1946 had proven the best summer yet for lake crowds. In the winter, the shops and resorts were boarded up, hibernating until May.

The old canal system, of course, had long since ceased operation, but bits of it were still evident here on the west end of the lake. A strip of the old towpath running along the canal remained as Towpath Island, connected to the larger Liebs Island by a footbridge. Rosie's grandfather had built his marina on one side of the footbridge, and he'd built the family farmhouse they lived in now on the towpath. Beside the two-story house was an old canal barge Hickory's own grandfather had won in a poker game, hauled up out of the canal onto Towpath Island and converted into the little cottage where Emily lived.

The barge house, as they called it, puffed smoke from its chimney in a determined way against the heavy fall of snow. Rosie could just make out the rooftop through the upstairs window of the farmhouse, from which she also spotted the figure of an elf-like man running through the storm.

This would be Hickory Graham.

The man who had been more father than grandfather to her banged in from his front porch just as Rosie bulleted down the stairs.

"Woooo-eee," Hickory was crooning as he paused inside the door, muscling it shut against a cloud of wet white.

Charlie pounded downstairs just behind his mother, overtaking her at the bottom. He had dressed with little finesse in his suit, one pleated pants leg bunched up in a boot.

"Can they still do it today?" Rosie asked her grandfather as she helped her son into a thick parka. Hickory did a little dance that involved stomping his feet and rubbing his gloved hands together. He looked like Santa in his bright red coat and bright red cheeks beneath shy, blue eyes. He was chuckling as he caught his breath.

"Never felt it quite this cold before," he observed. "But a wedding will be fun."

"Charlie wants to go with you guys from the barge house."

"Of course, he does. He belongs with the men."

Charlie puffed up.

"A man whose bow tie needs a bit of help," Rosie observed, done trying to chase her son around. "Will you ask Drew to help him with it?" Before she knew it, the pair left, sucked out into the storm by a sense of adventure.

Rosie flew into the kitchen, where she figured new plans were in order regarding the meal she'd been preparing. The original menu had seemed easy enough. A lovely turkey dinner for the wedding guests, with all the trimmings. But that plan had included Drew's mother, Aunt Cookie, Dottie Berkeley, and herself in the kitchen. Now, their club of cooks and grand plans had tanked with the temperature, and there would be few people to feed, anyway.

The morning, after all, had dawned with phrases like "storm of the century."

Rosie regarded the cake, still a bit too warm for frosting. Raw ingredients were everywhere, and the turkey still cooked. A full meal just wouldn't work. Even the few folks who'd made it to the church on Liebs Island could not get down here to the towpath in this weather. She decided to transport what she could to the chapel, where guests could have a quick snack to bolster them before nightfall made getting home in the storm even trickier. Cake and turkey would do the job. Cheese and relish trays had already been prepared. This could work.

The cuckoo clock on the kitchen wall indicated the cake would simply have to be iced, warm or not. Rosie still needed to dress herself and find a way to transport the basic fare, as well as the bride, to the church.

Would a vehicle even make it up the hill by the marina at this point?

Rosie drew a slow breath to settle her mind. Decorating things was her sweet spot. Making something simple into something delightful was what she'd been created for. So, she swirled the frosting she'd prepared before Drew's latest attempt to infiltrate the house. With steady, sure hands, she sea-shelled it onto the base of the white cake with a smooth knife that had belonged to her grandmother.

Nearly everything in Rosie's domestic life had once belonged to Grandma Louise, from the embroidered towels on the oven door to the woven rugs on the floor. Only Rosie's artistic life managed to be her own, which suited her just fine. She loved the photography dark room at her boardwalk studio on the north shore, she loved the little garage she shared with her mentor where they blew glass sculptures, and she loved her sketchpads, her pastels, and her charcoals, always waiting for her at the top of the stairway. With all of that, though, she also loved this kitchen and the way it kept Grandma Louise alive for her. Even the knife, as it swirled a design in the frosting, seemed to convey an abiding love.

She told herself being alone with this cake and a tight deadline, surrounded by the memories of the godliest woman she would ever know, could go a long way in chasing away the sense of loneliness that pressed so close lately.

Rosie turned the platter and kept applying frosting as fast as she could without getting messy, knowing all the while she had no right to feel lonely at all … which was likely why it had taken her so long to identify what she'd suspected, at first, was restlessness. Just a simmering frustration.

She loved living in the house where she'd grown up, after all, with her grandfather for company.

Then, there was Emily, who would at least begin her married life in the barge house next door, where she'd lived since returning from college to take over the local newspaper. Rosie knew she could talk freely with her sister. It had been the Graham Girls against the world more than once.

Then, of course, there was always Charlie, her bouncing not-so-baby boy, with his agile mind and his affectionate nature. Raising him alone demanded all her best energy.

Who could manage to feel lonely with all that in her life?

Certainly, her sister's relationship with Drew Mathison had probably helped Rosie redefine her own restlessness as loneliness.

Drew had shown up in early summer, seeking a witness to his brother's murder who could help him shut down a Reno gang and find some justice. It was, in fact, Emily who had hidden that witness Drew sought, for his safety and in the name of childhood love. It had taken weeks, along with a few threats from Reno, for Drew to earn Emily's trust.

And that was only *after* he'd won her heart.

Rosie was happy for them, even down in the deepest part of her heart where she expected to find envy. There was no envy there, though. Drew, who was now running the park's watercraft division of police, was just what Emily needed and deserved. He brought out the best in her sister, Rosie reflected as she swirled the top icing. A true partner.

It was just that, the part about partnership, that Rosie supposed had her feeling lonely. Not envious. Just lonely.

She'd had her own chance at marriage just a month before, after all. A proposal from a man she admired and liked ... but did not love. Perhaps it was as much her necessary "no," as it was her sister's enthusiastic "yes," that had Rosie flirting with self-pity.

She looked at the cuckoo again, and her heart stuttered as she yanked off Grandma's owl-print apron. There was a crimson, wrap-around dress waiting for her that would be more acceptable as wedding attire than the robe-apron combination.

As Rosie burst out through the kitchen's swinging door, though, she let out a cry of dismay.

It was her exclamation that broke up the kiss Emily Graham was sharing with Drew Mathison in the living room. They made quite the picture, embracing before the roaring flames of the fireplace.

Emily whirled around, her lipstick smeared onto her right cheek. She held up a hand at Rosie as if her big sister were an approaching beast who needed appeasing.

"Now, Rosie," she soothed, and her cheeks turned a sweet pink. "Our luck is already shot, and we don't do luck anyway."

"We're making up our own rules," Drew defended with a triumphant grin. The words sounded extra ironic from a man who'd spent years in the Army and law enforcement.

Rosie let her breath out in a huff and turned to go upstairs to her own dress. Maybe they were right. Maybe they needed to create, in some small way, a world that made sense to them. "You two deserve a blizzard, you know!"

Chapter Two

When electrical power snapped off around the lake, Gabe Adams stood at a window and watched little flames of light appear in the windows of the Liebs Island Chapel across the street.

"Who would be having a church service on a night like this?" he wondered out loud.

"Wedding," said Ruth as she lit a fourth oil lamp in the parlor.

"Still, though ..." he remarked. That looked like madness, in this storm.

By contrast, he was snug inside the inn, listening to the sluggish pulse of an ornate grandfather clock join the song of the storm that rattled the stone building's thick, expensive windows. Gabe knew how much those windows had cost. He oversaw purchasing, after all, for all the FH Resorts establishments, including the Fairchild Island Inn at Buckeye Lake.

Ruth, the inn's capable caretaker, blew out the match she'd used to light the final lamp and walked back to the kitchen.

FH only used the best materials, so it never occurred to Gabe the windows wouldn't stand up to this storm. He was also grateful he'd had the foresight to upgrade the coal-burning central heating just after the war had begun, so the electricity going out only meant lighting a couple of oil lamps for comfort. One of many convenient things he'd accomplished during the war.

Like just about every man his age, Gabe had intended to fight Hitler, of course. Yet, an injury to his lower leg while supervising a redesign five years before had kept him stateside, making money faster than he'd ever meant to.

The Lord did work in mysterious ways.

Now, the Christmas holiday promised to be quiet and restful. Especially if they ended up with a few feet of snow, and the view out the window seemed to hint at it. Gabe had ridden out to the lake early that morning with the Fairchild family: Camden, Margo, and their grown son, Keith.

Camden had wanted to get away, if only for a week, from the weight that came of owning hotels and resorts in Columbus, Cleveland, and New York City. This one at Buckeye Lake, smaller than the others, had promised to be otherwise empty for Christmas. Gabe had suggested it to his employer as the perfect spot for holiday relaxation. Then he'd bribed

Keith Fairchild to help sway his father.

The bribe had only cost Gabe a ticket to the fights.

"It's supposed to be an actual getaway," Keith had argued privately. "Tell me you're not going out there to work on the resort plans, Adams."

"If Dot Berkeley wants to work on the resort plans, I won't deny her the chance," Gabe had responded hopefully.

As operations manager of all the FH Resorts properties, Gabe Adams was always working, and he couldn't afford to leave behind the weight of it as Mr. Fairchild could. Yet, in this holiday "getaway" plan, he recognized a chance to combine both work and pleasure.

The proposed north shore resort at Buckeye Lake promised to be the company's finest, most lucrative property yet, even stacked against the New York City hotels. Though it would only operate at capacity from May to September, Gabe calculated the four-story, opulent family resort with its acres of gardens and docks extending into the lake so close to the amusement park would line the Fairchilds' pockets and, in turn, his own.

If he could just finally close the deal and get the thing *built*.

Zoning challenges from nature lovers and scathing editorials in the local paper had stalled the project to protect some kind of marsh, but no one at FH was worried that the hurdles would truly prevent zoning approval. Gabe wasn't, for sure. They had an ally in Dot Berkeley and her family, who were selling the chunk of north shore land alongside their boardwalk amusement park. Dot even wanted to invest in the resort itself, as part of the deal.

Which was where pleasure might mingle with business, Gabe hoped, this Christmas season.

Yes, if the lovely Dot wanted to come by the little island inn and work on the plans for the newer, grander resort, Gabe was happy to be on site to work alongside her. The pair had been meeting for dinner, off and on, both at the lake and in Columbus.

Dot was beautiful, capable, intelligent, driven, and polished.

Gabe wasn't sure when dinners had veered away from negotiations to flirting and dancing, but veered away, they had.

"Are you interested in her on a personal level?" Keith had asked, but he hardly needed an answer. He'd known it from the time Gabe had leaned on him, as a friend, to convince Camden and Margo that the Fairchild Island Inn would be the perfect place to get away for Christmas. "I suppose the two of you do make a dashing couple."

Gabe agreed, so all that remained was to make sure Dot Berkeley did.

This intense storm, however, had not been in his carefully laid plans.

"They're saying it's some kind of *blizzard*," Camden had huffed over their light lunch.

"Well, Columbus will be getting hit, too, Dad," Keith pointed out.

"Might as well be here as there, eh?"

"We're better off here," Gabe had assured them. The thick stone and amenities of the classy little inn would last several Fairchild lifetimes.

It never bothered Gabe that he wasn't a Fairchild himself. The family had helped build him into the man he was, as surely as he'd helped build their empire.

It was another snowstorm years before, in fact, that had marooned the wealthy Camden Fairchild within yards of Gabe Adams' family's cabin in the Hocking Hills. While he was still just a young man, he had been accidentally "discovered" by Mr. Fairchild when he'd dug the man out of his car and saved his life.

Gabe worried, though, that this blizzard would keep Dot Berkeley from coming out to Liebs Island, which caused him to worry that he might truly be in for a week of quiet refinement rather than romance.

The wind howled, the expensive windows shook, and the snow piled up.

Margo had carried on worse than the storm itself when the electricity had first blinked out, but she settled as the main parlor began to glow bright with firelight.

Gabe thought it was rather a shame there were no guests to enjoy the ambiance those warm flames provided against the darkness.

Chapter Three

When Levi "Smokey" Black had shown up with his enormous Allis-Chalmers tractor and wagon at midday, everyone at the towpath had laughed at the way he had decked it all out in jingle bells.

A farmer, Smokey had grown up with the Grahams and become fast friends with Drew Mathison since they'd both been in Europe during the war.

By late that December afternoon, however, no one was laughing at Smokey's tractor. Instead, his forward thinking made him a hero all over again. It was only this jingling wagon and the hardy, four-wheel power of the Allis-Chalmers that got the wedding party up the marina lot and across Liebs Island to the little chapel building, which was fast being buried in snow.

It was a short trip, really, made nearly impossible by the blizzard. Rosie, with help from Smokey and Hickory, had loaded baskets with the turkey, wedding cake, and platters into the wagon.

Candlelight flickered in the chapel's windows, and the few guests who had managed the drive out around the lake from town had one kerosene heater going. Bows and greenery were in place for the holiday season. A wedding was supposed to happen, and the people who loved Drew Mathison and Emily Graham were making sure it would still happen.

Rosie, who loved them very, very much, was delighted as she puffed warm breath onto her pink fingers.

"How nice the candles are!" Hickory laughed beneath a snow-encrusted scarf, and he embraced Cookie and Burt. "I'm not removing this coat for anything, though."

Pastor Skip was running in and out to help carry Rosie's baskets of food in, exclaiming over the scent of turkey while Cookie scolded him for tipping the cake sideways.

"The poor fellow slipped on the ice." Dot laughed, looking like a movie star, as usual, moving around to brush the snow off her friends' backs. "Smashed the cake to bits."

"And Rosie had it frosted so pretty," Smokey remarked.

"Don't fret," Rosie said from inside her own heavy hood, still trying to catch her breath. The door shut behind her, and she took comfort in the relative warmth of the little vestibule, smelling as it always did of wax and wood polish. "I've entirely let go of all my expectations for this event. Not that it was my expectations that ever mattered." She let the others arrange the baskets she'd just carried over to a side table.

Drew was unwrapping his bride from her heavy parka like she was, indeed, his Christmas gift. "This wedding is going to be whatever it ends up being. Right, Em?"

"If we're married at the end of it, all will be well," she said with a laugh, letting her old friend, Dot, exclaim over her gown.

Everyone talked at once.

"Can we change you out of those dreadful boots, though, honey?"

"I've got her heels here in this satchel! No, this one here!"

"Mild frostbite is all the rage for weddings this season, I heard."

"Not sure we'll be getting back out of here."

"Well, the turkey is already cold."

"Stay out of that. We can't eat until they're married, for crying out loud!"

"Might as well eat it before it freezes."

"Charlie, Delia. No running around with all these candles burning."

"Oh, a pianist! No way Claudia was ever making it from off island. Can we all just hum the wedding march, do you think?"

"Nonsense. I can play," Dottie said.

Rosie side-hugged her friend as she passed by. "Can you really?"

"Kind of. A little."

"The kerosene heater is warm. Ish. It's warmish."

"If the turkey doesn't last, we'll just have to eat one another to survive."

Pastor Skip begged his ward, Delia, to stop making morbid predictions about their fate. She had learned of the Donner Party in social studies just the week before, and she was determined to recount their demise in grisly detail even as Skip tried to get everyone in their places.

"Drew, you'll have to let go of your bride for five minutes if you want her to be able to walk down the aisle. Come up front with me now, young man." Pastor Skip's smile was as large as the storm. He would always be grateful to Drew Mathison for keeping his son, Gilbert, safe after he'd testified as a witness in Drew's brother's murder trial. To get to marry the officer to his sweetheart was making him glow.

"May I kiss the bride first?"

"For pity's sake," Rosie murmured, but she couldn't stop the bubble of laughter as she gave him a shove and guided her very blessed little sister in the opposite direction, toward the drafty rear of the sanctuary.

"Historians think the Donner party ate the weakest people first, when they knew they were completely trapped," Delia was saying, the ivory bow atop her head flopping sideways as she followed Rosie and Emily.

"That's what Ms. Bailey says. Maybe even children."

"Delia, *please*," Pastor Skip called in exasperation over the howling wind. "This is a wedding."

"If the children were anything like you and Charlie, they probably tasted a bit gamey," Rosie said, enjoying Emily's laugh as she tucked her sister's hand into Hickory's arm to keep things moving. The old man's blue eyes went wet with tears. A quiet settled over the sanctuary, in contrast to the cacophony of before.

Rosie blinked back her own tears once more. The storm took a backseat to the vision her sister made, the muff over her hands bedecked in mistletoe, the gold of her hair shining like the hope and certainty in her smile. Rosie let her arms encircle both Emily and her grandfather, and for a moment the three of them stood united.

This old man had given the sisters a home, together with his wife, and he'd later helped them make sense of her death, added to all the loss they had already experienced. Rosie would never forget the way Hickory and Emily had stood beside her, a unit like the one they made now, when little Charlie had arrived fatherless, and she herself had to face coming-of-age as an outcast.

How did a person thank other people for all that history? An embrace hardly seemed enough.

"I love you both," Rosie whispered, and Hickory swiped at the tears on her cheeks with the ratty handkerchief he could reliably produce at any moment. "I'm so happy for you, Em."

Up front, Dottie plucked out the wedding march. Pastor Skip raised his voice over the howling wind, as the temperature in the sanctuary dropped still more.

The vows were magical enough and brief enough to keep Delia temporarily quiet about their future as cannibals. Burt, in his hardy baritone, led the group in "How Great Thou Art," acapella.

They were only a verse in when the chapel door burst open and, in another cloudy explosion of snow, Police Chief Gunn clomped into the peaceful, candlelit scene.

"Gunn!" Pastor Skip called as the man wrestled a toboggan cap off his face.

"If you've come to object, you're too late," Drew called good-naturedly to his former boss, pulling Emily hand-in-hand down the aisle toward him. The couple stopped in front of him. "You okay, Chief? Sorry we had to start without you."

Chief Gunn had known the Grahams all his life, and he'd been the one to hire Drew when he'd appeared in Buckeye Lake last summer, on the hunt for Gil, the missing witness. "Congratulations, Mr. and Mrs. Mathison," the chief gasped, face red from the wind.

"Hey, now. I haven't officially introduced them yet," Pastor Skip hollered.

"Whatever their names now, they're going to need to seek shelter and fast. You all do," Gunn said, his expression somber.

"We'd noticed there's a bit of snow falling," Burt put in.

"More than a bit, I'm afraid," the chief continued as the party gathered around him. He coughed into his coat sleeve. "The latest from the weather service says we're in for a bad several days here, and power's out all over. Anyone without enough firewood isn't going to make it. Temperature keeps falling fast. I've got a lot of folks to check on. Possibly to move."

As if to punctuate this dire news, a fir tree that had been brushing one of the church windows blew right through the glass and shattered it over pews as the group cried out in alarm. Frigid air funneled in with a screaming sound.

Drew, who had been a light-hearted groom moments before, was suddenly a soldier again, moving fast. "Gather the food up again, everyone. Bundle up."

"For now, all of you should head across the road to the inn," Gunn instructed. "They have a working heating system, and I doubt you'll make it back down to the towpath in this. Not tonight."

A different but even less pleasant cold moved through Rosie's veins. "The inn?"

"The Fairchild Inn. They've got heat and room for you."

That was when Rosie decided, with some regret, that she would simply have to freeze to death.

Chapter Four

From the common room of the Fairchild Inn, there was no way to know that, outside, trees were falling and pipes were freezing.

Within the stone fortress, Gabe watched Margo Fairchild produce another porcelain sheep from a nest of newspaper wrappings and straw. The straw, in fact, was the only manger-like aspect of the nativity she was assembling on the polished oak table near the fireplace.

Gabe rested his chin on his hand and watched this latest sheep take its place alongside a porcelain section of fence. The pieces were all white and perfect, shiny in the candles and oil lamps Ruth had lit.

For his part, Keith Fairchild had surrendered to a nap, his own chin planted on his sweater. Soft gargling sounds came from the back of his throat. Camden Fairchild read a newspaper close to the opposite side of the fire from his wife, glasses perched on the tip of his nose. He cleared his throat approximately two times per minute.

Gabe had created a mental chart to track it.

Newsprint crinkled, this time from Margo's side of the fireplace. Gabe waited in expectation of the next shiny, delicate creature to emerge. At last, the paper gave birth to a cow. Careful with the twiggy little bovine legs, Margo inspected the porcelain for smudges before placing it on the other side of the fence from the sheep. Then she stepped back, considered, and moved the cow a quarter inch to the right.

The wind howled in contrast to the soft snore and the barely audible click of porcelain on polished oak.

Gabe thought he might run mad from boredom, and this was only their first day at the inn. Christmas was still days away.

He fantasized about rushing out into that storm, just catapulting himself from the overstuffed chair and pumping his arms and legs hard into what looked like a wall of wild white beyond the windowpane. No coat. How *alive* he would feel.

Until he froze to death.

"Gabriel? Are you all right, sweetheart?"

Margo was squinting at him across the room, a shining camel cradled in her hand.

"I'm fine. Why?"

"You just made a sound, is all. Are you warm enough?" Now Camden was also squinting in Gabe's direction, over the paper. Their son continued snoring softly.

Gabe had made *a sound*. Heaven forbid. He shook his head, hoping the sound hadn't been a growl.

He owed these people everything: his shoes as polished as the tabletop, his fine sweater vest over his tailored shirt. Restless, he rose and walked to the broad window with its cushioned seat. Besides the fireplace, this charming window seat was the showpiece of the common room. His job was to know exactly how much it cost to add an extravagance like this cozy seating to a hotel.

It was just *so quiet*. Quiet enough within to make the storm somehow appealing without.

Now he took to watching the stark white nativity scene take shape in reverse, reflected in the window glass before him with streamers of white snow like a backdrop in the darkness behind it. There was also the reflection of his own face, a shade or two darker than anyone else's in the room.

Then the quiet came to an end.

Beyond the archway behind him, the heavy inn doors slammed open, and the raucous sound of a dozen voices came rushing in with snow and frigid air.

Gabe's first thought was that a group of intoxicated Christmas carolers was attacking, but certainly no one would be caroling—drunk or sober—in a blizzard. Well-wrapped bodies kept tumbling through the doorway, though, one after another, exclaiming and coughing and making both alarmed and happy noises.

A middle-aged man and woman with their arms full of baskets, a very old man still managing to keep up with the others, a young boy and girl darting around the others, a woman with another large basket, the preacher Gabe recognized from town. A small cluster of others, unrecognizable in flapping winter hats, practically fell on top of one another as they slid across the now slick tile flooring.

It took two of them to shut the door against the storm once more.

Ruth, after lighting the oil lamps, had been down the hallway and in the kitchen, but she still made it to the foyer before the Fairchilds had roused themselves from their reading, their nap, and their shock, respectively.

"Here we come a wassailing," a deep voice rang out from the group, making them all laugh and forcing Gabe to wonder if his first impression had been correct.

Everyone was talking at once.

Somehow, it was through this indoor storm that Dot Berkeley appeared! *His* Dot Berkeley. The one he'd all but given up on getting to romance over his holiday trip. Now, she was here, and she pushed

Packed Together

through the cluster of chaos and spotted him through the fur-lined hood of a thick coat, her dark curls ice-encrusted to that fur.

"Bet you weren't expecting this," she called as they started toward one another. "The wedding managed to happen, believe it or not."

Wedding. It clicked for Gabe that Dot had said she was in a wedding, but he hadn't realized it was the blizzard wedding across the street.

"And now ... wouldn't you know it ... we're stranded!" someone declared.

"A tree crashed right through the stained-glass window!"

"I've never felt it this cold. Never."

"You're coming from ...? The church, then?" Camden Fairchild had found his voice in the choir, seeming to just remember he owned this place. Next to Gabe, Dot had removed a pair of fine gloves and was blowing on her fingers.

Gabe reached over and chafed them between his own to help warm them.

"Yes, forgive us!" The old man still standing in the foyer with the others pulled off a cap that covered what turned out to be a bald head with a tuft of white around the edges, his cheeks bright red and his blue eyes bright and vital. Gabe now decided this was somehow St. Nicholas leading the fray. "Sorry there are so many of us and that we just burst in like that, Fairchild."

At that, Camden seemed to recognize the old man and moved quickly toward him to shake the work glove he'd extended. "Why, Hickory Graham! Didn't know it was you. Been a while! Come in, come in."

Gabe recognized the name from Graham Marina, just down the hill and next door to the Fairchild Inn. The properties shared a beach on the lake, and Gabe figured the men must have seen one another off and on for decades.

"Good to see you again," Graham said cheerfully. "Mrs. Fairchild, hello ma'am. Chief Gunn said you had working heat here and advised us to come over."

Camden looked blank, and the refugees looked at one another as the room adjusted to the fact that Gunn had forgotten an important loop in the communication.

Gabe wondered how many more people the police chief would be sending to the inn. In his mind, he calculated beds.

"It makes sense, of course," Keith said, speaking for the first time. Gabe just now noticed his friend standing stiffly next to the sofa where he'd dozed a few minutes before. Though he spoke to the room in general, he watched his father.

"I'm so sorry to impose," Graham said. "Gunn didn't ask before he sent us here, did he?"

"No, but that doesn't change the fact you're perfectly welcome, Hickory," Camden said with extra warmth to make up for the silent beat of confusion they'd all just endured.

"It's only until Smokey gets back, anyway," Hickory informed the inn's owner, and everyone stood with coats still on in the foyer.

Pastor Skip, beside the man called Hickory, explained to the room: "Smokey, err, Smokey Black has a tractor and small wagon, which is how we all made it up to the church in the first place. He took the bride and groom and half of a turkey back down to the barge house for their honeymoon and was going to make sure their place and Hickory's are able to hold enough heat from the stoves."

"Well, come in for now and get comfortable, for heaven's sake," Margo decided, rubbing her arms from the chilly air they'd brought in. Gabe figured she'd rallied once she realized they were being picked back up again shortly.

Ruth materialized again with a mop for the snow falling off boots.

Gabe, inspired by Margo to remember his manners, took Dot's coat and draped it over the chair he'd been in minutes before. She smelled, as always, like very subtle and very expensive roses. Tucking her curls back away from her face, she grinned and assessed him. "I like your sweater."

"Thank you. You look lovely."

"If that's even close to true, it's a small miracle." She laughed. "I'd already climbed out of a ditch before this latest bout with the elements."

"It's a shame about this storm, but I'm glad I get to see you."

"Me too."

Gabe leaned in and placed a kiss on her cheekbone. She reached down and squeezed his hand affectionately, which wasn't pleasant. Her fingers still felt half frozen.

"Come stand closer to the fire," he insisted, which turned out to be a popular place to be.

With the whole group shivering their way over to the stone hearth, Gabe bent to feed the already lively fire some additional wood. If this inn was the only source of heat left on the lake, then he'd do his part to make sure there was plenty to go around.

Margo was quick to introduce herself to Dot, whom Gabe had told her about. The two women were a pair, standing together. He realized how natural Dot looked amidst the luxury of this waterfront inn, her pearls a match for Mrs. Fairchild's.

Perhaps that was what had his eyes tracking to another woman who did *not* look natural standing in this room.

Why he noticed her at all, he couldn't say, with all the commotion at the fireplace. She had put down the packed basket she'd carried in, but the young woman, apparently about the same age as Dot, stood off to the far side of the entryway, still wrapped tight against the storm.

Something about her posture conveyed misery.

Concerned, Gabe made his way over to help her off with her thick coat. He noticed how bright her eyes were against almost colorless skin. She could have been the white porcelain figure of the nativity Mary, were it not for her floppy, knitted cap and mismatched mittens. Her eyes, somehow haunted, tracked to his only when he was directly in front of her.

"Welcome," he said in a soft voice because he had the feeling she might run back into the storm as he'd just been imagining doing himself. "May I help you with your coat? It's a great deal warmer by the fire."

She shook her head. "Thank you, but no. I'm fine here. Smokey should be back any minute to get us and take us home." She softened the refusal with a smile but leaned back against the paneled wall to convey her determination.

"And how far is home?"

"Oh. Um. Just down the hill." She extended a mitten, crusted in ice as Dot's hair had been. "I'm sorry. I'm Rosie Graham."

"Rosie Graham ..." Gabe thought hard. He knew the name, perhaps from Dot. "Are you the bride, then?"

"No, that's my sister, Emily."

"Ah. So, the maid of honor. I'm Gabe Adams." He endured the handshake, wiping the bits of melting ice off his palm on his corduroy slacks.

It was sliding into place for him, now. Gabe had met Emily Graham over the summer. If he wasn't mistaken, she was the one publishing the articles about his resort project in her paper. She and her sister had grown up with Dot.

The woman in front of him seemed to be making the same connections.

"Oh," Rosie said with a nod of recognition. "You, you're Dottie's ... friend." She managed a small, polite smile, but he noticed her gaze darting around the room. It occurred to him he wasn't having any luck putting her at ease.

"That's right. Dot's over by the fire. Why don't you come join us?" He looked back toward the fireplace only to see Dot working the room in that way she always did. Poised, charming, mildly aggressive. There'd be no getting her attention.

Gabe tried to make sense of these two very opposite women as lifelong friends.

A boy of about ten scampered up, having shed his hat so that his sandy-blonde hair stuck up every which way, and the very nervous and cold Rosie Graham reached out and clamped one of her mittens around his arm.

"Charlie, please stay with me."

"Mom, have you ever seen a fireplace as big as that? And the lady said she's going to make cocoa to warm us all up!"

"I doubt we'll be here long enough for cocoa," she responded in a tight voice that matched her grip on his arm. "Just stay right here." It wasn't a suggestion.

"But..."

"Smokey will be back to take us home any minute."

"I wanna stay here for a while, though! It's fun! And warm!"

"We aren't staying, Charlie."

Gabe felt like an intruder into something he didn't understand.

Perhaps the woman was a recluse, which would explain the pallor and her general discomfort. He eased away, wishing himself back to the comparative vitality of the fireplace, but he found his path blocked by another child who had tumbled in with the group, this one a girl.

"I'm Delia," she said to Gabe, startling him a little. "It means I'm a good *deal*. Get it? *Delia*?" She was about the same age as Charlie and was missing a front tooth. Her floppy hat with pompoms hanging to her shoulders had remained on, though her coat was dragging behind her, seemingly stuck to one wrist.

"Nice to meet you, Miss Delia. I'm Gabe. May I help you with your coat?" He bent to pick most of it up from the floor and tried to tug it over her wrist, but it was blocked by her fist. She squirmed and opened that fist, revealing a bright shard of sharp, blue glass.

"Is that...?" Rosie asked, moving from the wall toward them.

"I picked it up when the window broke at the chapel. Look at the light through it!" Delia held it up toward the fireplace, but Rosie was busy inspecting the little girl's palm for cuts.

"That's sharp, Delia. Be careful."

Once she had shifted it to the other hand and Rosie released the one that, thankfully, wasn't bleeding, Gabe swept the entire plaid, woolen coat up from the floor as it fell. Delia thanked him even as she held the glass up for Charlie to admire.

Gabe smiled, the chaos of the room and these children reminding him of his family's little cabin in the Hocking Hills, bursting at the seams with large and small people who liked to make noise. Suddenly those memories felt so much closer.

He grinned at Rosie over Delia's braids. "Your children are fun."

Rosie's homemade hat was sideways from her battle for the shard of glass. "Children are fun, for sure," she said. "Delia belongs to Pastor Skip, though. Technically."

The pastor seemed to hear his name and headed over, along with Dot, but Delia had already scampered closer to the fire, taking Charlie with her. Gabe left the pastor chatting with the reluctant Rosie Graham, who hadn't so much as unbuttoned a button of the thick collar of her coat.

"To think," Gabe told Dot. "I was bored out of my mind a few minutes ago."

"I see you met Rosie," she said, leading him away a little.

"Yes. She doesn't seem to want to join us as much as the others do." Dot looked over to check on her friend and shrugged. Gabe tried to sort it out in his mind. "It's her sister that's down on the resort, right? The one who got married today?"

"Emily's the one you're used to dealing with from the newspaper, yes," Dot said, looking up at him now, "but don't kid yourself about Rosie over there being on board with it at all."

"What's her issue with it?"

"Nature lover. Photographer."

It clicked anew in Gabe's mind. Emily Graham's newspaper had run several photos and reports affiliated with a university or professor or something, an attempt to designate Cranberry Bog a nature preserve.

He reassessed the unusual woman still standing straight-backed near the entryway, who must be the "some photographer" in his briefs about opposition to his project. Things made a little more sense.

Did Rosie Graham despise FH Resorts so passionately that she wouldn't even take heat from their fireplace when offered during a blizzard?

"Adams, listen," Dot was saying. When she was in business tycoon mode, as he thought of it, she shifted to calling him by his last name. Like they were a couple of pals at a private club negotiating a deal. He imagined her smoking a cigar. "Emily just got married, right?"

"That's what I hear."

Her dark eyes were dancing. "Soooo ... she's going to be honeymooning through the holidays. Though I don't know how far they'll get in this weather."

"Umm. Okay?"

"Regardless, though, the paper isn't publishing this week *or* next."

"What are you saying, Dot?"

"So, that gives us a week here before Christmas to try to push the zoning through! We can really put our heads together, finalize the design, put it in front of the board again. With*out* Emily managing to get the town riled up."

Gabe squinted down at her. It was hard to believe this little lake surrounded by farm fields in Ohio had produced such a formidable woman. She was dazzling and frightening. "Isn't she your ... friend? I mean, didn't you just stand up with her at her wedding?"

Dot blinked her long lashes. "Yes. What's your point?"

He cast a searching look over in the direction of Rosie Graham and lowered his voice. "This doesn't seem disloyal to you? I mean, won't she be mad when she comes back after the first of the year and we're, what ... closing on the sale?"

"Closing on the sale! Wouldn't that be a great way to kick off 1947?" Dot's smile was broad, her teeth perfect. "And, sure. She'll be miffed. But she and I have always understood business and friendship as two different things."

A great way to kick off 1947. Not for the first time, he tried to gauge the source of Dot's interest in him. She'd been excited about the prospect of the sale to FH Resorts before she'd joined Keith and him for dinner the first time to talk over details. Keith had never been the detail man, though, so Dot had naturally sought Gabe out in the weeks and months that had followed.

She was going to pocket a good deal of the sale of the north bank acreage for her family and invest some of the profit back into the sprawling resort. She had a double interest in the project, which she didn't have the capital for on her own but desperately wanted to help shape.

After a few months, Dot had openly imagined the pair of them shaping it together. That was when Gabe had very naturally imagined them shaping a life together. Buying up properties, developing them through FH. Traveling. The vision had propelled him to the jeweler's for the ring currently fastened into his suitcase down the hall.

Just in case she was as serious about that vision as he was.

Still, Gabe found himself struggling now with this plan to sneak around with the zoning. It wasn't the way he liked to do business.

Anyway, what zoning board would be meeting at Christmas and during a blizzard?

A pounding at the door interrupted that train of thought and brought another wave of excitement to the now crowded common room. Camden Fairchild hurried to open it.

Keith, Gabe noticed, had mysteriously disappeared entirely from the room. *How strange.*

The man who shuffled into the entryway this time, as the storm howled behind him, was even more covered in snow than anyone else had been, top to bottom. And he was enormous, like the incarnation of the Sasquatch the folks down in the hills loved to imagine. Stiffly, he managed to pull a ski mask off his head as he tried to catch his breath.

"Smokey! Are you all right?" an older woman from the group exclaimed, rushing near him but visibly hesitating to touch him, as if she feared he'd break to pieces.

"Good. News. And." He tugged off his farmer's gloves to reveal gigantic, bright red hands he tried to breathe on. "Bad. News." The room was silent.

"Bad news first! Everyone knows that!" little Delia hollered, jumping up and down over the prospect of this latest game.

"Bad news is," he said, regaining enough breath for sentences. "A tree has also managed to throw itself through the upstairs of your home, Hickory. Tractor's stuck. Nobody's ... leaving this place. Not for the duration of the storm."

A beat of silence preceded another general uproar.

Amidst the exclamations, apologies for imposing, and wild celebrations from the kids, Gabe's gaze went inexplicably to Rosie Graham, standing just a few feet from the doorway. He saw her close her eyes as her posture sagged, a private moment of despair that set her apart even more than had her determination to remain bundled.

This was more than opposition to the partial destruction of a bog. More than the damage to her family home.

Had he ever seen someone look so alone? Gabe nearly returned to her side, if only to catch her if she fell.

"But what was the good news?"

The question quieted the room.

"Our newlyweds made it safely to the barge house." Then Smokey Black reached behind himself, muscled the door open a few feet, and produced a small evergreen tree that went to about his shoulder. It was more covered in snow than he was ... snow that slid off its boughs and splatted onto the entryway floor Ruth had just mopped. "I cut down a Christmas tree for us from the towpath! You know. Just in case."

The children cheered. The adults soberly considered how many days remained until Christmas and what "just in case" might mean.

Rosie Graham's head dropped back against the wall with a hopeless thud Gabe heard across the room.

A tugging at his shirtsleeve pulled his attention back to Dot Berkeley, though. "Guess we have plenty of planning time, Adams. Is this shirt Egyptian cotton?"

Chapter Five

The grandfather clock in the common room chimed twelve times, a lonely sound that wrapped around Rosie just as she was wrapped in a quilt on the inn's window seat.

The tolling of the hours rang much louder here than those from the cuckoo clock in the kitchen at home, so she wasn't surprised when she heard a sleepy, "Mama?" from near the fireplace. Charlie only called her "Mama" now when he was half-asleep or sick. His head rose from the mattress that had been placed on the floor by the fire for the children.

"It's fine, Sweetheart. Go back to sleep now." She watched his head sink back to its pillow as the final three chimes sounded the start of a new day. Technically, anyway. From the sound of the raging storm that shook the large window beside her, Rosie didn't figure anyone would spot a sunrise in the day ahead.

Margo Fairchild had been happy to share soft, flannel nightgowns with Dottie and Rosie. Ruth, the inn's manager, had distributed pieces of her own simpler wardrobe to Cookie and to Delia. In fact, the little girl slept in only Ruth's billowing top like a nightgown.

The refuge taken by the wedding party had turned into a true party, it seemed, and that party had come to an end just an hour before.

Rooms and supplies had been generously distributed. The inn, laid out with four branching hallways off this common room, boasted twenty-five rooms and suites on two floors, according to Ruth. Uncle Burt and Aunt Cookie claimed a suite. Smokey had a room, Dottie had a room, and Hickory had a room. In theory, with its coal heat and its space, this was the perfect place to spend a stormy night.

As payment for the hospitality, the wedding feast Rosie had prepared had been shared with the Fairchild family.

For her own part, Rosie had not managed to taste so much as a piece of the mangled wedding cake. She'd pretended to nibble from the relish tray, and she'd pushed a small piece of turkey around on her plate.

She'd insisted her own bed be on the sofa alongside the children's fireside mattress. Somehow, she couldn't imagine retreating into some room of the inn and leaving Charlie and Delia alone and vulnerable in this place. So, Rosie had been given a blanket and made up her sofa bed, but the same nerves that kept her from eating would not permit her the vulnerability of sleep yet, either. She'd yet to even attempt the sofa.

Instead, she kept watch like a soldier in hostile territory. Back to the wall at the window seat. Knees drawn up tight beneath the quilt. Every sense on high alert.

She had a secret, and her secret walked and talked.

The last time Rosie Graham had set foot inside the Fairchild Island Inn was a day in early October more than ten years before. It had taken courage for her to approach Ruth Drumgool, the innkeeper who'd devotedly packed picnics for the charming Keith Fairchild.

Keith, after all, had lounged away that summer before college at his family's inn.

Ruth had outwardly approved of Keith, who would one day be her boss, of course. She had not approved of him dallying with one of the Graham girls down on the beach by the marina all summer, but she'd still obediently packed picnics for the pair of them because Keith had asked her to.

When Rosie sought Ruth out a month after Keith left for college, she'd been trying hard not to cry.

"The family did not give me permission to share Keith's number at school with anyone," the innkeeper had told her. If she noticed the tears in Rosie's eyes, she said nothing about them.

Rosie, unlike her little sister, had never been one to press people too hard. She drew a shaking breath, trying to be bold as she insisted, "But I really need to talk with him."

"I'm sorry, dear, but I think we both know he's not for you." And with that, the old maid had turned her attention to refilling the coffee cups of a couple enjoying a bonus autumn weekend at the lake.

Rosie had stood in this same parlor when she realized she'd be doing the unthinkable—and even unspeakable—in the eyes of society: having a baby all by herself.

She'd *never* tried again to share that secret with anyone at the Fairchild Island Inn, nor with anyone in the Fairchild family.

Now, more than ten years later, Rosie sat wrapped not just in the borrowed nightgown and quilt but, also, in the reality that the son she loved more than anything in the world had Keith Fairchild's sandy hair and blue, blue eyes. And freckles.

It was obvious in Charlie's every feature.

How could she eat her sister's wedding cake tonight, waiting, tense, for any of the Fairchilds to really *look* at Charlie Graham?

When she'd spotted Keith across the parlor when she first arrived, Rosie had been surprised to find him changed from a decade before. He was a little larger than he'd been at eighteen, filled out. At first, he'd seemed bored by the arrival of an entire wedding party into the candlelit room, but Rosie saw the moment he recognized her where she stood at the door.

He did remember.

She still managed to be surprised, though, when he'd slipped out of the room.

Keith Fairchild hadn't been able to stomach wedding cake tonight either, apparently.

Rosie sat now, side by side with the storm and the pulse of that colossal clock, mildly surprised that Keith had remembered her enough to look uncomfortable. Over the years, she'd imagined him playing the same part in countless young women's stories, tossing each aside carelessly so she had to handle the consequences by herself.

Yet, the fact he seemed to remember Rosie at all or that he even managed to look a bit guilty flew in the face of the narrative she'd grown comfortable with.

She still needed him to be a villain, but she would need him to do a better job at cooperating with that role. Him looking uncomfortable wouldn't work.

"Can't sleep?"

Rosie startled. Wrapped up in the past, she had let down her guard.

In the large room lit only by the fireplace, Dottie's fellow, Gabe Adams, was little more than a shadow in an expensive vest. "Isn't it awfully cold there by the glass?"

"Um. Well. This blanket is thick," she said.

He came closer, trying hard to peer out the window, but Rosie knew he'd find nothing but darkness. Nearest to the glass, there was only a slashing pattern of horizontal, icy snowfall.

"You don't seem to have made an effort at sleep," Rosie observed, nodding toward the man's still buttoned-up clothing.

He shrugged. "I think I had too much coffee."

"Hmmm." She turned her attention back to the nothingness of the window, but now the nothingness was replaced by his reflection in the glass as he moved in silence across the room, sidestepping the children on their mattress, to feed another few logs to the fire. It seemed surprisingly natural for him, vest and all.

Expecting him to depart down the hallway that led to the rooms where the others were sleeping, she was disconcerted when Gabe Adams strolled back her way, hands in his pockets. This, she supposed, was the disadvantage of staying near the children overnight. No privacy for brooding.

When he spoke again, his voice was more than a whisper but still very soft. "I know I'm entirely out of line here, but ..." He paused, and her heart thumped. "You seem upset about more than the storm, Ms. Graham."

That drew a sigh.

Hiding her nerves over the unexpected twist of the day had required more from her than she'd had left. She'd woken, after all, to a sudden storm, thinking the biggest challenge would be finishing the food for the dinner after her sister's wedding. Then she'd found herself sheltering among enemies, and only she knew *why* they were enemies.

Rosie shut her eyes and shook her head to clear it.

"I'm sorry," he said quickly, kindly. "I shouldn't have said anything."

"No. Don't apologize. You're not wrong." *Had anyone else even noticed?* Rosie had wanted to be invisible and then, somehow, also resented being invisible once she'd accomplished it. Everyone, even nosy Cookie and Burt, had been too distracted by the disastrous storm to realize their capable niece was coming unraveled.

"I guess it's been quite a day," said the stranger who *had* noticed.

Rosie grudgingly understood why Dottie liked this man. "You could say that."

"May I sit for a few minutes? Until some of the coffee wears off?" When she didn't protest, he slid onto the opposite side of the window seat cushion, then made a show of adjusting a pillow behind his back. Once settled, he looked earnestly across the small space at her. "Are you in love with your sister's new husband, then?"

Rosie gaped at him and noticed the groove of a dimple gave his smile away before it bloomed.

"Why so surprised?" He stacked his arms behind his head and settled in, studying her. "Why else would a beautiful woman be so sad on her sister's wedding day?"

Rosie's eyes opened even wider. "I'm sorry. I can't seem to catch up, Mr. Adams. Are you *flirting* with me now?"

He laughed, low and rich. To his credit, he glanced over by the fire as though making sure he hadn't woken the children. "No, no. And don't get me wrong ... I don't *want* to be right about you pining away for Emily's better half."

"Well, you're *not* right." She directed her attention back to the window, wondering where she could go to escape.

"So. You're not in love. You despise the fellow, then?"

"Who? *Drew?*"

"That might make you sad, I suppose. If you deeply disliked the man your sister married."

"Are you always this pushy?" He and Dottie really were cut from the same cloth, she supposed. Good for her friend.

Not as good for Rosie, who was actively missing her own nightgown and her old cuckoo clock and her silent art studio.

"No, actually, I'm not a pushy person at all. Not about personal things," he said, like he was really considering it. "I guess I was trying to shock you into telling me why."

"Why I'm sad?"

"Why you're not eating. Or sleeping. Or talking to anyone. Until now, I guess."

"Why?" she countered.

"Why what?" He leaned forward and grinned.

"Why do you need me to *tell* you why I'm not eating or sleeping? And why did you even notice, anyway?"

He blinked warm, dark eyes, and there was the flash of a full, white smile again in the shadows. "You've got me there. Maybe I'm just bored."

"Dottie's here. Go bother her." Rosie was never, ever rude. It felt surprisingly freeing, and she bit back a smile.

"Scandalous suggestion. She's tucked up in one of the rooms." He settled his head back against the wall again and sighed. "So, if I understand this right, your sister and her new husband are just down the hill on the strip they call Towpath Island, holed up in what was once a *boat*?"

"A barge. From the old canal system." The wind howled outside the window and the pane rattled again. "This particular barge is winterized and has a woodburning stove."

"What a wedding night. Not that I don't blame them for not claiming a mattress on the floor here by the fire with all their friends and family."

If Rosie had considered smiling politely at the comment, another howl of wind sobered her.

"I'm worried about her," she admitted, almost a mumble. She cut him a glance to see if he'd heard, and then she wondered why she had trouble holding his gaze for long.

"You're worried about *her*? Or them?"

Maybe it was the late hour or the storm, but for whatever reason, Rosie told the truth. "About her."

His brows shot up, amusement gone. "You really *don't* like her new husband. Is your sister unsafe with him, then?"

"Oh, no. No. I don't mean that. Drew adores her. He's wonderful, and he'd lay down his life for anyone. That's the way he is. And he lives and breathes for Emily."

Gabe nodded and relaxed again. "Sounds like the perfect man to keep her safe in a blizzard, even if it's in a beached boat."

"Barge."

"He adores her, and the barge is winterized. But you're worried about her, just the same. Are you worried they don't have enough wood cut to feed the stove?"

Rosie shook her head and felt her face heat. She shouldn't have said anything. "I'm sure she'll be fine," she said, picking at the quilt. "I'm sure she'll ... get used to it."

This time only one of his dark brows rose. "Get used to it?"

"You know. To being a wife."

His face lit with understanding, and he laughed once more, a low and rich sound. Before she thought a thing about it, Rosie kicked at him across the window seat, issuing a loud, "Shhhhh!" Which made him laugh harder, trying to stifle it, even as he "oofed" as her heel connected with his thigh.

"Are you a grown man or a child?" she hissed. "Keep it down."

Gabe's eyes were dancing now, and Rosie either liked him very much for no good reason or disliked him completely for no good reason. She couldn't decide which.

"So, this is why you've looked like the hunted all evening? Because a man who adores your sister and whom your sister adores is consummating their marriage tonight?"

"*Stop.* We shouldn't even be talking about this." She drew her shoulders back and stared hard at the nothingness of the window again, hot from embarrassment.

She couldn't tell him she had practiced the part of wife once in an attempt to make sure a college co-ed didn't forget her in the fall. She couldn't tell him she had hated it and that nothing had gone according to the promised plan.

Well, she supposed Charlie must have been in the Lord's plans. But the college boy had forgotten her just the same.

What was Emily going through down there in her own initiation to married life? It nearly made Rosie shudder to think of it. The sisters had never been very far apart, except when Emily had gone to OSU for her degree, but even then, she'd been on the train home at least half the weekends for little Charlie's birthdays and school recitals and loose teeth. They'd mostly grown accustomed to telling one another everything, to shielding one another when it was called for ...

... which was why Emily had shot Rosie a desperate look when it was suggested most of the wedding party seek shelter at the hotel.

Emily, after all, was the only one who knew for sure who Charlie's father was.

Now, Rosie was here without a shield among painful secrets, and Emily was down the hill—a space impossible to cross in the storm—experiencing who *knew* what kind of discomfort and confusion?

Rosie, though very comfortable in the role of Mom, had not known how to prepare her sister for this night.

Now, she realized Gabe was studying her as the loud clock ticked, his playfulness gone.

She shut her eyes against his gaze. Neither did she bother to break the silence with polite conversation. It was too late for that.

With any luck, the storm would stop at daybreak, and she'd be home. They could board up the upstairs, couldn't they, to keep the cold out from the roof damage?

If she were going to huddle beside a fire over the holidays, it would be the Graham family's fireplace. Considering that, Rosie saw no reason for her to play nice with this businessman who noticed things.

She did not know how much time had passed before she heard him whisper, "Hey. Rosie Graham. I'm sorry I pried."

She nodded. "No apology is needed. Goodnight."

She forcefully closed her eyes and tried to slow her breath. Sitting upright in that window seat, she faked sleep for the first time since grade school. She hated that she thought she heard him chuckling as he slipped out of the room to bed.

Chapter Six

Delia Stimpson Grade Four
Christmas Journal Project
Buckeye Lake Public School
December 1946

    I said: Well, it looks like I won't have to do the Christmas journal for Ms. Bailey now because we are in a blizzard and we are not at home, where my journal is I'm supposed to write in. Then Rosie gave me this paper she found in what they call the study here at the inn. And this pencil.
    So, I am still doing this journal, even in a blizzard and not in the right journal.
    We got to eat whatever we wanted last night and stay up so late and drink hot cocoa! Chief Gunn said we had to come here to the inn. It is warm, and there are nice people here. Pretty much all my favorite people plus some new ones. Emily and Drew got married and they are the only ones not here. And Smokey got us a Christmas tree. A real one from the yard! Rosie said we can decorate it today. She keeps saying things about us taking naps like we were all little kids or something, but nobody seems like they're taking her too seriously.

~~~~~

    Gabe had never had cause to see Dot Berkeley in a state she referred to — rather benignly, he thought — as "focused."
    Early in the day, she unrolled the blueprints he had brought along, giddy like a child on Christmas morning. Next, she covered the expansive desk in the study with additional paper and supplies. There were several lanterns positioned on every surface of the book-lined room. A typewriter joined the mix, and no amount of fierce wind or relentless storm seemed to distract Dot from a degree of productivity Gabe found alarming.
    Nearly as alarming as the storm itself.
    The blizzard had settled over the inn like a thick, white blanket that prohibited movement. Almost everyone was on edge beneath the weight of it. Just when it might be expected to let up, it managed to blow stronger still.
    When Gabe shared the suffocating blanket analogy with Dot, she blinked up at him, called him "adorable," and declared the blizzard "a perfect chance for us to finally get ahead on this."

Pacing, he found himself envying the children.

Though the novelty of being trapped in a fancy inn had worn off soon after breakfast, the other storm refugees rallied to entertain the two youngest. Smokey, who made an enormous bronco, galloped them around the parlor on his back as they squealed. Charlie, whom Gabe knew was clearly Rosie Graham's son, and Delia, who was somehow in the custody of Pastor Skip, had next been put to work building sandwiches out of leftover wedding turkey. After that, they'd engaged in a surprisingly loud game of hide-and-seek in the east wing of the inn.

Through it all, Rosie made comedic threats about what would happen if anyone "so much as lay a finger on" the baby grand piano.

Gabe wandered out of the study to see what they were all up to as the afternoon wore on, certain Dot would not notice he'd left.

"I would really rather you didn't use the inn's nicer ornaments," Margo Fairchild said gently. She was standing in the parlor over a crate filled with the same shredded newspaper that had cradled the nativity figures. Gabe had lugged the tree decorations down from the attic before lunch.

Inside the crate, it turned out, was a collection of highly breakable, stark white porcelain spheres no one had a chance to touch before Margo slid the top right back on.

"Oh, of course not," Rosie Graham said politely. "We can make our own decorations, can't we?"

She seemed more composed today. Capable of interaction, at least. To Gabe's secret amusement, though, she barely looked directly at him, and she blushed whenever it couldn't be avoided. He assumed it was because of their conversation the night before. Despite his amusement, she continued to be a riddle.

Rosie wasn't a fussy old maid, clearly, because … well, Charlie. She'd had a child. Yet, she was apparently wrecked by the prospect of her sister's wedding night?

It didn't add up.

He assumed she must be a war widow. Had her departed husband been less than considerate with her? He couldn't help but imagine possibilities, none of which were humorous, and Rosie had caught him staring today more than once as he'd wondered.

"Let's pop popcorn for the tree," Gabe suggested as Margo oversaw the re-packing of the too-valuable tree ornaments. He'd have hung the nice ones, were it up to him, but the wife of the owner out-ranked FH Resorts General Facilities Manager. "Do you have popcorn in the pantry, Ruth?"

"Of course we do." She seemed offended he'd asked.

After all, Buckeye Lake was surrounded by miles of cornfields, so much so that the little town of Millersport on the opposite side of the lake had a grand festival in honor of corn at the end of every summer. Gabe had driven out with Keith to experience it, where he'd shared a non-business corn-on-the-cob dinner with Dot.

Indeed, corn for roasting, boiling, stewing, and popping was in *every* pantry at the lake.

Comfortably perched on the hearth, he enjoyed the scent of butter melting in the metal popper extended over the flames. When he'd reduced it to a golden soup, he pulled the popper back so Ruth could pour the kernels into the heated butter. Securing the mesh lid overtop the pan, he balanced it back over the fire.

The experience took Gabe back to those poverty-ridden holidays of his boyhood, happy and carefree. His father had taught him how to pop corn over a fire when he'd been little older than Charlie. "Keep it moving, Son. Never stop shifting it so it doesn't stick. Keep it moving."

His father had turned it into a sermon on Sunday, Gabe recalled. Something about moving, but he couldn't remember the exact spiritual point.

Churning the popcorn was a workout at any age, and Gabe was happy for the chance to do it today as Charlie and Delia danced around beside him, waiting for the telltale popping sounds from within the metal. Gripping the wooden handle in both hands, he undulated the contraption over the fireplace flames. Butter sloshed in its base even as the kernels rattled.

"Ruth has some old jar lids she said we can decorate for ornaments, too," Rosie announced, joining them at the hearth and placing an affectionate hand on each child's shoulder. Gabe looked up and found she was finally making eye contact with him, surprised even more when she offered him a soft smile.

He realized it was the first smile she'd produced in the day and night she'd been under this roof.

The fact was, Rosie Graham was lovely, whether she was looking worried or delivering this tentative, closed-mouth smile. Her hair was a dark strawberry-blonde, and her blue eyes had a dreamy, shimmery quality a person wanted to return to in a crowded room. There was some kind of ... magic there. She had the look of a fairy, with her fragile white neck like the porcelain creations Margo Fairchild guarded.

This particular fairy, though, had mysterious and intriguing things going on behind those eyes. He hadn't made any progress discovering those things in the middle of the night, either.

"Smokey said he'd poke holes in them, and we found some ribbon," she was saying. He stared blankly at her until she clarified, "The canning jar lids. For the ornaments?"

"Right." *Slosh, slosh, clatter, clatter.* He focused again on the popper over the fire, enjoying the burn in his arms and grateful to be able to move in any way.

"Can I try? Please?" Charlie asked, moving closer. Gabe sought Rosie's permission with a glance, and she gave a slight nod.

Even after Charlie and Delia had taken turns wearing themselves out dramatically, still not one kernel had popped. Gabe had guided them, repeating his father's mantra. "Keep it moving." When he was fully back on popping duty, Gabe sifted so vigorously that the children giggled. Which meant he had to whole-body dance with the motion, and they laughed harder.

Then, miracle of miracles—though it was barely discernable over the first intrepid "pops"—Rosie Graham laughed.

From that point, it was the usual frenzy of popping and dumping the fruits of his labor into a pan Ruth had produced from the kitchen. "Ruth," he said, shaking the mountain of popcorn into the pan she held. She echoed his motions with a saltshaker. "You've been such a help that you really should have the honor of the first handful." Before the little ones could protest fully, Gabe added playfully, "But I think *I'm* going to, instead!" He exaggerated smashing a heaping fistful to his mouth as popcorn pieces rained down around him.

Charlie and Delia collapsed into more giggles, diving for stray pieces. Gabe laughed with them. What better season than Christmas to behave like a child again? Or to make friends with children?

They seemed far more appealing as pals than did Keith, for example, who was hardly to be seen today.

It was all a little strange. Keith Fairchild generally enjoyed company more than Gabe did. Certainly, Gabe could charm and negotiate and ingratiate himself to businessmen—it was the quality Camden Fairchild had quickly seen and sought to develop to his hotel chain's advantage, after all. But, outside of a business scenario, Gabe knew himself to hang back socially far more than Keith ever did.

His friend should be the one reveling in this unexpected company.

That was Keith's loss, Gabe decided as Rosie Graham joined him on the hearth with a pincushion and three different colors of thread on spools.

Margo herself served them a tray of tea, perhaps to make up for her stinginess with the decorations. Gabe dropped some sugar into the cup his boss's wife handed him, winked at her, and watched Rosie help Delia thread her needle. He noticed the little girl snuggled right up to the woman.

"Moisten the tip of the thread a little first, Dee," Rosie was saying.

"I could thread a needle when I was half her age," Margo observed, placing a cup on the stones next to Rosie, who shot Margo a quelling look that was wasted on the older woman.

"You're doing fine," Rosie said softly as Delia tugged the thread through.

Delia was in the custody of an old widower, Gabe knew. She could probably recite the Lord's Prayer backward and forward, but something told him Pastor Skip had not handled this part of the girl's education.

"You can just do mine for me, Mom," Charlie said around a mouthful of popcorn, regarding the thread with disdain.

"I don't think so, Son. Here."

Charlie made a groaning sound and mumbled something about "girl stuff."

"I had to sew men up on battlefields, Charlie." This from Smokey, who had managed to get the tree to stand on two slabs of wood he'd found in the storeroom. He turned it a little this way and that until he was satisfied the bare spot faced the wall. Gabe had learned the night before that the enormous man made a living, at least partly, by selling Christmas trees this time of year. "Think I could've patched men back together during combat missions if my mama hadn't made sure I could thread a needle?"

"I thought that was the medics." Charlie frowned through his glasses at the eye of the needle and stuck his little tongue out in concentration.

"There weren't always medics where I was, Kid. We all knew just enough to hold men's arms and legs on 'til we got back to a ship."

"Oh my," Margo said, even as Charlie made it to the knotting stage of his little project with a triumphant cry.

"Were you in the war, too, Mr. Adams?" Charlie asked then, moving to where Gabe balanced the pan of popcorn on his knee.

"No." Gabe chewed and swallowed. "I wanted to go, but my leg was injured a few years before in an accident."

"Don't be modest, Gabriel," Margo put in. "Tell them how you hurt it."

"It's not that exciting. We were refurbishing one of the hotels in Columbus, and a pallet of slate slid off the roof. I was standing in the wrong spot, but it could've been worse. It could've been my pretty face, I guess."

Charlie and Delia giggled.

"The 'wrong spot,' as he says, was pushing one of the contractors out of harm's way. He was a hero," Margo insisted. "Now, Gabriel, could you take these ornaments back up to the attic when you get a moment?"

"Heroes don't rate too high on Mrs. Fairchild's scale," he told the kids, rising to take hold of the box of prized decorations he'd lugged down a few hours before. "I imagine there are some other less breakable things up there," he said. "Anyone want to go on an attic adventure and see if we can retrieve some?"

Charlie shot up so fast that he smashed the puffs of corn on the end of his mother's length of thread.

"Charlie, you complete numbskull!" Delia announced mournfully. "Don't worry, Rosie. I'll stay here with you and help you fix it."

"Fine by me! Let's go, Mr. Adams!"

While Delia snuggled in tighter with the apparently endlessly patient Rosie, Gabe had to hurry to catch up with Charlie. From the corner of his eye, he saw Rosie watching him as he hoisted the heavy box up onto his shoulder.

The inn was laid out like a bow tie, with the large central room branching off in four hallways that fanned away from one another and then joined again in a hall at the end. On the west side, the end was the large kitchen, formal dining area, and supply rooms. On the east, it was another hall of rooms and a second floor of rooms above that. Charlie scampered ahead while Gabe gave him directions from overtop the crate.

The hammer Gabe had used to open the lid was still propped against the doorjamb. They had to get on their hands and knees to shove the crate ahead of them into the attic storage.

"Boy, this is the tops," Charlie said as he explored the plywood that created a rough subfloor between the rafters.

"Literally the tops. It being an attic."

Around them were the dusty collections of one of the oldest inns on Buckeye Lake. A dress form on a lopsided pedestal. An ancient croquet set. A chest filled, for some reason, with boxing gloves.

"Don't even think about it," Gabe told Charlie, reading his mind. "No good can come of boxing gloves and a bunch of people snowed in together. Move along and see what else we find."

"Can we take these ice skates downstairs, then? Mine are at home."

"Tell you what. We'll come back up for them if at any point it seems like we can find the lake through the blizzard to skate on it."

The wind somehow managed to be even louder up here, a few feet from a roof insulated by feet of snow.

"You think it'll still be storming tomorrow?"

"I can't say." Gabe slid the box of ornaments next to a few other crates. "Let's see what's in these others."

Gabe worked on prying the lid off one.

"Drew always lets me use his hammer when we build docks," Charlie offered. Message received, Gabe got each corner started and handed the hammer over. Charlie eventually muscled the lid off, his glasses slipping down his freckled nose in the process. He had bright blue eyes, a different hue from his mom's, and his hair was much lighter than hers.

Packed Together

"You build docks, do you? Down at the marina, I assume?"

"Yes, at the marina. Grandpa says I'll have to run it one day. And Drew says it needs a bit of work."

"Do you call him Uncle Drew now?"

Charlie sat back on his haunches and bounced a little, looking up with eager eyes. "Oh. Yes! I hadn't thought of that. He's *Uncle Drew* now!"

"Nothing much in this box," Gabe pointed out as they peered in at patriotic china dishes. "Let's try that one over there. Anyway, sounds like you're gonna like your new neighbor just fine."

"Me and Uncle Drew do stuff together. Man stuff. Football, and also, he took me hunting last month, but he said I didn't have to shoot anything if I didn't want to, and I didn't want to."

"Your first time hunting?" Gabe started prying again with the back of the hammer. That was a little like Delia learning to thread a needle for the first time; most boys would have already been hunting by Charlie's age.

"Yes, first time. It was tops. Mom doesn't like that kind of thing. She's an artist," he said, as if that negatively correlated with hunting.

It fit, though, the artist bit. Maybe that was the magic he'd seen in those shimmery eyes of hers. Because he couldn't resist, Gabe shamelessly took advantage of the opening Charlie had given him. "What about your dad? Does he hunt?"

"I don't have a dad." He said it very simply.

"Did he ... was he in the war?"

"No," Charlie said cheerfully. "I just never had one. Hey, look! Look at this! This one's full of *hats*!"

Why in the world would the inn have saved a box of turn-of-the-century hats? Women's and men's alike.

And why in the world would any man walk out on Rosie Graham and a son who must have been too young to remember? The scenario had somehow gotten even more perplexing, rather than less.

Charlie dug out a woman's hat with enormous feathers and plopped it on his head, sneezing from the dust and making Gabe laugh. In the spirit, Gabe dug around and found a bowler that he knew must look ridiculous. They took turns trying on hats, many of them bedecked in flowers and little lace veils, until their laughter was louder than the wind howling just above them.

~~~~~

At the hearth, Delia had lost interest in poking sewing needles through popcorn kernels. When she'd left for the window seat to dream over Ruth's copy of the Sears Christmas Book, Smokey had also risen from his spot on the floor.

"You're deserting me too?" Rosie asked, poking a kernel through its heart.

Never one to sit still, Smokey had been a good sport with the popcorn garland. Rosie enjoyed seeing the enormous war hero and farmer sprawled out with his needle and thread.

"I'm coming back with reinforcements. I've had about enough of Dottie being rude."

Sure enough, he returned with Dottie in tow a few moments later and resumed his spot. "Give her a needle, there, Rosie."

"What power does he have over you that has you stringing popcorn against your will?" Rosie asked.

Dottie caught the spool of thread she tossed her. Then she settled down on a pillow on the stone hearth beside her friend. "He's right. I probably should take a break."

"Probably? You're like some kind of mad scientist in there," Smokey chided.

The three of them had known one another since their earliest school days, and Rosie thought it never showed as much as it did in the tension between big, sweet Smokey Black and the relentlessly driven Dottie Berkeley.

"She's hatching evil plots, for sure," Rosie added, eyeing her friend as she grabbed another piece of popcorn. "You're working on your fancy resort, I assume."

Dottie ate a handful of popcorn before settling into her task, unbothered as Rosie had known she'd be by accusations of evil. "It's not *my* fancy resort. It's FH's."

"Mmm hmm. But you out-worked Fairchild Hotel's glory boy a few hours back," Smokey noted. "What's going on with you two?"

Dottie was threading her needle now, making short work of it. She was good at everything she did. Then she shot Smokey a glance. "What do you care?"

"Whenever I sew, I feel the need to gossip like an old lady."

"Does that include when you're sewing on men's arms and legs, soldier?" Rosie asked.

"I don't even want to know what that means," Dottie replied.

"You miss all kinds of fun when you're hiding in your evil lab. So. You and Adams?"

"We have the same vision," Dottie said carefully. Smokey guffawed at that.

"Leave her alone, Smoke. Why don't we gossip about you?"

"I'm an open book, ladies."

"If only it were an interesting book."

"It just so happens I'm thinking about getting married, myself," he said, stretching his long legs out in front of him. "I decided yesterday, during Em's wedding."

"Who's the bride?" Rosie asked.

"Not sure yet."

Rosie and Dottie shared a look and managed not to laugh. "So, you've just decided you're in the market for one?" Dottie asked.

"Yes. I think it's time. The farm is really taking off, and I think I'll start building a real house out there in the next year or so."

"At least that gives you a few months to meet someone and fall in love."

"Exactly."

"Fascinating," Rosie muttered.

"What?"

"I just don't know about this approach to it. It feels so ... I don't know."

"Like Delia shopping the Sears catalog over there," Dottie supplied.

Smokey turned toward her. "And it's different from your little 'shared vision' with Gabe Adams how, Miss Berkeley?"

Dottie simply grinned. She was impossible to rile. "I wouldn't want to be off the market just when you decide to start shopping, Mr. Black."

He made a huffing sound. "I might consider Rosie, though," he said, moving that dark brow he raised when he was playing. "Only, rumor has it you might be off the market, yourself, Miss Graham."

Rosie dropped the needle and gaped at him. "What can you possibly mean by that?"

"I heard you might get yourself hitched to the good professor. What's his name?"

"Are you referring to Dr. Maxim Lamb?" Rosie deliberately relaxed her jaw. "Who in the world said that?"

"Better be a vicious rumor, Rose," Dottie said irritably. "Because I just know you wouldn't have neglected to tell me something big like that."

"I heard it from my friend Mathison," Smokey said happily, holding up about two-and-a-half feet of popcorn garland for their admiration.

"Who must have heard it from your sister," Dottie said on a gasp. "It must be true, then! How dare you fall in love without a word to me?"

Rosie growled, picking up her needle again. "It's not true at all." She would have to talk with Emily about blabbing everything to her Romeo, who seemed to get it all wrong in the re-telling, anyway. "Men really are worse gossips than women. Listen. Dr. Lamb and I have been good friends for several years, and that's all."

"They've been working out at Cranberry Bog, so she can illustrate that book he's doing. His bog botany book or whatever," Dottie supplied to Smokey, who didn't seem overly interested in the details anyway. "So they can get the marshy thing named a nature preserve."

"So that you and our delightful hosts can't destroy it with your new resort," Rosie pointed out. Dottie waved that off. "Anyway, I'm not marrying him, you two."

"Did he *ask*?" Dottie demanded.

Rosie flinched. Poor Maxim. He deserved better than to be rejected and then gossiped about, but Rosie didn't lie. She avoided things and kept secrets, but outright lying? No.

"He asked me to marry him just before Thanksgiving," she said calmly, not looking up from the popcorn that snaked over her lap. "I told him I couldn't do that."

"Why not?" Smokey wanted to know, as though taking notes for his own crusade.

"I don't want to get married," Rosie told them.

"At *all*?"

"Not especially. I'm okay as I am. I don't love Dr. Lamb."

"So, I shouldn't even ask you?" Smokey threw a piece of popcorn at her, and it stuck in her hair.

"You do make it hard to resist."

Chapter Seven

No one was keeping track of time anymore, Rosie realized that night as the grand old clock chimed out a series she did not bother to count over the noise in the parlor.

The inn's owners and the inn's refugees had been divided into two mixed teams for Christmas charades near the fireplace, the furniture parted as if for a stage.

Their homespun fir tree in the corner stood in contrast, with its finished popcorn garland and jar lid ornaments, to the otherwise posh decor of the inn: the expensive rug, the overstuffed, embroidered furniture with its polished wood. Oh, and the porcelain nativity near the tree over which Rosie had already had three episodes of heart failure when the children had almost toppled it.

How many framed photographs of the roller coaster would she have to sell on the boardwalk next season to pay for that many busted camels and shepherds?

"You're a lion!" Delia guessed, hopping up and down in front of Rosie as the game intensified.

Everyone watched Keith Fairchild, who was plodding around on his hands and knees in front of the fireplace.

"A lion?! Don't be a goose, Dee," Charlie argued. "What have lions got to do with Christmas?" Like Delia, he couldn't stay seated during his team's turn to guess, and he hovered near Keith, bouncing on the balls of his stocking feet.

Rosie tensed whenever her son got within a few feet of the man, petrified someone would notice the clear resemblance between them.

Now that she had the chance to study him more, she noticed Keith's youthful cockiness seemed to have been replaced with the easy confidence of a wealthy man who had traveled the world through both the Army and his family's business.

He seemed grounded, somehow.

She hadn't seen much of him since they'd arrived, which had been its own kind of Christmas gift. Right now, as he crawled around before the fire, she smiled a little at the appropriateness of the fact he was clearly portraying the donkey that carried Mary to Bethlehem.

She had personally experienced him in the role of donkey.

Even though she was on Keith's team, there weren't enough points in the world for Rosie to give him the satisfaction of ending his turn by guessing correctly.

"He's a reindeer! One of Santa's reindeer," Aunt Cookie said decisively. Keith shook his head in frustration.

Their charades team, captained by her grandfather, was made up of Rosie, Keith, Charlie, Delia, and Cookie. The opposing team, looking smug across the pricey rug, was captained by Gabe Adams, who had chosen — unsurprisingly — Dottie, along with Camden Fairchild, Smokey, Pastor Skip, and her Uncle Burt.

The other team was winning.

Rosie reconsidered guessing "donkey" for the sake of her team's point, but something kept her quiet as she watched Keith fashion a harness and reins for himself out of some discarded rope on the log pile. He gestured at his back, where he clearly imagined a pregnant Mary seated, but Rosie simply bounced her foot where it crossed over her other leg and remained silent.

"He does look like a reindeer," Delia said as Keith tried to steer himself with his own reins.

"I'm *not* a reindeer. You can ride on my back."

"Hey, now! No talking, no clues!" This from Smokey, who stood behind the sofa across the room, occasionally adding his deep chuckle.

"A horse!"

"No, no. A horse is not a Christmas animal."

"A horse can be any kind of animal it wants," Charlie argued. "That's like saying I'm not a Christmas boy, even though I'm a boy on Christmas like a horse is a horse on Christmas."

Rosie wished for the hundredth time that Emily was here. Emily would appreciate Keith in the role of donkey. She missed her sister's laugh and the fact she'd probably be making "ass" jokes to help Rosie feel better in general.

She thought again of Em snuggled into the barge house down the hill. Which made her think of honeymoons. Which made her glance over at Gabe Adams, only to find him watching her. Again.

He quickly looked away, back at Keith. Sometimes today when she'd found him watching her with those dark eyes, they'd been crinkled with kindness, like he was always on the verge of smiling. She couldn't find a way to partner that warm gaze with the kind of man who wore expensive executive-style shoes during a blizzard and whom she knew was waging war against a helpless, cranberry-producing bog.

Then Keith changed the rhythm of the game by suddenly pointing to the white porcelain donkey in the nativity scene. Delia and Charlie both yelled, "Donkey!" in response, and the room erupted, laughter from her team and outrage from the other.

"You can't do that!"

"Hey! He pointed at the donkey! That doesn't count!"

"That is blatant cheating!" Dottie protested, hopping up from her seat beside Gabe. They really were a perfect couple, Rosie thought. Both so polished, so tidy, so attractive. Neither would ever allow themselves to be cheated or taken advantage of. Or even allow themselves to lose.

Rosie loved Dottie, but she had never identified with her. Rosie, in fact, knew herself to be *often* taken advantage of.

"No point! No way!"

"He cannot help that his team was not getting it," Margo Fairchild said in defense of her baby boy, and half the room rolled their eyes. Margo hadn't wanted to play, but that didn't keep her from issuing an opinion almost constantly. "How long do you want this game to go on, anyway?"

"Where else do we have to be?" Smokey asked.

"Cheating is cheating," Dot insisted, her eyes flashing at Margo in annoyance. Beside her, Gabe was clearly enjoying himself, as he seemed to in all things. "If we're going to have some kind of time limit on guesses, fine, but let's agree on that at the outset."

"I'm sorry, but as my team's captain," Hickory ruled from Rosie's other side, "I must agree. Pointing at the nativity donkey was crossing a line. I don't think we should get the point."

"Awww, *Grandpa!*"

"Sorry, team," Keith said, looking repentant.

"So, what? Do we lose our turn too, then?"

"The only fair way to decide if Team A gets another turn might be a sudden death round," Gabe suggested.

"What's sudden death?" Delia asked, predictably intrigued by something that sounded morbid. Rosie's heart swelled with love for her.

"We put Dot here up against Keith, one team against another. They pick the same challenge paper, and the first team to guess gets the next turn."

"As long as I can watch Dottie instead of Keith for clues," Aunt Cookie grumbled with a pointed look at Margo.

Dottie hopped up with zeal. "I love it! I'm game!"

If there were someone who made an even better match for Dottie than Gabe, Rosie thought, it was Keith. The pair stood side by side in competition, looking ready for anything. Him all blonde and bronzed, her always so put together. But Rosie would never wish a donkey on her friend, no matter how rich he was. Dottie was a businesswoman, for sure, but she also deserved a man with kind eyes that crinkled on the ends.

Rosie stifled a yawn as the room got even louder with the "sudden death." Not sleeping much the night before, or even the night before that, had caught up with her, and she regretted insisting on bedding down out here by the fire with the kids the night before rather than claiming a room for herself.

She'd thought it would be for one night, but here they were still, even less able to leave this place than they'd been when she'd claimed the sofa. Somehow, they were even further from home tonight, and she had nowhere to retire.

Seeking the solace of the quiet and chilly kitchen, Rosie slipped from the room and down the left hallway as the teams were all on their feet shouting guesses and missing the mark on what was clearly "tinsel." *Sounds like pencil.* Dottie's clue had been clear.

Rosie found the large kitchen, with its steel-topped counter island, lit by just one oil lamp. Its flame danced over the clean surfaces. The rattling of the windowpane over the sink was louder in here, and she was surprised to see Ruth Drumgool placing a pot of what looked like milk on the stove. The older woman looked over.

"In the mood for some more cocoa?"

"You read my mind. I need something to keep me awake, and I've had all the coffee I can handle for one day," Rosie said. "Let me help you make it?"

They worked in companionable silence for a few minutes. "You know, you can make yourself at home in the kitchen for as long as you're here," Ruth offered. "I told Cookie the same thing, since she rents out rooms at her own house, from what I understand. You're all welcome to use anything."

What would it be like to be queen of this enormous space? To rattle around in this inn for the off-season, completely alone?

"I appreciate that offer." Rosie also wondered if the woman remembered her from the summer of 1935, when she'd been little more than a girl. Keith had requested all those romantic picnic lunches for the beach, after all.

Did she remember the way Rosie had no doubt looked adoringly at the young prince, the heir to all the inns and hotels the family owned and ran? Had Ruth known the way it would all end, and had she cared? Did she remember Rosie's last trip up here to the inn, when she'd been shaking and asking if Ruth had Keith's number at school?

Ruth's tight-lipped words that day confirmed she really *had* known all along how it would go.

If there were someone Rosie worried about making the connection between the illustrious Keith Fairchild and her own little Charlie, it was this woman who was measuring cocoa and sugar into cups arranged on two trays as the milk worked its way to a boil.

"I have to admit, I'm surprised you're quite so at home in a kitchen," Ruth said to Rosie.

"Surprised?" She hardly lived the kind of glamorous life that equated to private chefs, after all. "Why would that be?"

"Because of your art," Ruth said with a shrug, causing Rosie to gape. "Your work is impressive. I can hardly imagine you having time to keep up with lesser domestic tasks. I mean, the blown glass and the photography and the paintings. Your talent should be reserved for the studio. That's all I meant."

"Thank you," Rosie said, blinking and nonplussed by what felt like genuine respect. She couldn't help the smile. "Are you offering to cook for me, Ruth, once this is all over?"

"In exchange for one of your paintings of the bog? In a heartbeat."

"Careful what you offer. I didn't know you followed my work."

"I've been buying it up the last few months from the stores up town," Ruth said as though it were a simple thing. A cheer erupted from far down the hall as a charades point was presumably scored. "Mr. Adams insisted I stock up. He wants to fill the new resort with your work, after he spotted it in one of the dining rooms on the boardwalk."

Rosie tried to process this. Had she ever seen Gabe Adams in her boardwalk studio? She didn't think so. Nor had he mentioned anything about art last night when they'd spoken. He must not have made the connection, she realized, between the bizarre behavior of the woman in the window seat and an artist whose work he thought worthy of collecting.

"I admit I envy your talent," Ruth was saying, and though the words were kind, her tone never managed to be, no matter the words.

Rosie began to understand this as part of Ruth's nature, an important thing she'd missed as a young woman.

"I've never been able to draw. I must be content setting a lovely table."

"That's its own kind of creativity and satisfaction, for sure. I also love to cook and bake." They were quiet as Rosie poured milk into the cups as Ruth stirred. It would need to cool.

"It's not the only thing I envy you for," Ruth said as she stirred the final cup.

"Oh?"

"I'm an old maid."

Rosie laughed a little. "I am that, too, Ruth."

"Yes, but you have the gift of a child, don't you?"

Rosie met Ruth's eyes. The woman *did* know. And even though her tone was somehow still severe, there was a warmth there that promised secrecy and maybe even hinted at apology.

"Thank you for referring to my Charlie as a gift. People never do that."

~~~~~

Gabe watched Ruth and Rosie carefully move into the room balancing steaming cups on round trays, which they placed on a table at the opposite end of the room from the fireplace.

"Give the cocoa a minute to cool," Ruth warned the room sternly.

"Hot cocoa!" Charlie said happily, but Gabe saw him yawn immediately afterward.

"Camden's turn," Dot said from her spot on the sofa beside Gabe. She still smelled deliciously of her fine perfume.

Camden Fairchild took his place in the center of the room, having read and contemplated the slip of paper he'd pulled from the bowl. Gabe watched in horror as the man began — with a cradling gesture followed by a slashing motion — to aggressively mimic the killing of infants. The room fell into baffled silence.

"It's King Herrod," Gabe said quickly, happy to cut this pantomime short.

"Nice job," Dot said with delight, reaching over to pat his knee in approval. Gabe smiled.

It was little Charlie's turn on the other team, and the boy asked the room in general if he could elicit the help of his mother on this one.

"We never said anything about partners," Burt said skeptically, though he added a wink. "But perhaps an exception can be made if you promise to do twice as well."

"It will be hard to top the last one," Rosie mumbled, but those who heard her laughed off the memory of Camden's invisible babies. For his part, Camden looked pleased enough with himself.

As mother and son took their place and whispered a game plan, Gabe decided he could handle a too-hot cup of cocoa and got up to move across the room. Smokey joined him near the piano since their team was off duty this round.

They stood together and blew a little over the tops of their cups. Rosie, backlit by the roaring fire, was pretending to roll something along the carpet.

"She's a gem," Smokey said in his low, gruff voice, looking over at Gabe.

Charlie, who had also been following his mother's motions, now mimed picking up something hugely heavy and placing it in the air beside Rosie.

"So's the kid," Gabe said, smiling. He considered Smokey. "Have you known them long?"

"Sure. I grew up with Rosie and with Em. With your girlfriend, too," he responded with a wink. Gabe imagined the lot of them running wild at the amusement park, on the beaches, in the lake. What a way to grow up.

He appreciated for the first time how special that wedding day must have been, gathered in the same place with so many memories.

"You must be happy for Emily."

"Sure am. Mathison is one of the best men I know. I'm honored to call him a friend now, too."

They watched Rosie hoist her son up so he could mimic putting a carrot in the invisible snowman's invisible head, and the rest of Team A allowed little Delia to be the one to yell, "A snowman! You're building a snowman!"

"Charlie told me he doesn't have a dad," Gabe said, deciding this was easier explored with Smokey than with Dot.

"He's right."

"The man didn't own up to his responsibility?"

"Rosie never talked about it."

"So, she never did marry? Never found anyone? Because of Charlie?"

Smokey chuckled, and they moved in silent agreement toward the window as the others stopped the game for their own hot cocoa break. "Kid or no kid, Rosie could have any man she wanted. Make no mistake."

Gabe watched her laughing with Dot and found it easy to believe.

"Just about every man who meets Rosie falls in love with her," Smokey warned, his voice low and his eyes serious.

Gabe felt his neck heat. *He* wasn't falling in love with anyone. Not Rosie, anyway. He was merely curious.

"But I don't think she's one to fall in love back. I think she's good with it being her and Charlie and her family down on the towpath, you know?"

"How about you? Are you in love with her too?"

"I think I was once, like any man with sense. But we're not right, me and Rosie. You know when you're with the right person." Smokey's gray eyes tracked across the room, elsewhere entirely, but Gabe missed where they landed as he watched Rosie tousle her son's hair and laugh in that warm way that apparently made all men want to spend forever with her.

Save one, apparently.

Chapter Eight

Delia Stimpson Grade Four
Christmas Journal Project
Buckeye Lake Public School
December 1946

I don't know what to write today. Ice can be very loud. Charlie can also be loud and very irritating when you have to see him all day every day.

I like being here with everybody else, though.

~~~~~

By the following afternoon, the wind had finally died down enough for feet upon feet of snow to be visible from the inn's expansive windows. Though Rosie tried to feel optimistic about this development, the temperature stayed perilously low, accompanied by relentless sleet and vicious bursts of ice that coated the windows all over again.

No one, it seemed, was going anywhere any time soon.

The biggest alarm of the morning had them all gathering to watch Smokey try to open the outside door to bring in more firewood. Thick ice had sealed it shut from the outside, so they'd cheered as he shouldered and muscled it open.

As the reality of being literally sealed into the building hit the cheering refugees, they were surprised to find out Aunt Cookie didn't deal well with being trapped.

She'd started breathing strangely, pushing her hands through her orange hair, pacing around the kitchen like an agitated wildcat as Smokey had worked at the door. Her brief but dramatic midday meltdown ended when Uncle Burt administered brandy from the kitchen's medicinal supply.

After that, an uneasiness seemed to settle over the group. Most of them decided to nap.

Rosie, who had desperately needed a nap the day before, found she felt better now. She'd slept late on the sofa alongside the exhausted children, waking only to the hiss of heavy ice pummeling the inn on every side. Then she'd spent a quiet half hour taking deep breaths and telling herself everything was going to turn out fine.

She'd prayed that God agreed to *help* it turn out fine. He would. He was, after all, good.

Added to that peaceful start to the day was her discovery, with Ruth's help, of a large drawer of art supplies in the study. There were no oil or acrylic paints, but the inn kept a supply of postcards, small journals, blank paper, and even watercolor paper for guests. Rosie had been delighted to find a box of well-used watercolor tubes and some brushes of different sizes, half of which had been cleaned enough to still be used. Another small box contained charcoal stubs and a few pastel crayons.

These discoveries and a shelf with ink and pens with new tips had Rosie feeling more like herself by the hour.

Now, she had her legs folded beneath her on a cushion she'd dragged down in front of the sofa. She'd taped a watercolor paper scrap onto a lapboard, and she was sketching Delia's likeness where the little girl perched a few feet away on the hearth.

"Make my braids look pretty," Delia instructed, chin high. This would be her first time having her portrait made. Rosie nodded, biting back a grin at the reality of the child's braids. Bits of unruly layers stuck out at different points in each rope of hair, which Rosie had re-braided half a dozen times since the wedding.

It felt good moving her right hand over the soft texture of the pressed paper, watching the angle of a cheek and chin take shape there in the light gray of vine charcoal. Rosie loved the smell of the supplies, the way her senses seemed harnessed by some other power. Her hand, her eyes, every muscle moved in a dance she'd been doing since before she could remember, even as her mind was freed from the storm and the tension of secrets.

Within minutes, the outline of Delia's features lived on the page, and Rosie called the child over to inspect the first phase. "What do you think before the paint goes on, sweetie?"

Delia danced a little on her knees beside Rosie, bouncing her approval. "Will you make my dress green in this picture? Dark green?"

"Of course. I never knew you were so mindful of fashion."

"I want it to look like that one green dress *you* have," Delia said adoringly. "Can I draw you too, after you're done?"

"Sure, you can! In fact, we can do it at the same time." Before Rosie settled in with the paints, she took her time taping another piece of paper onto a narrow wooden chess box for Delia. She talked her through how to use the vine charcoal to get her design sketched out, showing her how the soft values of the gray could be wiped off easily with the swipe of a finger as she adjusted angles and shadows. "And if you face me here where you were sitting before, you can sketch me even as I'm working on getting the colors right for your face and hair," Rosie said.

Pastor Skip was off playing the chess game that had originated from inside the box Delia used for a desk.

Rosie knew he did the best he could with the little girl who had come to live with him as her only alternative to an orphanage. His wife had been in heaven for more than a year when her great-niece had been left fatherless by the earliest months of the war. Delia's mother had already died of some sickness when the child was just a toddler, and Pastor Skip told the congregation of the Community Church that he had no doubt God had sent Delia Stimpson to him so he'd have a constant reminder of his beloved wife.

Only, Delia wasn't anything like the mild, gentle Mrs. Reese had been.

Skip had been as shocked as his congregation by the little girl's rambunctious nature and as dismayed as his congregation by his utter lack of control over her.

"This isn't the way this story was supposed to go," he'd told Rosie once in confidence. "Delia was supposed to be solace for all of us. A blessing from God in the darkest times of the war. Instead, she might be worse than the war."

In truth, Rosie and the others knew Pastor Reese had not done the best of jobs raising his only son, Gilbert, who'd grown up alongside Rosie and Emily and the others on the lake. Gil had been a wild and rebellious boy who had recently redeemed himself by returning to a life of faith and testifying in Drew's brother's murder trial.

Gil was now hidden away somewhere in a witness protection program, leaving his father fretting over his own inability to "get it right" for a second time with young Delia.

"Look at it so far," the little girl exclaimed, turning the chess box around for Rosie to see. A nod of approval earned her Delia's partially toothless smile.

Delia spent most of her time on Towpath Island with Rosie and Hickory because she'd become fast friends with Charlie, and Rosie's heart had embraced the girl since their first meeting. Having been hungry herself for the love of a mother she had never known, Rosie understood the girl's need for cuddles and hugs and long talks ... things Pastor Skip simply was not equal to.

Not surprisingly, Delia behaved just fine for Rosie Graham.

Rosie longed to adopt Delia. Not just because she loved the girl but because she had lately experienced clear nudging from God to that end. Some of that nudging was in her own heart, but other things were pointing toward a grander plan. Pastor Skip had been praying lately over a calling he felt to join one of his seminary friends on a mission to the Philippines. He felt compelled to go, but he wondered how his little orphan ward would do overseas.

Meanwhile, here was Rosie, desperately wanting to add that little girl to her little family.

"I think this green is just the right shade for the dress you want me to paint you in," Rosie mused, holding up a tube. "I can mix some darker shades into it if you think it's too bright."

"I just want it to look like your dress."

Rosie knew she would never be able to adopt or be given custody of Delia Stimpson. She was, after all, a "fallen woman." She barely had a right to her own son in society's eyes, to say nothing of taking on another child. The legal system would not so much as entertain the idea.

At times like this, Rosie felt ashamed she had, in fact, briefly considered Maxim's proposal of marriage, if only because it would make an "acceptable" parent of her. Being Mrs. Doctor Lamb, wife of a tenured professor, could have allowed her to secure a home for Delia, one in which the little girl would never be passed around again.

It wasn't right to use a man that way, though, Rosie had decided, any more than she'd ever approve a man using a woman for his own designs.

As she mixed the soft tones of Delia's skin in her tray, Rosie prayed again. She dipped the brush in more water to dilute the mixture into a slightly paler color, testing it along the imperfect edge of the watercolor sheet. She would say "yes" to whatever God wanted her to say yes to, but she suspected a marriage of convenience was her own quick solution when what she was likely supposed to do was wait.

Rosie thought of the Christmas story in the Bible. One of her favorite verses was the one about Mary "cherishing all these things in her heart" as time passed. If Mary, an unconventional mother, could calmly trust God for her calling, certainly Rosie could take another deep breath and paint. And pray.

"So, what do you think Charlie's doin'?" Delia asked, looking up from her own sketching. The two friends had gotten into a quarrel earlier, but clearly Delia's limited attention span tended toward forgiveness.

"Last I heard, he was in the office with Dottie making his own design for a hotel," Rosie said, barely resisting an eyeroll.

Her son tended to love calculators and graphing paper, so he'd always loved spending time with Aunt Dottie. Still, that had been more endearing before Dottie had begun her evil development plans.

Now Rosie's own flesh and blood was playing at designing mega resorts with paper and rulers.

"I don't have the right color for your hair, Rosie," Delia said with a sigh.

"Watercolors mix easily."

"Will you show me?"

Rosie made a "wait" sound as she blended a stroke from her brush along a shadow of collar bone. Then she set her board aside again to give

Delia a quick lesson in color theory that had to do with wheat yellow and the same burgundy as the dress Rosie had been wearing for too many days now.

She longed for a change of day clothes. She had added a thick, brown sweater with patched elbows to her attire when the temperature had fallen further, compliments of Mr. Fairchild.

"Here, you test it on the very edge, like this. See if it's the color you're shooting for."

"But I don't want to mess up my page."

"The edges will be covered when you're done, honey. By a matte or frame."

"Can we really matte this when I'm done?" Delia asked in wonder. Rosie regarded the developing image of herself on the little girl's paper. The eyes were enormous and fringed with spiky lashes. The nose— arguably the hardest part of drawing any face—was comically narrow and nostril-dominated.

Exactly the way a ten-year-old should be drawing.

"Of course we can matte it. I have everything we need in the studio at the house." She'd moved all but her dark room home from the boardwalk showroom for the winter. "Once we get home, we'll matte this in whatever color you like. Now, just make a stroke right about here to see if you've got the hair color the way you like it."

Delia slashed a patch of red gold and cocked her head to contemplate it. Then she looked up at Rosie's head, wrinkling her nose. "It's the color of some of your hair, but there are darker parts too."

"Then what you can do is lay down this lighter shade first. And it should be easy to darken up this little mixture you've got for the darker spots. See?"

"By adding another bit of both colors?"

"And not diluting it with water as much, yes," Rosie said, dropping an approving kiss between Delia's unfortunate braids.

"What do you think? Of this color for Rosie's hair?" Delia asked in the other direction, and Rosie glanced up to see Gabe Adams had appeared with an armful of logs for the fire. The fabric of his fine shirt strained over his arm muscles as he shifted the heavy logs, but he made no move to put them down. She straightened and watched him mirror her earlier posture bending over Delia's sketch.

"I'd know that was Rosie anywhere," he said with an approving nod. His eyes tracked up to Rosie's in consideration, and she had no idea why she felt her cheeks heat. There was something about the way he *saw* her. "And I'd say you've got the hair color perfect."

"That part there will be covered by a matte," Delia explained with an eager glance at Rosie.

"Perfect," he said again, turning to stack the logs beside the hearth. Rosie returned to her seat and board to add shadows to her depiction of Delia's face, her eyes on Gabe as much as on her tray as she blotted some sepia into her mixture for the shadows under Delia's neck.

The sepia had her considering Gabe's skin tone, though, more than Delia's. His features were Caucasian, she thought, but his skin and hair were darker. He had some fortunate mixture of genes to him, and though she couldn't pinpoint it for all she knew of faces, she thought the man could only be grateful for his sparkling brown eyes and healthy pigmentation.

Once he'd carefully slid two logs into the arrangement of the fire, Gabe turned straight to her. "Your son has some excellent ideas for the hotel business, Rosie."

Lovely. Rosie felt her shoulders tighten and swiped her brush beneath Delia's jawline on her paper.

"A curving slide that takes you directly from the third floor of the hotel into the swimming pool, for example," he continued. "Or you can get down to the pool area by bicycle handlebars on a wire. But you can't get down to the pool via the stairway. Those are one-way only. Up."

"An elevator would be better," Delia determined, her gaze darting from Rosie's hair to her paper while Gabe watched.

"He's far more focused on getting *down* from the higher floors so far," Gabe said. "Though perhaps he'd be open to some of your suggestions when it comes time to get people back up there."

"There should be fish tanks everywhere in the hotel," Delia said as though she'd been giving it long thought. "So that you can bring the fishes you catch right out of the lake and inside, you know?"

"To eat later?"

"Or whatever you want. To name, maybe. Or to take home."

"To carry home on the train or bus?"

"You'd have to put the fish in a bag to get it home," Delia said patiently, cutting a glance up at Gabe. "And if you wanted to eat it, well, then you could eat it at the restaurant except it wouldn't cost you money 'cause it's your own fish."

"Who has to clean it?" Rosie asked.

"Mmm. Maybe you can charge a little money if folks don't wanna clean their own fish."

"I like this idea. It's decorative and practical all at once," Gabe decided, moving toward Rosie's setup. "Should the tanks of fish be in the dining room, so the fish understand their future right away?"

"Maybe," Delia said, pausing to consider. "But wouldn't they smell kind of bad?"

"I guess if people are—" Gabe began and then suddenly stopped.

Rosie heard him directly behind her and glanced back at him. He was staring at the paper on her board, mouth slightly opened in mid-sentence. After a long beat, his eyes shot to hers. "Oh. Oh wow, it's you. *You're* RG. Of course."

Rosie smiled. That was the way she signed her photos and paintings here at the lake, with a swooping and swirling duo of initials. The ones Ruth said he'd instructed her to buy up for his own resort design. She had to admit that she liked the whole new level of appreciation in his eyes.

She always preferred to be admired for what God did through her hands than for the way He'd designed her face or body.

"You're the artist from the shops uptown," he was saying. "You won't believe this, but I'm a big fan of your work."

"I do believe you," she said easily, smiling and returning to her board. It was nearly time to lay some ink texture over the soft wash of watercolor. Delia had scampered over again to see what all the fuss was about, and for some time Rosie let the pair of them watch her play with colors and shadows and the lovely way watercolors could depict the folds and shadows of fabric.

She was used to vacationers up on the boardwalk watching her work. It was a sure way to secure a sale, and Rosie had never been stingy with her gifts, anyway. In fact, it was the only part of her life she felt like sharing with anyone outside her family.

It was what had driven her to negotiate with Dottie for the boardwalk studio space. Also, that urge to share had inspired her to decorate the old canal way with romantic glasswork, lit by little spotlights at sunset through the busy season. It kept her fighting the sumac out on Cranberry Bog to sketch flora and fauna for the professor's book.

Artwork was easy to share.

"Unbelievable," Gabe said softly from time to time.

Delia, having set her own depiction of Rosie aside for now, melted down over the edge of the sofa to Rosie's left side, pressing against her as she settled her head on her shoulder and watched her own face grow more and more distinct. Rosie heard her yawn with contentment. "My eyes look almost like yours, don't they, Rosie?" she asked.

"They do, yes." They didn't. Not much. But Rosie heard the need in Delia's voice, recognizing it all too well. She, herself, only knew her own mother's face from distant, gray photos of a woman dancing on stage at the park.

"I'm gonna be an artist just like you some day." Delia reached up and slid her hand into Gabe's where he leaned over the back of the sofa. Rosie kept working, wondering what God had planned for Delia's life.

She was distracted by the little girl's quiet follow-up comment: "This must be what family feels like."

Startled, Rosie glanced back over her shoulder and shared a look with Gabe Adams that she was certain they both regretted immediately.

Chapter Nine

Gabe decided he needed to spend more time with Dot Berkeley as he weighed the idea of proposing marriage to the woman. Hadn't that been his entire mission for spending Christmas at the lake? To win her heart? Now, here they were, snowed in together, and he'd made no progress at all with her.

The problem, as he saw it, was that he'd allowed himself to become distracted by other … well, distractions.

Like the blizzard.

It was time to get back to business. To the business of love, anyway.

He considered the inn's study a real showpiece of a room. It opened to the far end of the parlor and boasted interior windows, even in the door, allowing a person to work in the smaller space while still feeling connected to the action in the large common room. The carpet was thick in the workspace, the room dominated by a heavy oak desk that could double as a conference table.

Dot had made herself very much at home there, her stylish shoes arranged in a row beside the desk. She had her stockinged feet tucked up under her in the broad, leather armchair, and she was re-pinning her bun when Gabe rejoined her.

Keith was sprawled on the day lounger nearby, reading the newspaper his father had already read three times through. He was saying something about human capital to Dot, whose face lit when Gabe reentered the room.

"Good! You're back!" She leaned forward and pushed a paper toward him. "We were thinking English-style gardens here on the west side of the resort. A stone wall there could be an easy way to separate the property from the vacation cottages that are going to butt up to it on that side. What do you think?"

Gabe glanced at the concept sketch of little paths snaking their way through labeled flower beds and shrubbery. "I like it." Next to it lay Charlie's fanciful drawings of slides. "Where'd our newest team member go?" he asked, gesturing.

"He hadn't cracked walnuts in the kitchen with Ruth for a full hour, so he ran off to do that."

Gabe tapped a finger on the paper the kid had been working on. It included detailed measurements, he noticed with a grin. "You know, he's not entirely off base with this slide concept."

Keith folded the newspaper down at top to look over at him. "What?"

"Listening to Charlie has got me thinking that we haven't been truly family friendly with any of our concepts for the resort so far," he said.

"So, you want a forty-foot slide running down the side of the brownstone?" Dot asked with the quirk of a brow.

"A variation of it, perhaps. If we've planned all these extensive docks, why wouldn't we allocate a portion of it for a wider platform over the water and create a play area for children there? With a slide?" He pushed a ruler aside and knocked on that section of blueprint with his knuckles.

"We give up a lot of boat space with something like that," Keith pointed out, letting the paper rest on his lap.

"From a safety standpoint, you'd have to rope off a section of water right here," Dot said, unfolding herself to lean forward more. "To create a swim area where the boat motors couldn't get close."

"Seems easy to me."

"Keith is right, though. You lose not just dock space all through here, but you're changing boat traffic flow."

"So put it over here, on the other side. Let it bump into the little patch of beach."

"Beach was up in the air, I thought," Keith said.

"It's already being used as a beach now," Gabe argued. "Seems like an easy way to draw families, especially if we put some money into it and extend the docks into a swimming platform off this way. With slides."

"Slides!" Charlie the master designer had returned, dropping a handful of broken walnuts directly onto the blueprints and making Dot cringe a little. Gabe tried not to laugh. "You want my slides in your hotel? I knew it!"

"Slides into the beach swimming area," Gabe said in response to Charlie's cheers.

"They've got to curve. You know?"

"I'm listening."

Charlie, armed with a fresh sheet of paper, was tasked with sketching what the dock extension over the swim area might look like for kids to truly have fun. He settled into the task with zeal, loudly crunching nuts. Keith returned to his paper, Dot to her garden wall calculations, and Gabe settled in on the edge of the desk with the most recent rates for supplies and materials.

"Will you let me come swim there?" Charlie asked after a time. Gabe looked up, blinking. "I mean, this play area and the beach are gonna be for just the families who stay in this fancy resort, right? So, can I ever come try it out, at least?"

"Sure, you can," Keith was the one to say, off-handedly.

"And my friends? They already use that beach now a lot. Can I invite them to come try out the slides and stuff?"

This was one of Emily Graham's chief criticisms of the project, Gabe knew, at least according to the scathing editorials she wrote in *The Buckeye Lake Beacon*. The beach area on the north shore had always been public access to the kids in town. Yet, when Dot and her family sold the large swath of land there to FH Resorts, there would be no marked, non-boater swim area on the village's north shore.

"As manager of the company's properties, I can assure you that you and your friends will be the first to use these slides you've designed," Gabe promised, feeling more than a little guilty. He assuaged that guilt by meaning that promise with his whole heart.

He thought, too, of the swimming hole on the Hocking River he and his friends had free access to growing up. The ropes they swung out and dropped from. The canoes. Public access to waterways seemed to him an essential of childhood.

Charlie Graham would be okay. The marina at the bottom of the hill here boasted a small beach of its own, but it was far removed from the village and the park where most children in the community lived. It was Charlie's "town" friends, as he'd pointed out, who would suffer.

On cue, Rosie Graham, artist and do-gooder naturalist, strolled into the study. The fingers of her right hand were dyed a rainbow of color from sketching. She moved directly to her son and to his project.

"Hey, Rosie," Dot said casually as she loaded paper in the typewriter.

"Mom! Look! They're letting me design a play platform by the beach!"

"The beach?" she asked, a little crease forming between her brows as she inspected her son's scratchy writing and shapes.

"The beach at the new resort. You know, where the beach is now? Except it'll be smaller 'cause it's just for the guests. But this platform ... see here? See here on the plans? This dock will have a platform on it, Gabe says, and he says it can have slides and stuff like that. That's my job," Charlie said with pride.

Gabe cringed as Rosie inspected where Charlie pointed, chewing on the bright rose of her lower lip, the crease between her brows going deeper.

"To make it more family friendly," he offered, hardly recognizing his own voice.

She looked up across the desk at him with those dreamy eyes and nodded. She cut a sharp glance at Keith where he lounged and watched her uneasily. "Of course." But her lips pursed now in disapproval, and her hand came to rest on her son's neck in that way he'd noticed she had of always grounding herself to the people she loved. "I wonder if you'd come help me with a project, Charlie," she said, turning.

And she swept her son from the study, firmly closing the door of the room behind her as they left, effectively cutting off a good deal of their source of heat from the main part of the hotel.

"Chilly in here," Dot said with a smile, and Gabe walked over to re-open the door.

"I take it she really is just as opposed to the resort and zoning change as her sister," he said.

"Maybe more so."

Terrific. "Hard to imagine."

"You've been reading Emily's editorials, which are impacting local opinions," Dot said dryly, leaning back again in her chair. "But Rosie's the one fighting at the state and federal level to protect the bog."

"I thought that was some professor from OSU," Keith said.

"Dr. Lamb is fighting for protected nature preserve status, yes, but who do you think does all the illustrations for his publications and his proposals?"

"Rosie," Gabe said. Today, it seemed, she had turned out to be both his favorite and least favorite artist.

"You got it. Rosie's a nature nut. Always has been," Dot said, stacking some of the papers spread out around her. She snagged the last of Charlie's walnuts. "Sounds like there's still a chance she and the professor will end up married someday." She shuddered. "An academic and an artist with no business sense. It's a match made in my nightmares."

"Too bad we can't tie a lead around their precious little bog and tow it to the other side of the lake," Keith said. "Then we could all live happily ever after. Isn't the thing just made of moss?"

"Can't do it," Dot said, rising from the chair and stretching. Though still clothed in her dress from the wedding, she managed to look fresh and lovely as ever. "So, the race is on. If we can get the permits in hand before the bog gets government protection, we'll be fine to close the deal. That's why we've got to get all this put together. Now, I'm headed to the kitchen, too. Charlie inspired me."

Keith folded the newspaper as Dot exited, and Gabe considered him. He also considered the way Rosie Graham's eyes narrowed whenever she glanced at the man.

"This is more than the resort," he said, wondering if Keith had damaged relations with key people in Buckeye Lake over the summer without Gabe knowing. "The way Rosie is about you. It's more than her being opposed to the resort, isn't it? Did you insult her somehow last summer?"

Keith sighed and rose, nodding. "You miss nothing."

"What exactly did I not miss?"

Packed Together

"It wasn't last summer, but she loved me once." Keith shrugged with the simple statement, looking a little embarrassed. Gabe blinked and felt his heart stutter for no good reason. "Long time ago. A kid thing, is all it was."

Kids? Did someone still avoid a person that determinedly if it was a "kid thing"?

"Did *every*one in this place grow up together?" Gabe asked, shaking his head.

"Not me. I was only here the one summer," Keith said. "Don't even remember Smokey or Dot back then. Pop sent me here to the inn just that one summer so I could learn the ropes before school. Made me spend a little time in a few of them through college, but then you were there for some of that chapter."

Gabe had been. Keith had finished his business degree just before he was drafted for the war, and by then Gabe was already taking over the day-to-day business of the hotels while Camden worked deals for expansions.

"One summer," Gabe repeated slowly, thinking back to those early years while he himself had been learning the business. "How old were you?"

"Right before university, I guess. Yeah. The summer before."

Hardly kids, Gabe thought as Keith got up too, mumbling something about a nap.

"Why's she still so angry with you if it's been ... what, a decade?"

"Let's just say I didn't exactly keep in touch," Keith replied. To his credit, there was no pride or humor in the statement. "You know how college is, and I was stupid." He shrugged. "Makes the whole thing uncomfortable. Nothing I can do about it now."

"Yeah. Guess not," Gabe made himself say from his spot on the edge of the oak desk, after Keith had already walked out.

His mind was going a thousand miles an hour. Keith had accused him of missing nothing, and suddenly Gabe was certain *Keith* had missed something Gabe now realized was obvious.

Keith Fairchild had left for college just before Camden Fairchild had found Gabe during a snowstorm in the hills of southeast Ohio and made him an offer he couldn't refuse. Gabe knew the timeline well.

Ten years ago.

If Keith was to be believed, Rosie Graham had fallen in love that summer.

And Keith, in return, hadn't kept in touch.

And Rosie now had a ten-year-old son who claimed his father had not died in the war and that he, in fact, had never had a father.

And what had Smokey told him the night before? That Rosie had never really said anything about Charlie's father?

Gabe's heart was flopping around in his chest like one of the fish Delia wanted living inside the resort.

Would Keith have ...? Had Keith and Rosie ...?

The eyes. The hair. The freckles. The lanky build. Charlie Graham looked quite a bit like the father he'd never heard of, Gabe thought, moving from the desk back to the doorway that led into the common room.

He watched Keith slink off toward the hall where his room was, carefully avoiding Rosie where she sat sketching again by the fire, bracketed by Charlie and Delia.

Keith — tall, sandy-haired, bright blue eyes, freckles — had spent a good deal of time in his room alone since the wedding party had arrived, Gabe reflected again, which he'd thought before had been out of character. His friend had been almost ... sheepish these last couple of days around their guests.

Yet, it didn't seem to have anything to do with the boy, only with a long-ago summer love he'd jilted.

Rosie Graham, meanwhile, had been virtually devastated when the storm had trapped her in the inn, like she was a minute away from flinging herself into the snow to escape. She hadn't eaten or slept that first day or night. Gabe thought about sitting with her in the dead of night in that window seat, when she'd looked longingly in the direction of her own home.

When she'd worried about her sister's initiation into the role of wife.

Now Gabe's stomach churned to match his pounding heart, as he realized he knew something that possibly only one other person in this house knew. He found himself wishing he could un-know it, wished he did not know that Charlie Graham's father was none other than Keith Fairchild.

Chapter Ten

Mealtimes were not on any kind of schedule during a blizzard.

Ruth had stocked up for Mr. and Mrs. Fairchild, Keith, and Gabe, factoring in occasional visits from local friends who might be invited to dine over the holiday. She had not, however, planned for this many appetites for this long, which was what Ruth confessed to Gabe urgently in the kitchen early that morning as the rain turned back to snow and the wind, blessedly, relented.

"Creativity will save the day," Gabe had told the inn's manager with more confidence than certainty. Ruth had always doted upon him, Gabe knew, so it was easy to relieve her anxiety with some jokes from the pantry and a couple of well-timed winks. He'd had her laughing—and baking bread alongside him—in minutes.

Now, as afternoon settled in, Gabe didn't know if they were eating midday dinner or an early supper, gathered as most of them were in front of another roaring fire ... this time with frankfurters on sticks over the flames. Cooked, they would be wrapped in Ruth's fresh bread with some seasoned mustard. Everyone, it seemed, was an expert in cooking a frank over a fire, and lectures varied from total charring to long, patient spit-style rotations far from the actual flame.

There was a good deal of much-needed laughter involved in this campfire tradition, as though the group had needed to be reminded that winter weather could not last forever and there would once again be fireflies and campfires.

Or even sunrises and sunsets, Gabe thought, hanging back a little in the constant shadows that came with having no electricity.

He'd been in a watchful mood today. And he'd noticed a few things.

He'd noticed Cookie had pulled herself together following yesterday's meltdown, after her husband assured her one of the doors still, in fact, opened ... not that anyone would dare open it to four feet of snow. Today she had formed a tentative if unlikely friendship with Margo over needle crafts, which had freed up Burt to tell stories to anyone who would listen. Newspaper publishing stories. Stories about some of his pet dogs over the years named after mythological creatures. Very alarming fishing and boating tales that made little Buckeye Lake sound like the Pacific Ocean.

Also clear to any onlooker was an easy familiarity between Dot and

Smokey Black, who had laughed until they cried after Ruth let them light a set of pilgrim candles left over from Thanksgiving. The result had been the melting of the pilgrims' faces in gruesome ways. Mrs. Pilgrim's nose ran straight down between her breasts and splattered onto her buckled shoes. It occurred to Gabe that he'd never seen Dot laugh like that.

Mostly, though, Gabe had noticed Keith and Rosie and Charlie.

Now, he was convinced Keith did not know he had fathered a child all those years ago. Though his friend seemed to be forcing himself to make small gestures in Rosie's direction in the name of peace, Keith never seemed to notice the woman even had a son. His friend was not the most observant of men.

How would Keith feel about having a son of his own? Gabe wondered. Especially one with glasses and a penchant for math? Keith's school stories, after all, were frequently about his glorious baseball accolades and the girls he'd dated.

To that end, how would Charlie feel about being a Fairchild? His life with Rosie appeared to be simple, wholesome, and happy. What if he suddenly had access to the family's wealth? If he knew, in fact, he was heir to a hotel empire? What would Camden and Margo do? Probably dote on the boy, show him off at galas, immediately start teaching him the things they'd taught their son ... but what *were* those things, really?

They'd neglected some of the more obvious lessons, Gabe thought sourly.

Like how not to break a young woman's heart. Or maybe how to honor her purity. How to acknowledge your bad behavior once you'd grown into a man and you came face-to-face with that same woman. How to look past the nose on your own face and notice a kid who looked just like you, running tame in your family's inn.

Gabe knew Keith had come to know the Lord during the war. They'd talked about it upon his return, attending services together whenever they found themselves in the same city. Keith's transgressions with Rosie Graham a decade before had been forgiven by God, but how did the man not grasp true repentance after all these years?

Instead, Keith regarded one of the most enchanting women in the world as something from his past he could brush aside. However uncomfortably.

Gabe also noticed Hickory Graham did not treat Keith with any particular distaste, making him further wonder if Rosie's grandfather was even aware of what had transpired between those "kids."

Had Rosie and Keith been quiet about their romance, if even Smokey Black seemed unaware of who Charlie's father was? Unless he did know and wasn't telling Gabe, who for all intents and purposes was Keith Fairchild's closest friend and business associate. It all came down to wondering just how good these lake folk were at acting.

Rosie was helping Delia arrange her dog on a stick beside the fire, her cheeks as pink as her name from being so close to the flames alongside the children for two rounds of hotdog cooking. The woman and little girl laughed about something now, while Charlie chewed an enormous mouthful behind them. Rosie kept telling him not to run around with food in his mouth, while Charlie seemed exultant about not sitting at a table for dinner. Or whatever meal this was.

"Do you think the blizzard is over now?" the boy asked, sidling up to Gabe. He was still running around with food in his mouth, despite Rosie's best efforts. In fact, he'd escalated to talking with food in his mouth, too.

"Well, the wind has finally died down a bit, I suppose." Gabe didn't know. Why was it so hard to tell a kid you didn't know something? "Fact is, I have no idea how you know when a blizzard has officially blown itself out."

Charlie bit off another mouthful of thick bread and half-burnt dog, contemplating the ice-glazed window and the lack of landscape visible beyond it. There was still very little light. Snow might be blowing from every direction. It was impossible to tell. At any rate, Charlie didn't have the patience to ponder what he could not see for another moment, and he was off again.

If Keith knew about Charlie, would he marry Rosie? Gabe noticed she was finally getting around to making a frankfurter for herself, wiping her fingers carefully on a towel. Her dress was beautiful on her, but the fabric was just light wool, and she seemed remarkably comfortable in a cast-off brown sweater whenever she strayed more than a few feet from the warmth of the fire. Her hands, undeniably graceful, still boasted ink stains.

Would Rosie like marrying into the Fairchild family? He tried to picture her at formal teas and elegant dinner parties. Certainly, she was lovely enough to hold her own there, but for all that she'd been dressed for a wedding for days, Gabe felt she was more suited to the open air. To scampering over fallen trees in the Hocking Hills or …

… well, not necessarily right where he himself had grown up, of course. He didn't mean the Hocking Hills or southeast Ohio, exactly. Any bit of nature, that was all. Any green, leafy place or dreamy, watery one would be a better backdrop for Rosie than dining at some investor's mansion.

He looked up again to find Dot beside him in the shadows, and she handed him a frankfurter wrapped in bread. "I made your supper," she said.

Gabe grinned. "Thank you. It looks delicious."

"Heard you helped Ruth bake the bread. She's smitten with you, you know."

"She always has been. Ruth and I understand one another. Are you?"

Dot arched a brow at him. "Am I what?"

"Smitten with me?"

"I'm not really the smitten type," she said with a shrug and a smile. "I think it's gone out of style with my generation."

"You ladies don't know what you're missing."

She laughed. Was it a flirty laugh? "You're probably right."

"I baked bread today and everything. What more could you want?"

"I don't know," she said, but she wasn't smiling anymore. She yawned, instead.

The yawn was contagious, and Gabe managed one of his own before taking a bite of the frankfurter she'd offered.

"You've been awfully quiet today," Dot told him.

Keith made his way over to them too, and Gabe experienced a longing to be back alone in this shadowy corner of the room. Soon the pair of them would be debating types of bricks for the resort's drive, and he was surprised to find he couldn't care less about it.

"Can't believe I ate two of those things," Keith said idly, leaning against a shelf filled with jigsaw puzzles. Gabe wondered why no one had taken to the puzzles yet. "Think the blizzard's over?"

The same question the man's son had asked just minutes before. How fitting.

Why hadn't Rosie made sure the Fairchilds knew she'd been carrying Keith's child? Gabe imagined her at just sixteen, frightened and facing a lifetime of rude labels and judgment. She should have been sent away to have the baby quietly and put him up for adoption. Instead, she'd been allowed to stay here at the lake, but in many ways, it had probably been so much harder socially.

If Keith had known, would he have married Rosie back then? As a college freshman? Would that even have mattered for a family like the Fairchilds, where he would just have moved sooner into the family business to support his young wife and child? Camden and Margo would have been disappointed, certainly, but Keith would have come out of the thing far from injured in terms of his prospects.

So, why hadn't Rosie made sure he knew? Did she not want those advantages for herself and her son?

Why, Gabe wondered as Keith did mention the bricks, was he making this his own problem, anyway?

~~~~

So far, Rosie's declaration that the baby grand piano was "off limits" had worked well.

"Discordant banging is the absolute last thing anyone needs right now," she had maintained.

The restriction worked, anyway, until that evening, when being stuffed full of frankfurters had inexplicably left some of the company feeling musical.

"No," she'd declared when Charlie and Delia insisted on practicing "Chopsticks." To help them avoid temptation, Rosie took up residence on the padded piano bench and sipped a cup of tea.

The perch gave her a good view of the whole parlor, so she could watch Gabe performing card tricks for Dottie and the kids near the fire, Smokey whittling with Hickory, Cookie and Burt arguing politics with Camden on the sofa, and Ruth offering tea to the others. Then she saw Margo Fairchild crossing the room to her in her embroidered, velvet dress. The woman had flawless style and her husband's money to support it.

"May I have my tea here with you, dear? It gets so warm over by the fire."

"Of course." Rosie scootched on the bench, making room. Both women were careful not to set their cups down on the impeccably polished piano. Rosie imagined Ruth playing it on the lonely nights when no guests were at the inn. "Do you play at all, Mrs. Fairchild?"

"Not for a time, I'm afraid," Margo said. "You?"

Rosie shook her head.

"Well, you're quite the talented artist, at any rate. You don't need one more talent."

Rosie laughed. That was one way of looking at it.

"Gabe was showing me the portrait you did today. It's quite good."

"Thank you."

"I wonder if I could pay you to do a sketch of Mr. Fairchild and myself. We have a big anniversary coming up, and your drawing got me thinking about invitations."

"It would be a pleasure, and I certainly would not expect payment. You've been so gracious to allow us to weather the storm ..."

"Oooh," Margo interrupted. "That puts me in mind of that song." She squinted at the ceiling, humming a few bars, then sang, "Hmmm ... *but I can weather the storm! What do I care how much it may storm? I've got my love to keep me wa-aa-aarm.*"

Rosie smiled. "Irving Berlin."

"Keith and Gabriel have done a duet to it, I believe. Before the war, they'd sing together whenever we happened to all be in New York at the same time. You know. At the hotel, I mean. The guests loved anything Irving Berlin."

Rosie arched a skeptical brow. "Your son and your property manager performed a floor show for hotel guests?"

Margo smiled hugely at her memories. "Just impromptu, you know? A couple of dashing young men playing around on the piano in the big lobby. They'd do it for the fun of it, and oh, those were some of my favorite times."

Rosie regarded the woman who was taking a humming sip of her tea, lost in happy memories. For the first time, she considered how lonely it might be, travelling constantly with her husband, more often in hotels than at home.

Having only one son.

That son being Keith.

Like magic or, more likely, a curse, Keith Fairchild appeared beside the piano. Rosie was startled. They had avoided one another with equal fervor so far. Now, she nodded at him when he tried a small smile on her.

"I was just reminiscing, Sweetheart," Margo said to him, "about you and Gabriel singing and playing."

"Yes," he said, clearing his throat but keeping his eyes on Rosie. "I hear nothing but good things about your studio up on the boardwalk."

"Thank you."

"She's quite talented," Margo reiterated.

What was going on? "Have you been into the studio?" Rosie knew he had not been. She'd have known.

"No, I'm afraid not. But I'd like to visit in the summer. If you wouldn't mind it." His polite uncertainty in small talk made Rosie see this as the act of courage it was on his part.

"Mind?" Margo giggled. "It's a business, for goodness's sake, Son. Why should she mind?"

"Miss Graham here might not be my biggest fan, Mother."

Rosie blanched.

"The proposed resort threatens her beloved cranberry marsh," he continued, and then he startled Rosie again by winking at her.

He'd always been given to winking.

"Well," Margo said after a careful sip of tea. "Progress demands sacrifice, I suppose. I don't see why it needs to be personal."

"True, Mother. But sometimes, in affairs like this, I haven't always behaved as well as I should have."

Rosie was staring into her cup now.

"Business can bring that out in many, I guess," Margo went on determinedly, clearly only willing to believe her son capable of bad behavior if the rest of the world did it first. "I still don't see why Miss Graham here wouldn't want you to visit her studio."

"I would understand if she did not," he said softly.

Rosie drew a breath and met his eyes. There was an apology there, and it was so far from anything she'd been expecting that she didn't know what to say.

"I'm going to fetch you both a chocolate to go with your tea," Keith said with yet another wink, this time aimed at both of them. "As a peace offering."

"Oooo. Did you bring some of the chocolate from German Village with you?"

"I did. I'll be back."

"Wait until you try this, dear," Margo told Rosie as Keith crossed the room. "Have you been to German Village in Columbus?"

"I haven't, actually. No."

"You'll have to go. Though I don't suppose you get away much, all things considered."

Rosie turned her attention back to the woman beside her on the bench, noticing the pearls on her ears were trimmed in tiny poinsettia leaves for the holiday. "You mean because of my artwork?"

"I mean because you have a child. And you're alone," the older woman said, reaching over to pat Rosie's hand as though she needed consolation. She dropped her voice when she said, "I understand you're not exactly a war widow."

Something about the statement struck Rosie as irresistibly funny, but she bit back her laughter. *"You're not exactly a war widow"* was one of the more subtle labels she'd been given. Emily would have enjoyed it greatly.

"No, indeed," Rosie agreed, watching Charlie sneak a piece of popcorn off the tree garland and pop it into his mouth. She supposed she should move over to that side of the room to get away from whatever Margo said next.

Because there was always something next.

"My own mother used to tell my sisters and me that ... um, closeness ... between a man and woman ... is like a fire," Margo said somberly.

That was racier than Rosie had expected. "Oh my."

"Yes, a fire. In a fireplace like that one, the fire warms and cheers everyone because the fire is burning where it is *supposed* to burn." Margo took a fortifying sip of tea, watching Rosie over the rim. "That's like marriage, you see? The fire bringing warmth because it's where it's supposed to be."

It was too late to leave, so Rosie nodded in encouragement, hoping to speed up the part of the analogy designed to sting.

"Outside of the fireplace, fire is dangerous," Margo pressed on. "People can be burned. Things get destroyed."

Rosie was accustomed to on-the-spot sermons about her misstep, which had turned out to be more visible than the missteps of others. Yet, this analogy at the knee of Keith Fairchild's mother was deliciously ironic.

"Thank you. I'll try to ... remember that."

"Chocolate, as promised!" Keith said as he returned, looking more relaxed. Rosie imagined him congratulating himself on smoothing over any lingering awkwardness concerned with the girl he'd used and cast off. "Real German chocolate!"

"Let your mother have mine," Rosie said kindly. "She was telling me Irving Berlin is something of a specialty for you and your friend."

Keith grinned. "We were as far off off-Broadway as you could get."

"Play that one song," Margo said, daintily nibbling at her chocolate. "The one about love keeping you warm."

"Not without Gabe. No way."

Apparently from out of nowhere, Camden Fairchild's booming voice filled the room. "Gabriel! They're wanting you to play!"

Gabe, still flipping cards for the entertainment of others, looked over in bafflement. He and Dottie made such a handsome couple, but Rosie wondered if they should be so close to the fire, given Margo's memorable lecture.

"Play?"

"Come do that Irving Berlin song with Keith," Margo called. "The one from the musical *On the Avenue*. Remember?"

"'I've Got My Love to Keep Me Warm,'" Keith provided. "Rather suiting, I guess, but I'm afraid we're rusty."

"It's been *years*," Gabe said.

Rosie saw this as the perfect opportunity to abandon the piano bench, slipping around the edge of the room. She snatched Charles Dickens off the bookshelf and made it to the window seat without attracting attention.

"Four lessons a week for years, and you can't be bothered to play for your mother when she asks?" Camden huffed at his son.

Gabe grinned, but he rose and stretched lazily. "That guilt might work on Keith, but you in no way paid for a single lesson for me."

"You're in no more position to refuse than he is, and you know it."

"Where did you learn to play and sing so well, anyway, Gabriel?" Margo wondered, moving off the bench herself with the certainty she would get what she wanted.

"My parents play," Gabe said.

"Are they musicians?" Cookie asked.

"Missionaries, ma'am. My father was well-trained in hymns, and he taught my mother and me both on the little, out-of-tune upright at their church."

"He had to learn the fun songs with me," Keith said.

"Just shows you've never sung 'He Arose' in a clapboard church in the valley," Gabe insisted. "Fun doesn't begin to describe it."

Suddenly Rosie found Gabe explaining context to her, directly, as he made his way toward the baby grand. "Camden found me when I rescued him from a snowstorm, so now he thinks of me as his performing monkey."

"Nonsense," Camden said, but he laughed. "My car went into a ditch in those cursed hills, and there he was, digging me out of it. Saw right away the boy would be a capable hotelier."

"I was the son he'd always wanted," Gabe said dramatically.

"Now, now." Keith laughed, too.

After some more resistance and some re-acclimation at the keyboard, Rosie watched Keith and Gabe fall into a routine they must have once known well.

The piano itself sounded just as lovely as someone had paid for it to sound. When Keith belted out the opening of the song, which was all about snow snowing and wind blowing, the room erupted in laughter and applause.

Gabe got them all going again when he sang, meaningfully, that he couldn't remember a worse December.

Then the others seemed inspired to belt out the chorus about their love keeping them warm.

Rosie smiled, snug in the window seat. The two men's voices melted right into one another, rich and full, and she could well imagine the pair of them dressed in tuxedos, surrounded by adoring guests of the New York Fairchild Hotel.

They were undeniably handsome: Keith with his flop of blonde hair over his brow, Gabe with his tan skin and white smile glowing over his white shirt. One by one, the room seemed pulled toward them, like they were a force. Rosie's aunt and uncle, Pastor Skip, Smokey, Charlie and Delia, and even Ruth.

Margo glowed in triumph watching them, her hands clasped at her embroidered breast.

Gabe sang about his heart being on fire, Keith about the flames growing higher.

What was with the whole flame thing tonight, anyway?

Which took them back to the chorus.

Keith kept playing as Gabe leaped off the bench, grabbed little Delia, and waltzed her around the piano while she squealed.

Rosie decided, if she were her friend Dottie, she'd throw herself right into Gabe Adam's arms that very moment and keep his voice and his smile to herself for a lifetime.

Dottie, still seated by the fire, only clapped politely.

Chapter Eleven

Rosie had only read the first chapter—or "stave," as the original text called it—of *A Christmas Carol* out loud to Charlie and Delia on their floor bed by the fire. Their lids had slid closed quickly, so she'd read on by the light of an oil lamp beside her in her trusty window seat, which she'd taken to thinking of as her own.

The clock chimed the hour again, which, combined with the snow and the specter of the evergreen across the room, had set the perfect backdrop for Marley's ghost to visit Scrooge before the children fell asleep. Delia had loved it, of course, launching into imaginative scenarios of dragging around chains for an eternity. Rosie hoped they didn't have nightmares about visits from tormented ghosts.

Yawning, she mentally prepared for Christmas Present, which had already proven to be a haunting of its own kind, for sure.

The passing of time had become strange, made more complicated by the unknowns. Had the storm truly broken? How bad *was* it out there? Was the second floor of their house on the towpath even still standing?

Then, there was Keith, like a polished and sophisticated ghost from her own past, who had tentatively spoken to her today. Twice. Once, following the duet, he'd offered to help heat water for the dishes after Rosie had taken on the chore alongside Ruth. She was so astonished by the gesture and the fact he'd acknowledged her again, she'd forgotten to stand back and watch to see if Keith Fairchild knew *how* to heat water.

After avoiding her for the first few days, this very minor change in behavior had her concerned. Was he just trying to be a decent human being? Or had he begun to imagine a repeat of their doomed love affair? The mere idea of the second option made her stomach churn all over again.

She needed to talk to Emily about so many things. Most confusing of all was the way Gabe Adams watched her, his eyes irresistibly warm. When she'd make eye contact, the corner of his mouth would pull up into a half-smile, and it seemed to take him some effort to look away. Rosie hated that she looked forward to these moments and hated even more that she did not know why she looked forward to them.

Emily would talk some sense into her. Rosie reminded herself she was not interested in romantic entanglements of any kind, but the fact remained ... her stomach churned in a very different way when it came to

Gabe. *The man who was Dottie's fellow.* What had gotten *into* her?

Rosie needed to talk to her sister.

She rested her head against the papered wall behind her, chilled from its proximity to the window, and snuggled deeper into the heavy blanket. Closing her eyes, her mind worked to conjure a framework for what this Christmas would be like. Would they be able to get back to the house? Should they start trying tomorrow? She had a few gifts stored under her iron framed bed, unwrapped still. An erector set for Charlie. A new coat for Hickory. Nothing yet for Emily and Drew. She'd made a delicate blown glass rose for Delia back in early fall and was glad for it now. Her plan to finish her shopping, baking, and holiday preparations after they'd made it through the wedding had not worked out.

Now, even if they could access those few gifts she had squirreled away, there would surely be no way to get to town for giftwrap or other supplies. Could they cut across the frozen lake, perhaps, tunneling through the snow? To what store? Would anyone be able to open the store in town if shoppers managed to make the journey?

Her breathing slowed, and the ticking of the clock dominated the room. She thought of snow. Broad blankets of it. Individual flakes. The patterns of snowflakes under a microscope. The symmetry ...

Rosie only realized she'd dozed off when she felt something against her blanket-wrapped foot. The something turned out to be a man.

Gasping, she pushed back harder against the wall, and she heard Gabe make a "shhhhhh" sound at the same time. Blinking, she registered him there—fully clothed and buttoned up as always—on the opposite side of the padded window seat.

"I'm sorry," he whispered. "I thought you were reading, so I sat down. I didn't realize you'd fallen asleep."

"I didn't realize it either." Embarrassed, she straightened herself and tucked the scrap of paper she'd used as a bookmark back into Dickens. She wrapped the blanket tighter around herself, as tight as Gabe's white collar against the soft tan of his neck.

With her brain too fuzzy to maintain its usual walls, she had a terrible moment admitting she was wildly attracted to this man. He wore the same pair of horn-rimmed glasses he'd had on earlier when she'd seen him working in the study, and those glasses somehow had her melting like the stupid pilgrim candles had melted so disastrously that afternoon.

Still, it was better to concentrate on the hornrims than it was to notice the shape of his lips and to wonder if they were as soft as they looked. She wasn't sure if she wanted to touch them with her own lips (she did) or just with her fingers (maybe that too), but she knew for certain that she did want very much to touch them.

"Do you want me to leave?" he asked, his voice soft.

"No."

"Are you doing all right, Rosie?"

She blinked. Nearly every time he spoke to her, he offered evidence that he noticed her, like that first night when he was so bothered that she hadn't really eaten. She thought she might like a man caring, like a man watching her the way he did, so carefully. It felt nice. "I'm all right. Thank you for asking."

He nodded.

"Are you, Gabe? All right, I mean?" It was the first time she'd casually called him by his first name, trying it out in the stillness. His eyes crinkled in that happy way they had.

"I believe I am." He cleared his throat, waited. "I wonder if I might talk with you about something, though."

"I doubt we'll have much interruption just now. What time is it?"

"After one."

"Time for the next ghost."

"What? Oh. Right. I heard you reading earlier. *A Christmas Carol*?"

"Yes. Sorry." She smiled. "What did you want to talk about?"

"It's ... difficult, I'm afraid." There was some kind of warning there. She watched his chest inflate under the fine wool sweater vest, as though he were drawing courage.

Rosie felt her heart give a slight flop in her chest, above the usual stomach churning. *Gabe was attracted to her, too.* She'd been afraid of that, with every long look, and it suddenly seemed a disastrous prospect. She hoisted the stone of her private walls, ones that were typically well in place when this kind of thing happened.

This man was Dottie's future, not her own, Rosie knew.

Just as she was steeling herself to make a noble sacrifice for her friend, though, Gabriel Adams changed the game entirely.

"Keith is Charlie's father," he said simply. Four simple words.

Four words.

Rosie didn't mean to jump up from the seat, but jump she did, wrapped too tightly in the cursed blanket. Suddenly she was on the floor instead of the window seat, her face hot—hot all over, really, with panic and embarrassment—and she was scooting away from Gabe, who followed her right down to the floor with concern. The blanket was less warm comfort than restrictive binding now, mummied around her knees and ankles. Her breath wasn't clearing her throat in the usual way. Gabe reached out once more, as he had when he'd woken her minutes before.

"Shhhh," he repeated. "I'm sorry, Rosie. It's okay. It's all okay. Where are you trying to go?"

"You don't know that's true," she heard herself say, not realizing she'd said it too loud until he'd put his finger up to his lips once more.

"If I didn't know for sure, your reaction just now would cinch it, darling." The words, spoken with his usual gentleness and mild amusement, somehow grounded her. Reassured her. And then his next words did even more. "He doesn't know, Rosie. Don't worry."

"Keith doesn't know?"

"No, no. He doesn't know."

"How, though? How do *you* know?"

"It's not very hard to figure out," he said gently.

Just as Rosie had feared any time Charlie got anywhere near Keith. She'd known someone would make the connection, but when they hadn't on the first day or so, she'd foolishly allowed herself to relax.

"Something Charlie told me about never having a dad. Something Keith told me yesterday about a summer romance ten years ago. And then ... well, Rosie, there's the way the pair of them *look*." Rosie closed her eyes at the truth in that, and he went on. "All I needed were those pieces, honey, and suddenly Charlie looks like a smaller version of Keith."

"Shhhh." It was her turn now, pushing down on the blanket and looking wildly in the direction of the children to make sure they were still sleeping. If Charlie were to overhear .... *God, help*, she prayed wildly.

Gabe Adams had found out the truth.

Having shed her wrapping, Rosie stood, tossed the blanket in the window seat, and gestured for Gabe to follow her across the room, the temperature falling as they moved farther from the fire. He'd stooped for the oil lamp, and the light threw her nightgowned shadow up against the wall ahead. Rosie took deep breaths.

Gabe said Keith *didn't* know, she reminded herself. Gabe seemed like a reasonable man. He seemed to like both her and Charlie, even. It could all still turn out okay. Once they were in the study, Rosie turned back to close the door softly.

When she turned back around, though, Gabe was standing close to her, and the lamp was on a nearby table. He was several inches taller than she was, still completely dressed. The light played now on the shadow of dark hair that had grown on his chin and jaw and around his lips.

"You figured it out," she said carefully, no longer having to whisper quite so softly. As though she had to repeat it to verify its truth. "Keith has not figured it out, though."

"That's correct."

"And you *won't* say anything to him."

Gabe blinked long lashes behind the hornrims. "I can't imagine that being my place. But, Rosie, I'm only asking ... don't you think Keith deserves to know he has a son?"

Rosie took a long breath that shook. "No. I don't believe he deserves to know."

"Some would disagree, that's all."

"*Having a son*, as you put it, is not a very accurate description of Keith Fairchild's status in this situation, Mr. Adams."

"You called me Gabe earlier. Please don't change things between us. I just wanted to talk."

"We're talking."

"He's a father and doesn't know. He's also my friend, but I'm worried about what he's done or didn't do. Did ... did he have a chance to step up and do the right thing?"

"The right thing being ...?"

"You were both young, but you must have been old enough to get married with your parents' permission. I mean, for him to give both you and Charlie his name. I guess that's what I mean about him doing the right thing."

Rosie felt her nostrils flare. "You say the right thing ten years ago was marriage. Tell me. Would *you* like being married to someone who'd promised you everything and then walked away and never contacted you again?"

"No, I don't think I would."

"Who wouldn't answer letters? Who said they loved you when it was convenient and then left you to the consequences? Is that the kind of man you'd have me spend *my life* with?"

Gabe put his hands up, almost defensively, shaking his head. "No, Rosie. I only hoped he ... All I'm saying is ..."

"All you're doing is swooping in with an answer to a question no one asked you," she said a little desperately. She stopped, stunned by a sudden urge to cry. She swallowed it.

When would a single mistake stop backing up on her?

"I've only been wondering why you wouldn't want Charlie to have the advantages that come with being a Fairchild," he said almost cautiously. "That's the other thing I was wondering about."

"About money."

"It's not just a little bit of money. I wonder if you'd ... I don't know. I guess I wondered if you'd thought about what those advantages would mean for Charlie. And you. Even if we take a boy getting to know his father out of the equation."

"Let's *not* take that out of the equation. Let's keep it in, by all means, because I think it's vital. Let's think about the kind of man I'd rather not be married to teaching my sweetheart of a son what kind of man to be as he grows up."

Gabe pushed a hand through his dark hair and sighed. "Aww, Rosie, do you even *know* what kind of man Keith is? You knew him as a boy. A boy who was wretched, apparently, I'll give you that, but are *you* the same person you were ten years ago?"

"It feels like you're excusing him."

"No way. Not at all."

"I haven't seen such a big change. If anything, the full-grown man's *less* charming than the boy was. And I don't like your implication about advantages."

"Sorry, but facts are facts. I don't make the rules."

"Yes, you *all* make the rules. And it's not a question of facts being facts. It's perception. The so-called advantages of the Fairchild family don't compare to the advantages of hard work and integrity and honesty and follow-through. Charlie is growing up to be a better man than Keith already, thanks to my grandfather and now, Drew Mathison."

"I won't argue with you there. Your son is terrific, but ..."

"But you don't have a right to argue with me about this *at all*, Mr. Adams." Rosie, close to tears, decided it was time to leave this room. Past time. "You might be a businessman, but this isn't your business."

Good parting line, she decided, turning to open the door and head back to ... the sofa. In the middle of the room. Where there was no privacy. "Don't you dare follow me out here, either," she threw back over her shoulder.

He tilted his head and crossed his arms, expensive fabric sliding over expensive fabric. "How, then, do you propose I get to my room?"

Rosie hesitated. "You go out first, then. Please go on, and don't bother me anymore."

Eyes sparking with irritation, Gabe left the lamp to her and made his way past her in the doorway. She watched him disappear. Then she headed back to retrieve the blanket and book from the window seat and made sure she was tucked into the sofa before she let the tears come. She hiccupped them into silence so as not to wake the kids.

Gabe hadn't wanted her at all. Instead, he'd only been determined to trap her with a lesser man.

Chapter Twelve

Delia Stimpson Grade Four
Christmas Journal Project
Buckeye Lake Public School
December 1946

Rosie is reading Scrooge to us before bed. It's a little scary, really. Dead people you knew coming to visit you in the night like Jacob Marley did? It doesn't sound anything like what Pastor Skip says heaven is like, which is where my mom and dad are, but I don't think Jacob Marley is in heaven. He has all those heavy trunks and chains. I don't like it. But I can't wait to hear more.

It makes me want to be good.

Also, it's almost Christmas, and I want presents.

~~~~~

The next morning was still frigid but quiet in terms of weather, and Gabe made two decisions upon rising from bed far later than he usually did.

One: He would dedicate his mental energy to his own personal life and no one else's—something he'd loosely resolved yesterday and then stupidly abandoned.

Two: He would stick to Dot Berkeley like glue because that would remind him how interesting she was and how well they worked together.

Resolved, he pulled a sweater over his button-up and went in search of her. It was an easy quest, accomplished by simply following the cheerful sound of a small crowd in the kitchen. Dot was there, dressed today somehow in a different dress than the one she'd worn to the wedding, icing cookies over the stainless-steel island in the kitchen. Charlie and Delia were on one side of her, Burt and Cookie on the other. Ruth, Queen of the Kitchen, was surprisingly missing in action, but Rosie sat on a stool by the stove.

She appeared to be whittling. Her eyes looked puffy, but he glanced away as fast as he could.

"Join us, Gabe!" Dot exclaimed when she saw him. By contrast with Rosie, she appeared rested and content.

"Yes, come help! Ruth made cutout cookies for us after breakfast!" Delia called as Gabe moved their direction.

"These wreath ones are easy," Charlie told him, sliding over to make room. "The green icing can be all lumpy and still look right. You know, like clumps of pine branches." His little lips were also tinted green, proving he was qualified to endorse the icing.

"And you can put these little cinnamon ball things all over the wreath, too," Delia instructed, pushing an icing-smeared cup of red balls in Gabe's direction. "Have you ever seen a thing like these?" she asked.

Gabe had, but it wasn't surprising the preacher raising her didn't dabble in baking accessories. Pastor Skip, admirably, was spending a good deal of these days in prayer and study. He'd managed to lead them in prayer at some point every day, praying for exactly what anyone would expect a group of house-bound victims of the worst blizzard in a century to pray about.

For it to stop.

Obedient to all their cookie decorating instructions, Gabe exchanged a smile with Dot and set about icing a wreath. The warmth of the kitchen's oven and the candlelight reflected on the stainless steel before them proved to be the mood lift he'd needed.

Everything seemed fine. Rosie Graham might as well not even be in the room.

Charlie's great aunt and uncle nodded a greeting from the opposite side of the island. "Is it stressful, trying to live up to your name while doing an endeavor like this, Cookie?" Gabe asked the older woman, whose hair was dyed bright orange.

She chuckled. "I'm confident enough in my abilities, Sonny Boy."

"Cookie sounds like the kind of name that comes with a story."

"Hickory and Louisa's boy called me Aunt Cookie when he was just a wee thing, is all."

"Probably because she gave him cookies every time she saw him," Burt said, pausing from his happy, tuneless humming. "She worked hard at being that kind of aunt."

"That would be my grandpa, right Mom?" Charlie called in Rosie's direction.

"Sure was. Your mama's daddy," Cookie answered Charlie before Rosie had a chance to. "I was honored to have him give me a brand new name. I loved that boy."

"He died in a 'splosion," Charlie informed Gabe solemnly.

Gabe automatically glanced at Rosie, little white chips working off the end of her knife as something took shape in her opposite hand. She was, in fact, whittling. Rosie looked up and met his glance. Her eyes were red rimmed, for sure, but he guessed it was not about her father. "I'm sorry," he said, knowing he sounded like an idiot.

"I was about two years old," was all she said.

"Your daddy's favorite cookie, Rose, was an oatmeal drop cookie, so I always had them on hand," Cookie recalled with a merry smile.

"Mine's molasses cookies," Delia said. "Aunt Cookie makes real good molasses cookies, too. And I like Rosie's sugar cookies a lot."

"Thanks, ma'am."

"These cookies are good, too," Burt put in, his mouth full.

"Stop eating every single one you ice, or we won't have any for later." This, from the man's wife, made Gabe laugh. He considered the wreath Dot iced beside him, over which she was carefully sprinkling colored sugar. She was entirely absorbed in her task, as she was entirely absorbed in everything she did.

Gabe waited until Dot had that cookie decorated to her usual high standards. Then he reached over, grabbed it, and had it in his own mouth before she could even exclaim.

"I agree with Burt," Gabe said with a full mouth to rival Cookie's laughing husband.

"You see the influence you are, old man?" Cookie said.

"I'd retaliate by swiping the one rather sloppy cookie you've managed," Dot told Gabe. "But I already had a few too many before you got in here. I don't usually hit cookies so hard before noon."

He smiled in appreciation. She was funny, he thought, and beautiful. He was lucky that she'd gladly held his hand a few times and didn't push him away when he'd pressed a kiss on her lips after their last elegant dinner at Maramor.

That dinner seemed like ages ago, somehow, but ... yes, he was a lucky man, indeed. Blizzard and all.

The kitchen door swung open to reveal Keith, who made an approving sound upon seeing the cookies. Without hesitation, he strolled to the cooking island, grabbed Gabe's freshly finished cookie wreath, and took a hearty bite, causing everyone to burst into laughter that had Keith pausing mid-chew.

"Need coffee," he said upon swallowing, his Adam's apple working the cookie down.

"Don't you wanna ice cookies, too?" Delia asked. "We've got lots more to go."

"Coffee first."

"Just made a fresh pot a half-hour ago," Dot said, this time selecting a cutout cookie to ice that appeared to be in the shape of ... nothing. Gabe squinted at it.

"What is that supposed to be? That cookie?"

"It's Santa walking with his pack on his back." She rotated it. "See?"

"Hmm. Not as obvious as you make it sound. How do you go about icing a thing like that?"

"This way," Charlie said, holding up something equally nondescript with a hideous mound of yellow on it. More laughter.

Gabe noticed Keith, armed with a steaming white mug, meander toward Rosie by the stove.

"You're not icing cookies," he said by way of a greeting. He watched her for a beat. "What in the world *are* you doing?"

Rosie, who didn't seem any more jazzed at seeing Keith than she'd been to see Gabe, held up a small white shape. "It's Joseph."

"Joseph?" Keith leaned over her for a closer look. Gabe tried hard not to imagine the pair of them, younger, or the way Rosie might have looked at Keith back then.

"Joseph. Mary's husband?"

"Oh, right. And is that ... soap?" A short stack of Ivory bars was, in fact, beside her on the counter.

Rosie smiled. "Yes, it's soap. I'm making a nativity scene from it."

"Okay. Why?"

"What else is there to do?"

"She makes a nativity every year," Charlie said with pride, licking the side of his hand.

"Out of soap," Keith repeated, amused, and mildly condescending.

"No, not out of soap every year! Last year's was clear glass."

"I love the clay one you gave us a few years ago," Cookie told Rosie.

"Soap is what I have to work with here," Rosie said, returning to her task. The line of her neck beneath her pulled-back curls was pale and delicate. Gabe noticed that, like Dot, she'd somehow been able to change into a new dress, this one a green-checked cotton with a wide, white collar. Reminding himself to pay more attention to Dot and less to Rosie, he noticed Dot's dress was a plaid skirt suit of gray. Both women looked to be swimming in their dresses a bit.

"Where'd you ladies get your new duds this morning?" he asked Dot beside him as he reached for another un-iced cookie.

"Ruth took pity on us. And she's generous, too. I think these are two of her favorites, right, Rosie?"

"We're having a hair washing party later," Cookie put in. "No men allowed."

"Keith, prove last night's caroling stunt at the piano wasn't a Christmas spirit anomaly," Dot said. "Show us what you can do with a cookie, now you've had a bit of coffee."

Charlie was quick with his usual advice. "The wreaths are the easiest."

Keith, seeming more at ease all the time, settled in beside Cookie and reminisced about making cookies for Santa as a boy. "We had this cook at our Columbus house who told me Santa wouldn't leave me a present if *she* made the cookies for him. She said I had to do it if I wanted a present."

"You had a cook?" Burt asked.

"Is that true, though? About Santa?" Delia asked, pursing her lips. "You have to bake the cookies yourself?"

"I don't think so," Charlie answered his friend. "I never baked the cookies myself, and Santa keeps bringing me stuff. Right, Mom?"

Rosie nodded without looking up from her soap. Gabe's stomach was beginning to hurt, he supposed from the guilt of keeping a secret and having made Charlie's mom cry.

"Did your cookies turn out all right back then, Keith?" Cookie asked.

"Guess so. I got a Radio Flyer and a crate of Army men."

"Good thing Santa doesn't mind snow and cold," Delia said then. "He might be the only one who can get around with the blizzard and everything."

Gabe watched the adults share quick, concerned looks. From her stool, Rosie added the finished soap figure of Joseph to what he was just noticing was a small collection of soap sheep and what was surely, from where he sat, a little Ivory Christ child.

He experienced a strange moment, thinking of watching Margo set up the expensive, porcelain nativity scene just days before, and now watching these similarly white figures take shape from cheap bars of soap. He wondered what Margo would do if he switched out her shiny Baby Jesus for the crude but somehow more fitting one Rosie had carved.

With a kind of grim focus, Rosie moved on to the next bar of soap.

"When I was a boy, my father would design a new fishing pole for me every year," Burt remembered.

"What about Santa? What did he bring you?"

"Best gift Santa ever gave me was about the smallest rowboat you ever saw. I couldn't wait for the lake to thaw that spring," Burt went on. "My brother and I used to row it out to Cranberry Bog and fish from there. Pop didn't let us row out any farther than the bog in those days."

"Is there good fishing there?" Keith asked.

Burt and Cookie looked around, seeming to remember the other adults gathered round the icing bowls wanted to remove a good chunk of that bog to make way for elaborate boat docks for a new resort.

"Yes, the fish like it there," Burt said, his tone a little tighter.

"People could still fish there off a dock at our new resort," Dot pointed out, reading the room and unafraid to wade right into the muck. "Actually, a dock extending out that way from north bank would make it even easier to reach those particular fish."

"If you're one of the rich folks staying in the new resort," Cookie countered.

"Don't start down this road," Burt put in around another bite of cookie wreath. "We're all having a fine time. The last thing we need is a speech about it from our little bog champion over there," he teased in

Rosie's direction.

"Maybe we could all give our causes a rest for the holidays," Keith said, and Gabe cringed.

"And what is your cause, Keith?" Cookie asked.

"Money, I guess." A spattering of forced laughter.

Gabe did not look up at Rosie this time.

"Attitude like that, you can forget about ever getting anything as good as a Radio Flyer from Santa," Burt said. "You're a candidate for a lump of coal, I'm afraid, Scrooge."

Gabe iced cookie after cookie as the banter continued around him, punctuated by Burt's occasional humming and assessments from Dot beside him. The kids started getting restless after a time, perhaps partly because of all the sugar they'd managed to ingest.

"Ooo!" Delia exclaimed from beside the stove. "Look at the camel Rosie is making!"

"She can make killer diller stuff out of about anything," Charlie boasted with pride.

Keith glanced over and leaned against the stove. "You said it, son. Your mother is a woman of many talents."

At that, Gabe did look up at Rosie ... just in time to see the knife slip right off the camel's hump and into the fleshy part of her hand between her thumb and fingers.

He was up and around the island before the knife clattered to the floor in a trail of bright red blood.

Delia shrieked dramatically.

Gabe was only partly aware of what ensued in the kitchen in general after that. Keith declared they would need towels and ran off in search of some (forgetting the kitchen was full of towels). Unlikely he would return. Dot, mesmerized, declared her intent to follow him but didn't make it to the door before collapsing in a faint. Burt simply disappeared.

"You've got Rosie?" Cookie rushed to Dot but called over her shoulder. "Gabe, you have my niece?"

"Yes, ma'am," he said, and Cookie knelt to the floor beside Dot as Gabe took in the mess directly before him. "Charlie, you and Delia scram."

"But ..."

"I'll take care of your mother. Now get."

Rosie had stood from her stool and, having carefully set the bloody Ivory camel on the counter, stooped to pick up the knife she'd dropped. She dripped blood everywhere in the process.

"Oh, dear," she said like a woman who had spilled some milk while baking. "Hand me that towel by the sink, will you?"

"Sweetheart, I'm going to need you to sit down here." Gabe guided her back onto the stool, managing an assessment of her hand in the process. The cut gaped, its opening difficult to measure for all the thick blood pouring from it. "Hands and heads bleed a lot," he said, more to reassure himself.

But there was no reassurance in being trapped in this inn, in having no access to real medical help, nor in the very real threat of infection. Clinging to that last thought, Gabe moved his gaze to Rosie's face to make sure she wasn't going to follow Dot to the floor. Then, he opened the cupboard from which he'd seen Ruth produce the brandy administered to Cookie during her claustrophobic episode.

"I don't need brandy," Rosie said softly on his return. He'd snagged two clean towels from a drawer by the sink, as well.

"You may not need the brandy, but your hand does. Here. Let me see." Her narrow wrist and forearm were slick and hot with blood, and he set about wiping at it with one of the towels. "Scoot a little closer to the sink here." He doused her, wiped, doused her. She made a little hissing sound. "Can't have you getting an infection, now, can we?"

"I'm sure the knife was clean. It was covered in soap, after all," she replied.

Gabe, leaning over her, raised his eyes to find her face so near his that he could see the little twinkle in her eyes. Astonishing. The twinkle had no business being there when she was bleeding.

"There is that," he said, his voice thick. He hated the size of the gash in her hand, which looked so white cradled in his darker ones. He pressed the wet cloth hard on that gash, partly to stop the bleeding and partly to pretend it away.

The door burst open then, and Smokey Black ducked into the kitchen, all business. "Heard we have a man down," he said, waving the thread left from Rosie's popcorn garland project in one hand. "I sewed up fellas on the battlefield when there was no other choice, remember." He nearly tripped over Dot, who had just regained consciousness.

"What ...? Dottie?" He dropped beside Cookie, who eased Dot's head to her lap. Dot's fresh, new dress was flayed out in every direction where she'd fallen.

"Slowly, now," Cookie was telling her.

"More than one wounded, I see," Smokey said, running his hands over Dot in assessment. "Did she hurt her head?"

"I'm fine," Dot said weakly.

"Cookie, is she truly fine?" Gabe called from the sink, and the older woman smiled and nodded. "Good. Rosie's got quite a gash over here, though."

"It does *not* need to be sewn up," she protested in Smokey's direction. "Look. It's hardly bleeding now." She went to pull her hand away, blood puddling beneath it.

"For goodness' sake, woman. Here." Gabe re-wrapped the towel tightly on her hand and moved behind her on the stool, raising her hand up above her head and pulling her back against him. He applied pressure to her elevated hand, even as he despised himself for having to do so. "Relax a minute and let's see if we can get this bleeding to slow down a bit."

"Classic Christmas cookie battle," Smokey observed, finally making his way to the counter and sink area like he hadn't a care in the world. "We've lost many a fine soldier to this kind of thing. Not that a sharp knife seems particularly relevant to cookie icing, but who am I to judge?"

"I was whittling a camel out of soap," Rosie said, settling back against Gabe in a way he did not mind.

"Classic soap camel whittling battle," Smokey repeated with a chuckle, shaking his head. "You think it needs stitching up, Adams?"

"Yes."

"Let's just bandage it," Rosie said.

"I rinsed it in brandy."

"Did she take a swig?" Smokey asked. "She looks pale."

"*She* is sitting right here," Rosie snapped. "And I'm always pale. I was born that way."

"Give some to Dottie over there, then."

"I'm fine too," came Dottie's voice. "If she's fine, I'm fine."

"All right, all right. Let's take a look, then."

Gabe angled himself to her side, never breaking contact, and positioned her hand back over the sink.

"Mmm. It'll take a few passes. Going to hurt more than a little with this needle, Rose," Smokey said, somber now as he peered in for a closer look. "Then we'll wash it in alcohol again when we're done. Here, scoot your stool closer. Gabe, can you ... keep her steady?"

While Smokey threaded the needle, Rosie drew a shaky breath. Gabe looked down at her long lashes and was surprised when she leaned into him again. "Do you want to lie down?"

"No. I can do this."

"You're really something, you know it?"

She made some sound in response, and Gabe's heart stuttered as Smokey scrubbed the needle and thread in more of the diminishing brandy supply. Gabe realized he didn't want to see Rosie cry. He hoped she wouldn't.

"Not to be pushing it on you, honey, but you really could take a gulp of that before he gets started here. It would help," he said.

"No, thank you. I can do pain."

"I don't doubt that."

"I might not watch though," she said in a small voice, turning her head into the space between Gabe's arm and ribs. He kept one arm securely around her, the other even more firm on her forearm. Then he dipped his chin and pressed a thoughtless kiss to the very top of her head.

Fortunately, that was the moment Smokey inserted the needle into tender flesh, so the man didn't see his childhood friend casually kissed on the head to initiate a medical procedure. Resisting Rosie's shuddering sound of pain, Gabe shot a look to the other side of the kitchen space and was relieved to see Dot too distracted to have seen that tender gesture, as well. She was trying to rise with Cookie's help.

"We'll just head on out to a soft chair for a spell," the old woman said, trying to remove Dot from the still-bloody scene before she lost her again.

"Cookie, when you get a chance, would you mind asking Ruth for any bandages the inn might keep on hand?" When she'd agreed on her way out, Gabe dipped his head toward Rosie again. "Get it, Rosie? Keep bandages *on hand*?"

"She really has no sense of humor to speak of," Smokey said, chuckling as he pulled the thread tight. Rosie only managed a helpless sound.

Blood oozed. Gabe stopped watching. He thought he should make small talk to distract her, but his mind was empty. He fought the urge to rock her, to soothe, to gather her in his arms and take her ... away. Just away. Where there were no broken promises or hard decisions or sharp knives.

Rosie Graham had never been meant for those things.

"Here I am! Here I am!" Ruth rushed in, arms loaded with ridiculously large, striped beach towels at, no doubt, Keith's suggestion.

~~~~~

An hour later, the sugar cookies had been cleared away. So, too, had the blood.

Rosie and Dot had been propped on chairs at the same kitchen island. They were "patients" being monitored, they'd been told, given a choice between what was left of the brandy and some strong coffee.

Rosie, who an hour before thought she might never laugh again as the needle stabbed and tugged, stabbed and tugged, now reconsidered that conviction. She *wanted* to laugh. Gabe had offered to help Ruth make dinner for them all, which was proving entertaining, indeed.

The steel island's surface was now largely covered with flour. Gabe was rolling out dough with a large rolling pin, a floral-print apron trimmed in lace saving his sweater vest, if not his sleeves, from the worst of the flour. Some flour had made its way up to his face, much to the satisfaction of the young women watching.

Ruth was at the stove with what was left of the turkey broth and bits of meat that hadn't worked for sandwiches. She stirred and called instructions to Gabe in her deep, strong voice.

"Tell me once you get it all rolled out."

"Yes, ma'am."

"It's certainly taking you some time, I must say."

"I'm trying to impress you," Gabe countered, and Rosie thought it was hardly possible to offend the man. He'd rolled up his flour- and dough-splattered shirtsleeves to reveal ropey, muscled forearms as he pushed the pin over the dough. "How thick should it be, Boss?"

"Thick as a *noodle*, for heaven's sake."

Gabe looked up at Rosie and Dot, who snickered. "Don't look to me for guidance," Dottie said. "You know I'm a restaurant sort of girl, not a noodle-making sort of girl. I was too busy collecting rent on the boardwalk and managed to miss my mother's cooking lessons."

"You're fine right about there," Rosie advised, peering at the rolled dough. "Don't go any thinner."

"'Bout time. Now just cut them," Ruth called.

"'Just cut them,' she says," Gabe grumbled. "Do you have specs for the size, Boss?"

"Size of a *noodle*."

Rosie and Dot dissolved into laughter. Rosie, for all that her entire left hand was thickly bandaged and throbbing, wondered how she could be having such a fine time. But the kitchen was warm from the oven and stove, filled with the aroma of broth and baking bread, and it made Rosie think of holidays in her grandmother's fragrant kitchen, watching the woman dance around the room to songs on the record player. Louisa had adored music.

The coffee Ruth brewed was strong enough to have Rosie's system humming, and she was grateful not to have a headache like Dottie had from crashing into the floor. Keith had surprised Rosie by graciously offering to gather both women a bag of blizzard snow to help relieve their pain, but they'd declined the snow bags for now.

Resting her chin contentedly on the base of her raised palm, Rosie watched Gabe move the knife through the field of powdery dough, first one way and then the other until he'd created dozens of rectangles the size of fingers. He made some remark about knives and fingers that she promised herself she would not give him the satisfaction of laughing over.

"Well, that's one way to go about it," Ruth said with disappointment, joining Gabe at the other side of the island with an enormous metal cookie sheet.

Gabe shared another hen-pecked look with the girls, and Rosie hid her smile behind her over-large bandage. She was having trouble remembering why she'd been so angry with him the night before, and whenever she did begin to remember ... well, she shoved that reality right down again.

If she thought about what he knew and the fact her secret was out, she started to panic all over again.

Ruth directed Gabe in pushing the cut noodles onto the sheet so she could transfer them into the giant pot. Rosie lost the battle against laughter as first one and two and then three raw noodles splattered onto the floor rather than the pan, each splat marked by a huff from Ruth.

"Men do not have a single instinct in the kitchen," the housekeeper declared.

"Hey, now, Ruth! Tell that to the great chefs of the world," Dottie argued, taking a gulp of coffee. "Why would most of them be men, were that true?"

"That's enough sass." She spared Gabe a glance. "You're wearing more flour than you managed to spread on the counter, Mister."

"You can say that again. How do you *do* it, Ruth?"

"Do what?"

"Keep yourself looking so fresh and lovely despite slaving over a hot stove and all this flour." He said it with his mouth and, also, with his big, mesmerizing brown eyes.

Ruth softened like a noodle in boiling water.

So did Rosie, over and over again, no matter how she resisted.

She only kept wondering why Dottie didn't seem to, as well. Maybe the perfect man was something a person took for granted once she'd caught his interest.

Chapter Thirteen

Delia Stimpson Grade Four
Christmas Journal Project
Buckeye Lake Public School
December 1946

I got up in the middle of the night and ate more than ten cookies. I lost count after ten cookies.

We are still in the inn, and it is somehow still snowing. I am getting nervous and wish we hadn't learned about the Donner party right before this snowstorm happened, Ms. Bailey. Maybe teach that to your students from now on in the springtime when there won't be snow for a long time.

In our Dickens book, we are up to the Ghost of Christmas Present now, and he seems way less scary than the others. Everyone says your stomach will hurt if you eat too many cookies when they have lots of icing on them, but my stomach hasn't hurt one single time.

~~~~~

They were another day closer to Christmas when more snow blew in.

A hopelessness settled in over the inn as thick as the cloud of precipitation that pushed down from Canada, cutting them off from the world and the town and the lake and a dozen holiday plans.

Gabe had to re-wear a pair of wool slacks today and knew he needed to do something about his facial hair. He typically shaved daily but hadn't bothered in recent days, and he was beginning to feel a little wild.

He wasn't the only one.

Armed with the iron poker, Charlie Graham persisted in messing with the logs in the fireplace, irritating his mother and everyone in the inn as thumps of collapsing wood were inevitably followed by a fireworks explosion of cinders.

"That's just what we need, Charlie," Rosie had grumbled from the sofa. "A fire to burn down the one source of shelter we have in what appears to be a never-ending storm."

The throbbing of her hand, Gabe supposed, had put Rosie out of sorts. He had urged her to rest in a blanket with her copy of Dickens, but she looked no happier with this arrangement than anyone else did with their own.

At a none-too-gentle urging from Cookie, whose composure had once more cracked with the new snow, Pastor Skip stopped sermon writing and engaged young Delia in several games of rummy. Many of the adults were hiding in their rooms, probably afraid their despair was catching.

That included Keith Fairchild, Gabe thought irritably, whose secret son would not leave the fireplace logs alone. The mother of that son clearly lacked her usual ability to induce maternal fear.

Another log got catapulted from the pile deeper into the hearth in a puff of embers.

Rosie shifted positions again to try to prop her bandage-wrapped hand onto an extra pillow. Gabe, taking pity on her, decided to approach the young fire king. The one who had no idea that he should, by rights, inherit this inn and many others one day. Which did not give him the right, Gabe thought, to burn the place down with all of them in it.

Hands in pockets, he asked casually, "You know how to do flips, Charlie?"

Pausing with the iron poker mid-air, the boy looked up. "Flips? With firewood?"

"No, not with firewood. Can *you* flip? Your body. You know, heels over head or what not?"

"'Course I can. You know ... long as I have a running start."

Gabe considered the kid whose sandy hair was always sticking up in unpredictable places. "You sure haven't gotten the chance for a running start into *anything* this week, have you?"

Another poke at a log. "No, sir."

"Let's go see about that." Gabe strolled off, hands still in the pockets of his second time-around slacks, knowing Charlie would follow. He led him down the hall, up the stairs to the second-floor hallway on the west end of the inn, and into a room clearly not intended for occupation until Memorial Day and later. There were no linens on the mattresses in this area. Exactly as Gabe had calculated.

"What are we doing, Gabe?" Charlie asked, excitement in his voice.

"Grab that side of the mattress."

Together, they hauled twin-size mattresses into the hallway, stacking them two-thick and four-wide. Then, Gabe led Charlie down to the far opposite end of the hall and explained they would run as fast as they could, jump into the air, and do a front flip and land on the mattresses.

"Best landing wins."

Charlie jumped up and down, one leg of his trousers half-tucked into one of his wool stockings. "Who decides the best landing?"

"I do."

"But you're competing!"

"And I'm three times older than you, Kid. We both have our advantages here."

"Okay, okay."

"Just be careful. Smokey can't stitch your head back on. Don't break your neck or anything."

"I won't." With that, Charlie gave in to being ten and tore down the hallway, sliding this way and that on the wooden floor, pinwheeling his little arms.

"You won't be careful? Or you won't break your neck?" Gabe called, laughing. He leaned against the wall and laughed harder as Charlie slid into a wild leap and half-turn in midair on the opposite end of the hall. It looked nothing like a flip, but it had the kid bouncing across all four mattresses and squealing with delight.

Objective met. How many times would he have to do that before he got too tired to antagonize the fireplace?

"Your turn!" Charlie yelled. Gabe reminded himself that as many as a quarter of FH Resorts' customers were children ... not paying customers, of course, but customers just the same, and as he barreled down the polished wood of the hallway himself, he vowed to revisit the resort plans once more through the eyes of a child.

After several terrible flips, a questionable handstand, a wrestling match, and a few deadfalls, the pair splayed across the mattress stack trying to catch their breath.

"Phew. I needed that," Charlie said like he was a sixty-year-old man tossing back his first cup of black coffee for the day. Gabe looked at him and couldn't help smiling. The little boy's hair, besides standing up in funny little sprigs here and there, was now also matted to his forehead with sweat.

"Physical activity is important," Gabe agreed.

"I never thought about it much before this," Charlie admitted. "I'm always going to school or up to the park or out to swim or fishing or whatever. Hey. You think the schoolhouse will be all collapsed now? From the snow or the trees falling?"

"Your guess is as good as mine. Is that what you're hoping for?"

Charlie shrugged. "There's plenty to learn without being in school."

"You sound like my father, and you're only ten years old."

"Your *dad* told you not to go to school?"

"No, no. It's just that we grew up deep in the hills in the southern part of the state. My pops thought it was just as important I learned to trap a critter as it was to learn to talk Latin."

"Yeah. You gotta be outside to learn like that, though. Don't know why my mom won't let me and Delia go check things out, even though it's snowing again."

"It's cold, Charlie. Real cold. Like freeze-your-lungs cold."

"Cold's not that big a deal. Doesn't bother me."

"There will be people who don't live through this," Gabe said. His voice softened as he stacked his hands behind his head and realized he'd grown so used to the howl of the wind that he didn't hear it any longer unless he listened for it.

"People will die?"

"Already have, I bet. And more will."

That led to a few beats of silence. "From trees crashing through their roofs? Like at our house?"

"Maybe that. Getting lost or trapped outside for more than a minute or so. Not having a source of heat, water, food. Getting stuck in a car, early on."

"That's sad." Charlie, sober now, stacked his hands just like Gabe's. "I'm glad we're here, I guess."

"We are warm enough, and we have food," Gabe agreed.

"And Mama's hand's gonna be okay, isn't it? Pastor Skip prayed it wouldn't get affected. What happens if it gets affected, Gabe?"

"It won't get infected. I washed it good in alcohol to kill the germs."

"So, she's fine. That's what I thought and that's what I told Delia last night. Delia's mom died, you know, and she told me all about it."

"Your mom will be fine."

Charlie drew a long breath. "Also, thank you," he said somberly. "For taking care of her yesterday. And not letting her die."

"You don't owe me any thanks, my friend," Gabe said, touched as he always was by the kid's earnestness. Charlie was still small but managed to be a great human being. "I'd do the same for anyone."

The boy was silent for a moment.

"My mama's awful pretty, though. Doncha think?"

Gabe rolled his head on his hands to glance in Charlie's direction, only to see the kid had propped himself up on his right elbow to look at him more closely. "Your mother is a pretty woman, indeed, Charlie. But I'd have helped anyone with a bleeding hand."

"I just think she'd make a really good wife, that's all," Charlie went on. "Because she's pretty and ... you know. She's pretty."

Gabe squashed his grin. He remembered when he was ten and had decided that's all a man could possibly want in a wife. When he had no idea there even were other traits, let alone that they should be weighed in the decision to spend a lifetime together.

He also loved the idea that this boy thought he had to advertise his mother when, by all accounts, Rosie Graham had every chance in the world of finding a husband should she want one. "I'm sure she'd make a fine wife, indeed. Maybe we should put these mattresses back and go see if we can move some more firewood in from the breezeway. Unless Smokey beat us to it."

The pair rose and had moved two of the mattresses back to beds before Charlie spoke again, this time with a question. "You think if you decide to marry a woman, she'll be pretty, Gabe?"

The next mattress, lifted near his face, helped Gabe hide another grin. "That's how most men want it, I guess. Here, you back in the doorway this time."

"Is that how *you* want it?"

"I haven't given it too much thought," Gabe lied, thinking about the engagement ring he'd brought along in case the very attractive Dot Berkeley might agree to marry him. Yes, he was planning on a pretty wife.

The kid wasn't wrong, of course. Charlie's own mother was as pretty as they came.

"But you're gonna want a wife, aren't you?"

"I'm thinking I will. Someday."

"Why wouldn't you want her to be pretty like my mom?"

"Pretty isn't the only thing." Gabe considered wrapping himself in the mattress they carried and flinging himself out the window.

"What else is a thing? I mean, I gotta get married too."

"Charlie."

"Someday."

"There are lots of things. Too many to cover right now. Let's get that last mattress, Partner."

"Like being a good artist?"

Gabe's mouth twitched. "There's that, of course."

"And a good cook?"

"Always nice."

"And a good mom?"

"Usually so hard to tell ahead of time. But yes."

"You can tell with my mom, and that's a fact. She's a *real* good mom."

"I can't argue with that." They muscled the last and largest mattress back onto the bed frame in room 210 and shut the door against the chill of the unheated rooms on this side of the inn.

"You probably want to have kids, too."

Would this never end? "Yes, I suppose I would."

"Boys are really good to have. I mean, if you're gonna have one, you'd want a boy, wouldn't you?"

"Hadn't considered it."

"A boy to wrestle on stacked mattresses in the hall or help you carry firewood like we are gonna go do."

"Boys are just fine, yes."

"My mama is pretty and a good cook and a good artist and a good mom and she already *has* a boy."

"And I can tell you love her so much," Gabe said, moving down the hall at a clip.

"I'm a decent boy to have, too. Some folks don't want their boys to be friends with me 'cause they think I'm bad, but I'm really not bad."

"They think you're bad?"

"'Cause I don't have a dad."

"Oh. I see." Gabe slowed down, and Charlie caught up.

Gabe did see.

"I'm not bad, though. I do what my mama tells me to do. What Grandpa tells me to do too. I would do what you told me to do. You know, if you wanted to have me and my mom with you."

Gabe blinked down at the boy's bright eyes and felt too much. The load this little guy was carrying — one his mother didn't fully realize, Gabe was certain — was heavy, indeed. Could he blame him for wanting to bring someone else into the mix to spread the responsibility? Ten was too young to see yourself as the Man of the House, grandpa or no grandpa in residence.

"I think you're top-notch, Kid. Your mom too. No need to sell me on either of you, I promise," Gabe said, stopping to clear his throat. "Let's go get that firewood, eh?"

~~~~

Rosie regarded Charlie, curled like a pretzel in a chair across from the sofa she'd been on most of the day. How had he fallen asleep in that position in the late afternoon?

How was it this dark and quiet already? And what day was it, anyway?

Sometimes a love so powerful it hurt crept up on her when she looked at the details of her little boy. The indent of his bottom lip. The pink of his earlobes. All the cowlicks that made his hair such a perpetual mess. The pattern of freckles on his nose and cheeks. The hole he'd already worn in the right leg of the trousers she'd made him for the wedding.

She could hardly describe it *as* love. Love seemed too mild a term for it.

Words were Emily's thing, anyway.

Rosie's hand still ached. Everyone had left her alone to "rest," which meant all she had to think about was that plate of cookies sitting in the kitchen.

Well, that plate of cookies and whether or not she was an awful person.

Sitting there, watching her son sleep, she reminded herself again and again that she *had* tried to tell Keith about Charlie. She had written, but her letters were returned unopened from the university. She had told herself he'd contact her as he'd promised to do, once he got settled with his classes, but he never did.

He simply had not wanted her.

But ... would he have wanted a son? Rosie didn't think so, had never thought so, but her conversation with Gabe the night before left her wondering.

Had Keith given up his right to make the choice, truly? Was that the price of a promise broken? Or had she just been telling herself that her actions were fair, continued to be fair, based on the fact he didn't want to marry her?

For the first time since she'd held her baby boy in her arms, Rosie dared to imagine what it would be like if she told Keith Fairchild now that he was a father. How would he react? His denial would be a fresh, new insult. He'd known how innocent she'd been at sixteen. Denying Charlie as the product of their summer romance would be insulting in the extreme.

Still, she'd already been insulted, hadn't she?

His acceptance of Charlie as his son, though, could be much more painful. It was the fear of that acceptance, she had to admit, that might have kept her silent all these years.

There were so many things to consider, the simplest of all being Charlie's last name. Rosie couldn't bring herself to think of the more complicated aspects, which had to do with the power the Fairchild family held. Could they take Charlie to live with them? Send him away to boarding schools for the wealthy?

Not for the first time, Rosie wondered if it were more compassionate to all of them for her to continue to keep this secret.

Charlie was a bright, happy kid. Keith seemed content with his life and freedom. She, herself, could not deny she was more qualified and much preferred to call the shots when it came to her son.

Rosie rubbed at an ache in her chest, cringed at the ache in her hand, and, for the first time, found herself in a position where she knew she must pray seriously about whether to tell Keith about Charlie's existence.

She closed her eyes and tried to pray for guidance.

But she didn't *want* to tell Keith.

She opened her eyes again.

There was that plate of sugar cookies in the kitchen. Cookies with glorious amounts of icing and sprinkles.

She rose, yawned, and felt her way down the dark hallway, wondering idly if Hickory was enjoying having his fill of playing rummy in the study. She swung the door into the lamp-lit kitchen ...

... to find Gabe Adams shaving.

Dressed in a white undershirt, he turned in surprise to reveal a face partly frothy with shaving cream. His smile was just as white when he saw her. It occurred to her that, even after what he knew and their words two nights before, Gabe still only looked at her with warmth.

"No need to stitch *me* up just yet," he said pleasantly, gesturing at the steel pan he'd propped up next to the lantern. She realized he was using it as a mirror as he bent to it again, squinting at his reflection.

Rosie approached to see how he was making out, all thoughts of cookies forgotten. "Why don't you let your beard grow like the other men?"

He pulled his lips to the side to make a small swipe with the razor near the corner of his mouth, then stepped back. "Men with darker skin like mine aren't always viewed as trustworthy at the best of times," he explained, still amused. He swished the razor in a second pot of steaming water she realized he would not have wanted to carry to a bathroom. "Anything more than a five-o'clock shadow and someone's likely to call the law."

"Oh, dear. That's not funny, is it?"

"No, it's not."

"Where does your complexion come from, if you don't mind me asking?"

"My mama," he said, leaning against the counter to face her and smiling again. "She's wonderful. She's from Mexico."

"She is? How …?"

"My father—he's from Ohio originally—was a missionary, and he fell in love with her on a mission down there after seminary. Married her. Had me. When he was asked to start a church in rural southeast Ohio … I was maybe three years old? He moved us up there, and I think it's safe to say my mama is the only Mexican woman in all the hills around our cabin. That's a fact."

"Does she mind that?"

"She minds the cold, I can tell you. Gives stirring speeches about it from October through March. She's an angel, though, and I guess it doesn't occur to anyone down there that she's different anymore. My brothers and sisters and I vary from mostly white to mostly brown to me, somewhere in the middle. But mostly what we've always been is loved."

It was Rosie's turn to smile. "I can tell they mean the world to you. Is it hard, not seeing them for Christmas?"

"I wasn't going to get to anyway," Gabe said with a shrug. "I'll go down after the first of the year, once the roads clear. From the looks of things, that will only take until April."

"You'll miss all of your mother's winter speeches." When he smiled this time, she saw that he still had a shadow of scruff where the razor must already have passed. The steel pot was not doing its job as a mirror, and he'd been so kind to her when she'd cut her hand. No one ever took care of her like that, which she told herself was the reason she suddenly felt bold.

Rosie glanced at the steaming soup of shaving bubbles before him and, since her dominant hand was still in working order, reached down for the razor.

"You missed a spot."

"What are you doing?"

She glanced up and grinned. "Nervous?"

"I've seen you do some gruesome work with a knife in this very room, ma'am."

"Hold still." Rosie took two steps to close the short distance between them. Bracing his head against her bandaged hand for resistance, she rose on her toes and moved the blade carefully down past the right corner of his mouth. This moment, she thought, her breath thick as she went for another pass, was the reward she was giving herself for not openly complaining about her hand once all day.

Hadn't she done this often for her grandfather in the heat of summers, when he got impatient with his beard? This was just its own kind of comfort, she told herself, for both of them, after the heated conversation they'd last had.

Some of that comfort, it seemed, involved stealing glances at the way his arms were made and the way his undershirt fit the muscles beneath it. The way his brown hair curled a little over his ear where he'd gotten it wet. The flutter of his pulse in the hollow of his throat. Rosie thought she might be very, very attracted to him, and the thought annoyed her.

But not so much that she didn't carefully and gently return with the razor to the left side of his face.

Chapter Fourteen

Delia Stimpson Grade Four
Christmas Journal Project
Buckeye Lake Public School
December 1946

I am starting to get worried about Santa Claus, and the grownups aren't making me feel any better about his chances. Charlie is sure he'll come, but I keep seeing the others look funny at each other.

No way he knows I'm here. Last Christmas was my first one with Pastor Skip, and I was sort of worried Santa wouldn't know I'd come to live in Buckeye Lake, but I did get a brand-new stuffed bear and a Bible. Before that, I was other places at Christmas, but I have to say, Santa did find me. So, maybe he'll know I accidentally ended up in this hotel. I don't care what he brings me anymore. I just want to know he can find me.

~~~~~

A fitful night of sleep kept Gabe in bed longer than usual, and he awoke on the 23rd of December to the firm rap of knuckles against the door to his room. Blinking bleary eyes, he shuffled across the room. Confused, he hoped somehow Rosie Graham waited on the other side, though even his jumbled mind knew she wouldn't knock like that.

His mind also knew, as it began to engage, she should not be his first thought upon waking.

At any rate, he opened the door to the still unshaved but eager faces of Smokey Black and Keith Fairchild.

"Get your clothes on," Smokey said simply. That's when Gabe noticed the two men were dressed as though panning for gold in the Klondike. In January. "The storm finally broke. We're headed out to see what's what."

"Come on," Keith urged. "Coffee's in the kitchen."

As they walked off, the hallway window behind them still seemed crusted with ice, but between frozen globs Gabe could see ... orange light? Was it *sunshine*? A surge of energy shot through him that reminded him how sluggish cabin fever made a soul. Or fancy-inn fever, in this case. Either way, he spun around and dug for the quilted long underwear in his trunk.

Ten minutes later, he moved silently down the hall and out into the common area, where Charlie and Delia were silent, sleeping mounds beneath heavy counterpanes before the fire. He first glanced at the window seat for Rosie, but she was tucked in on the sofa, instead, her left forearm wedged between support cushions so that the white bandage marked her position like a flag. As he tiptoed by, he was treated to her eyes — puffy with sleep — blinking open.

"What …?" she whispered groggily, trying to prop herself up with her other arm.

"Storm stopped, apparently," he said in a happy hush, and he watched her face light up.

"We're leaving?"

Gabe couldn't help but smile. She clearly wasn't firing on all cylinders yet, herself. "I'll let you know what we discover on our expedition."

Just getting out the back door from the mudroom area was a brief project once the men had finished their coffee. Because they'd been in and out this back door to move stacks of firewood, it still opened easier than the front door would have. Nor would they have wanted to wake the children with a blast of frigid air that waited on the other side.

Hickory showed up to join them, more eager to get out of doors than he was even for hot coffee. He'd save it for after, he said.

None of the men said anything once they'd climbed out into the inn's yard over drifts of snow, the most manageable mounds of which were nearly to their waists. Gabe, breathing hard in the painfully cold air, looked around in disbelief. The world was nearly unrecognizable, the Liebs Island neighborhood he'd known on his business trips to the lake now just strange, snow-covered shapes, like a land of chilly monsters standing stark and still. He supposed he was looking at vehicles, sheds, porches and even houses under the white, though there was hardly any telling except for the occasional chimney releasing pale gray smoke into the pale gray sky.

"Let's see about the tractor," Smokey called up ahead, breathing hard, too. It was twenty below, at least, and the wind was still blowing a little. Sounds were muted, not traveling the way they usually did. Gabe tugged the heavy, knit scarf tighter around his nose and mouth but was sure his cheeks and lips were getting chapped beneath it. Why had he chosen last night to remove that extra layer of facial hair that would have provided more warmth?

The tractor, Gabe supposed, was the party's best bet for moving about in a world piled high in feet upon feet of icy snow. He'd heard Smokey say the Allis-Chalmers had chains on its tires and that he could drive the beast over the frozen lake itself.

"Had I not known where I'd left it, I swear we'd never find the thing at all," the big man huffed as he attacked the tractor-shaped drift with a shovel. Keith and Hickory laboriously pushed through the drifts to position themselves on the other side, and Gabe joined in the effort beside Smokey to uncover the frozen mass.

They barely lasted fifteen minutes before they headed back indoors.

After that unproductive session, not one of them was very eager to leave the fireplace hearth, while Charlie and Delia hopped around nearby, begging to go out with them again.

"You won't be seeing me step foot back out in it today, you scamps," Smokey said. "Believe me when I say your only move would be to tunnel around in it in temperatures like to freeze off your toes."

"Tunneling around sounds kind of like fun," Charlie argued.

"Look at my fingers," Keith said, holding out manicured but bright red fingertips that had to ache as badly as Gabe's. "I swear, I still can hardly feel them."

"Tractor's covered in ice," Smokey told Rosie, who'd risen and dressed while they'd been outdoors.

"You think Em and Drew are okay? It's been days," she pointed out, casting a worried glance toward the big picture window.

"The chimney down on the barge house is smoking away, darling," Smokey said. "I checked while we were out there."

"So, we really, truly can't go out?" Delia asked on a whine. "Not even with it stopped snowing and all?"

"No way. Not today. No chance," Smokey said, immune to their protests.

"Should we still write the letters to Santa?" Charlie asked Rosie, who brushed her fingers through his hair. "And leave them out for him? Just in case *he* can make it out there?"

"He's even tougher than Smokey," Delia reasoned. "Let's write them."

Smokey was thawed enough to flip the little girl around and tickle her until she screamed out a laugh that no doubt woke the rest of the house.

"You're quiet this morning," Rosie said to Gabe after she'd handed her grandfather a steaming mug. She must have had some coffee herself because the sleepiness around her eyes had cleared.

Gabe still didn't know what to say at times like this, when he was in the vicinity of Rosie, Keith, and Charlie together. All the history, the unspoken truths. He just wasn't used to secrets of this magnitude. "Um. How's your hand today?"

"Sore and stiff but still attached. Dottie's up and getting dressed. She's probably going to beg to get out of here even more than the kids. Just to warn you. She's never loved sitting still."

Gabe smiled. "I'll let Smokey deliver the news to her in that charming way of his. It worked so well with the kids."

"So. We're really not getting out of here today, are we?"

"We're really, really not." He studied her to see if she'd pout.

Instead, she sighed and shrugged. "I guess that means we'll have to put on a play," she announced at a volume that intentionally garnered Charlie's and Delia's attention.

"A play?" Delia squealed, rushing to fling herself at Rosie. "I love when you do plays with us! What's this one about? And can I play the villain again?"

"How would I know what it's about until you two write it?" Rosie asked. "I assume something about Christmas so you can perform it later for everyone?"

"Yeah, Christmas," Charlie said, running to get paper. "And also, bandits."

"I'll be the bandit!"

"There can be more than one bandit, Dee," he called back. "And pirates."

"What kind of Christmas play is this?" Keith asked, laughing. Gabe thought it was only the second time he'd noticed there were children here in the inn.

"You can be in it," Delia told Keith magnanimously, looking up at him. "You can be the evil prince."

Keith frowned. "Evil prince? Why do I have to be evil?"

"I'm not sure you've noticed," Rosie said consolingly, and Gabe felt a pang any time she addressed the man. "But *every*one in this play seems to be evil."

"The pirates can be good," Charlie argued.

"How disappointing," Rosie said. "Come on, you two. Help me get your bedding put away so we have room to stage this thing."

The kids babbled about costumes and passed Dot in the hall as she came out. Not wanting to hear another round of placating about the forbidden outdoors, Gabe bid her a cheerful "good morning" and then slipped away into the study, where he found Pastor Skip playing checkers against himself and dipping a sloppy roll in coffee.

The older man looked up and smiled a greeting. "Still bad out there, eh? Come, sit."

Gabe settled opposite him. "Need an opponent?"

"It's more entertaining that way, although I've been winning every time with this method." He laughed uproariously at himself as he plucked up the black discs off the board. "You can be red."

"Very festive. Thank you." Gabe settled in. They set up the board in comfortable silence, the chatter in the main parlor soothing background noise. Someone was fooling around on the piano again out there. Gabe studied the kind but tired eyes of the pastor and the creases between his brows. "Are you worried about your flock out there in the world, Pastor Skip?"

A resigned smile. "I know better than to worry, Son." He winked. "But it's safe to say I'm ... concerned."

"My own father preaches at a couple of tiny churches, and I know how 'concerned' he gets when things are tough in their community. Storms, floods, fires. They love their church family, he and my mama, and even the prospect of a funeral gets them shaken."

"But not worried." Skip chuckled, sliding one of his checkers over to a new square.

"Of course not. Never worried." Gabe smiled.

"You weren't tempted to follow him into the ministry? Your father?"

"I never felt that calling, no."

"Neither did my son. But there's plenty of work that needs doing beyond that, isn't there? The trick is figuring it out, I guess."

Gabe felt almost guilty jumping his checker and swiping it off the board. As a peace offering, he said, "I thought I had it figured out until this past year, to be honest."

Those pale eyes lit, just like Gabe's dad's when he thought there was counsel to give. And, just like his dad's, they urged him on without words.

"There's not much money flowing for ministry in the hills of southeast Ohio. That's where my parents planted first one and then another church."

Pastor Skip made the connection before Gabe had to explain. "And you're providing some of that money."

"Ever since I stumbled into the hotel business with the Fairchilds, I seem to make plenty of money, plenty fast," he said with a shrug, knowing the man would understand the nature of the blessing. "So, yes. My family is invested in that ministry, but I am too, in a different way. From farther away. And I'm very invested in my family, of course."

"You've got a big one?"

"Six brothers and sisters quite a bit younger than me."

"That's a load of blessings. I imagine it's hard to be away this time of year."

Gabe wondered why everyone kept pitying him for that. They didn't know how little nine souls in a cabin could feel like a blessing for an extended period, but the thought still had him grinning. He'd talked his father into adding three rooms onto the home in the coming summer, and he figured he'd be camped out there helping with the project even as plans to start the new resort here were developing. "Holidays are always ... loud there," he told Skip, and they both laughed when there was a squeal and crash out in the parlor of the inn.

"Louder than this? I admit I'll miss the Christmas Eve service at midnight. Doesn't look like anyone will make it there, least of all me." He glanced up, made a searching kind of eye contact. "Does it?"

"No, sir. It's just not possible yet."

A nod. "It's my favorite service of the year."

"Candlelight?"

"And singing, yes. Nothing like the faces of your neighbors glowing over candles at midnight singing 'Silent Night.'"

"Sounds beautiful." He could hear Rosie laughing with the kids in the other room, making the best of another day of captivity. They were making their own kind of beauty, he supposed. "If we're still stuck, we'll make it work here, though, won't we? We're already lighting with candles, I guess. Adding some 'Silent Night' won't be too hard."

Pastor Skip double-jumped Gabe's pieces with a smirk. "Reckon we'll make it work, at that. Did you have a midnight service with your folks, too? On Christmas Eve?"

"No. Meeting at midnight wouldn't have worked too well on those dark roads in the hills. They're dangerous in the daylight."

"Of course."

"Christmas morning there were services, though, at the church. The night before we celebrated as a family. It was always my job, growing up, to recite the Christmas story from Luke."

"Ahh. An honor."

"Notice I said recite, not read."

Pastor Skip chuckled, even though he lost another checker. "You were a smart one, clearly. Who does the recitation now that you're away?"

"My next oldest sister, at least last year."

Another double jump, another smirk. "What's changed in the past year?"

"Hmm?"

Pastor Skip was watching him. "You said you'd felt pretty certain about your work for the Lord until this past year. What's changed?"

Ah, the man was good. Gabe smiled to acknowledge it. "It's hard to explain. It sounds crazy to say it out loud."

"Always a good indication it's from God."

Gabe had never said it out loud, in fact. "I've been feeling this tug, ever since I arrived here in Buckeye Lake this past summer. Again, it sounds crazy, but I can't shake the feeling that I'm *supposed* to be here. That there's something I'm supposed to do, a reason I keep coming back."

Visibly pleased, as though he were some sort of local ambassador to the lake, Pastor Skip moved a checker, pressed on. "Wonderful. But you don't know what it is? The reason?"

"I can only assume it's the resort?" Gabe looked over at the desk, where the plans were spread. Dot would be back there after she had breakfast, he figured, working and reworking. She was probably guzzling coffee even now, gearing up for it. Only in that moment, having said it out loud, did Gabe begin to wonder if it *was* the resort that was tugging on him, though. If it were, wouldn't he have felt pulled toward those plans in the past week with as much zeal as Dot?

And what did God want with the resort, he wondered. It was hardly a clapboard church in Appalachia, so why did his parents' church and Buckeye Lake fill him with the same urge to say, "Yes, Lord, I will"?

"All you can do is keep praying about it, stay open to whatever you're being asked to do," the preacher reasoned, and with that advice, he proceeded to win the checkers game. "All that lonely practice did me good, I guess."

Gabe politely agreed.

"I've been feeling a pull that doesn't make the best kind of sense, either," Pastor Skip said, leaning back and finishing his roll in one bite.

"What's that, sir?"

"Old seminary friend. He's asked me to go with him to the Philippines come spring on an indefinite mission, but there are a dozen reasons I shouldn't go. Mostly little Delia. It may not be safe for her, the situation we'd be in, but God gave me her to care for, no matter how badly I seem to be messing that up." He shook his fuzzy head in a self-deprecating way that probably made him a good preacher, Gabe thought. "And there's my ministry here. I don't know."

"But you keep praying about those things."

"I do because I can't shake the feeling I'm supposed to be moving in that direction. Like you, it sounds crazy to say out loud. It doesn't make sense. But sometimes I convince myself it *does* make sense, you know. There's Roscoe, just out of seminary, who could take the church here. He preaches for me sometimes. And there's Rosie, who loves Delia like her own child."

Gabe nodded. "Would she be able to take her for a time? Do you think she'd agree to it?"

"I know she would," Skip said with conviction. "But it could be months or years. Not that it would change Rosie's feelings about Delia, but is it right to saddle her with all the girl's health and educational decisions when I'm her legal guardian? I've thought about asking Rosie to just adopt Delia, but of course, no court would allow that. Not with Rosie being an unmarried mother already."

Gabe stared at the checkerboard. "And you think Rosie would do it. Permanently?"

"She's told me before she'd love to. She's been more a parent to Delia than I could ever be."

Gabe's head swam at the thought of it. *What was wrong with that woman?* She was already raising her own son alone, she refused to ask Keith to share the responsibility, and here she was actively seeking to raise someone *else's* child. She had no one to lean on as it was. Someone needed to talk some sense into her.

It's not my business, he reminded himself, as happy sounds of the crazy woman and the children continued to leak into the study.

She had people. Of course, she did. Her grandfather's marina seemed to keep a roof over their heads. She was clearly a successful artist here at the lake. She and her sister were close. *Rosie was not alone.* Someone else would talk some sense into her, right?

Though Delia deserved a mother like Rosie.

Meanwhile, there were those plans sprawled across the desk just a few feet away. *That* was his business. That was his role. Surely, that was the tug, the force that seemed to keep calling him to this little midwestern lake. The lake had a princess, and the princess was Dot Berkeley, and she wanted to build a castle on her family's land. Gabe happened to be in the business of building and running castles.

The happily-ever-after was all set to go.

Gabe blamed his humble upbringing for the fact that the idea of Rosie Graham sketching in a simple house surrounded by children seemed infinitely more appealing, suddenly, than princesses and castles.

Chapter Fifteen

That night, when the clock struck midnight and ushered in the earliest hour of the strangest of Christmas Eves, an air of hushed hilarity filled the kitchen.

Four women washing one another's hair in a sink in relative darkness seemed to induce confessions. And laughter.

Rosie had a private theory that everything interesting happened in the inn's kitchen.

"So, she'd instructed her attorney," Cookie was saying, "to deliver the quilt to him exactly three months after her death, which happened to be ..."

"Christmas!" they all said as a chorus and on a collective gasp.

"How delicious," Dottie said, bending at the waist to re-wrap the towel around her yard of dark, rope-like curls. "Listen, we need to heat more water before we do Rosie's. That was on the border of uncomfortable. Chilly even."

The hand-pump in the sink in the corner from the "old" side of the kitchen had proved an unexpected blessing throughout the blizzard, and Ruth set about pumping more as Cookie carried the first pot to the sink for dumping.

Rosie had been instructed to keep her bandage dry, which meant she'd been little help. She was also the last to get her hair scrubbed, which meant their midnight party would end soon. Still, it would take some time to heat a new pot of water.

Ruth had already told romantic tales she'd read about the war. Cookie had told ghost stories, most of which Rosie had already heard from her aunt growing up, but they were all the more soothing for it.

Dottie had shocked them with her own stories of behavior she'd witnessed during the season on the boardwalk, growing up, prompting renewed outrage from Cookie that the Berkeleys had exposed a child to any of that. Rosie knew the complete truth was even sadder than Cookie guessed, but that knowledge stayed in the quiet space of long friendship.

At any rate, Dottie's outrageous stories still had the group hushing one another in laughter so as not to wake the children in the parlor.

"I'll say what no one has wanted to say out loud yet," Dottie said as she muscled the pot of water back over the stove. She wore a robe and a towel turban, and she looked very young with her makeup scrubbed off.

"We're all still going to be here for Christmas."

Cookie sighed. "Those poor little ones. What a Christmas morning."

"We don't know what the day ahead might hold, though," Rosie insisted.

"Your grandfather didn't think they could get down the hill and back to get presents, to say nothing about the hole in the roof," Dottie told her friend, sidling up beside her and leaning in. "I don't see how you could head back home, and your house is by far the closest of any of us."

"What will you tell the children?" Cookie worried.

"There's a sled in the garage that's never really been used," Ruth said with determination, joining them at the center counter. "We could rig up a bow for that, and that would be something for the kids on Christmas morning. You know, from Santa."

"Seems like the sledding might be good for months to come, with all this snow."

"They'd like that, I'm sure. Thank you, Ruth."

"Come to think of it, there are some dolls up in the attic. A little outdated but in good shape if I dust one off and dress it up," Ruth went on. "Reckon Santa could bring a doll for little Delia and the sled for Charlie?"

"The pair of them really have been angels, all things considered," Cookie said fondly. "I'd have paid good money to see that play they put on for us tonight for free."

Ruth applauded her agreement. She had played an essential and natural role as "innkeeper" in the play, which had to do with Mary and Joseph arriving at an inn already crowded with bandits and pirates. After that, there had been a lot of plank walking and yuletide bank robberies.

"I'll tell you what I'd like Santa to bring," Dottie said. "Electricity. And a long, hot bath."

"Same. But at least my hair feels better," Ruth said.

"I'd ask Santa for a toaster that works and something to drag my bosom back up to where it belongs," Cookie said, sending them into another round of laughter.

"We'll look through the catalog for something once we get Rosie's hair done. Speaking of which, what about you, Rosie? What do you want Santa to bring?"

This was different, Rosie thought, from the things people prayed for. *That* was a very different list that centered around her son's well-being and Delia's uncertain future. But from Santa? "Art supplies," she told the group with a shrug. It was the same every year, so Dottie rolled her eyes. "Well, it's true. Especially for the glasswork. It's been hard to get the right tools, but with the war over ... I've got some projects planned."

"Projects." Dottie clapped her hands. "Oooh, I've got some hopes for the coming year, all right."

"If you say one thing about that resort and ruin the night..." Cookie warned.

"No, no. I mean with the rebuilding of the pier, from the fire, we'll be opening so many new and better attractions. You should see the plans for the new ballroom." She was lit up, carried away with the magic of her own visions.

"But will it be done in time?"

"In time for summer? No. Not the ballroom, anyway, but hopefully they'll complete it near the end of the season."

"And how about romance, ladies?" Cookie cooed, leaning across the counter and wiggling her painted-on eyebrows, which had lost a good deal of their paint over the past few days.

Rosie looked at Dot to field that one, but Dottie grinned. "What? She asked you, too, Rosie."

"You know I don't even go out with anyone, so romance really isn't applicable for me." If she'd had some confusing feelings these past few days, she told herself those feelings were just symptoms of the holiday.

"I don't know," Ruth said cryptically, narrowing her eyes at Rosie but adding a wink to settle Rosie's heart flop.

"Dottie. You're up."

"I guess I have some ... expectations," she said.

"Of course you do. Haven't you been seeing Gabriel?" Cookie pressed. More suggestive eyebrow movement. "He's a fine-looking Christmas gift, I must say."

Dottie grinned, though perhaps not with as much verve as she'd done about the rebuilding of the pier.

Rosie busied herself pretending she hadn't been obsessing about that same man's throat in this very room the night before.

"Well, this is going to sound sorry indeed," Ruth put in, and Rosie found herself eager for the interruption. "I know you're all desperate to be home. But if I could have one thing for Christmas, it would be that none of you all would ever have to leave here."

A chorus of warm exclamations ended in another round of hugs, and then the fresh water started to steam at last.

"I didn't realize how lonely I got here in the winter until now, when I haven't been lonely at all."

"Ruth, you must promise, when the weather does clear, that you'll come down to the towpath and share dinner with us now and then. Sunday dinner, at least," Rosie offered.

As she leaned her bright hair over the sink, holding her left hand behind her to keep it from being splashed, Rosie thought about how much good could come of an otherwise devastating blizzard.

Ruth had loomed judgmental and frightening in her mind all these years, a woman she'd passed with a friendly nod but then sped by after that fateful autumn a decade before.

Even Keith, whom Rosie had worked hard to fashion into a one-dimensional playboy over all these years, had been nothing but polite and respectful the past week—solicitous, even—reminding Rosie that people were more complex than a bad day or bad decision.

Which was true for herself, as well. She knew it, always, but a new appreciation for that kind of grace was turning out to be as decent a Christmas gift as any art supply could be.

Chapter Sixteen

Delia Stimpson Grade Four
Christmas Journal Project
Buckeye Lake Public School
December 1946

It's Christmas Eve, and there's not much to say except THE SUN CAME OUT! I don't want to write because we get to go outside! In the snow! I will write in this little book later when it starts getting dark again! I've got to go now! Outside!

~~~~~

Rosie didn't even mind the cold the next day. She was just happy it had been decided the temperature had risen enough for those of the party who wanted to venture outdoors to do so. At long last.

It wasn't exactly a free-for-all, to be sure, with Charlie, Delia, and her restricted to the stone patio that looked out over the lake. The worst of the wind hadn't turned the corner of the inn, leaving the snow a manageable foot-deep here rather than several feet deep as it was everywhere else.

Still, the snow had stopped falling, the sky had cleared, and the air was finally breathable for more than five minutes at a time.

The rising temperature even had the snow getting somewhat packable.

Which meant haphazard snow people were forming here on the patio amidst laughter and silliness. The children had been wrapped and re-wrapped in not just the outer clothes they'd originally worn to the wedding but also in additional scarves Ruth had produced for them.

Rosie, who had always played vigorously and unapologetically with her son and his friend, was doing her part with the snow friends. She'd lost feeling in her nose but had no desire at all to go back inside. Instead, she rolled and patted and pushed mounds of snow together, breath coming in foggy puffs, until she had created a kind of frozen warrior queen.

"Yours is a little bit scary," Delia declared, taking it in. "I like it."

"She just got taller than I intended her to, that's all. She's missing a sword now, I think."

"She can be the mommy snowman to my snowgirl. This is a girl, not a man."

"I can tell from the longer snow hair."

"Mine is two boys," Charlie said, "but they're joined together. See?

Like those twins Pastor Skip was telling us about who were born attached. Remember, Mom?"

"That's a creative way to deal with your first snowman's torso sliding off," Rosie praised. "The conjoined twins look quite healthy, Charlie. All things considered."

"Thank you." What little of her son's face she could see was pink from a combination of cold and happiness. Delia's was, too, though a glance at her had Rosie tugging the ear flap down over the too-red tip of one ear.

"The twins can have the big snowman as their mama too," Delia declared magnanimously. "They can be a family. Families look all different ways, don't they?"

"They sure do." Rosie's heart ached as it often did for Delia's underlying hunger for a traditional family, for something solid in a young life that had changed so often and so fast. Now she wondered what would come next for the little girl.

Rosie had been urging Pastor Skip not to subject Delia to a possibly dangerous mission trip, during which he would be more distracted from the girl's needs than he already was here. Patting some loose snow along Mama Snowman's hip, Rosie wished more than ever for the same thing as little Delia ... that she herself could offer that traditional home the child craved or that, at least, they lived in a world that would allow Rosie the privilege of adopting.

It was a world that barely acknowledged her role as mother to begin with, though.

Straightening, she was happy to be able to crane her neck and see down the hill, past what would have been the beach area at the marina to the little strip of Towpath Island, where the barge house chimney did, indeed, still puff in the distance, as Smokey had assured her it did the day before.

Emily and Drew would build that traditional family that Rosie and Emily had craved while they were growing up.

They'd spent so many years wishing their father back from the dead, wishing their wayward mother returned. Wishing. Now, it pleased her to think that her sister would have children and that those children would have devoted parents—a mother and a father—and that no one would look at those children askance.

The newlyweds, Rosie prayed, might just change the story of the family.

What would it be like, she wondered, to be loved with the kind of assurance her sister was now, in marriage? To have a strong ally? Was it restful, somehow? Rosie longed to ask these very questions, to sit with her sister and talk, but even she could not imagine a way through that deep,

deep snow yet.

"I've got a surprise for you!" Ruth, wrapped in her own coat but without hat or gloves, shuffled out a few steps to the patio armed with three rather rough looking carrots. "I've brought your snowmen some noses, and here's some of the food dye left from our cookies! Blue for the eyes and red for mouths. How's *that* for a face?"

Cheers greeted this announcement, and Ruth was quickly divested of her treasures and was back inside as fast as she could manage it, even as she laughed with her own glee.

"I don't see why the *eyes* can't be red," Delia mumbled.

"Depends on if your snowperson has been trying to sleep in the same room as wild little snow creatures and howling wind," Rosie said. "Then her eyes might be red, indeed, like mine."

Rosie used the swab Ruth provided to plop bright blue dye in two great circles on her Amazonian snow mother's face.

She thought of Gabe Adams's eyes, though, and wondered what it would be like to live in a world that assumed eyes should be blue. His own irises were dark-rimmed but swimming in shades of caramel near the pupils.

"One more surprise!" Gabe arrived on the patio now, as though Rosie had conjured him, armed with three of the silliest hats she'd ever seen. He'd been helping dig out the tractor around front and checking on the neighbor families on either side, she knew.

Now, he explained he'd managed a trip back up to the attic to top off the equally important work that had taken place here on the patio.

"We found these hats the other day, didn't we, Gabe?" Charlie exclaimed with pride.

Delia chose a red-feathered bonnet for her frozen girl. The bonnet exactly matched the gruesome red swath of mouth below its seeping eyes.

"Aw, man. The twins are gonna have to fight over a hat," Charlie determined, selecting a rust-colored bowler.

"You can have Mama Snowman's hat for the other twin," Rosie offered. "She's too fierce to need any other ornamentation."

Rosie warmed under Gabe's bright smile, even as she heard Delia exclaim, "Oh, no! Rosie, you must've gotten some red food dye on your bandage!"

It certainly looked like it. Rosie angled her body away and inspected the bandage. She realized with dismay that what she'd really done was opened up the gash beneath the bandage again during her snow playing adventures. It was now actively bleeding through thick layers of gauze and tape.

Too embarrassed to acknowledge she'd messed up Smokey's and Gabe's sewing handiwork, she simply tugged her coat sleeve down over it.

~~~~~

"Who wants more cocoa by the fire?" This time it was only Ruth's head poking out the patio door, and her sing-song suggestion was met with more cheers from Charlie and Delia.

"This is a *great* Christmas Eve!" Charlie called as the pair of them rushed in, and Ruth beamed over her success.

Gabe looked over at Rosie, who somehow managed to be more beautiful than ever with her eyes sparkling and her cheeks ... well, rosy. When neither of them responded, the door closed, and Gabe found himself content to remain in the fresh, if chilly, air. He made a show of inspecting the snow creations as he moved nearer to her, the patio part-cleared by all the giant snowball rolling that had taken place in such a compact area.

"You win the award for the tallest snowman I've seen all season," he determined.

"It's a her."

"Well, she's an intimidating creation. How are you, Rosie?" He liked the familiarity of her first name. He liked meeting her eyes, couldn't seem to resist the energy that thrummed between them when it happened.

"Very well, thanks."

She'd been avoiding him, but neither had he sought her out the night before. Rosie was, for all her gentle humor, intimidating in her own way. She was the most natural and fun-loving mother he'd ever seen. She was one of the best artists he'd ever met. And she was irresistible to look at. He couldn't say any of those things to her, though, with all that stood between them.

"That's our family's marina down there," she said into the comfortable silence, gesturing with her head. She had her hands pulled up inside her sleeves and her arms hugged around herself, but she didn't appear cold.

Gabe had certainly seen Graham's Marina over the summer months he'd been in and out of The Fairchild Island Inn. The geographic high point of the island that featured the hotel sloped down to the marina's lot, outbuildings, and docks that stretched into the lake below. But a man would have to already know the layout to make out any distinguishing marks under the blanket of heavy snow there now.

"Even the docks are invisible," he noted, scanning all the white. "And that must be the towpath I've heard so much about."

"Yes." She pointed with her right glove. "You can just make out the bridge over the canal there."

"And the barge house where the honeymooners are."

"Yes."

"It's beautiful, even covered in white. Buckeye Lake has its hooks in me, so to speak," Gabe admitted to her. "It must have been something special, growing up here."

"This has been my whole world," Rosie said simply, still watching over it all beside him. "I was born down there. Lived there all my life. Charlie has, too."

Gabe drew in a breath and let it out slowly. "Please forgive me for making things strange between us," he said softly. He looked around to make sure they were still alone in the snow-covered silence. "It was none of my business."

She didn't look over but nodded. At first, he didn't think she'd reply, but then she suddenly went on, "That smooth curve there, that's the beach by the marina. That's where I met ... him. That summer."

He followed her gaze, but he couldn't make out much of anything. He could imagine a beach there. He could imagine the kids Rosie and Keith had been, too.

He'd known Keith Fairchild not terribly long after that summer, as the lackluster college son of Gabe's new boss. He could well imagine Keith's summer tan and his sandy hair and the charm he could turn on and off with such speed. The charm would have been on full wattage down on that beach, Gabe imagined, when the cocky kid had found himself faced with Hickory Graham's talented oldest granddaughter.

"He was here to learn the ropes of running the inn, that summer," she continued, still staring down the snow-covered hill. "But he was lifeguarding some, too."

"Rosie, you don't have to ..."

Now she did glance over. "I know." Her profile, when she turned again, struck him as so perfect he couldn't look away. "We had just lost my grandmother that spring. It was horrible." She paused like she was seeing it all again. "Emily spent the whole summer with Aunt Cookie and Uncle Burt at the newspaper. Hickory was numb and buried himself in work at the marina. I was sad and hurting, here on the island."

"And Keith was there, on your beach."

"Yes. He was right there. He wasn't shy about letting me know how pretty he thought I was. He seemed very eager to hear about how sad I was, too." The side of her mouth twitched a little, perhaps a show of some mercy for the children they'd been. "Then he started to make promises to me, started painting his own picture of the life the two of us could have together."

Gabe closed his eyes for a long moment. Now he wanted to walk away. He hated imagining it in *this* much detail, the things that reckless boy must had said to win her over on those long summer nights.

"He said he would go and get his degree, and then we would be married, and we would have a big family. I'd always wanted a big family, you know? A big, traditional one." She cut him another glance. "You're lucky that way."

Gabe shrugged. "Blessed."

"Yes, blessed." She sighed. "I believed it all, all the things he said."

"Why wouldn't you?"

"I would sit under an umbrella on the beach, pretending to read a book," Rosie continued, a wry and unhappy smile flitting around her mouth again. "But I'd really be watching him on his lifeguard's chair. I would imagine the house we would have and how I would decorate it. I felt so safe and hopeful, like the future was going to be better than the present I'd been living. I imagined our children, all ten of them," she said on a laugh, "with light hair and blue eyes like his. Everyone would marvel at how *respectable* we were. We'd be that family everyone envies, you know?"

Gabe let the silence stretch. She'd gotten shame, of course, instead of the life she'd imagined. "I think I can guess how it all went from there," he said softly.

"The only thing that turned out the way I imagined was that my son did, in fact, end up with light hair and blue eyes." She seemed to consider the carrot that was Delia's snow girl's nose. It was slowly sliding sideways, so Rosie reached over and twisted it further into the packed snow of the head. "At first, when he went to college and didn't write back, I thought I'd written his address down wrong. I was embarrassed I'd made a mistake like that."

"Rosie." Gabe hated Young Keith. He wished he'd punched him right in the face when he'd met him not long after that.

"Turns out that wasn't the mistake I made," she said with a sigh.

What could he say to that? *I wish it had been me. I wouldn't have treated you that way?*

"Gabe." She turned now, leaning a shoulder against the icy stone block of the inn. She met his eyes, and he somehow felt they had known one another forever. "Is Keith a good man?"

"Um ...?"

"Sorry, sorry. I mean, jump past what I was just telling you, and tell me about him *now*. You know him, and I don't. Tell me about your friend, your business partner. Did he grow into a good man?"

Gabe thought about it as he mirrored her posture against the stone with his opposite shoulder. She must trust him to ask. The fog of their breath mingled, and Gabe told her the truth as he saw it. "Yes, he's a good man now."

She nodded, looked mildly disappointed. "I suspected as much."

"He's very different since he got back from the war, like so many men. He doesn't talk a lot about it, except for some funny stories, but there's something different about the way he sees people now, you know? Like he's looking at them through a different lens."

"Hmmm." Rosie didn't break eye contact. "I like that. The idea of him seeing people. It sounds like maturity."

"I'd say so. But don't start thinking he's perfect, either."

Her smile was sudden and took his breath away, her tone gently sarcastic when she said, "I'll try not to think he's perfect." She coughed a little and hugged her arms harder.

"Cold?"

"Only a little. Anyway, thanks for being honest, Gabe. Now is more important than then, isn't it? The past is the past, as they say."

"I don't imagine you can feel too sorry for too long about the past when you ended up with a kid like Charlie."

"He's great. You've got that right. But of course, there are things I'm very sorry about," Rosie said, somber now. "I'm sorry for the judgment my little boy has known, growing up. No one should have to shoulder that."

Gabe thought it was a good thing she didn't know her son was trying to find her a husband. It would only make her feel worse.

"I was just out here thinking," she went on, "about how sorry I am that I couldn't offer him — or any other children — the cozy, traditional family I always wanted, myself."

He waved that away. "There are plenty of folks out there wishing themselves *out* of that so-called traditional family, to be fair. It's sometimes but not always what it seems to be from the outside."

She shrugged. "I wouldn't know, would I?" Then she smiled. "But no. I'm not sorry it happened, and not just because I have Charlie. I suppose ... I'm not sorry now that I've carried such a visible sign of sin."

"Rosie ..." he began again, praying the words would just be there in her pause. He had none, though.

"No, no. You don't need to say anything. All I mean is, it's always been right *out* there. Everyone knows. It's probably the first thing people say about me, at least for the past decade. But I've never been able to pretend, the way others do, that I don't desperately need grace. Every day. Thanks to all the judgment, I've been throwing myself at the feet of the cross every single day since I was sixteen, and the love I find there makes whatever others dish out sting way less."

Gabe didn't consciously reach for her, but he did suddenly have her arms in his hands. He was a heartbeat from pulling her into an ill-advised embrace when a flash of red on her bandage caught his attention and saved them from ... whatever he was about to do just outside the windows of the parlor where anyone inside could see.

His gaze went from the bandage back to her eyes. "That's not food coloring, Sweetheart."

"No. I guess the cut is bleeding a little."

"More than a little."

"I'm sorry. I probably shouldn't have been so fully committed to the tallest snow person you've seen this season." Her repentant smile tugged at his heart.

"I'd like to clean it and rewrap it for you, if you'll let me."

She nodded and followed him inside.

Chapter Seventeen

Inside, Dot was playing carols on the piano. That, the fire, and an abundance of more hot cocoa had the blizzard refugees so occupied that they hardly noticed when Gabe led Rosie through the parlor, down the hall, and back into the empty kitchen.

"Peel off your coat, there, while I see to our supplies," he told her, heading for the cupboard where they'd stashed what was left of the bandages, cloth, and even the thread. He vowed there would be no more needles on her sore hand if he could help it.

Gabe quickly set a small pan of water boiling. Shedding his own tailored winter coat, he met back up with Rosie near the same center island where she'd finished his shave.

Now, she was watching him in that contemplative way she had, and something about the quiet moment filled him with joy.

"We need to stop meeting like this," he said and winked at her.

Perched on a stool in her holiday red dress, she looked very young when she stretched out her hand once more for him to fix. Or perhaps her stories had just reminded him that she had been young when her life had changed so dramatically and was still rather young as she met his eyes now. For all that she was raising a young man of her own, he knew Rosie was still a few years younger than he was, himself.

It made Gabe wonder what he'd really been doing with his life. Building hotels didn't seem like such a big deal next to building a family out of what scraps could be found.

He swallowed and unfastened some of the safety pins holding the white cloth around the gauze, being as gentle as he could.

Neither of them said anything as he peeled the strips away with slow, careful movements. Nor when he used a fresh strip of cloth to soak the angry wound, pinched together with the thread that held in all but the end of the gash where the blood seeped.

"I don't think we need to re-stitch it."

"Thank you," she breathed in relief.

When he had it cleaned, Gabe pressed another clean patch onto the area, holding it there firmly for long minutes to slow the bleeding. In that time, he allowed himself to enjoy the scent of her hair so close to his nose.

The tug he felt to be closer, always closer, reminded him exactly of that pull he felt to Buckeye Lake itself, so it confused him.

He hoped she didn't hear his breath shake its way into his chest as he stepped back and began wrapping a fresh bandage between her thumb and fingers and down around her narrow wrist.

"Not too tight?" he asked, and even he heard that his voice was not normal. She made some sound that seemed to indicate she was fine. He focused on being gentle, very gentle.

Rosie Graham should always be treated gently. How could anyone hurt her, ever? His thoughts felt thick, blurry as he secured the pins again.

When her eyes slammed into his, he knew she'd noticed that he was breathing a little fast.

But then he noticed her breathing was just as erratic.

"Gabe," she said on one of those breaths.

He moved slowly, silently begging her to *stop* him. First, it was just his hand. A hand that would always bear the rough spots of building materials, no matter how fine his clothes. That hand rose so, so slowly to the side of her impossibly soft, perfect cheek.

Instead of stopping him, though, Rosie leaned forward. Leaned right toward him, leading with soft, perfect lips.

He supposed he must have leaned down, too, because they met with the same care and slowness. The same sweet softness.

Yes, it was the exact same pull he'd been feeling all year. Had it been *her* all along? Though he hadn't met her until the week before, had it been the force of her rather than that of the lake and park?

Gabe let his fingers glide back, dipping below her ear, tipping her head up to change the angle of the kiss, cupping the back of her head beneath that soft hair. She made a low sound in her throat that matched all the other softness about her, and that had him finally, finally pulling her all the way into him, head to toe.

That alignment brought the actual kiss to a halt, though.

Rosie pulled back, lips swollen, looking up at him from just an inch away as though looking for answers.

He looked back at her for the same.

For a moment, he thought her eyes were swimming in tears. "It hurts," she said, barely audibly.

Blinking, he looked down at the fresh bandage pressed against his chest. He cleared his throat. "That's because you've got so many nerves in your hands and fingers."

"No. No. Feeling this way. I ... I love Dottie, Gabe. She's my friend." There was such sadness in the statement, and her eyes were shimmering with unshed tears, but then her arms snaked over his shoulders, and she dropped her head beneath his chin with a sorrowful sound.

A change in the commotion down the hall had Gabe tipping her chin up, though he was reluctant to let her go. "We need to avoid stumbling into one another beneath any mistletoe, I think. We did a little too well without it."

"There's no mistletoe in this inn, anyway," she said, pressing an absent-minded kiss to his jawline.

"Are you sure? It *feels* like there's mistletoe ... somewhere."

"Ruth decorated before we got here, right? No way Ruth hung mistletoe."

The sound of approaching voices was what it took to have them both stepping back.

Gabe quickly moved to the pan of hot water on the stove, his back to the door as it swung open. Rosie was tidying up cut bits of bandage, and from what felt like a very great distance, he heard her explaining to Dot and Cookie that everything was fine.

That she'd simply re-opened the same wound.

Chapter Eighteen

Pastor Skip was the one to announce there would be a formal Christmas Eve service late that night.

Rosie thought they all made quite the picture, sitting in firelight and candlelight around the hearth. Everyone—the Fairchilds and Keith, Cookie and Burt, Gabe, Dottie, Ruth, Smokey, Hickory, the eager little ones, and herself—had tidied up themselves and the parlor for their humble service.

Had a tree ever looked so festive?

Had Keith Fairchild ever looked so peaceful?

He perched on a footstool, one knee elevated in his linked hands, grinning. There was a quiet joy in him she hadn't allowed herself to see a week ago and that certainly hadn't been there a decade before. She supposed Gabe was right. The man had changed.

She tried not to think too much about Gabe.

What had either of them been thinking?

She'd never have guessed, the week before, that she'd be more comfortable considering her relationship with Keith than the one that had suddenly popped up with his friend.

The entire atmosphere felt different tonight, though, just as it always had at church when Christmas Eve slid with quiet song into Christmas morning. There was an air of holiness, perhaps more noticeable than ever with the awareness that the world around them was weighed down into true stillness. God's miracles, Rosie realized, felt somehow closer to the surface without electricity or roads.

Those miracles, in fact, did feel closer in a crowded inn, reminding her of the arrival of her Savior.

When Pastor Skip asked Gabe to share the story of Christ's birth with them all, the room was ripe for wonder, but there was still surprise when he did not open a Bible at all. Instead, his eyes dancing in the light of the fire, he stood next to the hearth and recited, "And it came to pass in those days, that there went out a decree from Ceasar Augustus that all the world should be taxed ..."

So, the fire crackled as the days were accomplished for Mary to be delivered.

"And she brought forth her firstborn son, and wrapped him in swaddling clothes, and laid him in a manger," Gabe recited from the second chapter of Luke, surprising them by reaching for the soap carving of the baby Jesus in a manger as his prop rather than the one from the Fairchilds' nativity. His eyes met Rosie's, and he smiled. She returned his smile, even as her heart did something strange in her chest.

Had she dreamed that kiss in the kitchen? No. Her lips still tingled.

"Because there was no room for them in the inn."

She watched Gabe's thumb as it smoothed the carve marks in the soap and as the shepherds heard from the angels not to be afraid. And then as they visited the babe and then as they praised the Lord. Gabe closed by remarking softly about this baby's blood eventually being spilled and all of them being made "clean" and flawless — which included a pun about soap — in God's eyes. He sat down on the edge of the hearth, to soft applause from around the room.

"Tell it again!" little Delia exclaimed, rushing to him and climbing in his lap. "And I'll hold up the animals, 'kay?"

Gabe smiled, natural as he bounced her and handed her two other hunks of carved soap barn animals. Delia began dramatically telling the story in her own way, amusing them all with her fresh and honest faith.

Then two very small things happened that made Rosie admit to herself that she was falling in love with Gabe Adams. Almost simultaneously, he dropped an absentminded kiss on the top of the little girl's braid and then mimicked the sound of cattle lowing to enhance her story.

She didn't know if it was the cow sounds or the natural affection for a child that did her in, but Rosie uncomfortably pondered these things in her heart as they sang "Silent Night" and Christmas arrived.

Chapter Nineteen

"Come to my room once you've tucked the kids in," Dottie whispered to Rosie as the others dispersed from their makeshift candlelight service for a long winter's nap.

Rosie jerked her head around, knowing she looked guilty as she set about arranging the mattress for the kids in front of the fire.

Oh, no. Dot must have seen *it* all over her face. *Love!*

Rosie had been so distracted by powerful feelings and the memory of that kiss in the kitchen that she'd never even looked over at her dear friend who, after all, had romantic "expectations" for the coming year. Wasn't that what she'd said? No doubt, those involved Gabriel Adams, General Manager for FH Resorts.

Rosie's stomach clenched. *What had she become?* The first time she'd found herself attracted to anyone in a decade, and it must be the man who'd been seeing the woman who'd given her a way to make a living when the rest of the community had shunned her years ago.

Watching Dottie retreat down the hallway, Rosie knew this was no way to repay an old friend.

She made a point not to look for Gabe as she helped the children place blankets on their bed, their fatigue clearly warring with their holiday excitement. Hickory was building up the fire to last well into the night, yawning himself as he advised them on the placement of the two cookies for Santa.

"You really think he'll get here?" Charlie asked his grandfather.

"I've seen many a storm and never saw a Christmas without at least one gift under the tree, I'm blessed to say," was the wise response. Charlie grinned and flopped onto the mattress.

When the little ones had settled and the other lamps had gone out, when hugs had been exchanged with her aunt and uncle, Rosie padded down the cool hallway to find the door to Dottie's room open. She placed a steadying hand—the one that wasn't still throbbing—against her stomach to settle the flutters.

Her friend had predictably made her bed with care, as Rosie was certain she had every day of their blizzard confinement, and she was wrapping a scarf around her curls. When Rosie knuckle-knocked on the doorframe, Dottie smiled and, rising, shut the door behind Rosie.

"I've got something for you," she said on a burst of childlike excitement, catching Rosie off guard. This seemed a strange reaction from a woman who could easily have spotted another woman mooning over her fella. Grabbing her wrists to draw her over to the bed like they had when they were girls, Dottie startled at the press of the bulky bandage. "Oh my. Sorry. How's your hand? I forgot to ask."

"It'll be okay."

Dottie gave a little bounce on the mattress. "I got you the most luscious silk robe! You're going to *love* it," she said. "I ordered it for you and have it wrapped so pretty ... back at my apartment. It's a soft rose color, which seemed appropriate."

Rosie smiled. "Thank you." She leaned in with a grateful hug, hating her own undisciplined heart.

"What'd you get me?" Dottie grinned, her doll baby dimple always making her easy to adore. *Why*, Rosie wondered wildly, when he apparently had a girl as stunning as this, had Gabe been kissing *her* tonight? Dottie was the better catch, by far.

"I made your gift."

"Well, I'd sure *hope* so! What is it? What is it?"

Rosie shook her head. "I think I'll make you wait. I don't want to ruin the surprise."

Dottie swatted her. "Aw, now. Are you mad I ruined yours, then?"

"Not in the least. It gives me something to look forward to, besides getting to sleep in my own bed someday."

"Seriously, Rose. I'm always grateful for the way you and Emily include me in your sister world. I'd be so lonely without you." Dottie had younger sisters, Rosie knew, but their lives—and their ideas about what their big sister's life should be as a woman—were so different from Dottie's that they might have been strangers. "Even with all this business with the bog, I know the two of you are still there for me, just as I'll always be for you."

"Don't bring up the bog, Dottie," Rosie said with a grin. "Not on Christmas. And not when you're alone with me. You know, with no witnesses." That sent them into girlish giggles. The idea of Rosie, who literally released household insects back into the outdoors rather than killing them, being any kind of threat was just too much for the late hour. "Anyway, don't think I'll ever forget the way you've stood beside me through everything, helped me get my art in front of people. We do this life together, friend."

"You bet we do. Merry Christmas."

"Merry Christmas." They hugged again, registering the stillness of the night.

"Can I tell you a secret?" Dottie asked in a whisper, pulling back but leaving her hands resting on Rosie's forearms.

"You'd better."

"Margo said, when they traveled here to the inn for the holidays, that Gabe packed a *ring*."

Rosie blinked, not understanding. "A ring?"

"Margo saw the ring! She told me tonight. Rosie, I think he might be going to propose tomorrow! I mean, today."

"Oh." Rosie felt her face heating, grateful for the low light, and she looked down at the bandage the same man had wrapped around her own fingers hours before. "That's ... nice." *No, no, no.* First, she'd been the unmarried mother, and now she was the *other woman*!

"I mean, why else would a man pack a ring for a holiday trip?"

"I can't imagine any other motive. And ... what will you say when he asks you, Dottie? I mean, have the two of you really spent time together?"

"I guess I'll agree to marry him," Dot said with a practical shrug, still half-whispering. She seemed to be considering her answer for the very first time, and her face wasn't exactly joyous. "I mean, I'm not getting any younger. Just ask my mother." The dimples flashed a little again. "Also, I don't cook, so I need someone who can afford to manage that some other way, like with a chef or something, and Gabe's got loads of money."

"That's an advantage," Rosie said woodenly.

"I intimidate most men, and the only truly feminine thing I do is faint sometimes, so I figure I'm a fool not to jump at this chance." Dottie looked over at the dancing wick in the oil lamp and finally sighed. "Life is so confusing, isn't it?"

"It really, really is."

Sober and serious, Dottie continued, "We can probably do good things for Buckeye Lake, together, Gabe and me. So, I figure I will probably say yes if he asks. Right?"

Rosie nodded, suddenly unable to speak. Leaning in for one more hug, she imagined her friend a bride as Emily had just been, only this wedding would be lavish, indeed. It would probably take place on the lawn of the extravagant resort they'd build together on the north shore, with a large brass band and fireworks over the water. Where Cranberry Bog had once been.

Wishing Dottie a merry Christmas and thanking her again for the robe she'd receive after the thaw, Rosie walked stiff-legged into the hallway, turning to softly close her friend's door.

Christmas.

She leaned against the cold paneling of the hallway, knowing, with an ache inside, that there were two things she needed to do to restore her own peace.

First, she could not return to the living room any time soon for bed.

Everything in her told her Gabe would seek her out there tonight on her window seat, and then the two of them would talk for hours, and then she would be even worse off by morning than she was now.

That was something she could do for herself: avoid emotional turmoil and a heart more broken than hers already was.

Next, she'd situate herself in a room down the hall where she could light a lamp without waking the children. She had a sketch to do. A drawing that would help her set to rights a long-ago wrong.

Determination fueled her now, pushing her shoulders off the wall and pushing down the strange ache in her heart.

A few minutes later, with the bed quilt wrapped around her shoulders and a piece of charcoal, Rosie sketched as the clock struck two. Now and then a tear trailed down her cheek, but she wiped it on the bandage on her left hand to keep it from dropping onto the paper and ruining the charcoal shadows.

Gabe and Dot each deserved more than she figured they were expecting from one another, but she was certainly in no position now to advise them of that.

Not when it turned out she loved them both.

Chapter Twenty

Delia Stimpson Grade Four
Christmas Journal Project
Buckeye Lake Public School
December 1946

> *Even with going outside and with it being Christmas, Rosie did not forget to make me sit down and write in this book again.*
> *I've been thinking about Jesus being born in a manger, in an inn like this one except not like this one. Pastor Skip says Jesus is God's son, and he sent him down to show us how to love each other and to make sure we couldn't ever be too bad that we couldn't go to heaven with him. Jesus is also Joseph's son, though. It's very complicated.*
> *I wonder how much Jesus missed his real dad when he was born down here on earth.*

~~~~~

Rosie beat Ruth into the kitchen in the stillness of Christmas morning, weary and sad but reminding herself to be grateful for what the holiday was all about: the birth of a baby that removed the fear of everything, even death.

She set about grinding coffee beans.

She'd stopped wondering when they'd be able to go home. She tried not to dwell on how much she missed her own space, her studio, her clothes, and Grandma's homey little kitchen.

The inn's kitchen was becoming complicated, emotionally.

And it was about to become more complicated still, she thought, as the door swung open. Keith Fairchild entered carrying a small lantern.

His face registered surprise at seeing her there. It was the first time they'd been alone together since the wedding party had arrived. He wore expensive-looking pajamas and a thick robe and slippers, his light hair already brushed and tidy.

"Merry Christmas, Rosie," he said in that bashful way he had now with her, audibly sniffing. "Coffee beans smell good even before they start brewing."

"They do," she agreed and finished grinding the beans in silence. She closed her eyes, searched once more for confirmation in her heart for the move she was about to make. "Wait here a minute, will you, Keith? I'll be right back."

Rosie padded out and down the hallway to retrieve the drawing board she'd spent the night with, deciding when she saw no sign of anyone else awake that God had opened this door for what she'd known needed to happen. She appreciated this divine confirmation as she returned to the kitchen, glad she was saying "yes" when she felt led.

"*You* know how to make coffee?" she asked, not bothering to hide her surprise when she found him beside the steaming pot.

"I was in the Army." He chuckled. "Not exactly the roughest of conditions, but I did develop a few skills."

"Of course," she said, trying to picture him in the mud with a weapon, and now it was her turn to enjoy the fragrance of the coffee. "Before we get to drink that, I have something for you."

His face blanched. He regarded the unadorned board in her hand. "Uh. I didn't get you anything. I'm sorry."

Rosie couldn't help laughing. Why in the world would he have shopped for a girl he hadn't seen in a decade? Especially when their paths would never have crossed were it not for the weather. "You can owe me," she said, and he relaxed. *You won't be relaxed for long*, she thought, passing him the board without ceremony.

Keith nodded vaguely as he took in the sketch that lived on the paper taped there. It had not been difficult for her to conjure a clear memory of little Charlie's baby face at about one or two: the chubby cheeks, the freckles, the grin. She'd sketched him in his favorite pair of overalls, which he'd loved to wear without a shirt even as a small boy. Rosie was satisfied with the likeness she'd captured, each shadow and every line dripping with the love she'd felt for her son since the day he'd been born.

A love she was at least partly responsible for denying the man who considered the sketch now.

"Is this your son as a little tyke?" he asked pleasantly and with open appreciation for her talent in his eyes.

"And yours," she replied simply.

Rosie's fatigue must have removed her nerves and emotions. That, or the Spirit had given her peace, enough so that she calmly watched Keith's light-colored brows draw together over the sketch.

Then he raised his eyes, his gaze slamming into hers in sudden comprehension. With an extra dose of Christmas compassion, Rosie walked him through it. "Charlie is yours, Keith. He was born the spring after you left for college."

Now his mouth opened, just slightly, and the board with the drawing shook in his hands. Keith looked back down at it, his distress obvious, like he didn't know what else to do. "I ..." he said the way people do when they have forgotten all the other words they know.

Rosie gave him time.

She remembered the day she'd realized what was wrong with her that early fall, when she'd vomited twice in the ladies' room at the school but felt fine after each episode. Then she'd done some basic math with the calendar on the science classroom wall.

She'd broken out in a sweat in that classroom, as she supposed Keith was doing now in his inn's kitchen. She'd felt confused.

Then she'd explained everything away in a hundred different ways inside her own mind until she was right back where she'd started.

"I know it's a lot to take in," she said, remembering the feeling so well. "Especially after all these years."

Her own surprise had been a vague concept of shame and an uncertain future. Keith's surprise, by contrast, walked and talked and giggled.

He finally looked up again, the drawing board still in his hands. She actually heard him swallow. His head was shaking "no," and his eyes were haunted. "I ... didn't know."

"I know you didn't."

"But. You didn't tell me, though. You never told me."

Ah, she'd known they'd get here fast. "I couldn't, Keith. You weren't answering my letters or calls. I tried leaving messages. I couldn't figure out how to reach you. You never wrote like you said you would."

When a man with a fair complexion felt shame, it started as a red neck, and the red crawled from there to his jaw and up his cheeks all the way to his hairline. Rosie watched it, still at peace in her own heart.

His gaze returned to the drawing, and one hand moved to massage its way up the back of his own neck.

"What if ... I mean, maybe I'm not ..." He looked up, back down at the sketch, back up to her.

"I'm in no way trying to convince you he's yours," she said simply. "I'm not asking for anything, anyway."

His eyes closed.

"I'm sorry," he whispered. "I mean, I don't ... I'm so sorry."

"I stopped trying to reach you," Rosie admitted, and now he looked at her, trying to understand. "Once I realized you didn't want to talk to me when you didn't know about a baby, I decided I didn't want to talk to you when you *did* know. That was a decision I made without you, and I'm sorry for that."

Keith shook his head, still red in the face. "You're apologizing?" He muttered a curse and then apologized again, himself.

"I wasn't ever going to tell you, truth be told," Rosie went on. "But these last few days, I've realized we were both very different people a decade ago. A lot has happened. Charlie. A war. You seem ... changed. I know I am."

"Changed. Yeah," he said miserably. "Changing now ... it doesn't change ... you know. What happened."

"No, it doesn't. You broke more than a few promises, Keith. But that was then, and I was part of it too, one way or another. I can't help thinking now that it's unfair of me to deny both you and Charlie the chance to know one another, since you don't have another family of your own yet."

Rosie knew she wouldn't have told him, had she discovered a Mrs. Fairchild and other children. She wondered for the first time, though, if he were seeing anyone.

He was silent for a long beat. "So." More silence. Then: "I'm someone's ... I'm Charlie's ... father."

He did not sound pleased or displeased. It was going to take him longer than she'd given him, Rosie knew, to wrap his mind around that.

"You'll need time," she told him out loud. "But, while you take that time, just know that Charlie is mine. He will always be mine. His last name is Graham, as it's been since he was born. I'm not asking for any of your money, Keith, for myself or for Charlie." She cringed just remembering Gabe's implications about what she and Charlie deserved. She'd never once wished for the Fairchild riches. Unlike Dottie, Rosie could cook her own food quite well. "He's an amazing boy, Keith. But I also wanted to give you that drawing as a piece of what you've missed because I think missing these ten years is punishment enough for past mistakes. *Consequence* enough, I should say, not punishment."

He nodded, mumbled something that ended with, "Punishment seems right." He swallowed again. "I don't know what to say, Rosie. I don't know. I don't know what ... what happens now?"

He looked panicked, like he needed someone to solve it all for him.

"Charlie doesn't know, of course. I'd like you to be part of the decision about whether he ever knows. Will you pray about it first, Keith? About the role you want to play in his life, if any? And if you decide you're in, will you make sure you'll stay the course with him, no matter what?" Rosie rubbed at her own neck with her good hand now, thinking about her own mother. About Delia's constant sense of rootlessness. She did not want rejection for her son. "I can't have him spend his life wondering why one of his parents didn't want to know him, once he'd had the chance."

Keith sighed, a shaky deep sigh, and then he nodded. He set the drawing down on the counter but did not stop staring at it. His coffee was cold, forgotten.

Rosie had expected denial from him. Then she'd expected anger. He wasn't moving as quickly through those emotions as she'd anticipated, which left her feeling a little confused.

She sipped her own cool coffee and noticed light at the lowest part of the kitchen window. Christmas morning had dawned. She hugged her arms around herself, keeping her bandaged hand high on her own shoulder. She heard him shuffle closer and turned to find him watching her.

"I'm not saying the right things, am I?" Keith asked gruffly.

"The bomb only just dropped," she reasoned, offering him a smile. "I definitely expect you to say the right thing eventually, but not until the dust has settled."

He shook his head, and she recognized lingering shame in the gesture. She recognized it very well. "Sorry," was all he managed. "I'm sorry for what I did and didn't do, Rosie."

If she'd imagined him making demands, she hadn't allowed herself to hope for a demand of forgiveness. Yet, that was something she was happy to give.

So, it seemed natural enough to step into Keith's conciliatory hug when he opened his arms to her. She blinked back tears, returning his awkward hug of friendship and moving a bit closer to real forgiveness even as she knew he would struggle to forgive her, too, on some level.

She told herself she'd been right to follow God's prompting, even if it had meant going without sleep.

~~~~~

Christmas morning felt a bit blurry, Gabe thought, because he had not slept much in the hours between midnight and dawn.

Admittedly, it was difficult to sleep while walking back and forth down the hallway of a dark, cold inn. When he tried to rest, all he thought about was the rightness of kissing Rosie Graham last night. Of the way everything felt like it was falling into place when she was nestled against him. Of the way it had him feeling a sense of home he'd somehow never felt so strongly.

Twice he had sought her out in her window seat in the parlor, only to find both the window seat and her sofa empty.

She must have needed a night in one of the rooms, in a real bed. He knew she was exhausted from tension and from entertaining the kids in the snow and certainly from the pain she had to be in from the deep slice in her hand.

Now, tugging on a wool sweater the color of his mama's morning oats, he headed back down the hallway once again, fighting the urge to whistle "O Come All Ye Faithful." The others in the inn would still be sleeping, but enough daylight was coming in through windows now that he didn't need a candle to find his way.

In the main parlor, a soft snore sounded from the mound of blankets on the mattress where the little ones slept. He smiled. The tree was a triangular shadow beside a hearth that was nearly as dark. Moving as silently as he could, Gabe added more wood and stooped for a time with the bellows, making sure the logs caught, the old Christmas hymn still running through his mind alongside happy thoughts of Rosie's soft, warm skin.

He thought of how perfect her lips were. The way she laughed easily at herself. How deeply she loved. It would be something to be on the receiving end of that, Gabe thought as he rose from the now cheerful fire.

A glance to the right showed him she must still be ensconced in a room somewhere getting much-needed rest. A glance to the left revealed a snow sled with a bow tied to it and, beside it, a doll boasting a similar red bow. His smile remained. Santa had come, indeed. He looked forward to Charlie's and Delia's wonder any minute now, remembering what a privilege it was to spend Christmas with children.

The scent of coffee claimed his attention as he stretched, achy from yesterday's relentless shoveling. Ruth or Cookie must already be up preparing the first of the many large pots the party had taken to drinking from morning to night during their entrapment. It would be another kind of quiet pleasure, Gabe thought as he headed toward the kitchen, to help with Christmas breakfast while he glubbed down his first cup.

He swung the kitchen door open, and there was Rosie. It took him a strange, frozen moment to make sense of the fact she was in Keith's arms in the kitchen, rather than in his own.

But there they were, embracing.

Gabe backed away silently, numb, and retreated down the hallway.

The sight of their embrace made it all too easy to imagine them a decade before the way he'd tried so hard not to: young and nearly as picture-perfect attractive as they both were now, clinging to one another in the desperate way of first love. Making promises to one another that it seemed to have taken ten years to keep, based on what he'd just seen.

Had he been blind these past few days? Had they rekindled that old romance that started on the little marina beach? Was that why she'd reminisced on the patio? Had he himself *oversold* Keith to Rosie when she'd asked him yesterday if he was a good man?

And when it came to the kiss he himself had shared with her ... Gabe shook his head. No. He couldn't think about that, but he did think in a new way about Rosie's comment even during the kiss: *It hurts.*

It really did.

"Santa came!" It was Charlie, shouting joyously from the parlor.

Gabe hurried down the hall toward the exclamation, worried the boy's parents would come rushing from the kitchen and stumble upon a grown man standing brokenhearted in the hallway.

Chapter Twenty-One

To most eyes, Gabe appeared to be extremely busy in the study during most of Christmas morning, which even he knew was a ridiculous ruse.

Why, after all, would the resort plans and prints he'd avoided for a week suddenly demand his attention during the most joyous holiday of the year?

Dot had come in to keep him company off and on, and then she, too, had wandered away to join the others milling about in the parlor. Ruth had surprised them all with her grandmother's famous coffee cake, a pastry stuffed with an almond paste and dripping vanilla icing that Gabe managed to enjoy even with a chronic churning in his gut.

Outside of the study, Christmas seemed to be unfolding in a surprisingly ordinary manner, from what he could tell.

Delia had concocted an elaborate backstory for the new doll she'd received, an orphan like herself but a "far more tragic one" because she'd been recovered from a gutter in New York City near death. With equal energy, Charlie had been begging to take his new sled outdoors, but his mother and grandfather were united in their argument that he wait for the sun to climb higher in the sky to warm things a bit.

Pastor Skip had just come into the study and suggested a chess game, for which Gabe was not in the mood, when a true commotion broke out in the main room. There was the explosive sound of a half-frozen door bursting open, breathless exclamations, and shouting ... reminding him of the wedding party's arrival days before.

Had it truly been mere days? It felt like some kind of lifetime.

As though he'd been a different person before they'd all come crashing in during a blizzard.

Gabe followed the pastor out and found a similar event to that first one, indeed, but this time standing in the doorway in a swirl of snow were none other than Mr. and Mrs. Drew Mathison, smiling their newlywed smiles and doing their best Ethel Waters impression of "Heat Wave" at the top of their lungs.

Everyone swarmed them with "Merry Christmas" shouts.

"Can you believe we made it up the hill?" Emily laughed, ripping a thick hat off her head and flinging it in the general direction of the already full coat tree. "We've brought presents, too, everyone!"

Drew helped her off with her coat even as he admired Charlie's new sled, carefully draping his wife's coat, her stray hat, and his own duds over a nearby bench. Then he retrieved a sled like Charlie's the couple had maneuvered into the foyer from outdoors, dropping thick snow chunks everywhere.

This sled was piled with cloth-wrapped bundles tied down by ropes like the pair of them had just finished a wilderness goldrush journey. A leather harness dotted with jingle bells was strapped across the top, doing its part to add to the general din.

"You've been married a whole week! Happy anniversary!" Cookie cooed as she hugged them.

Gabe contemplated retreating into the office once more amidst the greetings and stories all layered atop one another, a layering that made it impossible to follow any one conversation, which was saying a lot for a man who'd grown up in a tiny cabin with a far-from-tiny family.

"... and so, we thawed a ham and brought it ..."

"... so, then the knife went right into her hand! You should've seen it ..."

"... can't believe you didn't get stuck in the drifts ..."

"... almost out of firewood, which I thought would've been impossible ..."

"... potatoes to go with it ..."

"... and that snowman has a twin attached to it ..."

Before long, the ham that had traveled by sled to the house was cooking in the oven, and the entire group had settled into seats in the parlor by the roaring fire, apparently rejuvenated by the holiday and "new" people who had not been snowed in with them all week.

"If we can somehow partition off the second floor of your place while we work on repairing the roof, I don't know why you and Rosie and Charlie couldn't move back into the ground floor soon," Drew told Hickory, both men sitting near the chair Gabe had claimed when he'd given up hiding. Drew passed around a tin of deer jerky. "I went over and explored first thing this morning. An Army blanket tacked up at the bottom of the stairs might keep enough of the air out, if you keep the fire going strong to keep the downstairs warm."

Hickory lit up over the prospect of returning home, asking questions about the condition of the roof and talking through how they might temporarily patch things with supplies he had in the marina.

Gabe's first encounter with Drew Mathison had been watching the police officer sprint down a dock to attack Keith on the previous Fourth of July.

There had turned out to be a good reason for the misunderstanding, of course; regardless, Gabe had liked Mathison almost immediately. Drew had simply considered Keith a threat to Emily Graham. Gabe had only seen Mathison a few times since that soaking wet catastrophe, but each time the man had greeted him with an honest handshake and directness that put Gabe at ease. Having directed building projects for years himself now at inns and hotels, he appreciated Drew's similar background growing up in his own family's construction business. The familiar callouses on the man's hands were reassuring.

"Did you get more than you bargained for on your holiday at the lake?" Drew asked Gabe now, propping his ankle over his knee and drinking from his steaming mug of coffee.

"You could say so," Gabe acknowledged, thinking about the past week. "How about you?"

"You could say I got exactly what I bargained for." Drew chuckled as Emily waved to get his attention.

"I think we should hand out our gifts," she called.

"Go ahead, dear."

She stuck her tongue out at that, but she bounced over to the rest of the packages on the sled. The bells made a ruckus all over again as they fell to the floor.

"We don't have a thing for you two," Margo said woefully from beside the hearth. "Perhaps some of us should head to our rooms and let you all have your family time."

"Family time? We don't have any gifts to give them either," Hickory said with a laugh.

"Please stay," Emily insisted. "I have something for everyone, and we certainly don't expect or need anything. So many folks just sent or gave us wedding gifts, for crying out loud."

"Which is where half your gifts have come from today," Drew mumbled with a wry smile, so that only Gabe heard him.

"The ham was gift enough," Burt declared.

"Did she knit me something hideous, Drew?" Dot asked eagerly from her seat on the other side of Gabe.

"Only if you're lucky."

"For the Fairchilds, in appreciation for generously hosting our family and friends in a pinch," Emily announced, handing a gift-wrapped package to Margo.

"You really shouldn't have, dear."

It turned out to be a fancy salt and pepper shaker set that did look exactly like something the Fairchilds would want, Gabe thought.

"Get it?" Emily insisted. "Salt? In a *pinch*?"

"We got two sets of them from two different college friends of Emily's," Drew privately told Gabe with a wink. "They shipped them ahead last week."

"Genius."

"Em kept the ugly ones, of course, and wrapped up the decent ones to give away." He said it with a shake of his head and such love that Gabe was torn between envy and discomfort. He looked across the room at Rosie helping her sister hand out other gifts from the pile, the two of them laughing together and looking so in tandem.

Rosie seemed settled in a way she hadn't been all week.

Next, Gabe's eyes tracked to Keith, who sat on the edge of a chair far from the sisters, studying little Charlie with an absorbed, contemplative expression. The boy was hopping around on his knees in front of his mother and aunt, laughing and clapping, his eyes bright. Keith never took his eyes off the kid, a warmth in his eyes Gabe had never noticed there before.

And just like that, just as Gabe had realized suddenly that Charlie must secretly belong to his friend, he realized that the same secret was *out*. Rosie must have told Keith he was Charlie's father. There was no other explanation for the new paternal contemplation on Keith's face.

It also explained the couple's intimacy in the kitchen. More must have been happening than Gabe had understood.

What would that *mean*, Gabe wondered, his stomach churning again. Would Keith and Rosie marry now? Did Charlie know? *No.* Gabe noticed the little boy seemed completely indifferent to Keith Fairchild, as he had been all along.

"Ooh! A scarf for each of us! Thank you so much," Cookie exclaimed, as she and her husband unraveled the saddest looking rectangles of yarn perhaps ever looped together.

"I knitted them over the last few days," Emily explained. "I'm still learning, you know."

"They're lovely," her aunt said, even as Rosie laughed and side-hugged her sister. Beside Gabe, Dot had stood to also open a blob-shaped set of potholders that she admired with the same indulgent smile Rosie had.

"What about me? Do you have something for me?" Charlie danced around near Aunt Emily on his feet now.

"Drew needs to give you yours. And Delia's," Emily answered. She crossed the room with two matching packages and thrust them toward her husband, who uncrossed his legs and reluctantly set his coffee on the end table.

"All right, then. All right." The two children swarmed him. "Now, you both must promise before you open these that you won't cause trouble with them. Promise?"

"Um ..." Rosie inserted from beside the tree. "I don't love the sound of this, Drew."

"I promise!"

"I promise, too!"

"If I find out differently, I'm confiscating," Drew said. "Understood?"

"Yes, Uncle Drew!"

At his new title, Mathison's face split into a rare grin, and he handed over the packages.

Which, of course, turned out to be slingshots.

"While your auntie here was knitting scarves, I did a little whittling," Drew explained as the kids cheered and ran around immediately looking for ammunition.

"Oh, dear," said Rosie and Ruth at the same time.

"The snow is packing well now," Emily announced, still standing beside Drew's chair. "Maybe after we eat, you two can head out and make little snow missiles for your target practice?"

"Yay!"

Gabe watched Drew tug Emily down onto his lap, noting she seemed content to stay there. Her husband smiled with pride. "Told you they'd love them."

"I want one, too," she said, pressing a kiss to his forehead.

"I could probably make another, but you also have to promise you won't cause trouble with it."

Emily glanced over and seemed to notice Gabe for the first time. "I heard you helped Rosie with her cut hand. Thank you for that, and I'm sorry I didn't knit you something."

"She'll get to it, though," Drew offered. "Maybe while I'm carving her a slingshot."

"You'll want to stay on my good side, Adams." Emily winked. "I either knit you a scarf or sling something small and deadly at you." They both knew he was most definitely *not* on her good side, following months of zoning battles regarding the new resort, but Gabe couldn't help but like her anyway.

The Graham sisters were both extremely likeable, he thought morosely. It was a problem.

He glanced over to where the long fingers of Emily's left hand rested on the flannel of Drew's shoulder. A thin gold ring glinted there on her third finger with a bold yellow-orange stone in its center. Gabe had never seen anything like it.

"That's a unique ring," he said, wanting to distract her from shooting him ... or even knitting him anything, for that matter.

Emily pulled her hand back and admired the ring, tucking herself against Drew's chest. "Isn't it something? It's citrine. I love it."

"The color of sunshine," Mathison said as though he didn't care who knew how far gone he was over his wife. "It was my grandmother's ring.

I couldn't ever imagine it on another woman's finger until I met Em."

"It's nice," Gabe said lamely.

He remembered for the first time in days that he'd brought a ring with him in his trunk, but it was far from a family heirloom. No one he knew of on either side of his family had had enough money for stones of any kind, but he sure did. Dot Berkeley seemed like a Big Diamond kind of girl to him, so he'd picked out a dazzler when he'd prepared to come here to the lake for Christmas.

Gabe realized the ring he gave his own wife one day would perhaps be the one passed down for generations to come. At least, he hoped so.

Glancing over at Dot, he could well imagine the fancy diamond he'd purchased on her left hand. It suited her.

But he could not, for some reason, imagine their children and grandchildren and great-grandchildren. He just could not bring them into being in his head. Was that normal? Or was it a problem? And was it a bigger problem that he couldn't imagine being with her the easy way the couple beside him was nestled together?

The knot in his stomach grew.

In that moment, he knew that the morning had not only brought the loss of the strange new hope of Rosie Graham, but he'd also just lost the dimmer, more business-oriented hope of Dot Berkeley. The woman he'd all but forgotten he'd bought and packed a ring for until that very moment.

Gabe closed his eyes and rubbed the bridge of his nose. What was wrong with him?

Blocking out the mingling of Emily's and Drew's laughter beside him, Gabe decided the years ahead stretched long and lonely, indeed.

He rose and decided to go rest in his room for a bit, the smell of the ham only serving to remind him of better holidays. His head hurt a little, too. He'd nearly made his exit when Rosie stepped in front of him, offering a smile.

"Gabe," she said, and she seemed lighter, somehow. Her cheeks were the same glowing color as her hair in the light streaming in through the hall windows. "Merry Christmas. I just wanted to ... you know ..." She seemed to be waiting for something from him. "I wanted to tell you ... Merry Christmas."

"Yes." He spoke past the ache. "Merry Christmas." She still waited, and he'd never felt less able to offer something. "Your hand ... is it okay?"

Rosie looked down at it, as though to decide. "Yes, thanks."

More waiting. "I'm sorry I don't have a gift for you."

"Same. But, also, your friendship during such an unexpected week has been a gift itself," she said with a warmth that should have touched his very soul.

Instead, he was numb as he walked past her and down the hallway.

Chapter Twenty-Two

How long had it been since she'd felt at peace, really?

Rosie did feel it now, slumped into a leather chair across from her sister in the study while the ham finished baking. The kids had prevailed on the snowball-sling shot argument, so they were outside with Smokey, Drew, and Keith. Every now and then, there was the soft *thunk* of a well-packed snowball hitting the side of the inn.

Meanwhile, the Graham sisters had made themselves a plate of Ruth's coffee cake and fresh cups of coffee, and then, blessedly, shut the door of the study.

"I suppose they'd notice if I happened to spill my coffee all over these plans," Emily muttered, peering at the resort design spread out on the glossy top of the desk. "Then I could try to clean it up with bleach and steel wool."

"I really needed this moment of quiet," Rosie breathed, ignoring her sister. Emily snorted as she slid into a seat of her own, pulling her legs up beneath her. "Not that I ever thought I'd find your company restful," Rosie went on with a grin.

"I've had a lot of quiet the past week," Emily admitted. "And I can't imagine what it must have been like for you here. Has it been awful?"

"It was at first." Rosie took another deep breath. "But then it wasn't so bad."

"What kind of answer is that?"

"We'll get there. But first tell me how married life is treating you, Mrs. Mathison."

Emily's smile exploded in the way it generally tended to, taking up half her face in a split second. "I cannot complain." Despite the smile, she still managed to go all dreamy. "No complaints. He's taken very good care of me, blizzard and all, Rose."

Rosie felt another worry slide away. "Wonderful. I admit, I wished every night we could talk to one another, but what kind of honeymoon would that have been for you? Speaking of which, sorry you missed your trip."

"I'm not. It's been lovely." Emily's smile slid into a grin. "I *am* tired of eating turkey, though."

"That's really why you braved the drifts, isn't it? To retrieve that ham from our place?"

"I don't mind telling you, I've been thinking about ham every moment I've been trying to knit things."

"Smells like you won't have to wait much longer for your dinner. Drew said your firewood's running low?"

"We just needed to haul more over from Hickory's shed. There's plenty. Speaking of which, you're ready to get home, I suppose? Away from ... certain people?"

Rosie shrugged, even as Gabe Adams popped into her head. Though he was never far from her thoughts at any point. Leaving him behind was the right thing to do, for her dear friend's sake.

Did she want to, though? *Absolutely not.*

And, anyway, she knew that was not whom Emily was hinting at. As to that ...

"Ems," she said on a determined rush. "I told Keith that Charlie is his son."

Emily's legs were untucked in a flash, and she sat forward. "What? You *what*? When? What did he say? How did he react? *Why*'d you tell him?"

Rosie couldn't help a small laugh, though she could well understand her sister's jumbled response. If someone had told Rosie herself last week that she'd reveal this decade-old secret to Keith Fairchild, of all people, she'd have laughed a very different sort of laugh.

"Keith isn't quite who he used to be, Ems."

Emily fell back into her chair, sloshing coffee onto her lap and groaning. "You'd better start at the beginning. I've clearly missed a lot."

So, Rosie told her what Gabe had said about Keith. She told her Keith had been very respectful, that he seemed a very different man than the boy he'd been. Finally, all she ultimately had to offer was a shrug. "Charlie asks more and more questions all the time," she said somberly. "You've seen the way he clings to men like he's just craving a father. And with Keith turning out to be more ... I don't know ... *decent* than I'd imagined, I started to feel a bit guilty." Rosie tried again to forget the night Gabe had confronted her about her secret. "I started to wonder if it's really my place to deny them both the chance to know one another, you know?"

Emily narrowed her eyes at that statement. "I'm not judging anyone here, you least of all, but ... *yes*. It is *completely* your place to make that decision. As it's been all along, Rose. *You* had to do all that on your own, so it was your place from the start."

"You know better than anyone I hardly did it on my own."

Emily waved that off. "You know what I mean. So? What did Keith say?"

"It was just this morning, so it's new. He seemed like he felt guilty, himself."

"I should hope so!"

"Emily."

"Well. Go on."

"He apologized."

Emily snorted but stayed quiet.

"I told him to think about it, to pray about it. Whether he wants Charlie to know, what he wants his role to be. I told him I'm not wanting any of his money."

Emily dropped her forehead into her palm. "Go on."

"That's all. I feel like we made things right. Or started to. I think I might have finally forgiven him."

"You don't have ... *feelings* for him again, do you?" Emily looked like her coffee cake might come back up.

"Oh, no. No. Absolutely not." Rosie conjured both young Keith and full-grown Keith in her mind and was pleased to feel nothing for either version. Not even pain. "It's baffling to me that I'd been so invested in him at sixteen, truth be told."

"It was a complicated time," Emily allowed with another wave of her hand. "We'd just lost Grandma. Keith was charming and good looking. Smooth talker. Give Young You a break."

"I think I can finally do that."

"As long as none of that charm works on you now," Emily warned.

Rosie thought of Gabe again. He, too, was full of charm. Good looking? Definitely. Perhaps this was some kind of lifelong temptation she'd have to fight? Was she too susceptible to a certain kind of man, when she was probably too good at ignoring the others?

No. He wasn't the same kind of man as Keith. She thought of Gabe's tenderness as he'd wrapped her hand. Of the way those expressive eyes of his made her feel like exactly the kind of woman she'd always wanted to be, even after—especially after—he knew the truth of her life. Of his deep, rich voice bringing the Christmas story to life and the way he'd smiled at her over a carved piece of Ivory soap.

"No, charm doesn't work on me now," she told Emily frankly. "Nothing Keith Fairchild could say or do would work at all."

"Well, I suppose it's a Merry Christmas, indeed, then. I wonder what he'll decide. What do you think?"

"He seemed kind of ... dazzled? Is that the right word? I think his ego might not mind the thought of having a son. You know how men can be."

"But he doesn't *have* to do anything. You know how the world can be, too."

"If I wanted him to *have* to do a thing, we'd have had this conversation years ago, Emily."

"True. Sorry." Emily crossed one leg over the other impatiently, studying Rosie. Her foot bobbed up and down. Rosie waited, familiar with her sister's mind. But Emily still managed to surprise her when she asked, "What else is going on?"

Rosie blinked. "What?"

"What else? Something else is on your mind since last time I saw you. I can tell."

"Something else? Wasn't all that enough?" Rosie hedged. *Curse Emily*, she thought, *and her reporter eyes*. But the fact was, she just didn't know what to say about what else was going on.

It was Gabe Adams, of course. He would be the "what else" Emily was poking for. How to talk about that, though? *I fell in love with another wealthy businessman who has been going out with our good friend Dottie and might be planning to propose to her because he has a ring with him, and I might have made him fall in love with me, too, and I'm a terrible person who doesn't even want to be in love with anyone anyway, ever again.*

Rosie was not ready to say that out loud, and she hoped she never would be. "Nothing else is up, Em."

"Nope. That's my role," Emily said with a grin. "I'm the mysterious sister, remember?"

"I thought you changed your ways after tangling with the mob." Rosie grinned back, deciding it wasn't that hard to placate Emily with some of the truth, if not all of it. "Okay, so ... I've been thinking a lot about Delia this week. It goes without saying we've been together even more than usual."

Emily visibly caught up with this new twist. "Delia. Okay. Keep going. Is she all right?"

"Sure, of course she is. She's fine."

"She seemed really happy this morning."

"You gave her a weapon. Why wouldn't she be?"

"What's up with her, then?"

"Keep an open mind when I say this, Emily. The thing is, I feel like I'm supposed to be a real mother to that little girl. I feel that way more and more all the time."

"Is that all? You *are* a real mother to Delia."

"Not enough for either of us, though. Not really. You see, Pastor Skip feels like he's being called to a life that doesn't include a little girl."

"That Philippines mission?"

"Yes. And I feel like the Lord may be calling me to be a parent to her."

"I don't see the problem. Seems like God's already worked out everyone's role here, and Delia adores you."

"I don't want her to feel like she's just been passed around one more time, though," Rosie explained. "I think she feels like a burden on people, and it seems like death just nips at her heels through every phase of her little life ... I don't know. I guess I just want more for her than a temporary guardianship, another hand-off for an indefinite time."

"What else is there?"

"I want to adopt her."

"Ohhh." Emily nodded her understanding, looking off toward nothing in the corner of the room. "Oh," she repeated.

"I see I don't need to tell you why that's complicated."

"Unmarried women don't adopt orphans."

"Unmarried women with illegitimate children of their own certainly do not."

"Rosie."

"What? It's what you were thinking. Anyway, tell me that's not true, that it's not who I am in the eyes of almost everyone. Especially in any court. Keeping and raising Charlie was shocking enough, you know? In this case, there's a very respectable preacher — comparatively — who already is her guardian."

"God wants you to have her, though? To be a mother to her. And if it's God's will, it will work out."

"You make it sound rather simple."

Emily shrugged. "Wait and see. Maybe Drew and I can adopt her, and you can raise her?"

Rosie shook her head. "More of the same. Tossing her around. Feeling unwanted."

"We'd never make her feel that way."

"I know you'd never mean to. But we both know how disappointing that is, to crave a family and always know your own is ... different."

"Her situation is already different. But I follow what you're saying. I'll pray about it, too, Rosie." Emily picked up her plate of cake again, swiping a dollop of almond paste with her finger and licking it off. "Speaking of mothers, I didn't hear from ours regarding the wedding."

"Did you expect to? It was right to invite her, of course. You did the right thing there."

"I was hoping she'd ship another set of salt and pepper shakers, at least." Emily winked, knowing they both were comfortable now talking about their missing mother, as they hadn't been just last Christmas.

"Real life just isn't like the movies," Rosie said out loud, something that had become a kind of mantra for them.

"Not for us, anyway."

"I wonder if it is for anybody."

"I'll probably never give up hoping she'll stroll back in, desperate to get to know her long-lost daughters," Emily admitted.

"And I gave up on that so long ago," Rosie admitted in turn. "I envy you your hope, I think. Or maybe I don't."

"Well," Emily said, setting the plate aside again and resting a hand on her flat belly. "Maybe she'll make it for the birth of her second grandchild." The sisters shared a laugh. "Or, if we count our darling Delia, her third?"

"Don't be ridiculous," Rosie said with the wisdom of experience, however difficult those experiences had been. "You can't possibly know if you're ... you know."

"Having a blessed event?" Emily wiggled her brows in an imitation of their aunt. "If we're not, it won't be for lack of trying."

"*Please*, Emily," Rosie scolded with a wink of her own. "*I'm* supposed to be the scandalous sister, remember?"

Chapter Twenty-Three

The Christmas sunshine was about to give way again to the gloom of early evening, Gabe figured with a glance behind him over Towpath Island.

Drew was behind him, as well, the two of them using a two-man gas-powered tree feller to separate the enormous tree that had crashed into Hickory Graham's roof from the base of its trunk. The sweet smell of maple wood flavored the icy air as Gabe reluctantly worked to ensure Rosie and her family could safely stay in their home tonight.

He could see Rosie's form as she moved inside past windows, the house lit from within by a raging fire in the living room hearth and lanterns lighting the removal of snow and ice from places those frozen piles should not have settled. It had been an all-hands-on-deck holiday endeavor, slowed by the depth of the snow drifts.

As it was, Gabe still could barely make out the cut of the old canal nearby for the way the snow and ice had overflowed it.

"Let's start cutting it into logs," Mathison called, his words visible in thick puffs of breath. "Big ones for now. Then we'll pull down what's left out of the roof."

The tree had left a respectable hole in half the roof and part of the house itself, all in the second floor. Smokey and Hickory had hauled sheet lumber from the marina using the tractor, and they were shoring up the damage indoors with canvas and boards. The lonely sound of their hammers was drowned out when the gas saw started again.

Across the lake, the sound was echoed by other saws as Buckeye Lake's year-round residents emerged for the first time.

After a week of inactivity beyond occasional shoveling, Gabe told himself physical work was welcome. He enjoyed feeling his muscles engage, the vibration of the saw singing through his arms even as his feet went numb in his boots.

What would it be like, back at the inn tonight?

No dragging a mattress before the fire for the kids. No Rosie in the window seat, contemplating a storm or her past or her future. No silly traditions. No sleepy, stir-crazy whining.

Ruth would not be going out of her way to entertain and distract the little ones, which probably meant no freshly iced cookies. Now, to the Fairchilds and to their general manager, Ruth would serve fancy tea cakes and scones.

Gabe scowled over the saw. He *preferred* cookies in strange shapes with clumpy icing.

Margo and Camden would insist Gabe and Keith join them for bridge and rummy, sedate games punctuated by musings about their business cohorts and world news, stock trends and investments. Not that they had a clue of any updates regarding those, since they hadn't had a fresh newspaper in over a week, but they would still ponder it all.

There would be port wine in stemless glasses. Quiet so quiet he would be able to hear the wicks of the candles burning.

Gabe packed fresh-cut logs onto the pallet they'd tied to the tractor earlier so Drew could transport them to the shed. Without a connection to the ground, the length of maple stretched onto the Graham family's roof finally tipped and slid back to earth with a loud scratching and an eruption of snow that blanketed Gabe and Drew.

Drew brushed it off, laughing.

"Past time for you two to take a turn by the fire," Hickory called from the wrap-around porch. "Not much daylight left, anyway."

"You have enough tarps to block off the stairway from the bottom?" Drew inquired, out of breath, as they entered the house.

"Sure do. It's not bad in here at all, now that the fire's really going."

Gabe agreed the contrast between the air outside and the orange heat in the living area was striking. He tugged off his first glove with his teeth and used his own cold hand to wipe the melting snow from his face.

The entrance area and living room of the Graham family home were so different from that of the inn. Here, scuffed wood floors were covered by outdated but colorful area rugs, walls papered in green leaf patterns and blue blossoms. The fire did a fine job heating the space, flickering on blue chairs and a green sofa, all fronted by mismatched footstools.

Charlie ran through and greeted Gabe and Drew, his arms full of blankets and a one-eyed teddy bear.

"Guess what! We still get to sleep on a floor mattress by the fire, Mom says!"

"The party continues," Gabe said, figuring Rosie and her grandfather would also have to find a way to sleep here in this room. The upstairs would be out of the question until the heat was back on and more substantial repairs made. Delia, he thought, must be off in the kitchen with Rosie, based on sounds of clanking pans and chatter.

"Make yourself at home, boys," Hickory said happily, clearly more at peace now that he was king of his own space again.

"Thank you, sir, but I can't stay too long," Gabe apologized, putting his hands closer to the fire before starting the daunting climb back up the bank in hip-deep snow. Drew disappeared somewhere, clearly at home with his in-laws.

A tea kettle whistled now from the back of the house.

"Still need help with a tarp in the hall upstairs," Hickory insisted to Gabe, heading in the direction of the whistling. "But let's get some hot tea in you first."

At the mantle, Gabe took in a soft portrait of Charlie as a wee, happy baby. There was a photograph of a middle-aged couple, and Gabe recognized Hickory with his arm around what could only be Rosie's late grandmother. There were a few knickknacks and blown-glass trinkets. A dried blossom of some kind pinned to a card.

Then another photo, this one of Rosie, dressed in rubber waders and wide suspenders, a kerchief in her hair and a monstrous camera around her neck. She was surrounded by greenery and swamp, her smile more dazzling than shy. Was this taken at the bog? By whom? Someone else had been wading in the waters around blossoms with a fine camera of their own, capturing her in this sweet moment.

Gabe wished he could somehow turn back time. Not have followed that "gut" feeling that he somehow belonged in Buckeye Lake, nor that a grand resort also belonged there.

No, he wanted Rosie Graham to be able to continue exulting in that natural wonderland all her life. Along with that, he wished hard he could have gone all *his* life without knowing her. There wasn't another Rosie out there, after all.

He regretted the way not just this one evening would go without her, up at the inn, but all the evenings to come. There was regret not only for those quiet bridge games but for all the playfulness he would not get to experience.

He regretted that now he knew what his life had been missing, that it was *her*, of all people. He would always know that now. There was no turning back from the knowledge.

"I heard you'd earned a warm cup."

Gabe heard her come into the room behind him and turned his head. "You changed your dress."

"Finally," she said on a pleased smile. "I never want to see that maroon dress again. Nor Ruth's checkered one, grateful as I was for it. Are you thawing out some?"

"Getting there." He blew over the cup that helped warm his hands more.

"Thank you for lending a hand, getting us back down here. For removing that very unwanted tree. That big, old sliver of wood stuck where it shouldn't be. Could we call it a splinter, do you think?"

"Having chopped at the thing, I can assure you it's more than a sliver or splinter. Are you happy to be home, then?" As he ventured a sip of strong, black tea, he knew the answer. It was there in the way her eyes danced over a turtleneck sweater. He might easily have guessed she was, by nature, a home body, but he was certain of it now.

"Very happy."

What if Keith did what he should have done all those years ago and married Rosie Graham now? Would she whither, away from this place and from her family?

Yet, was Gabe even right about what he'd seen in the kitchen that morning? *Had* she told Keith about Charlie? And, if so, where was Keith now? Gabe couldn't help but notice he hadn't trudged down here with them to work.

He should not ask her about it. He'd stuck his nose in where it didn't belong before, and there was no good reason to do so again.

Still.

Had it really been just twenty-four hours before that they'd kissed in the kitchen of the inn?

"I was wondering," he said carefully, and he watched the way she tilted her head in curiosity.

The kitchen door swung in interruption. "When you finish the tea, we'll go up and work on the tarp at the top of the steps," Hickory told Gabe as he entered the room, Drew behind him. "But then promise you'll sit down to a cup of hot coffee after that. A man's drink, eh, Drew?"

"Oh, Grandpa," Rosie said.

Drew laughed. "Can you handle it, Adams? I need to take more of the dry wood over to the barge and then go help my wife back down the hill to home before it gets too late."

"No problem. It's one tarp. Won't take but a few minutes."

"Just keep an eye on the time, or you'll be stuck on that mattress between Charlie and Delia all night," Drew said, eyes crinkling as he zipped his work coat again.

The children, having just entered from the kitchen themselves, issued delighted cheers over the prospect.

~~~~~

As a busy single mother, Rosie allowed herself few indulgences in life.

An occasional long bath with homemade rose leaf soap. An annual shopping trip with her sister in Columbus, during which she bought a new dress. Or, if she'd sold plenty of artwork the season before, three dresses.

She permitted herself a second cup of coffee now and then in the morning.

This Christmas evening, though, Rosie allowed herself a new indulgence. She let herself watch Gabe Adams do manual labor in the upstairs landing, which she decided qualified as the most decadent treat she'd yet discovered.

Though it was cold up here from the patched, tree-induced hole, the man had shed his bulky coat and draped it over the top of the banister to allow him to maneuver better. Hickory's eight-foot ladder was arranged on the stairway, leaning against the wall. One boot on the ladder and the other on the railing, Gabe straddled the open stairs adeptly.

He was making too-short work of tapping nails into the canvas.

"That flow of chilly air won't make it through both tarps," he said around one of the nails he still held in his lips.

He always looked good, of course. Yet, work pants slightly damp from the snow drifts looked good in a new sort of way.

Rosie felt her stomach flutter, watching him, and she told herself the flutter was because she was nervous about his safety.

He'd likely navigated far more frightening divides growing up in the foothills, though.

An expensive leather belt held the woolen pants tight around his hips, and layers of flannel and sweater stretched with his arms to reveal a strip of his lower back as he tacked the last nail into place.

"It's not as chilly up here as it might be," she mumbled, letting the blanket she'd draped around her shoulders for warmth slip forgotten to her elbows.

She wished she could invent something else for him to do. Something that involved more stretching.

She felt a pang of guilt.

He will soon build a house for your dear friend, Dottie. He will be her husband. Had he proposed yet?

"Have you had a nice Christmas, Gabe?" she asked as she watched him swing back down to the landing and push a short piece of dark hair off his forehead.

He seemed to consider her question longer than she might have expected. "It was a fine day," he said a little reluctantly. Sometimes when he looked at her the way he was now, she got the feeling he had questions.

She longed for him to ask them, whether she had answers or not. After all, she had questions, herself.

"How about you?" he finally asked. There was a beat of disappointment between them, as though the couple who had shared that kiss the night before was frowning at them now. "Was your Christmas a good one?"

"An unforgettable one, anyway. I loved getting to talk with Em. And it's awfully nice being back home, of course."

"I'm sure it is."

"Where do you consider home, anyway, Gabe?"

"Coffee is ready!" Hickory yelled up the stairway, peeling back a bit of the lower tarp.

"I'll see you down there," Rosie said, taking her blanket with her down the steps and reminding herself that their wonderful talks—in which she felt she could be herself—needed to end. He had packed a ring in his trunk, and Dottie had "hopes." Rosie didn't need any more bits of Gabe's life than she'd already accumulated, so questions meant to reveal more of him needed to end, too.

To say nothing of ogling the poor man while he volunteered labor.

"I'll secure the base of this tarp, and then I'll be right behind you."

Frustrated with herself, Rosie squeezed through the give in the tarp below the stairs and went to help her grandfather.

He'd always kept plenty of lanterns, of course, from his growing up years on the island and from the years he'd taken his son, her own father, camping. Now, those handy Colemans lit her kitchen space, along with the old Stonebridge folding lantern she'd always loved, now glowing beside the sink.

"You take the couch tonight," Hickory was saying as he counted out cups for the serving tray. "I'll curl up in Grandma's sewing room among the quilts."

His tired smile shut down the argument she was about to make. He'd love the excuse to hole up surrounded by Louise's patterns and projects.

"You already have the little woodstove in there going, don't you?"

"I've looked forward to it all day, my dear. It's my Christmas gift to myself."

Rosie stretched to give him a peck on his dry cheek, placing the sugar dish on his tray, and then she led the way back to the living room with the pot of coffee.

Gabe was there now, having pulled a footstool up close to the fire. Charlie and Delia were playing a low-energy game of jacks on a wooden side table, taking turns yawning and talking softly.

"Thank you again for your help today," Rosie said as she poured a cup for Gabe.

"That'll warm your insides before you hike back up the hill," Hickory said decisively, reaching for his own.

"I don't like the idea of it," Rosie said, worried. "How will we know you made it safely?"

"We'll work out a lamp code from the inn's windows, and you can watch for it from here," Gabe said, peering out and up. "You can see the corner of the inn up there, I believe."

"Yes, we can." Rosie thought of the summer nights she'd sat on the porch, waiting for her grandparents to go to bed and watching for a signal from Keith Fairchild. She shook her head, wondering for the dozenth time today if she'd done the right thing in telling the man about Charlie.

What would he do now? What had been going through his mind all day? They'd never had a minute together again.

"The Rock Basket," Gabe said suddenly, pulling Rosie from her thoughts. She looked around, only to find he'd directed the statement at her.

"I'm sorry. The what?"

"You asked where I consider home," Gabe reminded her, sipping his coffee. "The Rock Basket. It's an outcropping of sandstone over a ravine a mile or so north of the cabin I grew up in."

"In the Hocking Hills."

"Right. Not an official name or anything. My family always just called it the Rock Basket."

Rosie smiled. "You feel more at home there than at the family cabin itself?"

He smiled back, and she tried not to enjoy their old rhythm too much. "I love my parents and the home they made. But the Basket was all mine, the only area where I wasn't crowded by my brothers and sisters. No one ever ventured there, that I could tell. I'd keep supplies in the little cave area. Blankets, books, lanterns. I'd camp out there by myself so much, sometimes hunting. Mostly thinking."

She could see him, skinnier like Charlie, imagining himself an adventurer in the wilderness. "When was the last time you were back there?"

"Couple years ago."

She wished she could see it. She was seldom happier, herself, than when surrounded by nature. "Do you get homesick for it?"

He shrugged. "Not homesick, no. I guess I'm used to traveling around, now that I've been doing it so long. I'm comfortable anywhere."

But she thought he seemed sad. "Even the city?"

"Why not the city?"

"It just seems like the opposite of that basket of rocks."

"The Rock Basket." The corner of his mouth twitched.

She tried not to think about the fact he needed another shave, nor about how warm his skin was to the touch. She knew what it felt like, after all.

"I guess it's not as different as you might think. There are quiet places in the city, adventures to be had."

"But no hunting."

"No, no hunting. Eating involves less work in general, I suppose."

"Do you eat in restaurants all the time, Gabe?"

"Why are you questioning this poor boy so much?" Hickory said, sighing into his cup and propping his feet up.

"I'm sorry," Rosie said, shaking her head because she didn't know why she was. In fact, she shouldn't be at all. But would he expect Dottie to cook for him, or would he like that she nearly always ate in restaurants? Had they discussed that yet?

Could anything be less her business?

"I mostly eat in the hotels."

Rosie made a sound into her own cup. She wanted to know if he liked that and would be willing to keep doing it for the rest of his life. She knew Dottie would. Dottie would love moving from one hotel to another. Or would they put down roots there on the north shore where the resort would be?

She stayed silent, listening to Hickory's rocking chair.

Gabe straightened off the foot stool, peering again at the window. "If I'm going to be off, it had better be now," he announced. Rosie followed him to the window, and together they looked far up the rise to the edge of the inn that overlooked the lake.

"There's the parlor window," she said. "Do you see it?"

"Yes."

She thought of the first night they'd talked there in that window. She wondered if he thought of it, too.

"Put a lantern there so we know you've made it back safe and sound." Rosie reached into her apron pocket—the festive, red-checker ribbon-bordered apron her grandmother had made when Rosie had been just a girl. She drew out a small box to which she'd attached a bow and handed it to Gabe.

"What's this?"

"A gift for you. I made it more than a month ago, in the glass studio."

Rosie watched with satisfaction as Gabe slid the lid off and discovered the three small, clear-blue figures within.

"It's ... a nativity," he said softly and with a sort of awe that pleased her.

"Just Joseph, Mary, and Jesus. They were this year's homemade nativity."

"I can't take these, Rosie."

"I didn't realize I was meant to be working in Ivory soap, instead." Rosie thought of the balmy day she'd blown and worked the little figures, never expecting a blizzard for the upcoming holiday. "The glass pieces are yours, Gabe."

Their eyes met, another shared memory of an Ivory camel and the slip of a knife.

"Did you bring the soap figures home with you?"

"No. You can have those too. Unless Mrs. Fairchild wants to fight you for them."

"But then you won't have a nativity scene from this Christmas."

"I don't need one to remember this Christmas. I'll always have the scar on my hand, don't forget."

Gabe laughed at that, his Adam's apple moving in his throat. "Well, thank you. I'll treasure this."

"And you'll remember, too."

He looked down at the smooth, simple glass he held in his hand and placed it back in the box. "I will, yes. I guess it really is over now."

He sounded sad. For her own part, Rosie could only nod.

Chapter Twenty-Four

Delia Stimpson Grade Four
Christmas Journal Project
Buckeye Lake Public School
December 1946

It won't be December much longer, and Ms. Bailey said this is a Christmas Journal anyway, so I think even if they clear up the roads and we have to go to school again, I should be allowed to stop writing in this pretty soon. When it's January, I think. I only need Rosie to forget about it because otherwise she'll probably say it can't hurt me to keep doing it.

I got to go back to Towpath Island with Charlie and his family. Rosie said I could, and Pastor Skip said yes, too. There was a tree in the roof of Hickory's house, though. There is a hole there. So, we are still staying close to a fire. It really is a little colder here than it was at the inn, so I guess I'm glad we got to be there when it was blizzarding real bad. Plus, we had a Christmas tree there. We don't have any decorations in the house here, and I know we won't because Christmas is over anyway.

I brought my doll Santa brought me, Bernadette, with me here. She has a bad, bad past, but Rosie says she can move ahead and have the kind of life she wants. I'm trying to figure out what kind of life Bernadette might want. Right now, she only seems to want to go ice fishing because she never has before.

~~~~~

It was the little lamb made from soap that Gabe held the following night when sleep again refused to come.

He listened to the ticking of the clock, just as he had that night when the blizzard had only been brewing. His life somehow seemed predictable then, though he'd hardly have described it that way at the time.

Hadn't he felt like crawling right out of his own skin as the clock had ticked before the blizzard had arrived?

The crawling out of his own skin feeling, at least, hadn't changed.

This day had brought still more changes to the Christmas inn refugees. Pastor Skip had donned snowshoes and treaded straight across the frozen lake in case any of his flock would be able to make it to church in the morning. Without Delia underfoot—or snowshoe, in this case—the old man seemed to regard his journey as a rugged adventure. He had set off with cheerful prayers for and thanks to the Fairchilds for their hospitality.

Smokey had a farm to return to, so he'd fired up the tractor early, calculating he'd have to help with half a dozen emergencies on his way home. He figured his father and brother could use a hand managing damage at the expansive Black-Pool Farms, and his mother would have worried herself sick through the holiday. It was time to brave the roads and fields to put her at ease, he'd informed them.

Burt and Cookie kept Camden and Margo company at the bridge table, in no hurry to leave, though Gabe noticed the couples had taken to squabbling more and more about the score.

Keith had joined them from time to time, but he'd disappeared somewhere after dinner.

That left the plans for the resort stretched between Gabe and Dot as the hour crept once more toward midnight. Gabe rubbed the pad of his thumb against the soap lamb's bumpy wool while Dot tattooed a cadence on the desk with a ruler.

The two of them had reached an impasse about the docks.

"I just don't see why they have to extend straight out that way toward the bog," he said again. He rubbed his eyes and felt the slight sting of Ivory soap residue. He blinked it away. "There's enough frontage to take them farther east."

"We'll run short on space for events if we do that, though. You'll want folks to be able to pull up there for concerts and hog roasts and things like that."

He dropped the lamb figurine onto the inky lines that represented the north shore, pushing it around there while he imagined himself overseeing the plucking of delicate water lilies to clear space. The blooms would whither on a barge, and he would watch.

To that end, what equipment would they use to hack up Cranberry Bog? He could well envision Rosie Graham standing there in her waders, while he personally devastated the bog's rare beauty so rich people could pull their cruisers up to hear jazz music.

He sighed in frustration and inadvertently sent the lamb skidding off the edge of the paper.

"What's wrong?" Dot asked. The glow of the lamp she'd placed in the middle of the desk highlighted her perfect nose and neck and eyes.

"It just seems like a lousy exchange," he said softly.

With that, he got up and poured himself a finger of brandy from a tumbler kept on the sidebar of the study, like he was some kind of eighteenth-century British aristocrat instead of the strong-backed kid of a preacher and an immigrant from the hills and hollers.

He'd felt so certain that God had called him here to Buckeye Lake, but now he wondered. Had that been his own ambition run amuck? He was afraid now it was easy to mistakenly attribute strong feelings to some kind of life purpose. *I'm supposed to be here, to do things here*, his soul had announced to his head. What had those "things" been about, though? Building a vacation empire for the wealthy? Running it like some kind of king with a pretty queen on his arm?

Discernment. The word had slid into his thinking more and more lately, a word his father had liked to toss about when Gabe had pretended to listen.

He knew what it meant, though. It meant he needed to figure out what it was God wanted him to do rather than charging ahead toward a bottom line. He should get serious about what these diagrams and plans spread across the desk truly meant. He had thought he'd known, just a couple weeks before, but everything about the vision felt off now, rather than inspired.

Dot did not rise with him but smoothed her hand across the lines representing the dream that had brought the pair of them together. Frowning, he wished she had gone home, too, when Skip or Smokey had left. He wished fervently she'd taken the resort plans with her.

"Rosie got to you, didn't she?"

He glanced over, never having taken a sip of the brandy. He'd have to be careful answering a question like that. "What do you mean?"

"She's so sentimental about that swampy bog. She and Emily both."

Gabe wondered if he could purchase crates of fresh cranberries from Canada and ship them to Buckeye Lake once they'd carved up and ruined the bog. He had the money to make that right, perhaps. The Fairchilds had the money. Dot Berkeley had the money.

"I guess we could extend the docks east, to minimize the impact on the bog," Dot said with resignation, running her finger across that part of the drawing, but Gabe didn't follow the line with his eyes. Instead, he watched her. She was so lovely, so tidy, so clear-minded. "If it's a sticking point for you."

Her gaze slammed into his.

Gabe tried to respond but had no idea what to say.

"I don't think you're that excited by the project in general anymore, though." Because she was Dot and used to playing hardball all her life, she pressed on. "Are you, Gabe?"

His head was shaking before he spoke, wondering if she'd been reading his thoughts moments before. "No. I guess I'm not."

She sighed, but that was her only reaction. "What about Keith?"

"We haven't talked about it."

"So, you're not speaking on behalf of FH Resorts right now?"

"Not at all."

"Just on behalf of yourself."

"Yes."

Dot nodded, studying him. She drew in a deep breath, stretched. Blew the breath out slowly. "I don't think that leaves us with much, somehow, do you? I'm only now realizing it."

The coolness of it chilled him, and Gabe couldn't remember what it had been like to hold her hand when they'd gone to the theater or whether her hand had even been warm in his.

"Now that you mention it, have we ever talked about ... *us* ... outside the framework of that resort?" he asked, needing to turn the whole thing back around to her. What did she feel or not feel, anyway?

"It honestly seemed like a good plan to me," she said as though to herself, as though she struggled to consider the possibility that she'd been wrong about something. "The whole thing. You and me, the resort. It seemed like it made sense. I mean ... didn't it?"

"It did, yes. It did make so much sense."

"Well. Maybe too much sense." She stood and stretched again as though she weren't tossing their future aside with his enthusiastic help.

He regarded her figure in her trim skirt and expensive sweater, knowing anyone would think him a madman for letting her leave the room this way.

"I honestly thought we would be dazzling together, Gabe Adams."

"We honestly would be, Dot Berkeley."

"But dazzling isn't as much your style as you thought it was." She crossed to him and reached down to take his hand. Yes, her hands were, in fact, warm.

He remembered that now, as she squeezed his.

"Maybe it's just not my style when it comes to love."

"We never mentioned that, did we?" She studied him, clear-eyed. "Love?"

"No."

"I think a lot of fuss has been made about love lately, because of the war and whatnot," she said, a little line of concentration between her perfect brows. "Yet, somehow, I had forgotten to let it matter."

"Do you love me, Dottie?"

"That's the first time you've called me Dottie." She smiled. "I forgot to ask myself if I loved you because we would have been so dazzling together. Had you asked yourself if you loved me yet?"

"Not until very lately."

She sighed. "Well, it might be worth the fuss. Love, I mean. In which case ..." Dot lifted the hand of his she still held and pecked a kiss on his knuckles. "Maybe we shouldn't let ourselves get drawn permanently into the plans rolled out on that desk."

"I'm a little embarrassed that we got it all mushed up together," Gabe admitted. A lightness filled him, seeming to spring from his stomach that ached a little less. "You deserve better than that."

"Do I?" She grinned again, her teeth as perfect as the rest of her. "I think I'm a business girl at heart, Gabe. I worry I might deserve exactly the kind of romantic future that can be approved by a zoning commission."

That surprised a laugh out of him. "You know that's not true."

She shrugged. "The fact I'm willing to settle for it says otherwise."

He raised the snifter, the splash of amber liquid whirling on the bottom of the glass. "Here's to neither of us settling for that."

She pressed a quick kiss to his closed lips, but neither of them drank from the cup. "Here's to not settling."

~~~~~

At the same time, just down the snowy slope and on the other side of the old canal, Rosie braided Delia's hair and realized the children should be getting ready to settle in for bed.

"It's getting late," she observed aloud, finger-combing a section of hair from the center part of Delia's head. The little girl swam in one of Rosie's own flannel nightgowns, curled in front of her on the mattress by the fire. She made happy little sounds, always content to have her hair fussed with. In the corner, Charlie played with the erector set Santa had left as a treat at the house, humming to himself, and Hickory smoked his cherry-scented pipe in his favorite chair.

"Days and nights managed to get all confused during the storm, didn't they?" her grandfather asked in response, the soft creak of the rocker accompanying his words.

"I want the snow to stay and for us not to be able to go back to school and for me to stay here forever and ever," Delia said. She yawned. "And ever."

"I've been here forever and ever, and I like it just fine," Hickory said pleasantly, blowing out a little ring of smoke.

Rosie noticed his cheeks were more crimson than usual. "I think you wind-burnt your cheeks today, Grandpa, ice fishing." They'd enjoyed fresh-caught fish for supper as they still waited for power to come back out on the island. This evening, they had spotted part of the north shore in the far distance flickering back to life.

"It wasn't the fishing what did it," he said. "It was clearing the path to the shanty on the ice. Nasty wind still blowing over the lake. Once I was in there, I was just fine and dandy, and woo-ee, were they bitin'."

Rosie told herself not to ask. She twisted two strands of hair with a third. It was none of her business. "And how did Gabe Adams like ice fishing?"

"Ah, he liked it, I daresay. Boy only ever fished the rivers in winter. Can you imagine?"

~~~~~

Earlier that day, Rosie had been heating water on the stove for laundry when Charlie had banged in the front door. He had stomped back to the kitchen, his face barely visible above his snowsuit and scarf and below his thick hat.

"How's your day in the ice shanty? Are the fish biting?"

When he shoved the scarf down with his glove, he was grinning. "I told Gabe how you baked early this morning."

Rosie blinked from the sink. "What? Gabe's out there? Ice fishing?"

"Uh-huh. He made you something."

She watched him wrench off his right glove, reach into his pocket, and produce a small figure. Rosie crossed the room to take it, "he made you something" hanging in the air like the steam from the stove top.

Perplexed, she took in what appeared to be a human figure made from a round wooden fishing bobber, with hooks where arms and legs would be. The hooks had been bent into hands and feet on the sharp ends. Most bizarre of all, a face had apparently been carved into the wood with a knife to create a forlorn expression. She hiccupped a little laugh.

Was this some kind of thank you for her glass nativity scene?

"Here's the note."

"Note?" She took the scrap of paper Charlie produced next. On it was written: *I am sending you my latest work, Man Contemplates Hunger, in the hopes you'll consider displaying it in your gallery on the boardwalk. You may keep the entirety of the proceeds in exchange for a hunk of the cinnamon bread I heard you made this morning. Yours, G.A.*

"He told me to wait for your response," Charlie said, but he had already used his one glove-free hand to grab a slice of the bread.

Smiling, Rosie decided this was a game she could play.

Just three minutes later, she had arranged the bobber man inside of a Dixie Mix fruit cake tin, complete with a matchbox for a table and a teeny piece of cinnamon bread. Beside him was the note she'd scribbled in return: *Sir, your work is impressive, but forgive me if I resist getting mixed up in any of your north shore business endeavors (though I like the idea of you as an artist so much more than you as a destroyer of natural wonders). I return the piece with a slightly altered title: Man Contemplates a Full Belly. Enjoy!*

Then, she tied half the cinnamon bread loaf into a towel and sent it along with Charlie to share.

An hour later, she'd just washed and hung Delia's wedding garb to dry when Charlie returned with the tin and the empty towel. He declared his intention of staying inside for a time to get warm. Mumbling something even she didn't understand in response, Rosie pried up the lid to find the bobber man's face bearing a single blue tear inked beneath its eyeball. This time, the scrap of paper in there with him read: *Man Contemplates Rejection.*

Laughing to herself, Rosie realized there were some things (or people) she could miss even more than she'd missed home last week.

~~~~~

"Anyway, Gabe managed to take Ruth up a passel of his own catches for dinner tonight," Hickory recounted later as he smoked his pipe.

"Can *we* go see Ruth tomorrow?" Delia asked Rosie without turning her head. Rosie tied off one of the braids.

"I'm sure she'd like that."

"Ruth isn't nobody's mama, is she?"

"You mean anybody's. And, no. Ruth never had a family of her own, dear."

"She'd have made a good mom. She makes the best hot cocoa."

"I agree. Hold still."

"Where is your mom again, Rosie?"

"She's out in California."

"Oh, yeah. On the edge of the us."

"Come again?" Hickory asked, pausing in rocking.

"I think you mean the U.S.," Rosie said helpfully, winking at her grandfather over the little girl's head.

"Does she live in Sacramento?"

"I don't think so."

"Sacramento is the capital of California."

"Very good."

"She isn't a very good mom if she's all the way there on the edge, and you're here, you and Emily," Delia said. "Is she?"

"I was hardly with her long enough to know if she's a good mom or not, sweet girl."

"Your mom isn't dead in heaven like my mom, so does that make you mad that she's not here and she doesn't have a good reason?"

"You're right. Your mom's alive in heaven, which is a comfort, isn't it? I don't feel mad anymore about my mom not being here with us, Delia. All we can do is pray for her."

"I will."

"Thank you."

"You're a good mom anyway, though."

Rosie's heart clenched. She wanted to be the one this girl leaned into all her life, and she told herself she didn't need any legal papers for that to happen. It was another matter of prayer. "Thanks again for that, Delia Divine. Isn't it lovely the way God fills gaps and holes in our lives with other people if we let Him?"

Delia made a sound of agreement, followed by the sound of a yawn, and Rosie finished the second braid.

"Come help hold this, 'kay?" Charlie demanded to Delia now that her hair was contained, and he didn't wait for her agreement before he thrust a metal piece of building material into her hand.

Sore from hunching over on the mattress for so long, Rosie stood and stretched her lower back. She loved the scent of Hickory's pipe. It said "home" to her. Yet, there was emptiness that hadn't been in this house before, and she resisted putting a name to it. She suspected it was one of those gaps she'd just spoken of, that God filled unexpectedly with people.

The gap had nothing to do with the hole in the roof.

"Penny for your thoughts." It was a phrase her grandfather had used her whole life, an occasional invitation to his granddaughters that she'd always interpreted as "I don't have anything better to do, so entertain me."

Emily had always loved to tell stories, in that animated way of hers, and her stories had always been good for several pennies. Rosie, more visual and philosophical by nature, rarely earned her penny. Hickory hardly ever asked her, especially now, when the two of them were typically content to sit before the fire. He would smoke his pipe while she would draw or paint.

"I was just thinking how strange it feels, only the four of us. You know. After being packed together with so many people for so very long."

"Ah, yes. It does feel strange, at that." He rocked in silence, but Rosie knew she hadn't earned the proverbial penny. A glance at Hickory confirmed he was watching her even as she watched out the frost-edged window.

"I'm not sad or anything."

"You never are, dearest. You never are." He stopped rocking and looked at her. "It's hard when you get a glimpse of something you want, and then you have to tell yourself it's not for you. Again."

It wasn't a question. It asked nothing of her, so Rosie didn't respond.

What did the old man think he knew? She tried to fit in what he said like a puzzle piece against her desire to adopt Delia. Then she tested it against the life she couldn't even let herself imagine with Gabe Adams, the deep comfort in being near him.

Unsurprisingly, Hickory's comment fit snugly in both places.

She would not earn a penny with her thoughts tonight, though. She ran her hand over the side of the fireplace mantle and deliberately grinned at her grandpa.

"You know, I'm kind of glad I never got around to getting the Christmas decorations up this year, with the wedding preparations." She watched him take a long draw on his pipe. "Since we weren't here to enjoy them, anyway."

A knock sounded at the door across the room, making Rosie jump in surprise. Her first thought was maybe it was Gabe. Maybe he was restless. She'd hoped he would stop in after he'd fished out on the ice today, but maybe he'd been too cold, and now he was warm and he …

Charlie pulled the carved oak door open to reveal Keith Fairchild, bundled in a parka and a thick hat.

Rosie was frozen by the fireplace, trying to register that he was standing there. How had she managed to forget about him?

"Come in, come in," her grandfather called, pushing up to standing and waving the inn's heir toward the fire.

Keith looked strange in their living room, in his long, expensive coat.

Rosie's stomach clenched tighter when she noticed Keith had a boy's baseball glove tucked against his side, decorated with a blue bow.

Charlie had immediately returned to the erector set project, far from guessing that his life was about to change.

Chapter Twenty-Five

Delia Stimpson Grade Four
Christmas Journal Project
Buckeye Lake Public School
December 1946

It's almost 1947, so Christmas is officially over, I think, and that means this journal is over too. Hickory says he is rigging up something so fun for us to do, and it is something fun outside. So, I hope you had a good holiday, Ms. Bailey. That's all. (Did I use the floating commas right? The ones that make one word out of two words?)

~~~~~

Gabe awoke with the conviction that he'd lend a hand where he could around the island. He figured some know-how, some restless energy, and some spare time were all the ingredients needed to help folks bounce back from the blizzard.

After all, there was no resort to plan, at least not today. Certainly no woman to win over (not that he'd expended much energy in the right direction there, anyway). In fact, getting out of the inn in general seemed quite appealing, indeed.

As he passed through the tidy parlor area, Gabe looked longingly at the window seat, knowing Rosie would not be there, but imagining her there anyway.

She'd left some kind of warm glow behind in that window that he figured might always remain.

Outside the bay window, the snow still sat heavy on evergreen boughs and made a deep carpet that hid all manner of terrain beneath it. It stretched white over the pool of Buckeye Lake, where ice fishing shanties could be spotted here and there, tiny fingers of smoke already rising from their crude pipe chimneys. The morning sun was its own ball of cold white over the scene.

He'd spent yesterday wrapped inside a shanty like that, a blanket around his shoulders, staring with Hickory Graham into a dark hole in the ice and waiting for a bite. Between tugs on the line, he'd amused himself making a sculpture for Rosie. He smiled thinking of it and thinking of the fish that had been as restless under the ice as he was, himself, to find a new landscape. In their case, the new landscape had been a tease in the form of bait.

Hungry like those fish, he followed the scent of sausage now, hoping

Dot was still in bed so he wouldn't have to eat breakfast with her.

Post-blizzard, the Fairchilds had begun taking their meals in the dining room once more, served by Ruth. It struck Gabe how the sense of togetherness and unity demanded by the storm had reverted to formality after the Graham family had departed.

Something else felt off in that dining room, though, when Gabe arrived. He stopped walking halfway across the plush carpet, unease thick in the air.

It had nothing to do with Dot Berkeley.

Camden and Margo Fairchild were sitting before full plates, each with silverware poised mid-air, faces similarly frozen as they regarded their son standing behind the chair across from them. Keith ran a nervous hand down the back of his own neck and turned to regard Gabe's entry with something like relief on his face.

"Gabe! Good! Come on in, come. I'm so glad you're here." He cleared his throat. Was he sweating? "I was just sharing some rather big news with my parents, and since you're practically part of the family ..." He didn't finish but gestured to a chair next to his mother.

Ruth was nowhere to be seen. Wise woman.

Gabe, suspended in place, wondered if he might already know this "rather big news."

"I do. Not. Understand," Margo said, blinking like the motion of her eyelids might help life make sense.

"What's there to not understand?" Camden said in a huff. "He claims to have a son."

"I just told them. I was just telling them, Gabe, that it turns out ... I do, in fact, have a son." He took a deep breath that trembled a little in his throat. "Rosie's son, in fact. Charlie. As it turns out, little Charlie is my son."

So, Gabe had guessed correctly once more. Rosie had told Keith the truth.

Gabe thought of his own role in this little scene, of the guilt he'd inadvertently laid upon Rosie for the long-kept secret, of what he'd said to her that night in the window seat. What had his own goal even been, he wondered now?

"But how is that possible? It just is not possible. Little boys don't just appear. You didn't *know* any of them until Christmas!" Margo was pale, with two blotches of crimson near each side of her jaw. "*Right?*"

"Margo, dear, don't make me spell this out for you," Camden mumbled, scowling.

Gabe, taking some pity on Keith's equally splotchy red cheeks and feeling no small amount of responsibility in the most illogical way, walked forward and extended his hand. "Congratulations, Fairchild. Charlie's a fine boy."

There, just that. Recognize the fact of it and move forward.

"But. But." Margo stared down at her food. "We don't know that! How do you even know that, Keith? That he's your son? Because some pretty woman says it's true, it must be true?"

Gabe had been afraid since he'd walked into the room that Rosie would somehow be maligned before this was over, and here it began. He gripped a chairback and told himself not to talk.

"I mean, she spends a week here, eating our food ..."

"Mother!"

"Mother what? What wouldn't a mother do to see her son ahead in life, I ask you?"

"What, indeed," Gabe muttered.

"Charlie is my son." Keith seemed to deliberately pull his shoulders back with the firm statement. "Come now, Mother. His age. And his looks. You cannot tell me you don't see it."

Camden massaged his temples. Margo moved her lips like a fish a few times before dropping her forehead into her hand. She had no defense against the fact Charlie Graham was a small replica of her own son.

"What will people say?" was the moan she finally produced. It was, Gabe thought, the best concession they could hope for from her.

"*I'm* people," Gabe put in boldly. "And I say anyone would be proud to call that young man family."

"Thanks, Adams."

Gabe nodded to his friend.

Margo slammed her fork back down and turned on her husband beside her. "I blame you for this, Camden."

Camden's head turned more slowly in her direction. "You blame *me*?"

"Well, you sent him out here with *what* kind of supervision? He was just a boy himself, all those years ago, and you just sent him here with ... what? No advice about life? No defenses against women like that?"

Gabe stiffened, reminded himself he had no business speaking.

"He'd graduated school," Camden said from between gritted molars.

"I was in the wrong, Mother," Keith said, almost wearily. "I assure you, I was no one's victim. As it happened ..."

"Spare me!" Margo burst out. "Instead of telling me how it happened, which I do *not* need explained," she hissed at her husband again. "Perhaps you might tell me how we might explain this to *other* people, hmm? The sudden appearance of a son, a grandson? How does that even work, I ask you?"

It could make next year's Christmas card more interesting, Gabe thought. Curious at how all this would go for young Charlie—and prepared to fight for him if need be—he finally made his way around the table and took the chair that had been indicated for him next to Margo.

She wasn't a bad woman, he knew. She was simply having a very bad moment.

"I'm trying to tell you," Keith said, taking another shaking breath. "I spent last evening talking more with Rosie about it."

"How lovely," Margo grumbled.

Gabe, however, felt a pang of envy. Keith had spent last evening with Rosie. He wondered what she'd been doing, if she'd seemed happy and well. Was her hand healing as it should? It had taken every bit of his own will not to stop in after his fishing excursion yesterday to check the stitches.

"Anyway, I decided the right thing is to face up to ... to what I did," Keith went on. "To do the right thing. We didn't tell Charlie the truth yet, of course, but I decided I really do want to do the right thing."

"All right, then." Camden patted his mouth with his napkin, though he'd managed to eat nothing. "She wants money. The boy's mother, I mean."

Gabe shoved a triangle of toast in his mouth. Of course she didn't just want money. If she had, she'd have said something a long time ago. He remembered her, with her legs all twisted up in the blanket, falling out of the window seat when he'd indicated he knew.

"How in the world was she allowed to raise him by herself, anyway?" Margo suddenly mumbled beside Gabe, censure in her tone. "There are places you send girls for that. They don't raise ..." She trailed off, making a helpless gesture with her hand.

Gabe chewed his toast. Of course, Hickory hadn't sent Rosie away when she'd realized she was pregnant. The family had already lost so much, so many people. His own wife had just passed. He was doing his best out on that little island, and the old man had probably simply closed ranks against the world.

But Gabe couldn't offer any of that insight. Instead, he braced himself as he decided to clarify for the table in general: "What do you mean when you say you want to do the right thing, Keith?"

Keith cleared his throat, nodded. "I'll marry Rosie Graham, of course."

It was Gabe's turn to stare down at his plate.

Camden nodded, but more as though he couldn't hold the weight of his own head up any longer than as though he agreed.

Margo—refined, cultured Margo—might have growled.

"I'll marry Rosie, and Charlie will have two parents," Keith went on with determination. "We'll move to the house in Columbus, and Charlie can go to the best schools. He's smart. I talked to him last night while I was over there, and he's very, very smart. And no one in Columbus will know, you know ... they won't know that he's ... well, that I ... anyway, that he was ..."

Thankfully, no one said the word. Gabe closed his eyes, imagining it. *What had he done?*

"I'll give him the name he deserves," Keith said, his energy seeming to flag, though he tried to keep his chin parallel to the table.

"Why didn't she say anything before now?" Margo asked.

"I admit, that bothers me too, but I know she had her reasons," Keith said. "And I suppose I will stop feeling angry with her about it over time."

So, Rosie would be married to a man harboring anger toward her. Anger that she hadn't worked hard enough to get him to respond to her when he'd taken her innocence and cut her out of his life completely. Gabe desperately wanted to turn back time, but to which moment in time, exactly?

"And Rosie is fine with this plan?" Gabe asked, trying hard to control his voice. "With leaving the lake and moving to Columbus? With leaving her art business and family behind?"

Gabe just couldn't imagine it.

"I don't know." Keith looked baffled. "Why wouldn't she be fine with it? She can sketch anywhere, I guess."

It occurred to Gabe he would have to see her. Company dinners, benefit galas, Fairchild family events. As long as Gabe was affiliated with the FH resorts and hotels, his path would cross Mrs. Keith Fairchild's path regularly.

"There's a lot to think through here," Camden said in the calm, reflective manner that had built a small but growing empire.

"What about Delia?" Gabe couldn't help himself.

"Who's Delia?" Margo squealed as though another unexpected grandchild might fall upon her from the sky.

"The little girl who practically lives with Rosie, the one who belongs to Pastor Skip?"

Keith looked confused. "I don't see what the girl has to do with anything."

That statement, more than the "she can sketch anywhere," made Gabe wonder if Rosie herself knew of Keith's plans.

Chapter Twenty-Six

New Year's Eve 1946 was still young when a knock on the inn's front door distracted Gabe from his sleepy pursuit of Keith's bishop on the chess board.

The sound was followed immediately by the creak of the door's huge hinges. Then there were rapid footsteps that could only be those of a child.

Charlie Graham—the very one who had been much talked of in this inn lately—came skidding to a halt on the wood floor beyond the study, puddles forming around his snow boots. Gabe knew the kid had no idea he was tracking the outdoors into what would be his own property one day. Under the boy's hand-knit hat (probably made by his mother rather than his Aunt Emily because it had the form of a serviceable hat), Keith's look-alike eyes flashed a reminder of how much a week could change things.

"Well, hello there," Keith said uncertainly to Charlie, rising from the chess game.

"You guys gotta get your stuff on and come out. It's so … *wow!*" He was breathless. "Human slingshot!" he managed, gasping with delight.

Then, to Gabe's surprise, Charlie turned and sprinted right back out the front door. He managed, somehow, to shut it as he went.

Keith glanced over the chess pieces, amused. "Did you understand any of that?"

"Only that we gotta get our stuff on." Gabe yawned and stretched. Smokey had returned the day before with his unstoppable tractor to haul Dot to her apartment and Cookie and Burt to their home. Everyone left had clustered together and saved him an uncomfortable farewell with the woman he'd tried so hard to imagine marrying.

"What happened?" Margo had whispered, clearly confused by life in general at this point.

"Nothing," he'd whispered back, and he felt like that said it all.

Smokey had reported back to them about the post-blizzard world, but now the inn was even more silent.

"I say we go figure out what a human slingshot is," Gabe said.

Half an hour later, having swallowed a sandwich in two bites, Gabe followed Keith down the slope to the sound of happy screaming near the marina. Every step was still laborious, as temperatures hadn't risen enough to melt even one of the feet upon feet of snow, but that didn't stop

Delia from running part of the way toward them, gesturing and calling something loudly as she plowed through snow at least up to her waist.

Gabe trekked down the barely-there path, trying to process what he was seeing.

It seemed the Graham family had cleared a pathway on the lake's ice off the tip of Towpath Island. A strip of ... rubber? A strip of what appeared to be rubber was stretched low between the trunk of a leafless tree and some kind of wooden post.

A human slingshot. Charlie's words came back, helping it make sense.

A marina would have rubber on hand.

"It's just like the ones Uncle Drew ... made for Christmas ... but big enough for *us*," Delia called breathlessly when she got closer. Once they'd exclaimed over it, she pivoted and ran back in the direction from which she'd come.

Gabe watched Charlie, mounted on a tire innertube and positioned before the stretched strip of rubber. Behind him, Drew Mathison and Hickory Graham pulled the rubber and the tube back ... back ... back ...

Gabe could hear them counting down loudly, even from a distance. Three. Two. One. *Release.*

Charlie and his tube shot down the smooth, snowy slope of the towpath, gliding onto the cleared section of thick ice, where he seemed, if anything, to gain speed. From there, his objective was clear because, at the end of a thirty-yard slick of ice were six large, cork buoys balanced like bowling pins. Rosie and Emily were positioned several feet from the buoys, applauding the boy's bullet-like progress.

His roar of delight echoed around the lake as he and his tube sent the buoys flying and came to a stop in a poof of snow. Apparently, the snow cleared off the ice had been plowed into a backstop that did its job admirably. Charlie was laughing as he pulled the tube out of the snow and moved to help his mom and aunt right the buoys again.

"My turn! My turn!" Delia was already exclaiming.

Gabe and Keith weren't close enough yet to hear what Hickory was telling her as the men prepared the slingshot. She had her own tube, it seemed.

Charlie was trudging back up through the snow, rather than on the ice, for traction, but it was a long walk back to the towpath from that far out on the lake. The children would sleep well tonight.

"So, you haven't told him yet?" Gabe asked as he and Keith crossed the little bridge cleared over the canal.

Keith sniffed against the cold and rubbed his glove under his nose. "Not yet. Rosie wants me to pray about it more."

"What's she think? About the whole moving to Columbus business?"

Keith shrugged. "Nothing's been decided."

The power had returned to the island the night before, and the windows of Hickory's home and the little barge house glowed with lamplight now. The laughter and exclamations grew clearer once they'd made it to the towpath. Fascinated, Gabe watched little Delia's braids under her hat flying behind her as she and her tube rocketed toward the buoys, her buckled boots leading the way.

"I wanted to give him my old ball mitt, you know?" Keith was saying. Gabe tried to orient himself to that. Nothing about this pseudo-sledding scene seemed remotely baseball like. But he supposed the old baseball glove was all Keith had here at the inn, probably dug up in the shed from boyhood summers of his own. "I think he likes baseball."

"You came!" Charlie exclaimed now that he'd climbed back up onto the little strip of island and the men were closer. He ran up and hugged Gabe first. Then waved to Keith. "Did you see me? Watch! I'm going again now. Watch, Gabe!"

"Now that you two are here, I can finally take a turn," Drew said cheerfully as he positioned Charlie's innertube again.

"Use Delia's tube, okay?" Charlie told him. The little girl was lugging her own back through the snow over the ice, but she was slowing down in the deep, white powder.

"I haven't laughed this hard in years," Hickory was saying as he grabbed the strip of rubber not far off the ground. Gabe admired how strong and agile the old man was. That was his *great*-grandson on that tube, and Hickory seemed to have nearly equal boyish energy.

Still, the pulling back of the band looked a bit demanding.

"We can take over on slingshot duty, sure," Gabe said, laughing with them as they released Charlie and his tube spun in a dizzying circle down the groove of snow the rings had carved over the towpath to the lake. The boy howled with delight. He left two "pins" standing on that run.

Gabe watched the Graham sisters across the distance haul the buoys back into place, laughing themselves, especially when Emily's feet shot out from under her, and she knocked two of them back down again as she fell.

"You okay?" Drew shouted in his booming voice across the distance. Her response was a mittened thumbs-up after Rosie righted her like one of the buoys.

It didn't take long to learn the ropes of the slingshot crew. Delia insisted on another ride so Gabe and Keith could watch her "close up." Then Charlie had to go again because Delia had knocked every pin down on her turn, and he was not to be outdone.

Gabe noticed Keith watching the boy with unmistakable pride, which made Gabe uneasy.

He thought of the relationship Keith had with Camden, his own father. Gabe knew better than anyone that Camden's affections for his only son were mixed up in ego and ambition. In fact, Gabe had long been convinced Camden had only picked him up and propelled him forward in the business to inspire Keith to try harder.

Camden Fairchild was a good man, but he believed strongly in competition in all things.

Over the years, Gabe was very aware of the strain between the Fairchild men. Keith tried hard to win his father's approval, and it almost worked. Sometimes.

Now Gabe wondered: what kind of father would Keith be to Charlie? Could he imagine another way?

Charlie and Delia relinquished their tubes to the overgrown boys. Charlie's cheeks were red, his eyes bright, his hat sitting lopsided on his sandy hair. A father should be proud of him every day, no matter what. Not because he'd scored highest on a test or won a bigger trophy or closed a property deal.

"Get ready to be amazed, Dear!" This was a bellow from Drew Mathison, eager to claim Delia's tube, calling across the ice to his wife.

Emily cupped her gloves around her mouth and shouted something in return that got lost across the distance.

"Assume your posts, men."

Keith rolled his eyes and Gabe laughed as they pulled back on the thick rubber.

"More." Drew pushed his tube back into it with a grunt. "A little more."

"Grow up, Mathison."

"You first!"

They released the slingshot, which had a very different feel with a full-grown man's weight against it. Still, the officer made good time down the hill. When he came up on his target and the tube was too far right, he simply flung his body out of the center and rolled into the buoys with whole-body exuberance, sending them flying.

"Wanna see the igloo we built yesterday?" Charlie was back, tugging on Gabe's scarf.

"Definitely." Keith inserted himself with too much enthusiasm, sending a less-than-subtle look Gabe's way that begged him not to tag along. Gabe understood the kid's preference for him probably wasn't sitting well now that Keith knew Charlie was his "boy."

Still, it wasn't Gabe's fault he'd been the one to acknowledge the kid's existence from the beginning of the storm that had trapped them all.

"You go ahead. I'll ... I think I'll take a go at this slingshot."

Keith stayed long enough to help Hickory pull back the band. Drew had just finished setting the buoys back up (apparently, unlike the children, the women had left him to his own devices) when Gabe was launched atop Charlie's tube down the hill. The chill of the wind stole his breath a little, but he still managed to laugh as the donut spun and hissed wildly across the thick ice.

In the end, he had to settle for five of the six buoys falling.

"Nothing to be ashamed of, Adams." Drew reached down to pull him out of the tube and the drifted backstop. "We can't all be winners."

"He stayed on the sled," Emily pointed out, already setting the buoys back up.

"Nothing in the rules about that."

"It's on page fifty-two of *The Graham Guide to Winter Body Bowling*," Rosie said, eyes sparkling. "Or was it page fifty-six?"

Gabe still hadn't caught his breath, and it was because of her, not the cold. He simply stood and drank her in, the colors of her. Her red-gold hair peeked in and out of a thick, lined hat with ear flaps anchored by yellow and purple pom-poms that dangled below her chin. She was wrapped in a scarf made of an entirely different palette, and she managed to be adorable in what looked like one of her granddad's long work coats.

Maybe it wasn't just the colors, though. It was also knowing what her mouth tasted like.

He had missed her intensely.

"How are you, Gabe?" she asked, studying him right back. "What have you been doing now that your holiday vacation has finally started?"

"I'm well, thanks. Helped some of the fellas repair the bridge back to the road yesterday. How are you?"

"Wonderful."

They nodded at the same time, smiling at one another.

"Adams, are you staying down here to set up pins?" Emily interrupted from right beside him. "I was thinking of walking back up with Drew to thaw out, but I won't leave unless you'll assist the Body Bowling Referee here."

"Go. I'm happy to help." Having Rosie Graham all to himself on the middle of an icy lake? It sounded bizarre but, also, like everything he wanted from life just now.

As soon as the newlyweds began trudging back toward the towpath, Delia came shooting down the ice lane as if on cue.

Even as she did, Gabe took in the change in perspective being on the ice gave him. The canal entrance was easy to see from here, even with all the snow. He could follow the shape of the lake's bank, the inn looking cheerful and inviting up the slope, lights on in many windows now, as well. Smoke still puffed from the chimney.

Rosie followed his gaze as they moved to set up Delia's buoys. "Wish I had time to paint it from out here."

"It's different. Helps you see the real shape of things."

"We don't go past the turn there." Rosie nodded in the direction past the canal entrance, then bent to pick up another buoy. "I mean, we don't go past there when the lake is frozen. You never want to trust the ice below that other side of the inn because a warm spring runs off from the west bank and makes channels of moving water. The ice can be eight inches thick everywhere around it and less than an inch thick right there."

"There are two spots like that in the lake," Delia joined in with a lecturing tone. "Uncle Drew says a boy drowneded near Picnic Point 'cause of that. That's one spot. And the other's over there."

"I'll try hard to avoid it." The forbidden area seemed far from anywhere an innertube slingshot would take them. "Thank you, ladies."

Delia snorted, mumbled "ladies," and set off through the snow back toward the island.

Rosie squinted across the ice to see if anyone was queuing up.

"You've got to be cold," Gabe observed. "How long have you been out here?"

"I'm bundled better than my sister." She smiled at him. "Are you enjoying the wonders of electricity once more?"

"Oh, certainly. Thrilling games of chess now by bulb instead of flame."

"How is Dottie? I haven't seen her."

"She left for home yesterday. Smokey was able to take her, and your aunt and uncle, back more safely once we shored up that side of the bridge."

"I see. And Dottie is doing ... well?"

"She seems to be." Why did she want to talk about Dot? "I hear the phone lines are going to be up again within the week, so then you can check on her yourself."

"Mmmm." She chewed on her lip and watched as her son returned to the slingshot for another go.

~~~~~

Rosie tried to determine if Gabe Adams of the perfect eyelashes and delicious jaw stubble had become engaged to her dear friend.

Wouldn't he have said so? She pondered the possibilities as Charlie crashed into the buoys and the three of them worked together to set them back up again.

"Grandpa says he's getting out the motorbikes, Gabe! You can ride them right on top of the ice and go *so fast*. You gotta stay!" With that, Charlie grabbed his tube and struggled back through the snow. Rosie grimly considered that her son had latched onto yet another man, as he had with Drew Mathison.

At least he chose the good ones.

If Gabe had given Dottie the ring he'd packed and she'd said yes, surely Rosie and Emily would have heard about it. Dottie would have come rolling down the hill to them like a human snowball with a diamond ring headlight flashing her news.

Or would she?

Their friend hadn't seemed as excited as Rosie would have thought when she'd talked about her reasons for saying yes to marriage.

If he *had* given her the ring and she'd said yes, wouldn't he also be feeling remarkably guilty long about now for the kiss they'd shared on Christmas Eve? So guilty that he wouldn't be standing so close to her, out here on the frozen lake, studying her in that way he did that she wished she didn't like so much?

The truth was that she'd missed him. Rather desperately. It had never mattered to whom he'd belonged or would eventually belong ... on some level, there was simply some sense of connection there. Now she appreciated how a person missed that magic once they'd been close to it.

It made her want to dismantle at least one layer of formality she'd put between them for Dottie's sake.

"So. Did Keith tell you?" she asked, casting off the polite distance and pinning him with the most personal thing she could think of. What was more personal than her son?

He nodded slowly.

"Well?"

"Well?"

"What did he tell you?" She huffed a bit. *Men.* "What are *your* thoughts?"

"I know you told him the truth about Charlie, and now the two of you are deciding what comes next."

"And are you ... I mean, do you still think it was the right thing?"

Gabe studied his boot. "Why does it matter what I think?"

"Gabe."

He looked up again, and Rosie wanted more than anything to read what was behind his eyes. There was a lot there. A lot of *what*, though?

"It will be 1947 pretty soon," he said simply, disorienting her even more. The change of topic confirmed that distance between them was still necessary, probably because of Dottie.

"Yes. Well." He annoyed her as much as he intrigued her, but still she said, "Happy New Year."

"What do you think the year ahead holds for you, Rosie?"

"I suppose I can only hope."

A cheerful call up on the strip of the towpath drew their attention, and there was Keith Fairchild, waving to them as he settled in for his first turn in the slingshot. Drew and Hickory were pulling the band back. He would be beside them in seconds.

Rosie couldn't help but sigh.

"Don't rush into anything," Gabe said, low, so low she almost didn't hear him.

Rosie was looking at him, but he was deliberately avoiding her gaze when the cork pins went flying into the air.

~~~~~

An hour later, Rosie was still preoccupied with what he'd said to her just before Keith had joined them on the ice and stayed. No amount of encouragement on her part could get Keith to trudge back up for another go at the slingshot, so eventually Gabe had looked pained and wandered away himself.

Maybe she'd misunderstood what he'd said.

Keith had been howling with the fun of flying down that snowy hill toward them, after all. Maybe Gabe had said something entirely different than what she'd heard.

She had not misunderstood, though.

He'd clearly said, "Don't rush into anything."

Did he mean telling Keith about Charlie? Because she'd already done that, and he knew she'd already done that.

Now she worked the knife over the potatoes Emily had just scrubbed, reducing them to bite-sized pieces for beef stew. Warm stew had been a terrific excuse to come indoors, away from the new game out on the ice involving motorbikes with chains on the wheels for traction.

Rosie had admitted to her sister that the ice racing made her nervous. She was certain Charlie was going to accelerate into someone's ice shanty or just wipe out and break his little body.

She'd sent up a prayer, though, and reminded herself that folks had been racing motorbikes around on the frozen lake for as long as there had been gasoline and motors. She'd grown up doing it herself.

Rosie couldn't help but admit the fact everyone had been doing it so long did *not* add logic to it, though.

Through the window, she saw Gabe Adams taking his turn, his face creased in laughter as he revved the loud toy. His thick hat flew off in a cloud of snow when he shot forward.

He was afraid she'd what... marry Keith?

They'd been talking about Keith just before he'd asked her what the year would hold and cautioned her not to rush into anything. What else could it be but marriage?

She wondered why he thought she would even consider it. Why, too, was he *opposed* to it? Hadn't he assured her Keith was a man to be trusted? Not that she wanted to marry Charlie's father, no matter how trustworthy his friend said he was these days.

Unfortunately, for the one-thousand-and-sixth time, she was mentally in Gabe's arms again. She could conjure up his scent and his warmth by closing her eyes. Had he been doing the same in the week since then?

If he did think about it, did he also worry Keith had convinced her to spend her life with *him*?

"I'm not the cook you are," Emily said, "but even I know slicing vegetables with your eyes closed is inviting trouble."

Rosie sighed and focused.

"Unless, of course, the goal is to cut your hand again."

"Hardly," Rosie mumbled. She'd applied a fresh bandage when they'd come in and she'd washed. This was a small, tidy wrap compared to the initial triage job from the inn. She supposed the stitches would need to come out soon.

Emily cheerfully attacked a carrot with the peeler. "I just wonder which of the rich men in your life you'd choose to come stitch it up for you this time."

Rosie glanced up, remembering why she needed to stay alert when her sister was around. "Shows what you know. It was Smokey who stitched it up the first time, and I wouldn't choose 'rich' as his leading characteristic." She transported the cutting board over to the roasting pan and guided the potato cubes in with the side of her knife.

"Well, that's up for debate, since he and his family own everything west of the lake to the Grand Canyon or something," Emily exaggerated. "But I know Gabe Adams played a role in the first aid. You told me as much. And I hear he's quite rich, indeed."

Rosie thought fondly of the role he'd played, holding her against him during the pain, offering her strength when she hadn't any. The memory almost made her disregard her sister's suggestive tone, but Emily's smug expression as Rosie turned from the pot thrust her back into the moment.

"So," she responded with a sigh, grabbing the first peeled carrot. "You suppose I'm in here dreaming up ways to trap a rich man into marriage?"

"Hmmm." Emily snagged a strip of carrot and cracked a bite of it. "When you put it like that, it seems a little out of character, I suppose. I guess you've had your chance before today." She chewed loudly as she peeled another. "Speaking of which, do you think Keith will want to marry you now?"

"He's hinted at it, and I shut that down every chance I get."

"You wouldn't even think about it?"

"No, I wouldn't even think about it."

"Because of what happened ten years ago? I thought you'd forgiven him."

"You're testing me. I *know* you can't be trying to talk me into it."

"Not even a little." Emily rinsed a few peeled carrots and lined them up along the cutting board.

"Well, anyway, I'd hardly consider marrying him when I already said no to Lamb."

"Is Dr. Lamb rich?"

"Does it matter? What's come over you? Since when are you so motivated by money?"

"I'm not. Not for my own sake, anyway. I just think you deserve everything."

Rosie stopped chopping and met Emily's eyes. "I agree I do. And I *have* everything."

Emily waved that away with her knife, swallowing her carrot. "You know what I mean. Maybe I'm devil's advocate here, but if you marry Keith, the pair of you could adopt Delia and make a cozy, little home."

"Big home."

"A cozy, big home."

"A cold, big home filled with over-priced furniture and pale walls and weird echoes."

Emily snorted. "Glad to see you're true to yourself."

A motorcycle hummed by near the tip of the towpath, and Rosie glanced out the window.

Emily followed her gaze. "I noticed you steered the conversation tidily away from the *other* rich man in question."

"You are steering every aspect of this conversation, Em, clearly."

"You know who I mean, though." Another loud bite of raw carrot punctuated Emily's impish grin.

"Gabe?" Rosie slid the carrots she'd managed to cut into the pot on top of the potatoes and meat. Then she muscled the roaster into the oven. "You can't possibly be rooting for him, no matter how mercenary you've become."

"Why wouldn't I be? Want me to top your coffee off?"

"Please." Rosie pressed her shoulders back and stretched her neck. "Anyway, you wouldn't be rooting for him because of the resort, maybe? Hasn't he been your nemesis since last summer?"

"Then he'd have been yours, too." Emily managed to shrug and pour without spilling a drop. "I still don't love that whole resort plan, but I don't think it's going to happen, anyway. Not with me keeping everyone stirred up over the zoning and the book you and Lamb put out. The bog will be protected by the government any day now." The sisters wordlessly agreed to slide into chairs at the small kitchen table. "I didn't bother getting to know Gabe before, and that was a mistake."

"I don't know why you would have bothered at any point."

"Well, there's that business about keeping your enemies closer." Emily sipped. "Only, I don't think he's my enemy, now that I tried getting closer."

She had Rosie's attention now. "What are you talking about? How have you managed to get 'close' to Gabe Adams in the past few days?"

"I went over to the Liebs bridge with Drew when they were working on it. He asked me to keep the park office warm and the coffee brewing so they could take breaks. Anyway, Gabe broke through some of the ice at the base of the bridge when they were shoring things up, and his feet and legs got soaked."

Rosie blinked. Why hadn't she heard about this? It was dangerous getting wet in this cold.

Also, why *would* she have heard about it? He was nothing to her.

"I dried his socks over the stove, which, you might imagine, gave us a bit of time to chat."

Rosie could see it all too well. Emily loved to talk to people. She asked questions shamelessly, with that mix of confidence and curiosity that won people over enough to relax and tell her more than they'd intended.

Then Rosie thought of her own talks with Gabe, and she felt envious of her sister for having surely drawn him out in detail. There was so much about him that Rosie still didn't know, which made it even stranger that she was so wildly attracted.

At any rate, the wave of envy felt foreign to her, and she didn't like it any more than she did the attraction. She gulped hot coffee, trying to drown her own insecurity.

God had given her gifts, too—different gifts than He'd given Emily, that was all. Curiosity helped her move past it. "So? What did you discover about him while his socks dried?"

"It's unfortunate, really," Emily said with a dramatic sigh. "It turns out, I like him enormously."

"He's a good man."

"Did you know he's the main financial support for his parents and their church down in the Hocking Hills?"

"He just came out and *said* that?" That didn't sound like him.

"Oh, not by a longshot. I had to niggle and prod." Emily was clearly pleased with herself. "He takes his financial obligation to the work they do seriously, which has fueled his business ambitions for years. It put the plan for the resort in perspective for me, I guess. Shows you can't make assumptions."

"You make assumptions all the time."

"Don't we all?"

"No. Yes. You're right." Rosie drew a deep breath. "Did he say anything about Dottie?"

"About Dottie? No, actually." Emily seemed to contemplate that for a moment. "It occurs to me I didn't direct the conversation there, like the dope I am lately. I tell you, a couple of weeks off the job, and I fall apart."

"You don't seem to be falling apart."

Emily winked. "You know whom he *did* want to talk about an awful lot? Without me asking?"

Rosie felt her cheeks heat. "Hmm?"

"You."

Now her heart heated, too, inside her rib cage, and the warmth spread. "What did he say?"

"Admit you *care* what he said, and I'll tell you."

Rosie didn't always like her sister. "I'll admit I care what he said."

"Why do you care?"

Rosie reminded herself she, in fact, loved her sister. She did not want bad things to happen to her. No way. There was no way, for example, she would ever imagine reaching over to the counter, picking up the knife she'd used to chop the vegetables ... "We got to be sort of ... friends. You know. Over Christmas."

"Friends, huh?" Emily studied her sister over the rim of her mug as she sipped. Rosie got even more uncomfortable when Emily sat back in her chair and grinned. "I admit, I never saw this coming. It's delicious."

"Stop it."

"I was distracted by getting married and getting snowed in with my own dreamboat," Emily continued. "That's probably why I never imagined you falling for Gabe Adams. Dr. Lamb ... it seemed likely. I was a little surprised when you turned him down, to be honest. Keith Fairchild ... well, it happened once, and with that history, I guess I wouldn't have been shocked if you slipped back into love with him again ..."

"I was never in love with him. I know that now."

"... but Gabe? I didn't see that coming at all. Not at first. With his fancy clothes and his business acumen and ten layers of polish."

"Emily. You don't know what you're talking about."

"Don't I? *Then* I end up discovering he turns out to be this salt-of-the-earth sort of fellow, underneath all that. Decent and faithful and devoted right down to his bones. I can see the attraction." She sipped again, shook her head. "But I still didn't suspect anything until he asked me if you'd been able to get back into your studio and work yet."

"That seems like a perfectly reasonable question." *Disappointingly so.*

"I agree. But on the heels of that, he asked me if you were taking care of your hand and keeping your stitches dry. Followed by wanting to know whether you like dogs."

"He did not."

"Sure did. And, from there, he wanted to know when your birthday was. What you like to eat when you're not snowed in. What kind of hours your studio on the boardwalk demands of you. Whether you're most happy working in the darkroom or with glass. 'Has she ever accidentally burned herself on the glass work?' he asked." Now Emily was laughing, which, combined with a sense of giddiness, made Rosie crack a smile along with her. "The man's got it bad."

Rosie drew a shaky breath and felt the giddiness pool with a sinking sensation into her stomach. "Em, he brought a ring with him."

"What?"

"He packed a ring when he came out to the inn for Christmas. For *Dottie*. He's going to propose to her."

Emily blinked, adjusting. "No, he's not."

"They've been going out. He bought a diamond ring and brought it out here for the holidays." Rosie desperately wanted her sister to tell her there were a dozen other reasons he might have done this. She'd be willing to latch onto almost anything. "Admit it. Gabe and Dottie make the perfect couple."

"But he didn't mention Dottie to me once."

"He did bring a ring."

"Well, he didn't *give* it to her."

"He didn't?" Hope had the sinking sensation in her stomach getting lighter again, converting back to something sparkly. "How do you know?"

"He would have said so, you big goof," Emily said dismissively.

"Because you and he are such great friends?"

"He told me a lot of things, Miss Know-it-all." Emily glanced out the window when the motorbike shot in a blur across the ice again. "Besides, Dottie would have told us. No way she'd have just taken off for her place without telling us she was engaged."

That was so true. Rosie had thought the same thing. There was no way Dottie wouldn't have rushed to share the news with them, regardless of how much snow had fallen.

"Dottie was expecting it, though. The proposal," Rosie pointed out. "She's the one who told me he'd brought the ring, because Margo told her."

"How tacky of Margo."

"That's beside the point. If he didn't propose, then that means Dottie is probably very disappointed."

"That's too bad," Emily agreed somberly. The sisters were quiet for a time. "Do you think she loves him? I got the feeling she was kind of dazzled by him, but that's about it."

"I don't think she loves him, no."

"Then how disappointed can she be?"

"She had quite a vision for turning the north shore into Vegas, side by side with him."

Emily shuddered. "Heaven forbid."

"That's the picture she painted. It was kind of ... sad, really."

"I'm not sure Dottie can separate any emotion from her amusement park. Though I'm one to talk. None of us are cut out for a fairy tale, I guess."

"Yet, you still fell head-over-heels in love," Rosie said with contentment. She adored her sister with Drew Mathison, and if Emily didn't recognize it as a sort of fairy tale, it was only because she was too clumsy to see herself starring in one.

"Fact is, you've fallen head-over-heels, too," Emily countered.

It was a little like aiming at her sister with a rock in a slingshot and having her catch the missile and over-hand throw it right back.

After all, Rosie knew Emily wasn't wrong about any of it, and she counted that as one more extremely irritating thing about falling in love.

Chapter Twenty-Seven

Dinner had been rowdy, marked by chapped cheeks and general hilarity. There was not one spoonful of beef stew left at the end of it, either.

While everyone pitched in on cleanup, Rosie slipped upstairs to her little studio space to continue tidying things up. She needed to draw. She needed the quiet of the gabled room and the familiarity of who she was in that space, of who she was in *any* space.

The tarp was still at the stairway with another nailed in place on the hall ceiling, but the air remained cold up on the second floor. Her escape time here would need to continue to be in small segments.

Yet, she figured she was comfortable enough with the lights on and a small coal stove she kept in the corner. The house, after all, was drafty in the best times. She'd made a pilgrimage to her chilly bedroom and layered up: an old pair of her granny's long underwear, a pair of wool work pants she'd rescued years ago from Hickory's cast-offs, now speckled with paint, a flannel shirt, a knit cardigan sweater, a scarf, and her flappy-eared winter cap.

Perfectly comfortable, indeed.

She finished the costume off with a pair of gloves from which she'd removed the fingertips.

Downstairs, she could hear the happy hum of laughter and conversation. There was still a little time until midnight, until 1946 became 1947, but there was an expectant energy that seemed to always come with the new year. She could hear that energy.

Though she loved those people downstairs more than anything—certainly, more than her artwork—she was content just now to listen from a floor away.

She began with the sketch paper that must have blown around in some kind of blizzard cyclone through the hole in the roof just around the corner of the hallway. Carefully cut and haphazardly torn sheets she'd tacked to the wall had fallen like their own layer of snow, revealing the whimsy of vine charcoal images.

Her first thoughts. Ideas she didn't want to lose.

Rosie was careful with them, each line and smudge a new beginning that took her back to the moment the little stub of charcoal had met paper. Everything before the blizzard seemed somehow alien now, like long-ago memories rather than recent concerns. She paused over one, in which she'd sketched her own arms around two children about the same age: a boy with multiple cowlicks in his hair and a girl with sloppy braids.

Other things had not changed.

"Need any help?"

Rosie looked up, unsurprised to find Gabe taking up most of the door frame.

She'd forgotten to close that door when she'd returned from her wardrobe layering adventure. That thought had her looking down at herself. What did he see as he stood there regarding her with those eyes that missed nothing?

A colorful hobo of a woman, probably.

One surrounded by two easels, a drawing table, several trunks stacked on top of one another, and a hundred odd things acquired through the years: dried hydrangea blooms, piles of books, slate roof tiles, notebooks and portfolios, a rusted school bell, a bicycle tire in the process of becoming a mobile, a saxophone she'd been painting, and the storm of ripped pages still littering the floor.

One shelf held a little wooden fishing bobber with hooks for feet.

"Um." That didn't sound very smart.

Rosie wished wildly that she was another kind of woman. That she was more like Dottie, with her pretty curls always tidily arranged in a bun. Dottie would never be caught dead dressed like a scarecrow.

He wanted to know if he could help her?

"I don't know," she said stupidly. She didn't know *what*? If she needed him?

He was unbearably appealing, in his cable knit, soft gray sweater and with all that kindness that worked together to make up the features of his face.

"Rosie," was all he said. Nothing else. She had undoubtedly rendered him speechless, with her get-up and her mess. Just as speechless as she had rendered herself, in fact.

Don't rush into anything. That's what he'd told her earlier.

Don't marry her, she wanted to tell him, in exchange.

Don't settle for building a resort with a tidy woman who understands the intricacies of business economics when you could have love.

As though he'd heard her, Gabe moved from the door jamb toward her. Rosie made sure to meet him halfway, flinging the small stack of sketches back to the floor a heartbeat before her lips met his, which happened another heartbeat before they were in each other's arms.

He tasted a little like the honeyed biscuits she'd made to go with the stew, a taste she explored with a kind of greed that surprised her.

Rosie had never seen herself as powerful. Nurturing, yes. Capable, for sure. Imaginative, always. Power was nothing she had ever considered.

Until now. Until she realized she could make this man's heart pound inside his chest. Her good hand snaked up between them and felt the hammering there at his sternum. Such a rush of power. Her fingers journeyed toward the echo of his pulse in the hollow of his throat, where the skin was tender and hot to the touch.

"Rosie," he said again, this time as barely more than a breath against her jaw.

~~~~~

Gabe wasn't certain what exactly she was wearing, but it felt like it might be six to eight separate layers of clothing.

It somehow seemed like it wasn't nearly enough.

"I came up to check the canvas over the ..." he tried to say, but there were her lips again. He'd needed a breath, one long breath, but the woman was focused. She vibrated in his arms.

He held her tightly there, like someone or something might whisk her away if she weren't plastered against him. He loved the scent of her, something fresh and floral now mingled with the scent of wool and moth balls. Her lips felt like his own lips, like some kind of missing puzzle piece, like he'd known his whole life how they'd feel and taste ...

Somehow, he had backed her up until they met the resistance of stacked canvases propped against the wall.

He felt her breath fast against his ear. "You're not what I expected," he heard her whisper, and he wasn't sure from her tone if she felt that was a good or bad thing.

"Neither are you." He couldn't say what he meant either, but it was true. She surprised him in every moment. A woman so delectable also managing to be not just a mother to a great kid but to be a *great* mother to a great kid. A perfect face, surrounded by the most ridiculous pom-pom bedecked hat he'd ever seen.

He pulled the hat off her head, sunk his fingers into her soft, bright hair.

He'd missed her hair.

Everything about her was bright. Everything about her fit with everything plain brown about him.

Gabe imagined, as he dove into another kiss, living right here with her. What it might be like to have the right to embrace her any time, to wake her up with coffee in bed, to sit with her by the fire every evening. To carry her back to bed when she got tired. She'd probably laugh about it, but he'd make the gesture, for sure. Valentine's dinner and Easter egg hunts and backyard barbecues and harvest hayrides and carved turkeys and all the holidays they *hadn't* done together yet.

But mostly, all the ordinary days in between.

They flashed before him so clearly as he moved his lips off hers to catch his breath, and he could hardly help himself when, cradling her head in his hands, he whispered, with all his heart, "Marry me."

She blinked.

Then, like dominoes falling, her blue eyes cleared, and then her face hardened, and then her whole body stiffened.

Then she shoved him away.

"Rosie," he said for the half-dozenth time in this little studio. He reached for her, but she slipped out of his grasp and away from him.

"I think you ..." she said, breathing hard. She pressed the heel of her hand to her forehead, her narrow shoulders moving with that heavy breath. It occurred to Gabe that passion had become anger, suddenly. "I think you should go now."

Yes, it was anger.

"No, please. I'm sorry." He searched back over the moments before. What had he been *thinking*? He'd gotten it all out of order. "Oh, man. Rosie. I'm real sorry. Please talk to me."

Her eyes, so dreamy and magical before, flashed hard at him now. "I know about the ring," she said, her voice shaking.

It was Gabe's turn to blink and attempt to process. The ring? What ring? He'd stupidly blurted "marry me," yes, but he hadn't said anything about a ring. "What ring?"

"The ring you packed in your trunk to propose to my best friend," she said, visibly trying to control the shaking that had spread all over her. She hugged her arms against her own chest to clamp down on it, and Gabe was amazed at how much distance she could put between them with just that gesture.

It occurred to him she might be angry not just with him but with both of them.

In his mind, he could see the diamond ring she referred to, buried in his trunk at the inn. He'd forgotten about it since Christmas day, since he'd barely remembered even packing the thing.

He nodded. "I can't imagine how you know about that, but I can explain." He took a deep breath, wondering if he *could* explain, wondering if there was anything to say that didn't make him look like the worst kind of womanizer.

It was ironic, since he'd never even really been serious about a woman before arriving at this lake.

"I don't think I need you to explain," she said carefully. Her hands moved now to each side of her head, where his own hands had been before, and she pressed as though her head hurt. Almost to herself, he heard her groan the words, "I've been here before."

Now when his heart thumped, it was a beat of anger to match her own. "Wait just a minute. What does *that* mean?"

"How do I manage to be stupid over and over in the same way? I mean I've *been* here before. In a moment of ... of passion. In a moment where a man wants something from me and says, 'marry me' like it's some magic phrase that makes everything okay."

He bit down on his own outrage. She'd been hurt and betrayed. Not by him, but he supposed that didn't matter when emotions were high. "Rosie, be fair. That's not what happened just now."

"Isn't it? Were you going to offer me the ring you bought for Dottie? I'm already a fallen woman, so ..."

"Don't do this. Please don't." He took a step toward her. "You're selling us both short."

"Did you or did you not come here to the lake to ask Dottie to be your wife this Christmas?"

Gabe felt himself falling into an abyss, helpless to grasp hold of anything at all. "I did. Rather."

Rosie gave one short nod. "And I'd *rather* you leave."

"You love to do that. Just shut the whole thing down when it's getting too real."

"You don't know me well enough to make that accusation."

"But you can accuse me not only of courting multiple women but of seducing you just now with lies?"

"Please tell me in what ways that isn't true." She had stepped away now, and she looked small, even bundled in all those layers. Something in Gabe's heart throbbed hard enough to cut through his anger.

"Look, I understand Keith hurt you."

"Let's not talk about that. About him. Please."

"You're the one who opened with it, Rosie. Or did you mean something else when you said you'd been here before and talked about seduction?"

Her cheeks were fire red, and she suddenly looked like she might cry.

Gabe half feared he'd join her.

He understood he'd messed this up rather badly.

"I messed this up," he said out loud, softer now. Horrified, he watched a single tear make a path from the outer corner of her eye and down her cheek. It was happening, the thing he'd feared on the day she'd sliced her hand. Tears. "No, please. Don't cry. No, no. Come here."

Instead, she moved farther away. "I need to be alone, Gabe. Please. I don't cry in front of people."

"You can cry in front of me."

"I don't *want* to." Her chin came up, a tear dripping off it ridiculously.

"You really want me to leave."

"Yes."

"Really?"

Her breath shuddered. "Yes."

"Answer one question for me first." He could tell by her expression that she was afraid he'd ask her for forever again. "Are you planning to marry Keith? *Please* say no."

"What?"

"Please don't marry him, Rosie."

"I don't understand. Is that why you asked me just now?" She looked genuinely curious. A line formed between her brows as another lone tear tracked from the same eye as before. This time she swiped at it, the gesture one of annoyance. "What are you afraid of?"

"I'm afraid of you feeling trapped by what everyone else expects. I'm afraid of you not loving and being loved like you should be. I'm afraid of you withering up and not doing the things you love and not taking in lonely children and not ... dressing like that." He gestured toward her body. Frustrated, Gabe moved toward the door. Then he turned back. "Look, I brought a ring. I had a half-baked plan to marry Dot, and I suppose she might have thought about marrying me, too. But then I met you. And I never loved her, any more than she loves me."

Rosie stared at him. He couldn't read her face now.

"And I do *not* seduce women." Angry all over again, and a little embarrassed, Gabe went out to check the tarp over the hole in the hall ceiling to make sure no more cold air would get inside.

~~~~~

The tarp was holding. It was nearly midnight, and the Graham family had ventured outside. Gabe used their exit to bundle up and quietly slip away himself.

He was halfway across the footbridge from the towpath back to Liebs Island when the fireworks had him stopping and turning back.

Down on the dock that stretched out from Emily's little barge house, the figures of Hickory, Delia, and little Charlie were silhouetted against some kind of torch they were using to send off another explosion of sparks high above, these green and white.

As the sky popped and lit, Gabe also saw Keith standing near his son.

Drew and Emily appeared to be snuggled in an embrace on their doorstep.

Rosie, he noted, had just appeared wrapped in a quilt on her own porch, watching the fireworks just as he was. Or as he had been before he'd noticed her. He watched as another explosion, this one red, melted light over her hair and the patterns of the quilt. He hoped she wasn't still crying. He hoped she was warm enough.

He hoped Keith didn't win her in the end.

A series of three loud bangs from firecrackers preceded the next flickering canopies of white, gold, and blue. Gabe couldn't seem to move and couldn't seem to look away, not even when the last firework went off to a series of cheers, and he watched Keith walk back up to the house with Charlie. Rosie held the door for them as they went inside.

Just like that, 1947 found Gabe Adams standing on a bridge in the dark and feeling truly alone for the first time in his life.

~~~~~

Since the roads weren't clear enough to get the supplies needed to fix the roof of the Graham home correctly, Rosie was growing increasingly used to sleeping on a couch. She'd become accustomed to Delia's soft snoring and Charlie's breathing, as well as to falling into exhausted sleep staring into the fire.

This night, though — the first night of a fresh, new year — she lay on the couch looking not at the fire but, instead, up the slope of the marina property to the Fairchild Island Inn. A few lights were always on there, now that the power was back on, casting a warm glow against the distant stone walls.

It had been a little more than a decade since she'd last watched those lights and imagined a future, leading her now to wonder when she'd stop the cycle of falling for a man at that inn.

Would she be doomed over and over to long nights wondering if he were awake up there, if one of those lights were his?

If he were thinking of her.

Repositioning her spine over a couch spring, Rosie decided she was tired of herself and of her thoughts.

Still, that irritation did not stop her from wondering about Gabe Adams and what he was like at two in the morning. Did he wear tailored silk pajamas or something more practical to bed? Did his choice of nightclothes reflect his humble beginning or the wealth of the man he'd become?

Did he really want to *marry* her?

Also, what was *wrong* with her, anyway?

She thrashed around beneath her quilt, physically cringing from the memory of being in her studio today with Gabe, of all that had happened there.

"Mommy?" Charlie's sleepy voice came from the mattress near the fire.

"What is it, Charlie?" she whispered into the darkness.

"Are you okay? I heard a ... a growl."

"I'm sorry. I didn't mean to wake you. Go back to sleep."

"Nothing is eating you, then?"

He'd been spending too much time with Delia. "No, sweetie." *Not physically, anyway.* "Just having trouble getting comfortable. Go back to sleep."

His breathing announced he'd followed those instructions promptly.

Wasn't this just terrific? Rosie was accidentally *growling* now, and even that truth didn't seem to diminish the mortification of her time with Gabe.

She might never be able to work in her studio again. Her place of solace and creativity no longer existed. The space would now only remind her that she had participated fully in something tender, only to abruptly make it into something ugly.

The tender part had been a joint project, but she'd definitely handled the ugly all by herself.

Then, for extra fun, she had reflexively blamed the whole thing on a decent man. Her face burned in the darkness.

What had come over her? Though she'd said she'd "been there" before, the fact was the embrace with Gabe had been nothing like any prior experience.

Ten years ago, in the boathouse with Keith, she'd clung to the promises he was making. Promises of security and happily ever after, travel and adventures, children, and a home of her own. Tonight, though, had been different. Scarier. Tonight, she'd clung to a promise that seemed to come from her very soul and get all entangled in Gabe's. A promise of partnership.

Then she'd ruined it. She'd been profoundly unfair.

She owed Gabe Adams an apology. Perhaps several.

The cuckoo clock in the kitchen announced three a.m. Through gritty eyes, Rosie noted all the same lights on up at the inn.

Gabe wasn't going to marry Dottie. Nor did he want Rosie to marry Keith.

Was he serious when he'd breathlessly asked—no, told—her to marry him today? What if it hadn't been some kind of lie for him, to talk her into doing something she knew she shouldn't? What if his logic had simply crumbled and they both had seen what he really wanted now?

What if what he wanted really *was* forever?

She was too weary to tell herself, as her eyelids slid closed, not to build what her grandmother had called castles in the sky.

Rosie's last thought before sleep claimed her was of what it would be like to share both the best and hardest parts of life ... yard work, babies, budgets, flat tires, illness, private jokes, back pain, hand holding late at night ... with Gabe Adams.

What if he'd had those same things in mind? Had he actually known what he'd been asking for?

Chapter Twenty-Eight

On New Year's Day, Gabe stood in the parlor of the inn, fists on his hips, and decided it was time to get back to work.

He had meetings set up with investors, contractors, and hotel managers. Unlike the power, however, the phone lines were not up and running.

He needed to get back to Columbus.

His head ached from lack of sleep, and he was sick of his own thoughts. Whenever that happened, his father had always told him it was time to set his hands to something.

He decided to take down the haphazard Christmas tree, a process Camden Fairchild watched while smoking a cigar.

"Roads keep drifting over," the older man said, crossing one ankle over the other knee.

Gabe un-strung the popcorn garland, acutely back in the moment he'd sat next to Rosie and the kids on the hearth. Planning to gift the popcorn to the birds, he was careful not to lose a kernel.

"No sense trying to take the car back to the city yet," Camden continued. He drew more smoke in, let it out. "Don't worry about needles on the floor, son. Ruth will sweep them up."

"I'll get them. It's no trouble." Margo had already supervised Ruth's demolition of the rest of the holiday décor immediately after breakfast. Gabe had barely salvaged the soap nativity from the garbage. "I was supposed to meet with Stover and his crew tomorrow. You know, about the dining room renovation at the main hotel."

Another noxious cloud of smoke. "He'll understand. The world's still mostly shut down."

Gabe carried the pile of string and popcorn down the hall to the door, not bothering with a coat as he doubled back to the patio outside the bay window. The snow people in their hats joined a chorus of memories as he spread the popcorn out for the birds.

Ruth could watch those birds enjoy the treat if she ever managed to sit down today with a cup of tea.

Tea made him think of his mama and how she despised any kind of hot drink. Tea tasted like dirt—*suciedad*—and coffee like mud. She would stoop to hot cocoa when given the chance, but their little family hadn't often been given the chance. Which reminded him to ship her a container of cocoa powder when he got back to the city.

Gabe realized he was uncharacteristically homesick.

"Maybe the bus is running," he suggested when he returned to the parlor. Already, a bright red cardinal had found the treat on the little stone wall of the patio.

"Maybe."

Gabe shouldered the now un-ornamented tree and felt a scattering of pine needles slide past his shirt collar and down his back. Camden opened the main door for him, and Gabe set out for the burn pile, where the tree could dry out the rest of the way.

The air was noticeably warmer now, and the thick carpet of blizzard snow was growing damp in the afternoon. Prime snowman-building and snowball-making weather. He wished Charlie and Delia would wander up this way.

"Hey, neighbor."

Gabe glanced toward the hint of roadway to see Drew Mathison tromping by, apparently returning to the marina and towpath from his office here on Liebs Island. He wore a homely scarf in an impossible orange color, no doubt knitted by his bride.

"Hey. What's going on?"

"Not a thing," Drew said with regret. "Just went around to check on things, but it's pretty quiet."

"The roads cleared?"

Drew shook his head. "Some vehicles can make it on the highways, but most of the roads keep drifting over almost as soon as a way is made."

That sounded about right to Gabe, sort of like the way things had been with Rosie Graham all along. Clearing a way just to watch it drift over. He needed to leave here, get some distance, sort his thoughts out, remember who he was, figure out why he couldn't get this lake or these people out of his head.

"What about the bus? Is it running yet?"

"No idea." Drew's eyes tracked over the ice of the lake just before the corner of his mouth twitched. "But let's go find out. C'mon."

"To the bus stop?" It was by the amusement park. Not a short trip.

"We'll take the motorbikes across the lake and check it out. It's practically my job as a lawman out here, isn't it? What do you say, Adams?"

Drew didn't wait for him to answer, and Gabe felt his first moment of hope of the day.

"We'll be back in plenty of time for Rosie's pork roast and sauerkraut," Drew promised after Gabe had grabbed a coat, hat, and gloves. Together, they made their way down toward the marina.

"Wasn't invited."

"I'm inviting you. Unless y'all have something fancy planned at the inn."

"We'll see." In his heart, he hoped he'd pull up to the north shore to find a bus looping back to Columbus. He would jump right on, leaving his trunk and everything about the tease of Buckeye Lake behind.

He didn't think he'd be welcome for New Year's dinner, at any rate. Not after allegedly proposing his way into intimacy with the cook.

Maybe he should talk to her, explain that he wouldn't have done more than kiss her even if she'd said yes to his stupid, thoughtless proposal. He hated that she thought he was that kind of man, that all men were that kind of man.

What had he even been thinking?

Rosie deserved a proper proposal of marriage: asking permission from Hickory, kneeling with a bouquet of flowers, a ring purchased with only her in mind. An opal. Lovely and light and sparkling inside, surrounded by diamonds so she didn't doubt for a second he understood her value. She probably even deserved a verse or two of poetry.

"... finally going to start melting," Drew was saying as they crossed the footbridge to the towpath the man now called home.

Gabe disciplined himself not to look to his right in the hopes of seeing Rosie.

The men had left the motorbikes tied up to the dock like boats on the ice.

"How's life in a canal barge?" Gabe asked, realizing he'd been unusually morose in the face of his new friend's spirit of adventure.

Drew looked up and smiled his rare, full smile. "Good." This prompted him to dash up to the little house that fronted the dock. He stuck his head in the door and conducted a brief conversation. Gabe coiled the ropes up on the dock and waved back when Emily stuck her head and arm out the door.

Minutes later, they were off.

The afternoon before, they'd kept their races near the island because the children were riding, too. Today, though, they were grown men with distance to cover, and Gabe opened up the engine to keep pace with Mathison as they pushed across the frozen lake. He pretended it wasn't the second most enjoyable experience of the past twenty-four hours.

Rosie, close and perfect and completely in tune with him yesterday, was not to be outdone, even by chained tires digging into ice for speed.

They passed ice fishing shanties here and there, most with smoke puffing from their chimney pipes. Some folks would be eating fish for New Year's and for every meal until they were able to make it to town. Were the stores open? Were groceries able to be delivered to those stores yet?

As the men pulled up to the boat ramps at the amusement park, Gabe found himself eager to see what was going on in the world beyond a pretty woman's cut hand, a human slingshot, a tree falling through a roof, and a botched marriage proposal.

He killed the engine and angled the bike up next to Mathison's.

Construction on the new pier had halted, of course, and the rest of the park resembled everything else post-blizzard: snowy shapes only hinting at what was beneath. A roller coaster covered in snow and ice. A merry-go-round, its horses removed to some barn for the winter, sitting so still under all the white.

They clomped up the public docks to the boardwalk, just a deserted path of snow. The candy shops and shooting galleries were boarded up.

Gabe slowed as Mathison made his way to the park office, where a light indicated the only life on this section of the north shore.

Though they hadn't exactly argued, Gabe was not eager to see Dot.

Drew muscled the door open, anyway, and Dot looked up from the *Columbus Dispatch* spread over the counter. "Happy New Year, Dottie," Drew declared.

Gabe noticed her warm smile cooled a degree when she saw him behind Drew. He wished her a Happy New Year, as well, and realized that, while he'd never struggled to talk to women before, he'd been unusually effective lately when it came to making things uncomfortable with them.

"A truck got through at noon from Newark," she told them. "I'd have given my favorite handbag and everything in it for this paper. I've read it twice already."

"What's the word?"

"Turns out, there was a blizzard." She folded the newsprint and winked at them, pushing *The Columbus Evening Dispatch* toward Gabe. "Why don't you take this copy back to Cam and Margo? It will make their day."

"Everyone here in the village come through all right?" Drew asked. "Haven't seen Gunn back at the island since the storm first hit."

"He and the others have been busy digging out. So far everyone's alive. Here, anyway. Thank heavens."

Snagging a striped hard candy from a dish she slid across the counter, Gabe realized again how much she loved the people here. It had to be part of the reason she had plans and lists and sketches spread out around her on the counter. He rolled the newspaper and shoved it down in his coat pocket. "Are the buses running, by any chance?"

"Not yet. Roads keep drifting." She walked around the counter, a fuzzy gray sweater knotted with a matching cord around her waist. "But it's a good sign with the delivery truck making it through. Maybe tomorrow, what with the melting. Wet snow won't drift so much. How'd you two get here, anyway?"

"Bikes."

"Oh, of course. You been racing?"

"We played around yesterday," Drew told her. "Sorry you missed it."

Dot waved that away. "I'd hate to embarrass you by winning."

Drew suddenly moved toward the door again. "While I'm here, I figure I best check in on Cookie and Burt. Give you two a little time together," he said cheerfully. Then he was gone before Gabe and Dot could do little more than flap their surprised mouths at him.

When they turned toward one another, they both shut those mouths.

"He doesn't know," Gabe said lamely.

"Clearly."

"Sorry about that."

"Nothing to be sorry for," Dot said in her usual magnanimous way, but she made a project of crossing back around the front counter and reclaiming her perch. She eyed him. "We probably wouldn't have been terribly happy together, would we have?"

"No, I don't think so. We might be too much alike."

She tilted her head this time. "I don't know about that."

Gabe grinned. "I didn't mean to insult you, ma'am."

She grinned back, and for the first time he thought they could perhaps reclaim the friendship that had only started to grow between them.

"What are you doing stationed here at the counter, anyway?" he asked. "There can't be anyone coming by the park."

She shrugged. "When I live upstairs, coming down here and pretending to work is something to do, you know?" She took a hard candy for herself. "I love these candies."

"Me too." His was melting to a mere pebble on his tongue.

"They taste like being a kid," she said. "So, you're eager to get back to the city?"

"I've got meetings."

"Well, maybe you can't leave town, but you know what you can do?"

"What's that?"

"Make sure my friend, Rosie, knows she has options." She crunched the little candy loudly instead of letting it dissolve.

Gabe blinked and tried to keep up. "Rosie?"

"Before I left, I heard Keith was going to man up to his responsibilities." She rolled her eyes. "I lost some sleep about it last night."

"You don't approve?"

"I like Keith fine. I'm not entirely happy to say I understand him."

She looked down and rubbed at a spot on the counter with her perfect fingernail. When she looked back up, she said, "But I don't approve of him for Rosie."

"I don't know what this has to do with me."

"Really? We're not past that?"

"Dot." He dropped her name like that and found nothing waiting to follow it.

"I'm not saying she came between us in any way. Not at all."

"She didn't."

"I know. I think things would have ended for us sooner or later whether you'd ever known Rosie Graham."

"Yes. I mean, I know. We weren't in love."

"But, the fact is, you *do* know Rosie Graham. And if you and I aren't going to build an empire together at this little middle-of-Ohio lake, then I think I'd settle for seeing my best friend happy."

"You're suggesting I court Rosie." How strange, to get his almost-fiancée's blessing on the very thing he'd come to want most.

"Just make sure she knows she has options," Dot repeated.

~~~~~

He didn't wait for Drew to finish his check-ins. After a quick visit to the bus station to see if a notice was posted (it was not), Gabe drove the motorbike far more slowly back across the frozen lake toward Towpath Island.

A plan was forming. One that had nothing to do with a bus.

As the plan formed, something that had been heavy on his shoulders eased off.

Perhaps Rosie would let him explain what he'd meant during that kiss, when he'd fumbled a spur-of-the-moment proposal. He'd hardly let himself hope for it, but if Dot thought there was a chance ... well, she'd known her friend all her life. Perhaps Rosie would at least consider letting him date her with the intention of marriage. Someday.

He loved her, and there were times he thought she must be at least close to loving him.

Maybe she needed to know him longer than two weeks, was all. Then she'd trust him.

Still, his mind rushed ahead where he'd hardly let it go before. Together, they could adopt Delia if Pastor Skip's calling to the mission field remained unchanged. Gabe would proudly join in parenting Charlie, even as he cheered Keith stepping into his own role as father.

They could stay at the lake where he felt he belonged. Rosie could make all the art she wanted.

As he re-tied the bike to the dock on the towpath, he was mentally calculating his own investments, savings, and even his relationship with the Fairchilds. *This could work.*

The deep snow was even damper as he trudged up to Hickory Graham's house, where the fireplace chimney was puffing welcoming smoke, and the windows spilled warm light in the cloudy afternoon. It occurred to Gabe he needed some of that warmth, that the ride across the ice had chilled his nose and his gloved hands. The house, he imagined, would smell like the pork and sauerkraut Drew had mentioned. Perhaps enhanced by the scent of fresh rolls. His stomach growled.

The remnants of shoveled snow on the porch boards carpeted Gabe's approach to the front door. He raised his gloved fist to knock, but it stilled as he instinctively looked in through the window that made up the top half of the door.

The scene within was nothing less than a Norman Rockwell *Saturday Evening Post* illustration.

Sprawled in front of the fire, Keith and Charlie were building something with an erector set. Gabe was struck by how content his friend looked, how his face glowed as Charlie pieced something together and said something that made his father laugh. Only a few feet away, Rosie and Delia were cuddled up in a quilt. Delia seemed to be asleep, but Rosie was watching the scene between father and son with relaxed, heavy lids, like she might drift off herself at any moment.

Gabe lowered his hand and tried to swallow past the tightness in his throat.

That scene was *not* a Rockwell painting. It was a group of people he cared about enormously, happy together, figuring things out.

In the end, he simply could not imagine disturbing it. He did not fit in it.

Rosie might not welcome him, not after his clumsiness of the night before. Charlie was finally warming up to Keith, it seemed, and what would happen if Gabe inserted himself into the mini construction project on the floor? Could he really rob his friend of that settled, hopeful look? Would he dare wake up Delia?

Push in where he wasn't supposed to?

Sometimes there was a reason a road drifted back over after it had seemed clear.

Weary all over again, trapped, and incapable of returning to the inn, Gabe shuffled off the porch and back down to the dock. Clearly, there was more thinking to be done, but the ache in his stomach where there had been hunger minutes before told him he'd probably already thought too much and too long.

He untied the bike, started its engine again, and hoped he had enough gas to get out to Hickory's ice fishing shanty. If the old man was there, well, he was easy company. There was something healing about staring into a cut circle and looking for things in the shadowy water below.

Hickory, though, was not in the fishing shanty, which Gabe thought might be even better. He preferred solitude. He lit the little stove and lantern. It didn't occur to him to bait a line. Instead, he sat in silence. In the distance, he heard the other bike returning. Drew heading back for his New Year's supper with his cheerful new family.

Gabe reminded himself not to envy.

Gabe also told himself this was the best place to be just now. There were no memories in this fishing shanty, unlike the inn or the Graham residence. He was safe here for a while.

He wouldn't have to watch the only woman he'd ever loved lean into what might actually turn into happily-ever-after with his own friend.

He would just sit out here. A Chicano from an impoverished background, bundled in wool clothing in an ice shanty, despising himself for imagining, over and over, a future with a red-haired artist who lived on an enchanted island.

Chapter Twenty-Nine

Rosie understood why Delia was feeling left out, so she led the sleepy little girl back to the kitchen for a cookie.

Removing herself from the living room for a moment might also help her hold onto her own temper.

"Is Pastor Skip coming for supper?" Delia asked, climbing onto a stool at the end of the counter with a yawn. Outside, the afternoon was gray. Snow-turned-water was dripping from bare tree branches outside the window. This would be a soaking of a thaw.

"I don't know. He's certainly always welcome."

"But I don't have to go back with him, right? I can still stay here with you?"

"You're also always welcome here, if it's fine with him."

"It will be."

Rosie knew Pastor Skip was a good man, but Delia knew as everyone else did that the man saw his purpose as loftier than caring for an orphan. He was talented and inspired and probably right, Rosie knew. Still, she did not like the little girl feeling so keenly unwanted.

Which had been precisely the problem with how this day had gone.

"Oatmeal raisin," Rosie announced, prying the lid off the cookie tin in front of Delia.

"Can I have two?"

"I don't see why not."

Keith had arrived earlier. They had agreed this would be the day they would sit Charlie down and have a talk with him, explaining to him that he had a father, after all. The man had brought Charlie another boyish offering from the attic of the inn: some soldiers. And Charlie had been happy to share his new erector set.

Meanwhile, Keith had made up reasons to remove Delia from the scene. He hadn't understood that Delia liked building things, too, or that she also loved playing "war."

He hadn't understood that Delia was part of the family.

While the little girl munched her cookie dejectedly, Rosie pulled the pork roast out of the oven. She ladled some of the sauerkraut juices back over the top. Soon it would be time to peel potatoes to be mashed.

Idly, she wondered what Keith would think when she made Charlie come back to help peel.

"Can I go up and draw in your studio?" Delia asked, audibly swallowing half a cookie and brushing crumbs into her hand from the counter.

"You sure can. I cleaned the desk off the other night, so you've got all the room you could need to create."

Delia gave a hoot and shot off without another word. Rosie could hear the creak of hinges and the thuds of the little girl taking the wooden stairway in her usual relentless way. Having Delia here was a little like having Emily back under the roof.

Rosie returned to the living room to find Keith giving her a nervous, expectant look.

Dear Lord, I trust this was the right decision, she prayed, swaying wildly between certainty and doubt. Had she really been following His promptings on Christmas, or had she simply been sleep deprived?

Keith rose from the floor and positioned himself on the couch in his most paternal attitude, patting the cushion to indicate Rosie should join him there. He seemed very dependable now, she told herself. There was no reason a boy wouldn't be thrilled to have him as a father. This was a gift she was giving them both.

She forced herself to stop grinding her teeth.

"Charlie, can we talk?" Keith said gently.

Charlie looked up from the building they'd done so far. Rosie made a note somewhere in her mind to trim his hair before school started again. His blue eyes sought his mother's, as though he suddenly felt the change in the room, but he remained on the floor, one of his socks sliding off his heel. Rosie experienced another of those moments in which she loved him so much it hurt.

Then she found Keith also looking at her.

So, this was the way it was to be. She'd be the one to do the hard things. No surprise. She drew a deep breath.

"Charlie ..." He would despise her. There was no way to say this, especially since she couldn't explain to a boy that age the way he should at least despise them both equally. "Charlie, I've always told you God gave us each other as a family, which is true."

"And families look lots of different ways. I know," he said, repeating the words she'd so often said to both him and Delia.

"Well, your family is about to look different again, sweet boy." She swallowed. "Because Keith here ... he's your dad."

Rosie knew all her son's expressions very well, waiting while the vertical crease formed between his brows. He shifted his gaze to the man beside her on the couch, who was squeezing his own hands together in an attitude of white-knuckled prayer.

"Keith?"

"Yes," Keith said calmly. "I am."

"Like you're, you're marrying my mom now and becoming my dad?"

"We are not getting married, no," Rosie inserted quickly.

"Not yet, anyway," Keith said, and she resisted the urge to punch him. She had been quite clear about this.

"We knew each other a long time ago," Rosie said, the explanation sounding lame even to her own ears. "But Keith didn't know he was your dad until he met you now. And he's very proud to learn he has a son like you, Charlie. He wants to spend more time with you."

Keith nodded with nearly his whole body.

Charlie got up, yanking his sock back on. Not understanding the details of how people became parents was making this so much more complicated for him, Rosie knew, but how could it be helped? Charlie was studying Keith. Hard.

"How do you know you're my dad?"

"Your mom told me. And you ... you look like me, don't you think?"

More studying.

"Look, Charlie, please understand that what your mom said is right. I'm so proud to learn I have a son like you. It's been the best Christmas present I ever got, to tell you the truth. And I promise that, if you're okay with getting to know me, I'll be the best dad to you I can. Starting right away."

"That's why you brought me your ball glove. And the soldiers. And the money."

"The money?" Rosie blurted.

"Just a little New Year's Eve gift," Keith said. "I should have been giving you gifts and opportunities all this time, Charlie, and I'd like to from now on." The line appeared between Charlie's eyebrows again, but Keith pressed on. "I'd like to take you riding on an airplane. Maybe to see the Yankees play. Would you like that?"

"Uh."

"Or a train. Have you ever been on a train? And there's a really great academy near my house in Columbus. That's a fancy word for a special kind of school, and you could learn so much there."

"Keith," Rosie said.

Charlie's brows shot up in panic. He took a step back.

"You knew all this?" he said suddenly to Rosie, and she knew she'd never forget the betrayal in his eyes.

The three of them talked at once, then.

"Charlie, you don't have to go anywhere ..."

"No, I didn't mean ..."

"I don't want to go to a new school!"

Then, gasping as though he'd already run a mile, Charlie stabbed his stocking feet into his boots by the door and ran out, yelling, "You lied to me!"

The door slammed, rattling the glass.

Rosie's sigh was shaky as it left her lungs. "That did not go well."

"I'm sorry. I shouldn't have said anything about the school. I got carried away." Keith rose, rubbing his hand over the back of his neck. "Should we go after him?"

"He'll just run over to Emily's and cry, and she'll burn him some toast and let him beat her at checkers." Rosie ached, inside and outside.

"He didn't even put a coat on."

"Em and Drew will bring him back bundled in five layers for supper."

Then they heard the motorbike firing up again.

The look they shared united them in concern for the first time as parents.

~~~~

Stillness and silence were the magic of a frozen lake. Within the shanty, Gabe scrubbed at his eyes, determined not to engage in self-pity. He had so much to be thankful for, after all.

Loneliness was a choice, he told himself. He could change some things, now that he knew what he wanted.

For the second time, he heard the hum of one of Hickory's old motorbikes, but this time it was getting louder, like it was headed his way. Drew must have decided to ride out and drag him back for New Year's pork. Gabe was concocting an elaborate excuse about needing to help Ruth with something at the inn when the engine stopped, and the shanty's door swung open.

Little Charlie Graham, face beet red, ears all but frozen, flung himself inside, failing to close the door again against the cold.

"Charlie! Where's your coat?"

The kid's teeth were chattering hard as he made a brief survey of the hooks near the stove. "C-c-came to get my f-fishing knife." There was a wild wetness in his eyes as he picked up a little canvas sack and shoved the knife in.

"Sit there by the fire a minute," Gabe said, shrugging out of his own coat and wrapping it around the boy's narrow shoulders.

Charlie seemed to debate, but then shoved his arms into the sleeves. He had to haul half the length up over his hands to reclaim the canvas sack. "C-can't stay. Runnnning away."

"You're running away." Gabe calmly relatched the little door to hold in what heat he could. "To where?"

"Don't know." He shuddered, made a sound like a sob, and jammed an old woven blanket into the sack with determination.

"Can I ask why?"

"She l-lied to m-me," he said, and this time it was obvious he was crying, which seemed to make him even more angry.

"Who did?"

"Mom." He hiccupped.

"Will you let me make you a hot pot of coffee to warm you before you head out, at least?"

"N-no. No. I've gotta run away. They're gonna m-make me g-go to a rich school." He heaved in a breath and shouldered the sack. For the first time, he met Gabe's eyes. "Keith. He's my *dad*."

"Oh." Gabe blinked. How had the happy scene he'd witnessed in the living room culminated in this? What did he say to this "new" information? "You don't want him to be your dad?"

"He just *is*," Charlie hissed. "I'm n-not letting him t-take me away, though."

"Listen. I'm sure he's not planning to take you anywhere."

"They think I'm stupid. Like I'm some little k-kid," he said, and then he surprised Gabe by moving fast to the door.

"Charlie, where do you think you're running to on this lake? It doesn't *go* anywhere. Trust me, I'd have tried to get out of here myself if it did."

"The old canal does," he called, and then he was gone.

Gabe slipped on the ice trying to reach for the door before Charlie slammed it shut. As he pulled himself up, the bike outside roared to life again.

Over the course of a split second, Gabe thought of the old Ohio & Erie Canal system, wondered where the remains of it would even take a boy. Through Millersport's village? And then where?

Rising, Gabe knew Charlie would access the cut of the canal remnants over beyond the towpath ... below the inn ... on the hill ...

"Charlie! *No!*"

There was a spot there, wasn't there? Wasn't that what Rosie had told him? A spot where a warm spring dumped into the lake, and the ice was thin.

Alarm had Gabe's blood running so cold that he didn't notice how painful it was to be sliding, gloveless and coatless, toward the motorbike he'd brought out here himself. Bellowing the kid's name, he finally made it to his own bike, never taking his eyes off the weaving path the little boy was taking toward the northern tip of the island.

He couldn't yell anymore over the roar of the engine once he had it going, his lungs spasming from the cold air at a speed he'd never attempted. The chains dug into the ice again, spraying bits of it into a fog around him, and he could just make out the same cloud of spraying ice far ahead.

In the distance, to his left, he spotted figures scrambling to the end of the island, as if they could head Charlie off in his course. He could make out Drew leading the way. Rosie's bright coat, a blur. Hickory and Emily, their mouths and bodies giving the vague impression of yelling across the distance.

Gabe had run away, as a boy. To the rocks in the hills, where he could be alone.

Did Charlie know where the canal went? Would he even make it there?

No.

Just as Gabe had known it would, just as all of them had worried it would when Charlie had angled the bike that way, the ice thinned and thinned as the subtly warmer-than-freezing water moved beneath it. The boy was angling to turn toward the canal when there was a snap, a crack as a sound rather than a shape.

Yet, the shape was no crack. Instead, it was a hole.

A thousand cracks shattering to make room for a motorbike and its small rider.

The sudden change from two motors to one gave the effect of deafening silence.

Gabe kept his grip tight for speed, not slowing for a second, calling Charlie's name again and again until it was a chant.

~~~~~

Rosie knew Charlie had taken off on a motorbike, of course, but now, wrapping her coat around her as she ran, she tried to figure out who was on the second bike. Drew and Hickory were running alongside her. Keith was somewhere behind, also calling for Charlie.

Her son had a coat on now, she noticed, though he was barely a blur out on the frozen lake. She'd had no idea the bikes even went that fast, and he was so small on it. She called him like the others, her dress gathered in fists high above her boots. A few yards behind Charlie, the other motorbike seemed to be giving determined chase.

Drew and Emily came running out of the barge house.

"What's going on?"

"Charlie!"

"The ice is thin that way," Drew boomed, and he took off in a sprint that looked like flying over top of the snow on the towpath. He waved his arms wildly, as though he might dissuade his nephew, who was hunkered down over the handles in preparation for the turn into the canal.

Rosie, breathless, somehow stayed close behind Drew. *No, no, no. God, please. No.* It was the only prayer she had.

The ice seemed to vibrate. Then, as though it were something she'd known would happen all her life, she watched as the motorbike and her son seemed to up-end and slide fast down below the smooth ice. Swallowed whole. A strange silence.

Rosie's lungs seemed to deflate. A scream froze in her throat.

In slow motion, she watched the second rider launch himself off the second bike at an insane speed. The bike spun off, wheels still spinning, in the opposite direction as Gabe Adams's body—coatless, exposed—rolled and then slid purposefully toward the same broken, gaping part of the ice. He was yelling something. Drew was yelling something, too, using a blade from his pocket to cut down the thick rope that hung from the bare maple tree.

It was the rope Charlie would be swinging from, out over the water, just a few months from now.

Rosie didn't know if she moved or was moved by someone else, but she got closer, too. She could clearly see Charlie's gasping face surface for such a short time, and then down he went again. It was like a nightmare in which her feet were weighed down, only they really were by the deep snow. Rosie thought she might have stumbled, must have stumbled, and got a mouth full of that snow.

As she scrambled back up, she saw Gabe Adams turn his sliding from the bike into a purposeful dive at that same spot where Charlie's head was, Gabe suddenly engulfed by the same water.

There was tremendous splashing.

Rosie went from screaming to being unable to breathe.

Drew was sliding, too, on his belly, rope in hand, ten yards from the gaping hole. He twisted, torso rising. With a lasso-like motion, he sent the rope in the direction of the hole where the splashing had calmed nearly as quickly as it had begun.

"Charlie!" Rosie tried to scream once more, but her throat had closed. *Gabe, get him. God, guard them both. Please.*

Chapter Thirty

Gabe felt a warmth in his belly.

Soft blankets, heat.

No, the warmth wasn't in his belly. It was *on* his belly.

It was too hot, and his arms should have pushed it away, would have pushed it away, but they didn't obey. He wouldn't mind curling around the heat, only a vague impulse as he slipped away again.

The next time he became aware of it, the warmth was closer to his chest, and this time his hand made the journey to push at it. It was *too* warm. Some kind of fleecy, hot thing, like a ... creature? No, a toasty sack of some kind. He wondered, through a fog, how he would escape it.

"He moved his hand," he heard a small voice whisper.

"Did he?"

"Look, yeah. He moved his hand to the hot pad. Does this mean he might not die?" Ah, *Delia*. Gabe remembered this voice clearly, which he suddenly thought was a good sign, because the word "die" made him wonder. Recognizing a voice had to be good, surely. *He was not dead.*

"Why don't you go ask Ruth to boil the water now? We'll see if we can get him to take some hot tea."

Gabe did not open his eyes, but this was Rosie talking, so he held still. He felt her warm palm against his face, and he was afraid it wouldn't stay there if she thought he was awake.

He must be in the inn. Something about it smelled like the inn. There was the familiar scent of burning wood from the fireplace, but a voice he did not recognize suddenly entered the mix.

"Yes, heating him up from the inside is just as important as heating his outsides," the strange voice said. A doctor? It sounded like something a doctor would say. "We just warm him. That's it. Little by little."

Rosie's hand slid away, after all, but somehow Gabe knew that hand was critical to his survival, so he tried to say her name. He was surprised by how strange his lips felt, though.

"Gabe?" Her breath was near him, and he finally blinked open his eyes because he needed to see her.

"There you are," she said approvingly, and he felt a strange pride at making his own lids obey. Her hand was back, caressing his jaw now. Her sharp, clear eyes were ringed in smudges and shadows, like she'd been crying.

"Charlie," he managed to say. Or enough of a version of it that she responded.

"He's fine, Gabe. He's just fine."

He tried to talk to her again, but he didn't know what he was saying, and he was pretty sure she didn't either.

He wanted to tell her he'd seen her face there in the freezing water. Not only her face. He'd seen himself with her, known all over again why he needed to be at Buckeye Lake for the rest of his life. Instead of telling her this, though, he simply made a sound.

"Will you please try to stay awake for a few minutes to sip some tea for me?"

He would do anything for her.

"I need to thank you," she said, and it sounded like she started to choke. "I don't even know how. How to thank you for saving my son, I mean."

Charlie would be fine. Gabe let his eyelids slide closed again, snuggling into her warm hand.

"Please stay awake just a little while, darling." When he felt the heat of her lips against his temple, it was easy to open his eyes again. She'd used an endearment, and the warmth in her voice was better than the fire and the hot pad. "Here comes the tea."

Gabe knew Ruth was saying something, and the doctor was, too, but he couldn't seem to make himself understand. Somewhere, Camden Fairchild was insisting on a hospital.

Gabe was vaguely aware that it was Rosie who raised his head in the crook of her elbow, and she spoke gentle words as she helped him sip the hot, flavorless water.

"I want to stay," he managed to say when the heat of the tea opened his throat.

"Ignore Mr. Fairchild. You don't need to go to the hospital." *That wasn't what he'd meant.* She nestled him closer and tipped the cup against his lips. "You're going to be fine here."

~~~~~

After serving as her blizzard fortress, the Fairchild Island Inn felt something like a second home to Rosie.

Here she was once more, this time keeping vigil over the man who had charmed her and flustered her in the nearby window seat in the nights leading up to Christmas. It was night now, again, and the enormous fireplace crackled its soft song as the now familiar clock struck a late hour.

Gabe had slept for many hours after she'd all but dumped the hot tea down his throat and applied the heating pad to his core, heating and reheating it until even his arms and legs began to feel warm to the touch. Charlie, who had fared much better, had been settled in at their own house a few hours before.

Rosie had assured her son he would not be leaving Towpath Island for any trip or any school until he absolutely wanted to. Once he'd eaten heartily and slipped into a peaceful sleep, Rosie had stared up at the inn through the window for exactly two minutes before she groaned, donned her boots and coat once more, and decided to trudge back up the hill. She'd lived the equivalent of three lifetimes today alone.

"I'll be back for breakfast," she'd told Hickory, who had smiled as she pulled the door softly closed.

Returning to the inn, Rosie had come face to face with Margo Fairchild, who had been standing in her robe at the window as though waiting for her. A glance had assured Rosie that Gabe still slept beside the fire.

"How is he?" she'd asked.

"More tired than anything," the older woman said with an affectionate glance of her own. It occurred to Rosie, not for the first time, how much Gabe Adams seemed to mean to Keith's family.

Now Margo looked directly at Rosie, and Rosie was struck by the fact the woman's pale eyes were wet. So many walls felt suddenly stripped away after this day and at this hour.

"Are ... you all right?" Rosie asked her.

"Charlie," she said, her voice soft. "How is he?"

"Asleep and feeling fine. Otherwise, I'd never have ventured up here."

"Of course you wouldn't have." Margo had stared at the floorboards then. "You've done a good job with him."

Astonished, Rosie had swallowed and managed to nod. "Thank you for that."

"Keith told me." She sounded weary. "He told me what happened, why Charlie ran off. He felt bad."

Rosie wondered how Margo felt about Keith feeling any emotion like guilt. "Keith didn't do anything terribly wrong," she offered. "He just got ahead of everything, that's all. He had a vision and just tried to bring a little boy in on it too fast."

"That's broad-minded of you. My son doesn't always think things through," Margo offered wryly, meeting Rosie's eyes again. "Clearly."

Rosie grinned. "My son doesn't either. Clearly."

They shared a soft laugh and, at the end of it, Margo had reached for Rosie's hand in the soft light from the fire.

"Thank you," she said, and her grip squeezed a little. Rosie blinked and raised an eyebrow in question. "For offering us the chance to get to know Charlie. You didn't have to. I want you to know that I ... I understand that. After what happened today, knowing he might have been lost before we even got to know him ... Well, I wanted to thank you for giving us a chance."

Surprised, Rosie had watched the woman head off to bed, leaving her standing in the parlor with the ticking clock. She'd settled in by the fire, next to Gabe, wondering all over again what would come of her decision to tell Keith about their son. The sense of rightness remained, but she whispered another prayer about it. Then she'd begun to pray for Gabe to heal completely beneath his mountain of blankets.

After an hour had passed, she had thoroughly and unashamedly memorized the face of this man she loved. His nose seemed divinely chiseled, no less so than the similarly perfect indentation just over his top lip. A day of beard was back again, so strangely familiar and masculine, balancing out his impossibly long, dark lashes.

"My, but you're beautiful," she murmured, and she meant it. As an artist, she felt she was qualified to make the declaration.

The lashes blinked open again, and there was more *Gabe* in the dark eyes that opened than there had been earlier. She sat very still while he blinked a few times more, never looking anywhere but at her.

"Hi," he said gruffly, followed by the ghost of a cough.

"Hi. How do you feel?"

He drew a long breath and moved for the first time, apparently testing his arms and legs. He cleared his throat. "What time is it?" All was dark around them, save for a few large lanterns and the nearby fire. "Where ... is everyone?"

"It's very late. They've all gone off to bed for a bit."

"Rosie." The corner of his mouth quirked. "Have a care for your reputation. Sounds like you've gone to some lengths to get me alone." He coughed softly again and slowly rose up on his elbow.

"Not too fast." She watched him move around a little more. "Would you like some pillows for propping?"

"Very much."

She crossed to the sofa — her former bed — and pulled two embroidered pillows off. "You never answered me. How do you feel?"

"Strange," he said, after she'd wedged first one and then the other pillow beneath his torso and neck. "Cold, somehow. Like I'll never get warm. Otherwise, not bad."

Rosie nodded, sitting back down across from him on the edge of the mattress, her knees pulled up to her chest. "What do you remember?"

"Charlie. Is he really fine? Don't I remember you saying he's fine?"

"He's doing much better than you are," she said with a grin.

"That's as it should be. Even though I'm doing great, I promise. Did he finish running away once he was fished out?"

"I think he needs his rest before striking out on his own again. And he's out a motor bike, I guess." Rosie let her eyes close, comfortable with Gabe in a way she wasn't with anyone else. Behind her lids, she saw it all, all over again.

Her whole heart breaking away and sinking into the cold black.

"Hey, now. Are *you* all right?"

"Definitely." Boldly, she reached down and took hold of his fingers, which felt nearly as warm as her own now. The doctor said it would take a few hours for his body temperature to return to normal. "Do you remember it all? I mean, being in the water?"

He took a deep breath, letting his head settle into the pillow. "I remember sliding in, the shock of it. Grabbing Charlie. I remember Mathison in the distance. The rope. But that's all, I think. I suppose I owe the man my life."

"You owe no one a single thing, Gabe." She raised his fingers to her cheek. "You somehow managed to toss Charlie right up to that rope and helped him grab on. He was in the water for mere moments." She stopped to try to get her voice to stop shaking. "And then … then I thought we'd lost you."

He squeezed her hand, pulling it in turn to his own lips and smiling over her knuckles. "I do recall quite a lot of chilly water, now that you mention it."

"It's not a joke. You *sank*. You could have died."

He rubbed the pad of his thumb tenderly over the stitched thread knots still lining her injured palm. "But you've nursed me back to health. Thank you." His eyes were full of light. She'd been so afraid of not seeing that light again.

Gabe looked like he wanted to say more but stopped.

"What?"

"What *what*?" He grinned.

"What were you about to say?"

"Nothing. That I've missed you, I suppose."

"You suppose."

"I have. Missed you."

"Gabe." Rosie swallowed what little pride she had left where he was concerned. She wondered if they'd ever be on the same page. Well, beyond when they kissed. "Listen. I'm sorry about the other night. About what I said."

He shook his head, managed to clutch her other hand now too. "No, no. Please don't take responsibility for that scene, sweetheart." She watched his Adam's apple bob on his throat's caramel skin. "I messed that all up so badly."

"Maybe we both did. We got carried away." She tested that with him, to see his take on that level of attraction. Hoped he couldn't read her well enough to know how willing she'd be to repeat that part of it in the future.

"Some people," he said softly, "must be drawn like magnets to each other. That's all I can figure."

And some people must not be, Rosie thought, contemplating his split from Dot and her own complete indifference to Keith. So inconvenient.

Ah, what a mess they'd all made of a blizzard.

Gabe yawned, and Rosie looked beyond the lights in his eyes to the fatigue in them. They were a little sunken from his exertions under the ice. *Thank You, Lord, for giving me such good gifts to begin with,* she prayed. *And for giving them back to me all over again today.*

"You'd better sleep," she said out loud.

"I wish you could stay." His words were beginning to slur.

She wished she could stay, too. The doctor had said body heat was the best way to rewarm a hypothermia victim, but the residents of the inn had acknowledged there was no appropriate scenario for that treatment. That's when Rosie had heated the rice-filled pad over the stove, all the while regretting that Gabe Adams was not hers to warm as she saw fit.

"Ruth is just down the hall, and Camden has been in to check on you about every half hour." Seeing him slipping into slumber already, Rosie carefully removed one of the pillows from behind him. "Can I get you anything before I leave?"

He said something she didn't understand, but it sounded content enough. She decided to make herself happy, as well, and dropped a barely-there kiss on his forehead.

Boots fastened and wrapped in her hooded coat, Rosie turned back for one more glimpse of Gabe alive and well. One more prayer of praise. His eyes were closed, but as she slipped out the door, she thought she heard him mumble something else. Something that sounded like, "I love you."

Chapter Thirty-One

The new year remained heavy with low clouds, which contributed to Rosie sleeping much, much longer than she typically did the following day. The fact she'd managed to sleep late on a sofa in the middle of the family room when two children had apparently been up and around for hours helped her feel less guilty about it.

She supposed she must have needed the sleep to have accomplished it at all.

Still, it took time for her to move from under the heavy quilt and thermal blanket that weighed her down into the cushions. She yawned and stretched but remained there, listening to the sounds of the house around her. There was the hum of the furnace, which she'd never take for granted again. In the back, from the kitchen, came the soft sound of a muted record. Harry James, she thought, accompanied by the scrape of wood on cast iron. She smelled maple syrup. Heard Delia giggle and snort.

Rosie smiled.

Hickory had made his famous French toast and fried up some bacon, if her nose had it right. Soft footsteps and the scent of her son she'd recognized on some basic level since the day he'd been born completed the feeling of contentment she'd already started thanking the Lord for when he pounced on her.

"Good morning," he said, clambering across the quilt toward her head.

"Good morning. How are you today, sir?" She opened the covers so he could burrow in with her, and she hugged him tightly. He was warm, thank heaven. His hair smelled like syrup, so she and her pillow would end up sticky, but even that filled her heart with joy. She ran her hands down his arms, startled all over again by how small he still was.

"I'm good. There's French toast. We tried to wait, but you weren't waking up. Hickory said to let you sleep."

"Looks like half the day's gone. Sorry about that."

Charlie shrugged. "I don't care."

"You're not itching to go out for another swim today?"

He giggled. "I guess I can wait 'til things thaw a little."

She planted a loud, hard kiss on the back of his head. "Do you want to talk about anything, Charlie-kins? I mean from yesterday?"

He was quiet for a long moment. "You said I don't have to go anywhere. And you meant that?"

"I would never say something like that unless I meant it. Your place is here with me for as long as you want it to be."

"Does Keith ... does my father ... know that?"

"Yes. He doesn't want to upset your life. He just wants to add to it, you know?"

"I guess."

Rosie told herself it was a testimony to the way she'd raised him that he hadn't yet calculated or cared about just how wealthy his father's family was. Charlie still counted riches in worms dug out of the mud for bait and hours running on the boardwalk at the park with his friends.

"I'm sorry this is so hard for you."

"I'm okay, Mom."

She gave him another squeeze.

"Do I call him 'Dad' when I talk to him, then?"

"That's between you and him, I think."

"And you said you aren't gonna marry him?"

"No, I'm not. Is that all right with you?" She wondered if having a dad "counted" in Charlie's ten-year-old mind if his dad and mom were not a couple like other boys' parents.

"That's between you and him, I think," Charlie said, tossing her own words back at her and making her smile.

"You're really something, you know it? I'm glad Gabe and Drew managed to land you like a big, floppy fish from the lake."

"Is Gabe still doing better?"

"He was doing much better when I left the inn, but I thought I'd go over and check again later. Would you like to come with me?"

"Yeah. I think I should say sorry and, also, thanks. And I like Gabe."

"I imagine you do."

"We ran and jumped on a pile of mattresses at the inn. During the blizzard, I mean. He's fun. I kinda want to do that again some time."

"Well, you've got those mattresses over against the wall there you've been sleeping on. What's stopping you now?"

"It's not the same. We need that long, long hallway at the inn. And tons and tons of mattresses."

"Hmmm. I doubt he'll be feeling up to that today." She thought of the sparkle in the man's dark eyes. "Though, I suppose you never know."

Rosie finally stretched and wandered back to the kitchen, leaving the quilt around her shoulders. Once there, she enjoyed letting Hickory wait on her. He, too, wanted to know how Gabe fared during the night, as he brewed fresh coffee and reheated two slices of toast. Delia stood on a stool, helping with dishes, and she called Charlie in to dry. They all talked for some time about the accident.

"Charlie, my boy," his grandfather said, "I'm trying to think how to have you work out the replacement cost of that motorbike you sent to a watery grave."

"Sorry 'bout that. I can polish boats this spring," the boy said.

"Figured you'd do that anyhow." Hickory set the French toast in front of Rosie with a wink. "Naw, Wally up at the bait shop was telling me back in the fall he's got a couple of motorcycles that need work to get running again. I guess if I went and got them from him, you could maybe spend a bit of time learning how to get them running. You too, Delia."

Suds went flying from the sink as the children cheered over the idea.

"Don't get too excited. It'll be a lot of work." He placed a mug beside the toast. "What are your plans today, Rosebud?"

Rosie's mind had been wandering. The urge to return to the inn was strong. She'd wanted to jump off the couch and run straight over upon rising, but a woman needed some dignity. And a bath.

Had Gabe said "I love you" as she'd left? Or had she imagined it? Why, why, *why* was she always wondering what she thought she'd heard him say? Or what he meant by what she *did* hear him say?

"I thought I might bake a pie," she decided suddenly. "To thank Gabe for rescuing my favorite boy."

"If he hadn't pulled you out, they wouldn't have found your body 'til spring," Delia remarked.

Rosie shook her head at Delia, putting a stop to speculation she never wanted to think about. "I think a cherry pie should do it. Everyone likes cherry, don't they?"

~~~~~

She dropped a pie off to Drew and Emily first, tearing up as she thanked Drew for having the wherewithal to see that swinging rope and act so quickly. Charlie had hardly been in the water a minute.

"Job security," he said, waving it off. He challenged Charlie to a round of backgammon.

"I've got to get this other pie up to the inn while it's still warm," Rosie said. "Do you want to play first and meet me up there, Charlie?"

"Yeah! I'll be right up after I beat Uncle Drew."

"Hey, now," Drew said. "Don't forget I'm a hero, not easily beaten."

Emily saw Rosie off by wiggling her eyebrows in Aunt Cookie's suggestive manner. "Be sure to thank him thoroughly, sister dear."

Rosie ignored her but couldn't stop smiling as she crunched over the melting snow, up the incline by the marina, and along the roadside that stretched to the inn. It was just as well Charlie had stayed behind a few minutes for a game. It would give her time to get to the bottom of late-night mumblings that sounded like declarations.

She gave a cheerful knock on the main door, enjoying the scent of cherries and the heat of the pie pan through her mittens.

Ruth opened it, beaming with pleasure at seeing Rosie. "Come in! Oh, you've brought a pie!"

Rosie followed her back to the kitchen, where she placed the pie on the island. The place was quiet. She'd noticed Gabe's makeshift mattress by the fire had been tidied, but then, they'd always done that with the kids' beds during the blizzard in the daytime, as well.

"How is Gabe this afternoon, Ruth?"

Ruth's face fell, and she froze in the act of filling a kettle with water. She sent a searching look at Rosie over her shoulder. "He's well. Didn't he ... say goodbye?"

Rosie's heart stuttered. Her voice was hollow when she asked, "Goodbye?"

"Bus finally made it out here from Columbus. Camden and Margo headed into town with Gabe not an hour ago, and they all hopped on." Apologetically, she added, "Said something about important meetings."

"Ah," Rosie said as calmly as she could, but she turned away toward the high window as if to look out over Liebs Island. Her heart and her head were both thrust back to all those years ago, when out of frustration at no reply from Keith the college co-ed, she'd run up here to the inn, begging Ruth to ask him to respond. "It's very important," she'd insisted to the innkeeper back then, and she'd cried in front of the woman.

Rosie, accepting a cup of black tea from Ruth now, was struck by the sympathy in her eyes this time. They had both changed. Rosie seldom cried now because she didn't have the time, and Ruth had matured and softened in so many ways.

"There you are!"

Rosie jumped at the words, nearly spilling the tea. Keith stood in the kitchen doorway, smiling in his affable way.

"Keith! I ... I guess I assumed you'd left with your family."

"I have family here now, too," he said simply. "And I kept the car with me to take back to the city."

"Ah." Rosie cleared her throat. "Was Gabe well when he left, then?" she asked, trying not to wonder why he'd left without a word of farewell to her. That alone might answer the question she'd had since last night.

There could not have been a groggy declaration of love.

Not if he had just turned around and left. She must have been mistaken.

"He was a little weak but feeling well, otherwise," Ruth offered. "A hearty breakfast set him to rights."

"You brought us a pie," Keith observed happily, and Rosie thought he regarded her with an odd sort of ... pride? That made no sense, though. Had she stumbled into some Hitchcock film? "Ruth," Keith continued, "may I have a few moments with Rosie?"

"Oh. Of course." Ruth looked around uneasily, but then she shuffled out.

Keith moved nearer, and Rosie backed to the edge of the counter, setting her tea down there before she'd ever managed a sip. "What's going on, Keith?"

"How's Charlie today? I thought I'd give him some space this morning."

"He's better, now that he knows he doesn't have to be whisked away into sudden adventures and enrolled in top-notch schools he's never heard of."

Keith managed to look contrite. "I didn't handle it as well as I should have. Sorry again."

Rosie sighed, thinking again of her conversation with Margo the night before. She reached over to pat his arm awkwardly. "I'm not sure there's a good way to handle a thing like this, to be fair. We made some mistakes, both of us, back then and again now. Partly at Charlie's expense."

Then he startled her again by sliding his hand into hers. "That's what I wanted to talk with you about."

"What's that?"

"We need to talk seriously about getting married, Rosie. That's where we should have started."

Rosie pulled her hand away. Fast. "Keith."

"I promised you all those years ago, I know. And I didn't come through."

"To be clear, I'm not expecting you to come through now."

"But you *should* expect that."

"I don't."

"You wanted to get married, Rosie."

"A decade ago." She slid sideways against the counter to put some space between them. With the whole kitchen behind her, she was able to draw a shaky breath. She thought of the girl she'd been all those years ago, the life she'd imagined with him, and it seemed a lifetime had passed since then.

Well, Charlie's lifetime had, she supposed.

"I think the problem is," Keith was saying, pressing the fingertips of both his hands together, "I haven't packaged it quite right."

"*Packaged* it?"

"Just like I didn't package it right with Charlie last night."

"Packaged ... what? A vow to join our lives forever?"

"Yes, that."

Rosie closed her eyes. Anyone would say she was a fool not to consider the benefits of what Keith was tossing out there. He was so rich. She had once wanted him so much. She was half annoyed she couldn't make even a shadow of that matter in her heart. "It's not a business merger, Keith."

He was undaunted and strangely calm. "Be fair. It's not like I've offered you a check." He considered her. "But I can, if that will get you to hear me out."

Was this really happening? She'd come eager to talk about love with a man who had saved her son's life, then disappeared, and she ended up being accosted by the very man she'd wanted to propose to her a decade before.

Rosie sometimes found her life amusing, but today was not one of those times.

"I think Charlie needs a mom and a dad," Keith went on. "I've given it a lot of thought."

"Charlie has a mom and a dad."

"Living together. With him. In a house. You might pretend to be some free-spirit artist, Rosie, but you know the way this is supposed to go."

That hurt. She told herself he could not know the way she'd longed for a traditional family, longed for social acceptance, longed for love. She certainly *did* know the way it was "supposed to go."

"Our son deserves that," Keith went on.

Rosie felt her nostrils flare. "That's the life you're telling yourself will make things easier, but no boy deserves to have his existence uprooted, Keith."

"Rosie ..."

"Or to have to live with a mother and father who do not love one another. I don't see how Charlie remotely deserves such a thing. I've grown pretty used to the way things are, and I've been happy. So, I'm not sure we should be sentenced to a life like that, either, no matter how many mistakes we've made. That is *not* why I told you about Charlie."

She was breathing a little hard, watching Keith chew on the inside of his cheek and consider her. She saw the moment he decided to try another approach and braced herself for it.

"Love?" he asked. "We managed all right a few years ago. I don't see why we couldn't get that love back."

"More than a *few* years ago, and we were kids then. I don't think we've really grown in the same direction since, either."

"You just need to get to know me again, is all."

"I don't think that's it." Rosie blew out a breath. The hurt was still there. "Anyway, you haven't said a single thing about little Delia."

"What about Delia?"

"Delia stays with me almost all the time now, and Pastor Skip may be leaving for a mission journey. More than a brief trip. Keith, Delia is my daughter in all the ways that count."

"She can stay over sometimes." He shrugged, looking confused. "That's fine."

Rosie shook her head, feeling suddenly weary again. She was growing very, very tired of marriage proposals. Especially the ones she didn't want.

Which reminded her ... why had Gabe left without saying anything?

She glanced back over at Keith, who stood there looking strangely patient. It made her wonder how long she'd been standing just a couple of feet from him, daydreaming about his friend. "Did you ... tell Gabe you were going to propose marriage to me, Keith?"

She wondered if "propose" was the right word for what had happened in this room. It felt more like an agenda item.

"I did tell him, yes. Early this morning. I explained how I wanted us to be a family. You, me, Charlie."

Rosie closed her eyes again. Of course, Gabe would have left after that. Just when she needed someone to talk to who would understand why Keith Fairchild's well-intentioned plan would never work. To remind her that there was more than this. To remind her not to rush into anything.

"And what did Gabe say?"

"He asked me if I'd prayed about it."

"Have you?"

"Yes. You'd already asked me to, didn't you?"

"And you asking me to marry you now ... is where you feel led?"

Keith shoved his hands into his trouser pockets. Somehow, in spite of everything, Rosie felt sorry for him. The man really was trying to right a wrong. "I know I'm supposed to be part of Charlie's life. His whole life, for as long as he wants me in it."

"That *is* what I asked you to pray about," she said with a nod. Gently, she added, "I never asked you to offer to marry me, though."

"People do it all the time."

Rosie was fairly certain she'd never read that proverb in the Bible. "People do a lot of things, I guess."

He gave her a pleading look, but he let go of her hand.

She needed to go home.

"I need to go home," she said out loud. "I think we need to schedule a time to sit down and decide how we'll proceed from here, and I think Charlie should be involved in the conversation. But the two of us, marrying? I don't think that's the right thing. I'm sorry, and I don't mean to hurt you, but I can't imagine it feels right to you, either."

Keith nodded so slightly it was barely visible. He looked more tired than disappointed.

"You know, I think you deserve to be really loved." She realized she should start praying for the woman who would feel that way for him, since that woman might also influence Charlie's life one day. Rosie could not hug Keith to soften her refusal, afraid to set them back five minutes in the conversation. Instead, she thought again of another man. The man the woman wanted, rather than the girl. She said, "I think we both deserve to be loved."

Chapter Thirty-Two

In the days that followed, January's temperatures stayed above freezing enough to accomplish more melting of the blizzard snows. Buckeye Lake and the communities on its banks continued the process of digging out, making repairs, and settling back into the sleepy pace of off-season life.

Drew and Hickory repaired the roof of the house.

The school re-opened, and Delia turned her holiday journal in.

The Beacon was scheduled to go to press for the first time since its publisher became Mrs. Mathison, and Emily had emerged from her snowbound honeymoon full of ideas for her paper.

One of those ideas involved Rosie.

"We need photos! Lots of photos!" Emily had declared. "Before the snow all melts, for crying out loud!" She saw it as her responsibility not only to uncover injustice but, also, to document the history of the lake.

She just knew she didn't have the talent or the dark room for what a blizzard required. That was her sister.

So, on Charlie's and Delia's first day back to school, Rosie donned her wool ski suit, which had orange and green blossoms embroidered over its chest pockets. The sun shone on the snow, so she slid on a pair of round sunglasses and a warm, black hat. A pair of thin leather gloves made working with the camera easier.

The drive to the studio was revelatory, a world that seemed almost strange to Rosie, with roof collapses and drifts plowed into twenty-foot mountains all around. Children, too young still for school, had turned one such snow mountain into a toboggan sledding adventure. She kept mental notes on what she'd return to photograph.

Rosie left Hickory's truck on the village side of the amusement park and made her way up to the boardwalk. Only two lights were on in the little buildings that lined it: Dottie's park office, where she knew her friend would be angling to get construction going again on the new pier; and Emily's newspaper office, where her sister would be sorting through AP wires and press releases.

Rosie tapped on the window of each and waved but did not venture in. There were pictures to take, and her beloved Graflex camera had been too long off duty in the studio.

Other women feeling the level of sadness she felt these days might have wept, but Rosie had learned early how to stop the faucet on emotions.

When her grandmother had been dying, she'd come to understand there were times when crying only made things worse. So, she'd learned to manage her tears. Barely a year later, carrying a baby and barred from her school and friends, she practiced the art of it. Ironically, the art of not crying had led nicely into other types of art.

Art teachers, Rosie had found, had not been so fast to judge.

Now, as the world had come back to life, she'd managed to rise each day and dress and cook and create and clean and shovel and laugh with her family. No matter how confused she felt, the faucet nozzle on emotion was firmly turned to "off." She was so good at managing it, after all.

So, that was why, when she saw Gabe Adams shoveling a path to her studio on the boardwalk, Rosie was appalled to feel her eyes fill with tears.

He heard her coming, apparently, and turned with a wave and a smile. Rosie stood frozen in place. He tossed the shovel down, mid-scoop. She was mortified when she sobbed, wondered if she could turn and escape before he could witness whatever was happening with her emotions.

She pocketed her sunglasses. Through the haze of heavy tears, which Rosie tried furiously to wipe away, she saw Gabe rushing to her as best he could over the crunching snow. He was calling something to her which, as usual, she couldn't seem to make out, this time because of her own crying.

The invisible faucet dial that usually obeyed her had snapped off entirely.

Then his arms were around her, and her nose was running directly onto his fancy but warm city coat. He smelled like his aftershave, and she thought she might just let her legs give out to see if his arms were as strong as they felt wrapped around her.

She cried like that, trying to babble an apology, while he simply held tight and stayed silent.

"Well, my goodness!" She heard Dottie calling out from far behind her on the boardwalk. "Is she *crying*? Emily, get out here. She's crying!"

Rosie tried to ignore them. Like a child, she imagined they couldn't see her if she couldn't see them.

"Maybe he shouldn't have left for Columbus without saying goodbye," Emily called loudly, evidently to ensure Gabe heard her over Rosie's sobs, which mingled with laughter now.

She really was being a complete goose, and so were her sister and friend.

"Or she's mad he didn't get the walkway cleared before she got here," Dottie yelled.

Rosie tried to wipe her own nose, mumbling, when she felt Gabe press a hankie into her glove.

"Sweetheart," he said softly, in contrast to her friend's and sister's hollering. She felt his head resting, sideways, on top of her own head. "Please stop apologizing."

"There's ... my nose," she stuttered. "My nose ran all over your coat." She felt his deep, soft laugh beneath her ear.

"A small price to pay, I promise." Then he raised his head. "Go back into your caves, you harpies," he called loudly to their audience. "I've clearly got work to do here."

"See that you get to it."

"*Men.*"

Two doors shut down the boardwalk. Then, there was only mid-morning silence and the little hiccups of Rosie's tears. Mortifying. Knowing she'd have to have his fine coat laundered anyway, she scrubbed her face back and forth over Gabe's chest before raising her head. She could only imagine, once more, the sight she made.

Redheads didn't cry pretty. Not this one, anyway. Self-conscious, she jabbed her round sunglasses back over her eyes and finally looked up.

By contrast, the man looked amazing. He proceeded to draw Rosie's sunglasses right back off.

"I want to see you. I need to just drink you in."

"Gabe." She was embarrassed, but then she supposed he did rather *deserve* the sight of her red, puffy eyes.

"Please understand. I had to know you didn't want Keith," he explained. "I had to give the two of you a chance in case that's the way it was supposed to go."

"Couldn't you have *asked*, you fat head?"

He laughed. Rosie loved his laugh. "He told me how you turned him down. How you said you thought you deserved to be loved. How you both deserved that."

"What of it?" She wanted to punish him, but she thought she was sabotaging that mission by staying firmly nestled in his embrace. Couldn't she have it both ways?

Now there was the flash of his white smile. "What *of* it? Dot and I said the same thing to one another, so I agree with you. I suppose Keith does deserve to be loved. But I know without a doubt you do." He dipped his head and kissed the tip of her undoubtedly red nose. "I know without a doubt you *are.*"

"I'm tired of puzzles, Gabe."

"*I* love you, Rosie."

Her heart flopped in her chest, and she let herself feel what it was to truly belong there in that tight embrace. Afraid she would cry again and as irritated with herself as him, she let her head fall below his chin once more. She released a shuddering sigh, enjoying the patient trek of his gloved hand up and down her back.

"Rosie?"

"Yes?"

"I wonder if you'd show me Cranberry Bog."

That had her lifting her head back up to study him. He was always surprising her. "You want to see the bog?"

"Dot said we can walk right out to it over the ice from the other side of the little lake."

Gabe loved her. She let herself bask in it, and she realized she wanted to show him the bog he'd only ever seen as a hindrance to his plans for a resort. "You mean you've never seen it up close?"

"No. Will you show me?"

"Let me get my camera."

The day had taken a strange turn. Rosie, sunglasses back on, led Gabe in silence back down the boardwalk. She stopped twice to photograph the fantastic, other-worldly shapes of rides covered in snow. The Flying Bat looked like a frozen crib mobile, snow-crusted cars hanging and studded with icicles.

Rosie stopped to photograph parents and young children ice skating on the little lake, an extension off the main part of Buckeye Lake that boasted a beach and, on its other side, Picnic Point. Gabe took her hand when they crossed the footbridge, and Rosie begrudged the gloves that kept their skin so far from meeting.

From Picnic Point, it didn't take long to walk straight out to the bog when the lake was frozen like this. Idly, Rosie wondered if Gabe felt uneasy about ice now, but she didn't ask. She was tired of the past.

Besides, she knew where the ice was thickest.

"What you're not really seeing under all the snow is ten-thousand years of sphagnum moss," she told him as they crunched along to regard the acres of what simply looked like any other island but was Cranberry Bog. "When it all thaws, you need to come out and see what it's like to walk around on a giant sponge."

"I'd like to do that."

She tugged him farther to the bog, remembering he was in love with her, so perhaps she would get to be the one to watch him bounce on it the first time.

There was no wind today, really. A narrow dock, just a shape in the snow, was not normally visible because of all the green growth from the marsh. Rosie stepped up onto it. She turned and took a photo of the view behind them, now able to capture the entire amusement park post-blizzard. Gabe kicked snow off the wooden planks around her as she shot, then drew her down beside him to rest after their walk.

"I don't know why I cried all over you back there," she said, letting her shoulder rest against his. She placed the camera behind them.

"I didn't mind it."

"I didn't entirely understand why you'd just taken off like that. I hadn't let myself feel anything about it over the last couple of days, I guess."

"I needed to be sure, Rosie. I needed to remove myself and give Keith a chance with you," he repeated, "to be sure. It was the hardest thing I've ever done." He reached down and, as though he'd read her mind before, he slid his right glove off his hand. Then he tugged her left glove off and settled her hand inside his own warm palm. "I didn't know if you'd be grateful or angry."

"Try abandoned."

"Not for the first time." He made a sound like a sigh and a groan combined. "Look, I'm sorry. I also ... I had a lot of things to take care of before I could say the things I want to say."

Rosie nodded, wondered. Waited for *the things*.

"You're beautiful, you know."

That made her grin. He was always unexpected. "Thank you, I guess."

"But have I ever said that to you, really? I was so struck by it, from the night you first walked into the inn. The colors of you. Your hair, your eyes, your skin, your lips. You're just lit from within, and it's beautiful. By the firelight. Out here, against a backdrop of sun and white snow." He squeezed her hand. "Keith came to see me when he got back to the city yesterday, and that's when I knew I could really talk to you."

"Is he all right?"

"Yes."

"He's coming back to talk things over next week."

"That's what he told me, as well," Gabe said. "I think he's thinking pretty clearly about what he has to offer to Charlie and what he shouldn't try to offer just yet."

"You were right. He's become a good man."

"Mmm. Still, I think you made the right decision not marrying him."

Rosie laughed and looked up at him. "I assume you do, seeing as you practically *told* me not to marry him days ago."

"Thanks for paying attention."

"I didn't need to be told, though." A bright red cardinal landed on a branch four feet from them, twitched its head sideways to take them in. "What do you think of the bog so far? From what you can see?"

"I'm not going to carve it up, Sweetheart. Your Cranberry Bog is as safe as it can be."

Her heart thudded in a whole different way. Was this another kind of *I love you*? "Tell me."

"I talked to Dot, and I talked to Camden and Keith last night. The resort is going to end up looking different than originally intended." The cardinal flew away, and Gabe went on, nodding to the shoreline directly across from them where a beach still waited for children under that snow. "Smaller."

"FH Resorts is backing down?"

"We're switching plans up. We're all in agreement."

Rosie thought of the elaborate plans she'd seen drawn out in the study at the island inn, remembered Dottie pouring over them, adjusting and planning. "How will it change, though?"

"We went ahead with the purchase of the Berkeleys' land, which satisfied Dot. But I made a case to Camden and Keith about leaving the beach for the community and the bog for generations to come. A smaller resort can stand further east there, see? With the docks stretched longer in that direction. We might need to negotiate a little chunk of space from the property owner to the east, but not much. Dot feels they'll sell that little bit, too."

"She's still investing, though?"

"Smaller. She's got her hands full with the rebuild after the fire that took out the pier last summer. And I honestly think she's tired of fighting her best friends over the bog preservation," he added with a chuckle. "Anyway, I couldn't ask you to marry me while also playing the villain in the story of this marsh."

Rosie snapped her head toward him, somehow managing to feel even lighter. "What's that?"

"You haven't even told me you love me yet, and you don't need to, but I want to be absolutely clear, finally, about what I want from you, Rosie Graham. While we're not locked in a mind-numbing kiss, I mean." He leaned in and gave her a peck, softly and quickly. "Maybe just a tiny kiss. Regardless, I want forever."

"Oh." She blinked. Sighed. Three proposals in a week. Four in six weeks, if she counted Lamb's. Now she smiled. Finally, *this* one managed to make her blood heat and sing, despite the fact her bottom was in the snow. "Well. I do love you, too, Gabe."

Another flash of white smile, and he seemed to mumble "thank you" in the direction of the heavens.

"I loved you even when I thought you wanted to carve up this bog, you know." She leaned toward him, this time, and met his lips with hers. She trailed her fingers along his strong jaw, feeling proprietary now. Could this man really be hers for the taking?

He let her play, let her thumb trace his lower lip before she placed another small kiss on it. "There's more," he told her finally.

"This seems like plenty," Rosie said with her whole heart.

"Then you can let me know when you're ready for the rest." He settled into kissing her back.

"We can come out here and pick cranberries for Thanksgiving," she told him, pulling back and giving in to the giddy fact of this *forever* he spoke of. Just as she'd levered off the flow of most emotion, she'd also managed not to build much in the way of hopes.

Until now.

It still felt daring, somehow, to imagine it. Picking cranberries with him eleven months down the road?

Rosie was feeling reckless, indeed.

He would be here with her eleven months from now, and, God willing, eleven years from now. Eleven grandchildren from now? Anything was possible.

Had he proposed, though? She wasn't sure, and she'd had enough of not being sure.

"Gabe, when you say there's more ..."

"You seemed determined to wait."

"I'm done waiting now."

He threw his head back and laughed, then hauled her into his arms until she was half sprawled over his lap. Rosie grinned, enjoying the feeling of warmth rather than coolness through her ski suit. Gabe tried out this new angle for kissing and enjoyed it for another minute.

"If you'll eventually agree to marry me," he finally said, "I have some other plans in the works."

Rosie's smile grew. "And if I don't agree? What happens to your plans?"

"I'd better put the brakes on them, then, because those plans will make us both very uncomfortable if we're not man and wife."

Now she laughed. "I'm leaning toward agreeing to marry you," she lied. She knew she'd marry him that very day if he wanted to. "But I have some questions."

He nodded. "I do enjoy a good negotiation."

"Remember I'm an artist. You've more experience at negotiating than I do, so I just hope I come out all right." She tried to look worried, but it was hard while grinning.

"You have every advantage, Sweetheart. I assure you. What's your question? Or, I mean, your first question?"

"Where will we live? Not that it affects my answer, mind you. I love you enough to follow you back to the hills of southern Ohio or to the city, but I just need to know."

"You're right. You're not good at getting what you want in a negotiation," Gabe said, laughing. "How about I handle most of the business negotiating when we go to purchase things, eh?"

"Don't care about that."

"Well, I was hoping we could live here at Buckeye Lake if that suits you."

Rosie vibrated with pleasure. "I like that."

"I love it here," he said. "With you."

"I really like that."

"That's one of the plans in the works, actually," he said. "But I wanted to consult with you first. I drew up papers with Camden to purchase the inn."

Rosie blinked. "The Island Inn? You mean to *buy* it?"

"Yes. It's close to your family but with considerably more room than the towpath has available. And it allows me to really make the place into what I want it to be. What do you think?"

"Gracious, Gabe! How much money do you *have*?"

He laughed loud again at that. "Enough to keep you in art supplies. I wondered if maybe we could build a wing onto the inn, past the kitchen?" Rosie's mind flashed images of the memories that kitchen held for them now. "More of a house, you know, so you don't feel like you live in a hotel. But we'd manage the place, of course, in season. I know it's a stretch but ..."

"Oh, yes! It sounds perfect!"

Another grin. "You're nailing this negotiation."

"Or you are." Rosie let her imagination go. Saw herself baking sweet rolls in the mornings and welcoming families from the city for a summer escape. "But wait. What about Ruth?"

"Ruth, of course, would stay. I don't think you want all the care of cleaning and feeding folks when you could be in your studio, love."

Rosie's heart soared. *This was what it was like to be understood.* It gave her goosebumps in all the right ways.

"I think Ruth might enjoy having us right there with her," he continued.

"Yes." Which brought a new vision to Rosie's mind. One of family. She drew in a shaky breath and prayed the next question wouldn't shut down negotiations. "Um." How to ask this one?

"Delia will always have a home with us," he said before she could ask.

Another almost-sob swelled in Rosie's chest, but she swallowed it and embraced him, half fearing she'd hurt him. But he laughed against her neck again, filled with joy, even at being handled a bit roughly.

"I didn't know how to ask it."

"You've been pretty clear about Delia's place in your life," he said, pulling back a little to look down at her. "I adore her, myself. Do you suppose we can re-open the conversation with Pastor Skip about adopting her? I mean, if we're married?"

"I'd like that. I'd like to ask him about that."

"Then, that part is settled," Gabe said with a brisk nod and one more fast kiss. "Next? I assume you know I'll be honored to care for your son, as well, as my own. Even as I respect Keith's important role in Charlie's life, of course."

Rosie sniffled, capable of no more than a nod. She had no more questions.

"I'm afraid the boy will have more fathers than he'd bargained for if you agree, though," he continued with that characteristic twinkle in his eye. "Which reminds me. Are you … I mean, would you be open to having more children at some point, Rosie?"

She laughed. For the first time since she'd felt her life shrink to judgment and loneliness at sixteen, she dug out the dusty longings of her girlish heart. Longings for a home filled with children and filled with love. She sniffled, resisting the urge to wipe her nose on his coat again at such an important moment. "I always rather wanted a large family, in fact. How does that sit with you?"

He beamed. "It's exactly what I've wanted since I left my own large family."

"I can't wait to meet them all."

"They will love you to pieces. Charlie and Delia, too."

"So, you're proposing we get married, run a charming inn on Liebs Island just a stone's throw from all the people I love most, and we raise a big, loud collection of Adams kids to torment the lake area for generations to come?"

"I know it's quite the business plan, Miss Graham, so I understand if you need time to consider. Have I answered all your questions adequately?"

"You said you had plans in the works. I assume the inn was one. Was that it? Did we cover it?"

"Well, there was something else." He looked down, still holding her bare left hand in his right one. He wiggled her ring finger. "I'd like to put a ring on your finger with your permission."

Rosie smiled. "I don't want the ring you hauled out to the lake for my pal Dottie, Adams."

"I wouldn't think of it. That ring would've suited you poorly."

"Silk purse out of sow's ear and all that?"

"Hardly. You deserve something custom made. Before I left this morning, I visited a jeweler. I think it might take a week or so, but I designed a ring especially for you."

She blinked, imagining what it might be. "What's it look like?"

"Is that part of your decision? Do you need the details?" A smile played along the edge of his mouth.

"I definitely don't need them, but I'm curious. I suppose I'll say yes without them."

"You suppose?"

"I'll say yes."

"Opal. Full of fire and color and smooth, perfect white. Like your skin and your hair and your eyes and your whole soul. And then small diamonds, all around it and all around the band."

"Well, my goodness."

"You said you'd say yes."

"Yes, I'll marry you. But not because of any ring."

An hour later, the pair of them walked back across the ice, across the point, across the bridge, and along the boardwalk, different people than they'd been on the walk out. First, of course, there were the tender kisses, the cuddles, and the promise of so much more warmth they'd save for the spring wedding they'd agreed on.

"I feel changed, somehow," Rosie told him out loud. "Like I'm ... I don't know. Settled."

"Me, too. I've felt a tug in my soul since my first trip here, Rosie, but I think I just needed to wait for the right plan. I finally feel peaceful."

"Yes, *peace*. That's a good word for it."

"I know it's been my business for a while now to make money for the growing church my parents started when I was just a baby myself, and I'll always maintain that."

"Of course, you will."

"But now I feel like it's time for my business to be about a home. That's the obedient thing now, the thing I'm supposed to say yes to, and it's feeling like a remarkably easy 'yes,' you know? A home where I can share the wonderful weight of life with you. Where I can love you. A home where Charlie and Delia can continue growing into great, loved kids. It's an easy 'yes.'"

"Easier than some of the Good Lord's plans, for sure."

He squeezed her to his side. "This hasn't been completely easy, either. A little confusing, at times, even."

For Rosie, she thought it felt like God had found a way to give her the things she'd asked for — for Charlie and for Delia — with a great big something special thrown in for herself. She hadn't thought to ask for true love, but it seemed her Creator did, indeed, know how to give good gifts to His children.

Emily and Dottie were waiting for them in the window of the newspaper office as they strolled by, arm in arm. Rosie laughed when she saw their eager faces in the glass, and she drew Gabe to a stop on her way to return the camera to the studio.

The Beacon's door jingled open. "I have five inches on page three to announce an engagement," Emily declared. "He already asked Hickory's permission."

Rosie smiled up at Gabe, as Dottie ran out and pulled the camera's leather strap off Rosie's shoulders.

"Keep smiling just like that, and I'll get the picture. Don't move!"

"I look a wreck," Rosie said, remembering she'd cried hard at the start of all this.

"It's black and white," Emily said. "They won't be able to see how red you are."

"You're perfect," Gabe said softly.

"You didn't have to go to such drastic measures to shut the resort project down, though, Rosie," Dottie said, squinting into the viewfinder. "I mean, this is obviously quite the sacrifice."

They were all laughing hard when she took the photo of the pair of them locked in a kiss. Rosie thought the community would certainly find the image scandalous, indeed.

Epilogue

March 1947
Towpath Island

"It's bad luck to see the bride before the wedding," Drew lectured Gabe, the voice of experience.

Gabe swatted Drew's hands away from straightening his tie. He was trying to get a look at Rosie, whom he knew was just behind the white tent under the maple. He was tired of hearing mumblings from his younger siblings about how lovely she looked in her dress. "She's mine. I deserve to see her, to talk to her. This is stupid."

"Look, I've been given this one job, and I'm taking it seriously. Turn around here. Anyway, it's almost time to start. Settle down, man."

The wedding was to have taken place in the large parlor of the Island Inn, as it was now called. Gabe had dropped the "Fairchild" part of it after he'd signed the paperwork that gave him ownership. This week, the inn was housing his parents and siblings from the Hocking Hills, who were loving the novelty of staying in a fancy hotel, as well as loving the blossoming beauty of spring at Buckeye Lake.

To that end, the early spring day had turned out to be so unexpectedly fine that they'd made an impromptu decision to hold the ceremony on the grassy strip of towpath, surrounded by the water. The trees had early, mint-colored buds, and yellow daffodils already peppered the little stretch of island.

Though Gabe's father would perform the ceremony, Pastor Skip was busy getting everyone in place. The couple had all the paperwork drawn up for Delia's adoption, which would be finalized when they returned from their honeymoon.

Gabe planned to take Rosie to the nicest FH Resort in New York City so she could see the Metropolitan Museum and some shows on Broadway, and from there they'd take a train north to Niagara Falls for a week. Meanwhile, Charlie would have his own adventure visiting Keith and his newfound grandparents at their Columbus home for the first time.

Once Margo had come to know Charlie, she decided she didn't care quite as much what other people thought about his sudden appearance in their lives. As the weeks had gone by, she'd become eager to show him the city she loved.

Keith now took his own turn giving Gabe's tie a tug.

"Why is everyone so preoccupied with the straightness of my tie?" Gabe shrugged into his suitcoat. "I've been dressing myself for years."

"I'm honored to stand up with you today," Keith told him, producing the little rosebud that would decorate Gabe's lapel. Together, they managed to attach it. "You've been like a brother to me."

"Well, I'm glad you're not exactly rid of me, by any means." Gabe smiled.

"That's a fact."

Gratitude had laid the new foundation for this season of friendship: Keith grateful that Gabe would live the life he, himself, had not truly wanted, and Gabe grateful that Keith managed to be so reasonable in his own role as Charlie's father. The fact the two men already understood and loved one another kept an otherwise complex relationship simple for the boy.

Charlie stood nearby, scratching in his own suit.

"It's getting warm, Uncle Drew," he said out of nowhere. "Can we?"

"Not yet," Drew responded.

"Can we what?" Smokey asked, strolling over.

"Can we put the boats in the water this week? *Please*?"

Smokey laughed and crossed his arms in his dress shirt. "I have a very strong feeling we're not done with winter yet, Buddy."

Charlie groaned but forgot the farmer's prediction as soon as he spotted Delia scampering down the grassy side of the canal.

"He's ready for summer," Drew said. "We all are."

"That flower is crooked." Gabe's mother squeezed between the groom and his groomsman. Señora Adams was little, and she had to stretch to fix her son's boutonniere. Gabe found he didn't mind his mother fussing with him like he did his friends. "Your bride is lovely, son of mine."

"That's what everyone keeps saying. I think we need to get started already."

"Patience, patience."

~~~~~

On the other side of the tent, where a soft breeze blew, Rosie let Emily fasten the same color of tiny rose buds to her hair.

"All I'm saying is, I should have heard it from you first," Rosie admonished her, swiping at her eye. Once she'd started crying months ago, it seemed to happen much more easily. "I'm your sister."

"I can't help it my husband is a big blabbermouth," Emily said around a pin in her mouth. "Hold still."

"I'm going to be an aunt," Rosie said out loud, eager to hug Emily all over again. She imagined the joy of being Aunt Rosie, of more and more children crowding the island, and she couldn't stop smiling and dancing in her chair.

"Hold still." Emily worked more, fussing with the blossom until it lay right. "We didn't want to distract from your day, is all."

"Once Drew let it leak to Charlie, you were doomed," Dottie said.

"The day is all the more lovely for it," Rosie insisted. "What better blessing under which to start a marriage, after all? It's the only gift I even needed."

"Well, I'm sure you don't mean that, since I got you those dishes you wanted," Dottie said. "Oh, dear, would you girls look at Delia?"

The child had a dress designed to offset her new mother's gown, both of them a pale, spring pink with little lace overlays in a rose pattern. Instead of puffy little sleeves like the bride's, Delia's was sleeveless but was adorned with a delicate beige sweater ... which was currently being used to cradle ... something muddy.

"Look! Lester the toad survived the blizzard," Delia was yelling as she scrambled over the edge of the canal.

"Was Lester even on the guest list?" Emily called.

"Don't put the sweater back on now, you scamp," Dottie scolded. "You'll ruin your dress even more."

"You look beautiful," Rosie told her daughter. "But I do not want the toad so close to me."

"Um ... speaking of uninvited guests," Dottie said. She pointed to the little footbridge that led from the marina to the towpath. "Who is that?"

A thin woman in her late forties or fifties stood uncertainly at the apex of the bridge wearing a floral dress, a floppy hat, and a pair of travel gloves. A small suitcase, battered, sat at her feet.

Rosie heard Emily suck in a breath behind her.

Goosebumps rose on her own arms, though the spring sun was out in full. There was something familiar, after all, about the way the woman stood, one hip shot slightly to the side. Legs anyone could tell were long and strong even under the floral print of the dress, identical to the legs that were otherwise trademarks of the Graham sisters of Towpath Island. Long legs, short torso. A dancer's body.

"Is it ...?" Emily's hands had fallen away, and Rosie rose beside her. Unconsciously, they entwined their arms.

At the same moment, their mother looked directly over at them from across the space of the canal.

"It is. It's *Lillian*," Rosie said on a breath, clearly seeing her own coloring and her sister's nose under the shadow of the stranger's hat. The woman made no movement. "It's *her*."

"I think you're right. I think it is."

"Who?" Delia asked. "Want me to go find out?"

"No, we'll go," Emily said, her voice a little stronger now.

"But ... how?" Rosie asked. She glanced at her sister.

"Don't ask me. I didn't invite her this time, honest." Emily swallowed audibly. "Is it really her, do you think?"

Wordlessly, they walked from behind the tent and crossed to the bridge, forgetting that the bride was to stay hidden. Behind them, Dottie insisted Delia stay put.

"Don't go getting all invested right away, Em," Rosie warned in a low voice. She supposed she'd always feel protective of her kid sister.

They released arms to cross the narrow bridge, where the interloper still stood.

Up close, it was even more obvious. She was simply an older version of Hickory Graham's granddaughters. She was chewing worriedly on her bottom lip. There were lines at the corners of her eyes and bracketing her mouth. She looked tired, a little washed out, but still lovely. Rosie could only imagine what her life had been, in the decades since she'd left them on Towpath Island in the care of her in-laws to pursue her own dreams.

"I invited you to my wedding at Christmas," Emily blurted, shaking her head in astonishment rather than bitterness. "And you didn't come. But you weren't even invited to *this* one, and here you are."

"I didn't know there was a wedding," muttered Lillian Turnbull Graham. Or whatever she called herself now. Her eyes drank in her daughters, studying and storing details as though someone might drag her away against her will at any moment. She looked generally worried and more than a little embarrassed. "Is it ..." Her gaze landed on Rosie, the much more elaborate one today, in her lace and rose buds. "Rosie, dear?" She swallowed. "Is it your wedding day?"

So, she still knew them apart. Rosie imagined how they'd looked when this woman had last seen them, as toddlers. It could only be their hair that gave them away.

"Yes, it's my wedding day. You must be our mother, then?"

"Yes." She closed her eyes, and Rosie watched tears slip from the corner of the left one. Rosie sighed. There were days she wished she could still turn her own emotions on and off. This was an inconvenient day to cry complicated tears, and it seemed she wasn't done.

Emily was there to save the moment, though. "Well," she said with a kind of exhilarated joy. "Well, this is a day for surprises. We've got a lot to work out now, don't we? Rosie, is it fine for our mother to come watch you marry the man of your dreams?"

"Of course." It was a different answer than Rosie would have given this time last year, back when she hadn't known Emily had been corresponding with and sending money to this mysterious parent of theirs.

Still, Rosie couldn't help but think of her own son, of his reaction to learning just months ago that his father was in his life for the first time. Families, she'd said all along, could look different. They were complicated, too. Very complicated.

When she crossed back over the footbridge in her lovely wedding dress, her mother following behind, Gabe was waiting on the other side. His eyes drank her in, and a long, bright smile stretched across his face. He looked so polished in his suit, the sun shining on his dark hair.

"You're stunning," he said as she walked straight into his arms.

"Not my fault!" Drew yelled, hurrying to the scene and looking alarmed. "She came out from behind the tent! I couldn't keep him from seeing her!"

"Gabe, meet my mother, Lillian. Lillian, this is the man I'm marrying. Gabe Adams."

They greeted one another. Lillian hardly said a word as she met first Gabe, then an astonished Drew Mathison. Hickory stood off to the side, looking mildly stormy but like he was determined to play nice. He had lived too long for dramatic scenes, Rosie figured, and anyway, he'd always preached forgiveness.

She clung to that now, even as she clung to Gabe's hand. He tugged at it, turning her attention just to him.

"Do you still want to do this today, love? I'd understand if you didn't."

"What? Why, of course I do!" Rosie could not imagine postponing, her heart too filled with joy and anticipation to even consider such a thing. She looked around at Gabe's exuberant family, her own dear family and friends, and reflected on the surprise blessings the day had held so far. A new baby for Emily. The return of their mother, whom they knew next to nothing about.

Charlie was about to find out he had yet another grandmother, on top of everything else.

Then, there was Lester the toad, apparently alive and well for another summer in the old canal.

"Fantastic," Pastor Adams exclaimed, joining the scene and resting a large hand on his son's shoulder. "I think we ought to get things underway, then, because there seems to be a spring storm brewing on the horizon over there."

Gabe and Rosie looked to where he pointed, over to the west, where the bright sky was turning a dark pewter.

"A storm," Margo Fairchild sighed, hustling off to her seat. "*Not again.* How unlucky."

Gabe laughed and swung Rosie in a joyful arc. "On the contrary, I think storms have been rather a blessing for us. Don't you think?"

"I do!"

The End

ACKNOWLEDGEMENTS

Thank you, Reader, for journeying back to Buckeye Lake with me for Rosie's happy-ever-after! I appreciate all of you who messaged me asking me about Book Two after reading Pressed Together. That you love these characters the way I've felt they deserved to be loved has meant more to me than I can say.

This book is also dedicated to the women who didn't have the luxury Rosie had of raising her child "alone." In 1940s America (and for decades after that), young single girls expecting babies were still routinely sent away to give birth, and those children would usually be adopted away. The mothers would then return to their communities, and the whole business would supposedly not be talked of again. I doubt that last part was entirely true, but regardless, I do need to acknowledge that Rosie's situation with Charlie was more than a little unusual.

Specific thank-yous go to so many people who helped get this book to this point:

Thanks to my amazing critique partner and mentor, Penny Frost McGinnis, who always makes me feel safe in both support and in good "catches." From there, I owe a big thanks to my husband's brother, Brad, for helping me figure out the nuances of early 20th century home heating in thirty seconds after I'd spent an entire day researching it. I'm indebted to my beta readers: Jenn, Leah, Carmen, Cameo, and Lori. They are the best kind of balance and came in clutch, helping me get the tractor and the hot cocoa right. I am also so grateful to Cassidy, Ellaina, Megan, Caroline, Angie, Nicole, Lauren, Stacy, Janelle, Melanie, Abby, Kelly, Jan, Bev, Jackie, Linda, and so many others who helped me out of my little writer cocoon this past year. Thanks to my "Saved a Seat" ladies for praying (and making me laugh).

Michelle Levigne is just the queen of editors. She is the perfect balance of big-picture continuity, word-level perception, and humor. Everyone at Mount Zion Ridge is great to work with, in fact. Thank you, Tamera, for wanting more, and thanks to Jerah for general guidance. Talented cover artist Addie Stewart is a large part of the reason most people pick up the books in this series. She's just spot-on every time!

Finally, if I know anything about the blessings and joys of love and family, it's thanks to my own people: Brent, Graham, Emma, and Kora; my parents and my sister, Jen; the extended Garees. And, most of all, it's thanks to the God who blessed me with all of them. "Thanks," of course, never goes nearly far enough.

ABOUT THE AUTHOR

Kim Garee worked as a newspaper reporter in Buckeye Lake for years before becoming an English teacher and, most recently, a school librarian. Her husband, Brent, is a high school principal, and together the couple has three grown children and three grown pets. Kim is also a portrait artist and miniature enthusiast who will hike and bike with anyone willing to go with her. She welcomes connections at www.kimgaree.com.

Have you read *Pressed Together*, Book One of the "Together" series?

Emily Graham's story of love and suspense begins just after World War II, when the war-weary Army detective Drew Mathison finds himself searching for a witness in the summer chaos of the amusement park. When he suspects Emily, owner of the local newspaper, is in fact hiding that witness, the couple engages in a dangerous game of hide-and-seek in which trust could save lives. *Pressed Together* is available now at *MtZionRidgePress.com* and most online bookstores in paperback, audiobook, and ebook.

Coming September 2025
Patched Together, Book Three of the "Together" series

In the series' conclusion, the confident and capable Dottie Berkeley finds herself completely leveled by a tragedy that leaves her feeling enormous guilt. She may have been "princess" of Buckeye Lake's amusement park her whole life, but when her reputation is wrecked, she seeks redemption in the last place anyone would look for her: the fresh-tilled dirt and back-breaking work of a local farm. Plus, both Dottie and the man who owns those acres of pumpkins and evergreens were looking for very different people to love.

THANK YOU!

Thank you for reading this book from Mt. Zion Ridge Press.

If you enjoyed the experience, learned something, gained a new perspective, or made new friends through story, could you do us a favor and write a review on Goodreads or wherever you bought the book?

Thanks! We and our authors appreciate it.

We invite you to visit our website, MtZionRidgePress.com, and explore other titles in fiction and non-fiction. We always have something coming up that's new and off the beaten path.

And please check out our podcast, **Books on the Ridge,** where we chat with our authors and give them a chance to share what was in their hearts while they wrote their book, as well as fun anecdotes and glimpses into their lives and experiences and the writing process. And we always discuss a very important topic: *Tea!*

You can listen to the podcast on our website or find it at most of the usual places where podcasts are available online. Please subscribe so you don't miss a single episode!

Thanks for reading. We hope you come back soon!